T0197009

WINGS OF ACES

R. M. MEADE

iUniverse

WINGS OF ACES

iUniverse books may be ordered through booksellers or by contacting:

iUniverse
1663 Liberty Drive
Bloomington, IN 47403
www.iuniverse.com
1-800-Authors (1-800-288-4677)

ISBN: 978-1-5320-4663-6 (sc)
ISBN: 978-1-5320-4664-3 (e)

Library of Congress Control Number: 2018904566

Print information available on the last page.

iUniverse rev. date: 04/13/2018

CHAPTER ONE

KATYA PRESSED HER FOREHEAD AGAINST the window, her eyes only half-open from sleep. The two days on the train had taken its toll; her legs and neck were sore and stiff. Her head ached from the smell of pipes and cigarettes. Her back had stiffened from her failed attempts to sleep upright. She smiled; *these things aren't new to me*, she thought. She glanced out the window into the moving streaks of light. Many times, the smell of aircraft fuel had sickened her and on countless return flights to base, her lower back and legs had fallen asleep from lack of circulation. Through the darkness, she caught a glimmer of sunlight struggling to be seen, and across the horizon, the sky was turning from black to a pale blue. She closed her eyes and remembered another sunrise.

The sun was also rising on that October morn. The reflections from the instruments on the canopy glass grew dimmer with each ray of sun. *Only a few more minutes until takeoff* she thought as she looked over to her flight leader. The leader's plane was at an idle, warming up, like hers. She could still see the little blue and white exhaust flames, intermittently flashing with each cylinder blast. Lilya's plane's signature gradually stood out with the sun's growing brightness. The *White Rose* that was painted on her fuselage was notorious among the Germans. Many Nazis challenged her, but were soon outwitted and out-flown to their doom. So far, twelve of them had gone back to their Fuehrer in flames.

Katya saw Lilya turn to look at her; she nodded, and then

1

pointed forward. Katya looked over her gauges, then throttled forward. She was the wingman today; she remembered that Lilya liked her wingmen off to the left and to the rear.

As they taxied to the runway, she heard Lilya say over the radio, "Good hunting!" With the sun just rising over the church steeple, they took off and climbed to twenty thousand feet to put the sun to their backs. They were heading for the town of Orel—and any German bombers they came across.

They were about an hour out and cruising at one hundred sixty-eight knots when Lilya yelled out over the radio, "Stukas at seven o'clock! Do you see them, Katya?" There was a tremor of excitement in her voice.

"Do you think they see us, leader?" Her mind was a crazy mixture of hope and fear.

"We're in the sun... it is butchering time. Let's go and get some meat!" Death was in Lilya's voice as she leaned the plane over and lined up her first victim.

A powerful relief filled Katya. "I'm right behind you, leader." She banked and throttled up for the attack. Lilya got off the first burst, then another. Katya's first burst with her cannon blew away the cockpit and gunner's mount of the point Stuka. As she flew through their formation, she flamed one more. She didn't know if Lilya had gotten any hits but as they pulled up to get in position for another pass, she noticed the sky was nothing but smoke and flaming plane parts.

They got elevation on the remainder of the Stukas but as they centered them for another pass, Katya spotted something out of the corner of her eye. "Leader... there's 109s at ten o'clock!" she gasped, realizing a shiver of panic as she watched the German fighters set up for an attack.

"Stay on my wing, Katya... we're taking out the Stukas," she said with staid calmness. They both throttled up once again and Lilya flamed two more on their next pass.

"Did you see that, leader? Nothing but dead meat!" She gloried briefly in the shared moment. Lilya didn't answer but dove for the hard deck, and Katya followed. Soon the sky was filled with rounds, all German. A dozen or more Messerschmitt's were on the Russians' tails, firing burst after burst. Both of the Russian Yaks were taking hits. Katya could feel and hear the piercing of the Huns' rounds as she glanced at her gauges.

"Bank left and climb!" shouted the leader.

Katya pulled her stick back and throttled up. She climbed rapidly and then leveled off. None of the 109s were on her and she questioned why. She looked for Lilya and saw her being pursued by no less than eight 109s. Fear and anger knotted inside her. "Shit… I'm coming, leader." She lowered her aircraft's nose and started for the 109s. Glancing at her speed, she saw it was close to three hundred knots but it wasn't fast enough, for like a star bursting in the heavens, Lilya's plane suddenly exploded. Nothing but fire and smoke was left of it. Katya took a deep breath to hold her emotions but didn't hesitate; she bore into the Germans, firing burst after burst. "You goddamn Nazi sons of bitches!" She spat out the words contemptuously as she sighted in. "It took eight of you to do the job but it will only take one of me!"

The Messerschmitt's scattered as Katya made her pass. She flamed one, then got on the tail of the leader. Her crossbars were dead center on the cockpit and she pulled the trigger. There was nothing; she was out of rounds. But apparently so was the German, for as she came alongside him he turned and just smiled. Katya returned his smile with her finger and then tossed her head and eyed him with cold triumph. Examining his plane, she noted the yellow tail and yellow fuselage, with a black cross and red star in its center. She would remember that plane and there would be a next time. She banked and turned for home, relaxing a bit.

She knew better, but needed to feel her pain. Lilya was a leader, not just for her, but also to two hundred ninety-five other women pilots. She was the number one woman ace in the Soviet Air Force; she was also her friend. She felt the nauseating sinking of despair. How would she tell the others that the *White Rose of Stalingrad* was gone?

The sun's brightness shone through her closed eyelids and she opened them. A lingering frustration was still with her. The dream seemed so real, but the more she moved and stretched, the more her dream faded.

"Are you all right?"

Katya narrowed her eyes and tried to focus. "Yes... why?" She started to examine the woman more closely. She was dressed in slacks, a long-sleeve blouse and was wearing black gloves; it seemed odd in this kind of heat. She looked almost military, straight-laced. She was fairly good-looking, with beautiful, powder-blue eyes, but her hairstyle seemed a little strange. It was shoulder-length and covered most of the right side of her face. "I'm sorry if I bothered you, just a bad dream." Katya's Russian accent was stern and to the point.

The woman was moving her hair even more to her center. She turned and fell back down in her seat. Suddenly, pure hatred raged in the woman's face. Her eyes glared, her nostrils flared, and her face reddened. The leather on her gloves was stretched tightly on her now fists.

"Are you German?" The words almost sickened her as she asked.

Katya didn't answer at first; she just looked at her, bewildered and stunned. This woman was in pain, a tortured thing. She had seen this look before... sometimes even in the mirror. Katya spoke softly, almost in a whisper, concerned with the woman's attitude. "Russian... I'm Russian." A frown grew on her face.

The woman sank back in her seat and sighed. A small tear fell from her eye as the anger left her. She turned towards the window, trying to hide her sorrow. "I'm sorry... I shouldn't have spoken in that manner. Just because you used a foreign language that doesn't mean you're a Hun." She could see Katya's reflection in the window and wondered what military branch she was with. "I'm English," she said. She turned to see what expression Katya was wearing.

Katya raised her eyebrows and stiffened her jaw. "I believe you, and I flew in the Great Patriot War. I flew Yaks and Lavochkins." She forced a remote dignity into her voice.

Leaning towards Katya, wide-eyed, she asked, "You were

allowed to fight?" After seeing Katya nod her head and smile, she became more tranquil. "I'm sorry, my name is Amy Johnston." Amy raised herself, then offered her hand in friendship.

Katya's mouth widened and her forehead narrowed as she recalled the name. "I know who you are!" She got to the edge of the seat to accept Amy's handshake. A part of her was revealed in her open admiration of her. "Did you not fly solo from somewhere in England to Australia in a Gypsy Moth… right around 1931 or '32?" She took Amy's hand roughly and squeezed hard; she shook it almost violently in the pleasure of her acquaintance.

Amy could barely answer with all the jolting coming from Katya's handshake. "Yes, the trip was about eleven thousand miles." Her words seemed to hiccup out of her mouth, for Katya was still exuberant with the handshaking as she spoke.

The leather from Amy's gloves felt wet to Katya. She softened her grip and slowed the up-and-down motions of her hand. "Sorry, I didn't mean to hurt you."

Amy looked down at the two hands grasping each other. "Don't worry, they don't hurt anymore." Her faint smile held a touch of sadness. Amy was about to do something she never did with strangers, but she liked this one and she was, of course, a fellow flyer. She took off one of her gloves and showed Katya her hand. The hand was a mosaic of colors, mostly red, brown and pink, but had blackish outlines throughout. Some of the veins protruded, almost lying on top of the skin, and a few of her fingernails were gone. Those that were left were deformed.

Katya had seen this before, and it sickened her a bit. Amy had been burned badly. She raised her hand to her hairline and pulled it back. The whole right side of her face and down her neck had the same wounds as her hands. She lowered her hair back into place. "I was shot down over Hell's Corner… scarred, but I can still fly." As she put her gloves back on, she turned to Katya and gazed at her with a bland half-smile.

A smirk on her face cleared the air. "Why do you think I'm still in the air force?" The two women's laughter caught the attention of the rest of the passengers in the car. Katya rose, and then lifted the small Amy off her seat. "Are you hungry? Let's go have breakfast!"

Between giggles, Amy said, "The one thing the Yanks have is food, and plenty of it. No brains, but plenty of the old kippers." As the two women started down the aisle Amy asked, "Are you a contestant in the race?"

"Yes, there are about a dozen of us on this train from all over Europe." She patted Amy on the shoulder. "I'm glad to see another woman in the race… there might be some competition now!" She leaned over to whisper in Amy's ear, "You know these men can only fly with their sticks up!" Amy brought her hand up to stifle her giggling.

The train began to slow down, and as Katya started to go through to the next car, she looked and saw a station sign going by. It read Reno, Nevada, elevation… the car passed too quickly to get the number. She shouted to Amy over the screeching of the brakes, "How do you like the wild and woolly west of the Yanks?"

But before she could answer, Katya barked, "Too goddamn dusty for me!" They smiled at each other and then continued their quest for the dining car. Along the way, Katya spotted another contestant. Stanis Chalupa, a Polish flyer, was sitting with some other guys. As they passed Katya greeted Stanis and asked if he would like to have breakfast with them.

"Breakfast with two gorgeous women? Of course!" Another flyer asked to go, and then another, then another, and soon the whole aisle was filled with pilots looking to fill their stomachs.

The dining car was only half-full when they entered. The car had stopped just parallel to the main street in town, and as the group was being seated, a French pilot shouted, "Look!" He pointed out the window and down the street. A banner read: The New Mapes Hotel and Casino Welcomes the 1947 Reno Air Races - Sept. 16 thru Sept. 23. "What is Sept.?" the Frenchman asked.

"It's an abbreviation for *September*, you idiot."

The Frenchman frowned. "So, my English is not that good… it's a savage language anyway."

"Maybe Oakland is nearby... perhaps this was the race we were entered in."

The group turned to Katya. "Could be, but I know Oakland is on a bay. I looked on a map before we left, and I don't see any water around here." She looked at one of the Englishmen and asked, "Would you go get Captain Brevan? He'll be able to tell us." The Englishman nodded and then left through a door at the end of the car.

"If this is the place, let's hurry and eat. I don't want to fly on an empty stomach." The group started yelling orders at the two waiters.

"What's a goddamn omelet?"

"And you called me an idiot!" the Frenchman said nasally. "All you Russians are peasants... goat milk and rye bread is all you know." The Frenchman felt good about getting even. He grinned at the group.

All at once, the Russians' faces became solemn, then one of them lowered his eyebrows and the rest of their faces became hard. "There was a time that we would have thanked God for some milk and rye."

The pilots became quiet after hearing the Russian's words. They, too, remembered the bad times. They looked around the dining car to see Americans feeding themselves to excess, not even realizing there were still hungry children back in Europe. They slowly and calmly returned to ordering their breakfasts.

The door opened and a tall, stocky man in a wrinkled suit walked in. He recognized the group and walked up to them. The Englishman that was sent for the captain was bringing up the rear. "Someone needs some help with something?" Brevan was in an upbeat mood.

Stanis pointed out the window. "Are we at the race?"

Brevan read the banner and then with a smile turned to the table. "Just a coincidence. We're getting off in Oakland." He glanced at his watch. "That will be in about four more hours, give or take an hour or so. Then you'll meet up with the rest of the contestants." He turned to leave and then looked at Katya intently, smiled, then strode to the door and his car.

"I knew it. I've been wondering about it for days now." Katya's voice was not loud, but harsh.

"What… are you worried about something?" Viktor was young, and prone to feelings of anger.

Katya smacked her hands together. "Where in the hell are the Spaniards, the Italians, Romanians, and of course, the mighty Germans?" Katya looked over to Amy, and with a sneer said, "They're the rest of the contestants!"

A rumbling came over the room. "Good!" piped up one of the Polish men. "We beat them once; it will feel good to do it again. I wish I had my own plane though."

Their questions came fast and furious, and all at the top of their voices. The words were all meshing together, and no one could decipher or answer any of them. The other passengers looked in puzzlement as the group argued. The conductor started to come over. Katya saw him approaching, and warned her comrades. "Shut up… sit down… your food is coming! We're just going to have to wait till we get to Oakland." Katya was surprised that the men had allowed her to take over the conversation, but that was the Russian way. She looked over to Amy; she had hate in her eyes again. It was not becoming on her.

The train pulled out, and soon started to climb into the mountains. Katya could see there was some snow still on the tips of the peaks, but not much.

As the men finished their meals, they wandered back to the sitting cars, mumbling to themselves. Katya lingered through a pot of coffee. She had never tasted coffee before and she liked it, especially with cream and sugar. Tea was the hot drink back in Russia, with sugar if you could find it.

She enjoyed the pampering the pilots were given on the train and ship coming over to America. Never had she ordered food before, it was always just given to her. Like it or not, that was the meal of the day in the Russian military. She also had noticed the American women. Frail things. It seemed that if you would touch them too hard, they would break. The American men seemed to like it that way. Women were taken care of here in America, not like whores, but like prized possessions. Their men prided themselves on how good they treated their women. She felt a little out of place, too rough maybe, and military.

Looking from the window, she noticed a man looking at her. It made her feel uneasy; why, she didn't know. She'd had men look at her before, and it did not bother her. Why this one? Maybe it was his smile or the twinkle in his eye, or maybe just because he was noticing her! Out of uniform she could be very appealing, she thought. Not as frail as most of the American women here, but definitely feminine, with a pretty good shape. She was only twenty-six, an old maid back home; but something told her that here in America that wasn't so.

As she was examining her appeal, her admirer got up and left the car, not even glancing back at her. *Wishful thinking,* she thought, then started to daydream back to the beginning of the war.

The summer of 1937 was one of those magical times. The weather in Moscow was warm, as were the hearts of the people. Everyone was poor so everyone was rich, this being the Russian way of equality. They didn't have material things, but they had each other. The people played and loved hard and fast; even for a young girl just out of school, the world was good. Katya was working as a lab technician in a pharmaceutical company. She thought her life boring, and couldn't wait to go to university. She was proud to have won the honor and been picked to attend. The lower class seldom achieved this position, but her grades were extremely high.

She had met Mikhail Raskova at work. He was a striking young man, about two years older than she. His hair was as black as onyx, and he had the darkest blue eyes she had ever seen. His skin was that of a Georgian, smooth and dark, and his voice was always soft and low, like he was always whispering. He was the sexiest man she had ever seen. Though he didn't come on to her for the longest time, she tried to maneuver his attentions in many ways. Endless nights of dreaming filled her heart and her mind; she fantasized about lovemaking to an extreme. Many times, her father had opened her door in the middle of the night to strange moans and groans coming from her room.

"Are you all right? Are you sick or something?" he would say.

She would straighten her nightgown in the dark and with a breathless voice reply, "I'm all right, just a little nightmare."

Closing the door and returning to his own bed, she could hear him yelling at her mother, "Ida, you've got to have a doctor look at her or we'll never get any sleep!"

She was inexperienced and ignorant of most of the actual sex acts, except one, and that one she'd learned from a friend in sixth grade, which was the pleasure of playing with one's nipples. Her breasts had grown into a B cup then, and she felt that when the time came for sex, she was definitely woman enough for anything.

Katya was lucky, for Mikhail was a good and kind young man, taking her through their courtship slow and easy—sometimes too slow for Katya's way of thinking. They started with long walks in the park, then the cinema every once in a while. She liked the cinemas, for she loved those long, wet kisses in the dark. Mikhail didn't mind them either, and she found that her B cup didn't hurt the situation at all.

One afternoon, she was to meet Mikhail at a small café. She was running late, so she hurried. Sitting there sipping tea, he smiled as he caught sight of her and rose to embrace her. They sat down, and Katya began talking a mile a minute about something. He raised his finger over her mouth. "Shhhh." He went for something in his coat pocket, a small black box, and opened it. It was the smallest stone she could have ever imagined, but it didn't matter, for she knew what it meant.

Before he could even say a word, "Yes! Yes! Yes!" she yelled. Her lips quivered from her excitement as she tried to say more, but couldn't.

A single tear told him all he had to know. "I love you... I will always love you." It was a truth of all truths. They were one now, and would remain that way forever.

She rose from her seat and devoured his face with kisses. Suddenly, she stopped, and a devilish look came into her eyes. "When?"

He lowered his head and tilted it to one side in confusion. "When... what?"

She puckered her lips, and with a twinkle in her eyes said, "When's the wedding, and when's the bedding?"

He started to laugh. "You are a sex maniac, aren't you?"

Wearing a sneaky little grin, she said, "I don't know yet, but I would like to find out!"

"Come." They started back for home.

As they walked, she wondered what it was going to be like being married. Sex anytime you wanted. One could even talk about it without shaming one's self. Having someone to take care of you, but also performing your fair share… how wonderful to have someone to just talk to, and listen to your opinions and thoughts. Of course, always agreeing with you would be a must! Most importantly though, were the arms to hold you when times got bad. She thought she'd like being married.

"I think we'll marry in the spring," he said out of the blue. He stopped her, and then looked down at her lovely face. Her smooth skin glowed with a pale gold undertone. "You go to university, and I'll get my recruit training over with. That way we wouldn't be separated right after the marriage."

She puckered her lips once more. "Do we have to wait?"

He looked matter of fact. "You know I have to register for the army. I've been lucky to get an exemption to go to Medic School, but that's over in a month, and then I'll have to go." He held her close as they started walking again. He hoped the up-and-down motion as he massaged her arm would ease some of the tension. "What about university? You don't want to ruin a chance like that, do you?"

Across her pale and beautiful face, a dim flush raced like a fever. "I know… but my bed is so cold at night!" She glanced back up at him with that same twinkle in her eye.

He smiled. "Well, if it's only for warmth's sake!"

She giggled and rubbed his stomach.

A voice interrupted her thoughts. "Ma'am, will there be anything else?"

A black man dressed in all white, and with extremely bad timing, was standing over her saying something as she came out of her daydream. Her eyes were distant and remote, but then focused on the man. "Pardon… I didn't hear you."

The waiter smiled, realizing she had been somewhere else. "Sorry… can I get you anything else, ma'am?"

"No… I'm just leaving." She looked around to see if anyone else had caught her daydreaming, smiling as she saw the coach empty. She slid around and stood in the aisle, taking money out of her skirt and attempted to pay for her coffee.

The waiter touched her hand and said, "Mr. Brevan takes care of that. You have a nice day now, ma'am!" He hummed to himself as he started picking up the table.

Katya smiled, then turned for the door that led to the sitting cars. She left by the wrong door though, and found herself walking to the rear of the train, through a definitely lower class of ticket holder. They looked like farmers, definitely working-class people, and she felt more at home being surrounded by them. As she reached the door at the far end of the car she saw a sign that read "Colored Only." She didn't know what it meant and didn't care much, so she reached for the handle and started to go through the door.

A middle-aged white man dressed in coveralls stopped her and said, "You don't want to go in there, young lady!" His eyes were flat, hard, and cold.

She looked at him with aroused curiosity, then with a frown she said, "Why?"

His voice seemed commanding. "That's the niggers' car!"

She thought he was talking about some kind of animal car. She looked through the glass and saw no animals, then turning back to him she asked, "What is a nigger?" She laughed nervously when she asked the question; she thought he was joking with her.

The man became upset, and was almost shouting at her question as he rose to his feet. The rest of the people in the car were mumbling and staring at her, like she was some kind of freak. He pointed at the window of the door. "That car is for Negroes. Darkies, blacks, melon-eaters! A girl like you should stay out of there, if you know what's good for you!" His face was marked with loathing.

This man was scaring her, and so were the rest of the folks in the car. She hurriedly turned and left by the other door. As she went back through the dining car, she saw the same waiter; people were speaking to him, and even laughing with him. His color could not be the reason for that sign on the door. People didn't hate this man; why the hate of the others in the next car? As she approached the far door, she looked for a similar sign on this door, but found none. Just before she entered, the thought of black uniforms raced through her mind. The fear of police wearing black must be the answer! Gestapo-type policemen... she had learned to fear these men from her training. Always avoid the black uniforms if shot down in enemy territory. This must be what angered those people; she saw the fear and hatred in their eyes. She suddenly felt sorrow—no, more like disappointment. All of Europe was taught that America was the land of freedom and welcomed everyone. It saddened her to think there was no difference between the Gestapo in Germany and the American police. She would have to look out for these policemen in black. She'd better carry her papers with her at all times, she thought.

She regained her composure and went through the door to the next car. She saw that the groups of men were still in heavy discussions over, what else, flying. Katya suddenly remembered Amy. After Brevan had left the dining car earlier, she seemed to have vanished. She looked around the car for her, and not seeing her, strolled over to the men. There in the middle of the group was Captain Brevan, and sitting next to him was the guy that had been staring at her in the dining car.

Brevan looked up at her as he retrieved a file folder from the redheaded young man next to him. "Katya, this is Matthew Drew." Brevan turned to him. "Matthew, this is Katya Yegorova. She flew in the Soviet Air Force." Brevan grinned as he turned back to her. "Have my seat; I have to get my things in order before we get to Sacramento. By the way, he's American... and single."

As he got up to leave she said to him, "I hate to travel with fools!" but was uncertain this was an appropriate phrase.

He bent over to her ear and whispered, "He was asking about you." His voice was calm, his gaze steady.

She examined the redhead a little more before she sat down. He had green eyes, a somewhat pale complexion, the brightest smile she had ever seen, and those freckles; he must have a thousand of them. Except for his build, which was fairly muscular, he looked more like an Englander.

As she sat down he said something to her, but his accent blurred his meaning and she didn't reply. "I said good morning, ma'am!" He was a little embarrassed, and upset that she hadn't answered the first time.

"Dobraye ootro!" Viktor, Katya's fellow pilot, piped up out of nowhere. "Katya, darling, how could you? Are you sure he's your type?" The beginning of a smile tipped the corners of his mouth. The rest of the group looked confused as they stared at her, waiting for her response. Viktor leaned down to her and exclaimed with intense pleasure, "Maybe I'm not so much a pig?"

"You'll always be a pig… my pig!" She reached up, and took him by the face, and kissed him on the forehead. "Tebya ne ebut, ti ne podmakhivai!"

Viktor smiled and kissed her back. "Anyone for a drink?"

The men quickly got to the aisle and proceeded to the club car, leaving Katya and the American alone by the window.

"What did you say to him?" He raised his eyebrows to enhance his words.

"I told him to mind his own fucking business!"

His face reddened and his jaw went agape.

She sensed the American was upset. "What's wrong? You getting train sick or something?"

"It's just that women don't talk like that where I come from." His tone was coolly disapproving.

With just a hint of a grin she said, "You don't get out much, do you? Did not Brevan tell you that I was in the air force for over five years?" She turned from him and stared straight ahead. "And by the way, all women talk like that, they just have to keep the pretense up in front of men." Her words were playful but the meaning was not.

"I'm sorry... it just shocked me a little." His face went pale again as he apologized.

She was glad he had accepted the enlightenment on the female's use of the language, it being so different from that of males. Females think before they speak. "By the way... you talk funny too. What part of America speaks like you?"

The corner of his mouth rose and those beautiful white teeth showed through. With a cocky tone to his voice he said, "I'm a Southern boy, ma'am, from the deepest part of the South. I was born and raised in Tampa, Florida." Pointing a finger at her he said, "I wouldn't talk much about accents, yours being so thick, you might say." His grin turned into a full smile.

She was beginning to like this Southern American, freckles and all. She liked the way his green eyes twinkled when he was aroused. His way of speaking was different, but nice. It was sort of soothing hearing a different accent. Russian can be so hard and abrupt, but this Southern American's way of speaking was softer, elongated. The words were more gently spoken; you had to really listen to understand, and that was good. She started to wonder what the sounds of love would sound like from his lips. Fantasizing, she heard passion and lust, words spoken in a yielding, almost choral way. He could do wonders to the darkness of a bedroom, she thought.

"Hello... are you with me?" He snapped his fingers at her.

"Yes!" she retorted and then regained her composure.

She seemed a little angry coming out of her daydream, he thought, appearing to have enjoyed it better than the conversation she was having with him. "How did you get picked for the race?" He hoped the question would bring her back around. "Did you get a letter, like me?"

"A letter with a thousand-dollar cashier's check!" she snapped back at him.

"I bet you called the telephone number right away."

"Yes, I did." She raised her chin and turned slightly towards him. "A thousand dollars is a lot of rubles; almost three years' earnings in Moscow."

He smiled at her with a pitiful look on his face. "Yes."

"I know, that kind of money is nothing here in America… we've heard about your streets of gold, even in backward Russia."

His eyes widened and his body shuddered slightly. "You've got the wrong idea, Kat!" He touched her hand. "A thousand dollars is big money no matter where you are. And I got to tell you about those streets paved in gold… I haven't found them yet!"

She patted his hand. "What did you do with your money; give it to your wife for safekeeping?"

His eyes widened once more and that twinkle in his eyes came back. He shivered as he uttered the words, "I'm not married." Just the sound of the word brought fear to him. He calmed down after a few seconds and looked over at her smile; she looked so pleased about something. "I don't need a wife, I need a partner."

"A partner?" she asked.

"Here, let me show you!" He reached down and was searching for something in his bag. "Yes, here it is!" He pulled out a brochure and showed it to her. "Have you ever seen anything more beautiful in your life?" His eyes clung to hers, analyzing her reaction.

It was a plane, painted a bright yellow and white. It was an enormous, bulging, fat plane. It looked like an elephant. It could not possibly fly, she thought. "Oh… it's beautiful!" she said, trying not to hurt his feelings.

He gazed at the photo like it was a lost love. "Look, only sixty-five thousand dollars!" He took a deep breath. "It's navy surplus. They originally go for much more. I put the whole thousand and a couple of hundred that I had saved up to hold the sale." He dropped his shoulders and a slight frown came to his face. "I got ninety days to come up with the balance. So that's why I'm in this race. The letter I got said there would be a substantial prize for winning." His confidence became apparent as he raised his chin slightly.

She took him by the hand. "Why would you want an ugly plane like that one?"

He pulled his hand back and showed her the photo once more.

"That's a Grumman 'Goose,' G21-A. The best-built seaplane in the world!"

She pointed to the picture. "This thing lands and takes off in the sea?"

"You bet!" He kissed the picture and then started to fold it back up and put it back in his bag. "That's why I need a partner, to help me fly passengers from Tampa, or maybe even Miami, to the Caribbean Islands. We would make a fortune taxiing folks or bringing cargo to the hotels and resorts on the islands. The Goose has a 640-mile range. At 201 mph it could reach almost all the islands. There's a lot of money in Florida. All the big wheels from up north are going there to retire, and they all like that Caribbean action!"

He was talking so fast Katya was getting dizzy. His arms and hands were flailing around in mid-air… it reminded her of an Italian having a fit. "That sounds like a good opportunity and it means you can still fly. That's what I miss most… I hope you succeed in finding a partner."

A surprised look overtook his eagerness. "You don't fly anymore?" He looked like he was going to faint. "I thought you were in the Russian Air Force?"

She swallowed hard. "The war's over now. They don't need women flyers anymore. I retired last month from the air force—or rather was forced out by old-thinking men with stars on their shoulders. I'm going to use my money to start again."

"I'm not afraid of women pilots." He stared straight into her eyes. "Would you like to fly with me… fifty-fifty… a full partnership?" His stare softened as he waited for her to answer. "I know we just met, but sometimes first impressions tell a lot. At least think it over… or are you going back to Russia?"

She smiled discontentedly, her face suddenly worn, and sadness crept upon her lovely features. "There's nothing but destruction, hunger, and sad memories; not to mention the long lines in the streets. My Russia is sick, and I don't think it will be cured for a long time. No, I'm not going back." Katya turned from him and closed her eyes. She thought about the flyers she had met on her journey to America. Viktor and the other two Russians, Stanis the Pollock, even Amy—all of the Europeans had passports and travel visas. Those were the hardest documents to get anywhere in Europe. She wondered who could be behind this race. No one knew any details about the race; no one she had met had ever raced before. They were flyers but wartime pilots, not used to racing each other but killing one another. The money and the freedom had enticed all of them to come. Nothing to lose, they all said, and they all were thrilled to fly again. There was something strange about the whole thing. "Do you know who's behind the race?" Her voice shattered the silence. "You were looking at files when I first came up to you."

He turned towards her; she was still sitting with her eyes shut. "I've wondered about that myself. The papers in the file all had a Navy Intelligence letterhead. I'm an ex-navy pilot so I didn't think anything of it. It would be strange if the navy were putting on a race, though. We would have heard about it here in the newspapers. It would also be a little odd for the navy to give out thousands of dollars like that. It was hard enough to get your ninety-two dollars a month out of them during the war. But since we're almost there, I guess we'll just have to wait."

Suddenly, Katya blinked her eyes and turned to face him. "Yes… I will!"

A dumbfounded look appeared on his face. "Yes, what?"

She turned back to the comfort of the sleeper seat and closed her eyes again. "Yes… I will be your partner," she said in a clear and strong voice.

Picking his jaw up off the floor, he responded, "It's true… women are the same all over the world… thank God!"

His meaning was clear, and she just grinned and breathed easy as she returned to her daydreams.

The shadows passing by her eyelids and the roar of the train's engine climbing the mountains lulled her into memories of the days when she would receive the dark letters from Mikhail. The war was hell, he would write. Bloody, mishandled tragedies, where men's blood and lives were not worth the ground they stood on. The generals ran the war with maps. Lives were expendable. They were just tools to gain feet or yards on the front. The wounds were so bad and the supplies were so few. His tears intermingled with their blood as he would try to save them, but it was hopeless.

Then one day, the last letter (unfinished) arrived, two months late. The dirt and blood-stained paper started off with the words: "Darling, the memory of your beautiful face keeps me sane in these days of Armageddon. The love I have for you keeps me strong. The longing for your touch keeps me warm. My fear has turned to numbness as I watch our men die." His letter suddenly changed to a stranger's hand and it wrote: "Mikhail died trying to save a soldier. He was very brave and will be missed." The letter ended and her heart shattered but without tears, for she could feel him. Then and even now, he was with her, helping her and loving her.

"Katya… get up, we're almost there!" shouted Viktor. The group of men followed him to the front of the car. As he passed her, he gave her a shove. "Wake up and come on. The last one there is a Hitler!"

The train had been following the river and then it opened up to a large bay. They could see sailing ships and small boats from the window. The group rushed between cars so they could feel the mist from the bay. The mild breeze blew salty scents through their noses like a perfumed bouquet. The chilly air surprised them, coming from a land of cactus and rattlesnakes just a few hours ago.

Matt could see a great city on the far shore. "That's San Francisco," he said as he pointed it out to the rest of the flyers. The train started to slow down; it was coming into the station. Captain Brevan barked out orders to gather on the main boarding ramp and not to let anyone get separated. He would see to the bus and be right back.

"Will you sit with me on the bus?" a voice said to Katya.

She turned to find Amy standing there. "Of course! You want the window or the aisle?"

Amy moved her hair with her hand. "The window please. And can we sit in the back?"

When Amy played with her hair, it made Katya remember her burns. "Whatever you say. By the way, where did you vanish to earlier?"

19

Her mouth took on an unpleasant twist. "I'm not comfortable around other people, especially men."

Brevan came walking back with two other men to help him. They all picked up their things and followed him out to the bus. It was a gray bus, with US Navy painted on its sides. Matthew looked at Katya, shrugging in disappointment that she would be sitting with the Englishwoman, then got on the bus.

CHAPTER TWO

THE SKY WAS THE DEEPEST blue he had ever seen in all his years of flying. There were no clouds, only the silent soaring of gulls to contrast its enormity. The reflections off the water made the ship seem as blue as the sky. Through the window of his office he could see the ship being prepared for sea. The men on the docks were hurrying to complete their tasks. The other ships docked nearby seemed small in comparison to the aircraft-carrier he was spying.

He turned from the window and walked over to the far wall. There, for the last time, he reminisced on the dozen or two pictures that were hung there. The largest photo was that of the carrier, *Lexington*. He remembered the year he commanded her. September of 1932; that day was much like today. It was a bit warmer in San Diego harbor, as he recalled. He could still feel the pride in being the captain of a carrier, especially the *Gray Lady*. It was the largest vessel he had ever seen. He was in awe at its size. He glanced up and to the right and there was the battleship *Arizona*, his first command. The photo was of him and his first officer on the main deck. He looked really young. He was only forty-five, one of the youngest captains in the navy in 1930. He wandered along the wall and then stopped at the picture of his wife and son. The house in Honolulu was her pride and joy. She would stand out on the wooden deck and gaze at Diamond Head for hours. She never tired of the view, and he never tired of comparing the sunset's beauty to that of his wife.

She always won out, for in his eyes there was nothing to compare to her loveliness.

As he gently touched her image, he strained to remember when the photo was taken. Michael must have been about eight or nine; that made it 1928 or '29, he thought. As he stared at the photo, sadness flowed over his face, then turned to sheer hatred as he glanced at a nearby picture. The photo was of a Japanese Zero, with special markings; it had a Japanese name written across it. He turned from the photo and closed his eyes as he tried to get the Zero out of his mind. He returned to his wife's picture and tried to concentrate on her image. The photo became blurry with his tears as he spoke to her. "How are you doing today, love? See you soon, and tell Michael to behave himself."

The secretary was talking on the phone when Bill Morgan came into the office. "Chief of Naval Intelligence, may I help you?" she said. He waited till she was through with the phone call before he asked to see the admiral. He was told to go right in.

Bill knocked before he opened the door and stuck his head inside. Seeing Robert at the wall he asked, "Are you busy? I just need a minute."

The admiral turned and said, "Come on in, Bill, I've been expecting you." He strolled over to his desk, blew his nose, and put the handkerchief in his pocket as he took a seat. Bill was busy emptying his briefcase and piling the papers on the desk. "You need me to sign all these documents?" Robert asked.

Bill looked over his glasses and said, "You have to sign all of them, in duplicate." He then stood up erect and with a serious tone to his voice said, "Robert, I've run your businesses and we've been friends for thirty some-odd years now and I have to tell you, I think you're cracking up! Do you know what you've done?" His expression turned from serious to concern. "You're going to be broke if you go through with this!" He shook his head from side to side. "Your entire family fortune will be gone and for what, a kid's game?" he said with a significant lifting of his brow.

Robert was still signing the papers and did not look up as he said, "What good is a family fortune… without a family?"

Bill responded sharply, abandoning all pretenses. "Damn it, Robert, it's been five years now since Joanna died, and I know Michael wouldn't want you to do this stupid thing! For the past eighteen months I've watched as you sold everything with your name on it, for a race? You used your power and money to obtain that ship and the other materials so you could put on this charade."

Robert stood quickly, his eyes narrowing on Bill. "I know you don't understand, old friend, but it's something I have to do." He picked up the signed papers and handed them back to him. "Bill, in ten more days I wouldn't even have the navy anymore! What good is money... I need a purpose!" His voice was firm, and final.

Bill smiled halfheartedly. "You're now the proud owner of a goddamn aircraft carrier, for at least thirty more days." He closed the briefcase and extended his hand. "Good luck, old buddy... happy flying, sailing, or whatever." They shook hands and he turned and left, shaking his head all the way out.

Robert looked down at the letter from the Secretary of the Navy that confirmed his retirement. A lifetime of naval service... was it worth it? His thoughts flowed back in time, out to sea for years at a time with Joanna and Michael living on their own. He was constantly striving for combat but was always stuck behind a desk. Now he'd spent most of his days and all of his sad, lonely nights trying to deal with his feelings of torment and guilt for not being there when she died and not being there for Michael, either. What kind of man was he? Was his career more important? Was his commitment to the navy all-consuming? He wasn't a good father or husband, but he would be a good avenger! That thought alone burned in his mind.

A knock at the door brought him back from his rage and self-pity. The secretary opened the door and announced, "Mr. Norris is here. Can you see him now?"

The news that Norris was there made him happy. He smiled as he rose from the chair. "Commander, come right in!"

Using a cane, Norris walked into the room. "You're the only one that still calls me Commander, Admiral, sir!" He walked over to a chair in front of the desk.

The admiral noticed he was dressed in khaki trousers and a khaki shirt, with a long-sleeve black navy sweater. He was starched, with creases perfectly in line; his salt-and-pepper hair were regulation and his face clean-shaven. He was a civilian, but you wouldn't know it by looking at him. John had been the admiral's flight officer on the *Lexington*. He had been wounded when the ship went down in the Coral Sea. They found him in the water, clinging to a piece of teakwood from the flight deck. He had lost his right leg and had been discharged (not fit for duty). The admiral had a cane made of the teakwood, and John called it Old Lexington. They had become good friends over the years; both were navy through and through.

"Please sit down, John, take a load off your feet."

Norris smiled as he sat in the chair. "Take a load off... do you want me to take the whole leg off? You do know this prosthesis weighs a ton."

The admiral enjoyed this man's gentle camaraderie, his subtle wit. "You damn fool, quit kidding around. Is everything ready to go?"

John smiled, "Just as we planned. Everything's going smoothly. I'm really surprised it is, with all that could have gone wrong. But you've taken care of every roadblock that's come up."

The admiral returned the smile. "Why be head of Intelligence if you don't use it?" He had studied all the factors of the plan, having the Aussies and the Brits putting up most of the funds and the aircraft. He even chose pilots that flew against each other, which made it personal, and who had the same yearnings as he did for revenge. He had to cover up his own bloodthirstiness to succeed in his plans.

"The strings you must have pulled. I'm astonished you're not in the brig." He looked at him with amused wonder. "How much did it cost you to get the Europeans and the goddamn Japs their papers to get them out of their countries? Those Russians are playing hardball all the way... I know you're rich, but that rich?" He started to rub his upper leg, trying to get the circulation flowing.

The admiral's smile turned into laughter. "I've just been told that I'm broke and haven't got a dime!"

"You can laugh? You're a better man than I; but you don't have a wife and two daughters who want to go to college."

The admiral stopped laughing and stared at John.

John's face went red from embarrassment and he started to grit his teeth. "I'm sorry, Admiral. I'm an asshole. I didn't mean—"

"Nonsense, John, we've been friends too long." Smiling, he said, "You are an asshole though!" They both started laughing again. "By the way, where are Susan and the girls?"

"They'll be on the dock just before we sail." John's face brightened with just the thought of them.

"Good, I have something for her."

"What?"

"Never mind, it's a surprise for later."

John's face relaxed after the laughter and he became a little more solemn. "Could I ask you a question, Admiral?"

"Sure, John, go ahead."

"I was thinking… maybe you could tell me the details on how you pulled all this off. I know little bits and pieces, but not the whole picture. It might make a good book later. Susan and I might be able to get the girls through college after all."

The admiral put his elbows on the desk and leaned slightly forward on them. "The navy really fucked you over, didn't it?"

John had trouble answering. His love for the navy was evident, but his disdain for the policies regarding its wounded men was also apparent. "What do you do with a one-legged flyer with a wife and kids?" His voice was unsteady and a little garbled, like he had embarrassed himself. "The disability check barely buys food. To my disgrace, Susan even had to go to work. A man that can't take care of his own family… what kind of man is that? We had to sell the house… she loved that house… she lost everything. I only lost my leg." His eyes reddened and he started rubbing his leg once again. "Until you looked me up, what, eighteen months ago, I was ready to cash it in for the life insurance money." He paused and swallowed hard. "I'll always be grateful for what you've done for me, the past year and a half. You gave my life back to me. I felt like I was back in the navy again. I had purpose."

It was funny that John had used those words, the same words spoken just a few moments ago by him. "Do you want to know the whole story?" The admiral wanted to start up another subject; he didn't like seeing his friend like that. Self-pity didn't look good on that kind of man.

"Yeah! Give me the whole story, we got time." He looked down at his watch.

The admiral sat his chair in a backward position and stared at the ceiling, his forehead crushing downward in thought. "Where to start? Okay I think it was about ten days after the bomb and the Japanese finally surrendered. I got a memo from Staff that there was a problem with the next group of carriers that were being built. The contract the navy had with the builders stated they could cancel out on any ship not yet started. The memo stated that the navy didn't need any more Essex class carriers now that the war was over and they now needed a new class. Unfortunately, the keel had been laid on at least one. The navy needed relief from this project. We were ordered to put all available personnel on solving this matter." He looked at John with narrowing eyes. "You know what that means?" His eyes returned to the ceiling. "Use all means at your disposal: threats, bribery, the IRS, safety, or even the unions. That's why the navy gave the Intelligence Department the job. We're the behind-the-scenes part of the service, spying on everyone and everything. The Navy Department figured we could find a secretary in bed with the builder's president and blackmail its way out of the contract. I put three men on it but their results were negative. The builders were clean; they had dotted every 'i' and crossed every 't'. No girlfriends on the side, either. I found out how much the contract for the carrier was… $44,000,000. Not bad, a pre-war price. I was still being pressured from above to take care of this problem. The navy needed every dime they could get their hands on."

He lowered his head and pointed to the far wall. "I was sitting here staring at my pictures when the solution came to me. I ordered an ensign to put in a long-distance call. 'Make the call to the Royal Australian Navy Department, Chief of Staff, Admiral Deans, in Brisbane.' My guts turned with excitement, I was almost giddy with delight. I could get back into the war; not the last one but the next one, my own."

He leaned on the desktop and placed his face into his hands and pressed hard, trying to suppress his joy even now. Then he lowered his hands and stared back at John. His eyes were a little red from the pressure his hands made. "My next move came easily, then the next and then the next. If I moved quickly, it might work. I talked to their Secretary of the Navy and proposed a deal that they could buy an Essex class carrier for $50,000,000. They agreed in four days. In the meanwhile, I talked to our Secretary of the Navy and got the go-ahead. A call to my accountant was next. Liquidate everything I own, then turn it into cash; it turned out to be five million dollars. I then went to the builders and made the deal to buy the ship myself. I put the five million down as collateral for one hundred twenty days; the Aussies were to pay in ninety days. They were very happy not to lose the contract, no matter who bought it. To cover the Secretary's ass, I had to agree to retire before taking possession of the ship. So, the sale actually went to a civilian. The news made both Secretaries great heroes in their own services. Australia would have her first carrier, and the US Navy Department would save $44,000,000. After about three months, I figured I needed about another million to succeed with my scheme."

As the admiral continued, John could see his tempo quickening, the wheels in his mind turning over and over, like he was planning the next invasion of some Japanese-held island. He had turned his world into a war room, calculating every possible move. Just the texture of his voice as he told his story brought back memories of the ready room on the *Lexington*. It was pure enthusiasm; but to what end, and why?

"I was a little downhearted until I thought of the obvious; what good is a carrier without aircraft?" He stood, walked to the window, and opened it for some air. "I nosed around till I found out that Grumman had sixty F6F-3 Hellcats sitting at their plant, paid for and ready for delivery. I also found out that Grumman had come in under budget and was selling the aircraft for $35,000 each instead of the $50,000 that was contracted for.

"Then I made another call to my good friends at the Navy Department. Since I knew the production on the new Bearcats was in full swing, they might consider selling some Hellcats for a profit. They wanted to know what I wanted out of it. I told them one Bearcat, one Hellcat, the use of landing strips in the South Pacific, and of course, ship stores for two hundred men for thirty days and fuel to deliver the planes on the carrier to Australia. They balked a little at first, but after I showed them they would have to deliver the planes anyway, and the cost would be much more than my simple requests, they agreed.

"I contacted Australian authorities and made the deal for $50,000 a plane, which they jumped at. At the same time, they requested all manuals on the carrier and the aircraft, so they would have time to train personnel to operate the vessel when they received it. I suggested to them that they should train some officers and a small crew and send them over to sail the ship back to Australia. That way they could get hands-on experience. I would supply a small but expert crew of officers to break their people in.

"They agreed, and I arranged for the material to be sent. They also agreed to supply fuel for the aircraft. I recommended to their Secretary that he might want to see if he could strike a deal with the English for some of their Sea-hurricanes or Sea-fires, since those planes were already familiar to the Australians. I told them I would be happy to deliver them for a small fee. One month later, they agreed. I knew they would.

"I notified the English manufacturer about the deal with the Aussies and received one Sea-fire and one Sea Hurricane for my compensation. That's when I thought of you!" He closed the window and leaned against the file cabinet. His face grew serious. "I need a flyer, a good flyer, a leader, and someone who knows carriers. But most of all, a man that has a need, maybe even a vendetta. Someone that would not shun my ideas; that was you.

"As you know, I gave you the list of aircraft we needed, arranged for their purchase, and had you pick your eight men to help with the planes and training. I then went to work getting the warbirds that needed to be converted into carrier planes. The navy had files on all

28

the pilots already. It took some work to get their papers through. A little cash and some bribery worked wonders. So, when the carrier was ready for its shakedown, the Aussies had arrived two weeks earlier with a crew of about 125 men. I just sent it to Liverpool, where it also picked up the British aircraft that the Aussies wanted. The aircraft and half the pilots I acquired in Europe. The other half went by train and then by navy personnel carriers to New York. From there, they just hopped a train to Oakland. The whole thing was very simple, really."

The admiral walked over to the picture of the *Lexington* and took it off the wall. "Remember those F2s and F3s?"

With a wave of vivid recollection John said, "Sure I do! Trying to get those bi-wing F2s below the flight deck was a pain in my ass!" John's face had lit up with just the word *Lexington*. "Remember when the first Little Cats landed on the deck? There wasn't a better fighter in the world. I couldn't wait for the next war." He smiled as he rocked back and forth in his chair.

The admiral hung the picture back on the wall. "I shouldn't have accepted the promotion to work in Intelligence. I should have stayed at sea, where I belonged... but Joanna liked the idea of a desk job; it kept me closer to home, I guess. It made me miss the war... you too. I missed my chance in the first war; I was too young. But now I would be chained to a desk for the second." His heart grew heavy with the words.

"What was it, May of forty-two when the *Lexington* went down? Then you spent two more years in a hospital and then a forced discharged. It wasn't fair to either one of us! This race can fulfill a need in us again; a small war, I agree, but a war nonetheless."

"How do you figure this race a war?" The confusion in John's expression and his voice was obvious.

"Do you think these pilots, with all their anger, hatred, and prejudices, aren't going to bring them out in the race? They've spent four years killing each other. Yes, it will be a war. My war."

John sat grinding his teeth as he listened to him. "You've done all this just because you weren't able to command in combat?" He lowered his head and shook it. "I thought this was a true race of warriors, to find out which one was the best. I've read all the dossiers on the contestants; there are some really good flyers among them, all aces."

The admiral's face grew red and his nostrils flared. "It is a race, a race of convictions, just like the war was! They'll need tactics, maneuvers, and calculations. This will be their means of survival and their means to win, just like they were back in their squadrons. You forget these pilots are fighting men and women... they need to win. Above all, they need to win!" He knew he was getting angry with the wrong man, so he tried to calm down. "Look... the race is real, the prizes are real, and so will the conflicts be real, even those out of the air." He calmed himself even more with a smile. "John, this is a race, just like we discussed many times in the past. It will be fair, as fair as I can make it. But you do know the rules, and the second half will be war-like. They'll need all their fighting skills to win... you do know that, don't you? It's a new beginning for most of them. They've got nothing to go back to... their world is here and now."

"Yes, Admiral, I know and I approve of the rules. I just don't see it as strongly as you." His admission was dredged from a place beyond logic and reason.

"Someday I'll tell you why it's so important to me." The admiral looked down at his watch. "Shouldn't we be going?" As John looked at his own watch, the admiral walked to the wall once more. He took down the photo of his wife and one more, and put them in his briefcase.

"The car's just outside. We'd better get a move on." John was still a bit uneasy as they went through the outer office and to the car.

They didn't speak much on the short ride to the docks, but once they got there the admiral said, "Have you said your goodbyes to Susan?"

"Yes, this morning."

The car came to a stop and the driver got out and opened the door for the two men. "Kiss your wife and kids goodbye, then go get everything ready. I'll be right there. I have to look at some papers here in my briefcase."

"Okay!" John went through the door and walked up to his family, who were waiting by the ramp.

Robert watched through the window as he saw the tears fall from the females. He wished they were tears for him. Suddenly, John bolted up the ramp, leaving them all behind. Robert got out of the car and said, "Susan, can I talk to you a minute here in the car?"

She smiled and wiped the tears from her eyes. "Sure. You kids, stay close; we'll be leaving soon." She had a funny look on her face as she entered the car and took a seat. She was afraid of bad news, and almost didn't want to hear the next line. She had been disappointed so many times before.

Robert looked up the ramp and saw that John had vanished inside. He turned and joined Susan in the backseat. "I've got some things for you." He started going through his briefcase. He pulled out some papers and put them on his lap. "First, this picture." As they gazed at it, a tear flowed down his cheek and fell on the glass. "It's my wife and my son… I keep it with me always. It needs to go back home to Honolulu. Will you take it there for me?" His red eyes stared at her, waiting for an answer.

She was too startled by his request to offer any objection. His smile broke the tension between them. He handed the photo to her. "Please hang this in a good spot in your new house." He gave her the top paper on his lap. "It's the deed to my home in Honolulu. It's yours now."

Susan looked down at the photo of the house. The surprise siphoned the blood from her face. "I can't believe it!"

Robert was feeling very happy. It was the first time since his wife's death that happiness had been in his heart, and it felt good. "The party's not over yet!" He reached for the other document and gave it to her. Susan's hands were trembling; "These are two, four-year tuitions to the University of Hawaii for the girls. John is worried about the girls' education."

Susan's jaw was lying on her lap. She couldn't believe what was going on. She didn't even know Robert that well. He was giving her family a whole new life. *Thank you, God,* was all she could think.

Another paper flashed in front of her face. "Four tickets on

31

the clipper for tomorrow, leaving San Francisco Pier # 39 at eleven o'clock."

"There's only three of us, Robert." She was thinking much too logically.

"I thought you had a dog. You wouldn't leave the dog behind, would you?"

She started laughing; the emotions were swirling around inside her like a girl at her first prom.

The next piece of paper was pretty, a light blue, with little figures on it. It was folded in half. "Look at it. Go ahead and read it." He felt like one of Santa's helpers.

She gushed out an ungodly sound from deep in her throat. "One hundred thousand dollars. We're rich… my God, we're rich!" Susan's tears began to flow once more.

"Hang on, I don't have much time, and the most important thing is yet to come." The last paper was of a rich, satin texture and was written in gold lettering; he tried to sit erect as he read it. "'The Navy Department is happy to reinstate and reassign Commander John Norris as Harbor Master, Port of Pearl Harbor. Commander Norris hereby will receive all benefits and compensations due forthwith.' Tell John, when you see him, that the navy always corrects its mistakes." His voice had an infinitely compassionate tone.

Susan grabbed him and squeezed him till he could no longer breathe. Her tears bounced off his shoulders like rain in a storm. "Thank you, Admiral! May God bless you always!"

Robert raised his finger to her. "Just keep this a secret from John till the race is over. I'll have him call you from Australia when it's through. You go get the house all fixed up for him. I've got to go now or he'll get suspicious." He started to get out of the car when she gently took hold of his arm.

"I'll proudly hang the picture right where all can see it." She softly kissed him on the cheek. "Goodbye, sir."

He took her hand and kissed it. "Just enjoy the sunsets. They're beautiful, just like you." He stepped out of the car, called the girls over from their small boat and told them to get in. "Be happy, Susan!" Closing the door, he watched the car turn and go out of sight. He looked up into the blueness of the midday sky. "I hope you don't mind, Joanna!"

The ramp was steep, especially for someone of his age. As he reached the top, he passed a seaman running down with his arms full of papers. *Must be the insurance documents,* he thought. He then turned and entered the ship. The smell of diesel overcame his senses and as he walked, he noticed the hustle of the crew trying to get ready to sail. The shouting of orders over the loud speakers, the arms directing personnel here, then there... it all brought back earlier days. He felt young again and he smiled. The men were almost in awe as he passed; few of them had ever seen admiral insignias before. He was dismayed slightly. This would be his last day as a rear admiral but it was time for it to end, he thought. John was waiting at the entryway to officer country. "Is everything in order?"

"Yes, sir. The pilots are in the wardroom, all stores and fuel loading are completed, and the captain has been given orders to sail."

The admiral stopped and looked at the outer hatches being closed. "The pilots that sailed over with the ship from Liverpool haven't been told anything, have they?"

"No, sir. You wanted to explain everything to the whole lot. We haven't said a word, though they ask constantly!"

The admiral noticed the new black flight suit John was wearing. He reached up and rubbed the gold number two on his shoulders. "Looks good!"

"The pilots' suits are blue, with their numbers in white. They're being delivered to their quarters as we speak."

"Any trouble yet?"

"No, they're still trying to figure everything out, but I'm sure we will have some. You always have some trouble with flyers. You know that; you're a flyer yourself!" A grin crept onto his face.

"I'd better hurry and get dressed then. Give me ten minutes and I'll meet you in the wardroom. Better have a couple of the security men standing by, just in case."

"Yes, sir, I have just the ones, two ex-Marines that did brig duty with me on the *Lexington*. Real red-liners, if you know what I mean."

"In ten then!" The admiral turned and went through the

gangway, turning right, then left and then right again. He opened the door to a small room; everything was painted navy gray. Only the whiteness of the sink and the pillows stood out from the dullness. He took four steps and he was in front of a small locker. Inside were five black flight suits, all brand new, with a small number one on each shoulder, all hung up in a neat row. He looked down at the all-white uniform he was wearing, his shiny, white shoes and his bright brass. He touched the fruit salad that covered his left breast. "Get with it, old man." He started undressing. When he came to his shoulder boards and ribbons, he gently took them off the shirt and put them in the top drawer. He put the uniform in a laundry bag that was hanging on the door. He stood in the middle of the room for several moments, feeling cold, and goose bumps shot up his arms. He spotted a mirror over the sink. He moved to view himself. *You are an old bastard,* he thought.

His face seemed older than it should be; the white hair had somehow turned to silver, almost overnight. He glanced down to his arms. They were wrinkled with blemishes, age spots, and it looked like he had no muscles in them at all. He remembered when he was twenty and he would flex his arms for the girls to ooh and ah over.

He went close to the mirror; his eyes even looked dull to him. The deep blue of youth seemed to have faded to gray. "Those days are gone forever, you fool," he said to his reflection. He reached in the locker and brought out one of the suits. He quickly put it on, then sat down and put on his new shoes. They weren't shiny, and he didn't like that. He heard the foghorn blast. *That's my signal to get this game underway.* He stood and left the room.

The walkways were empty in officer country as he made his way to the wardroom. He entered to find his officials, in their black suits, lined up in front of the room. The pilots had all arrived and were all sitting in the pilot chairs that were lined in rows, six to each row and six rows. The admiral knew there were thirty-six contestants; he looked to the table as he passed it and he smiled to see everything in order; stacks of manuals and paperwork, all neatly piled in thirty-one stacks. The pilots didn't see him come in and they were mumbling to themselves.

One of them spotted him and stood up. "Attention!" All the pilots snapped to attention.

The admiral looked and then waved to John.

John spoke loudly and sharply. "There are no officers in this race! Be seated!"

Looks of confusion were everywhere and the mumbling started up again. Katya appeared uneasy with the black uniforms but the others didn't mind at all, so she would wait and see if these black-uniformed men were those dreaded police she had wondered about on the train.

"Some of you might think this is a military venture, being on an aircraft carrier and all. For the rest of you who don't know it, this vessel is a carrier, and you fly aircraft off of it." He finished his sentence just as he got to the front of the room. He stopped and stared at the group. "This contest is strictly a private endeavor. So, there are no officers to salute or stand to attention for. You will refer to these men in black by their numbers on their uniforms, no names. They will be your instructors and will be grading you." A grin crept onto his mouth. "Don't piss them off, if you know what's good for you!"

"Grading? What the fuck do I need grading on? Do I look like a schoolboy?" a pilot said in the back of the room.

"No, you don't look like a boy, just a fool!" The admiral scowled at the man for a few long seconds. "Please stand." He reached his hand out and Number Six quickly put a file in it. He opened it and started to read, letting the pilot stand there looking foolish for a bit. "You're a Romanian, Mr. Balan?"

"Yes… Admiral!"

One lowered the file and shot a look of disapproval towards the Romanian. "Were you not just told there are no officers in this contest?"

"Yes… but I saw you come onboard."

"On this trip we all will be recognized by numbers; us in black, and you, if you pass the test, will eventually be in blue. Even the aircraft you will be flying are numbered. I'm Number One, you are Number Twelve."

The flyer nodded his head. "Yes, Number One!"

Number One lowered his eyes back to the file. "Being a Romanian, I take it you've never seen an ocean or a carrier before this trip, is that true?"

"I've never seen so much water in my life!"

He slapped the file against his leg and in a soft and deliberate tone said, "Then you do need some schooling, don't you? Sit down and keep your mouth shut!" He gave the file back to Number Six. "Listen, people. Do me a favor, and listen before you speak. I can't stand stupidity, especially from a flyer." He took a deep breath and let it out slowly. "Let's start over; this is a privately run race. The start will be Hawaii and the finish will be Australia. It will take you about nine thousand miles, with ten legs. Half the legs will be on this vessel; the others will be on landing strips on South Pacific Islands."

"I don't understand," came another voice from the back of the room.

"We're going to hop from island to ship, probably alternating each time. Is that right, sir?" The woman's voice interrupted the low murmurings of the males.

"Exactly!" replied One.

The group started rustling around.

"Let me get some things out of the way. First, most of you are aces in your own right... the exceptions are some of the women, but their flying abilities are unquestionable. Anyway, there will be only nine contestants in the race."

Two or three pilots stood in protest and their shouting interrupted One's speech.

"Sit the fuck down and listen!" One stood erect with his hands on his hips. "The nine best pilots." He turned to Number Two and signaled him to remove the cover on the blackboard. "The nine best aircraft for this race!" There were large pictures of nine aircraft on the board. A Zero, Yak-7, a Sea Hurricane, a Sea-fire, Hellcat, Corsair, Polikarpov I-16, a Messerschmitt 109, and a Macchi MC 202.

"Gentlemen and Ladies; these are the warbirds of this race." Number One looked proud at this group of aircraft, his head tilted high. He turned to face the pilots. "You were all picked by me for several reasons. You all speak and read English… all information and instructions will be given in English; also, your commands in the air. Second, you all flew warbirds in the last war, and third, you all are good flyers."

Stanis stood. "What about the ones not picked for the race? We came all the way here for nothing?"

One clasped his hands behind him. "Weren't you all given a thousand American dollars?" One glanced down. "Dufresne, how much is that in French francs? Or you, Budanova, in Russian rubles? How about lira, marks, or pounds? I'll tell you. More than you all made in a year when you were in the military." He walked up to the standing Stanis and got close to his face. "Didn't you negotiate with me for your wife to be brought from Poland to England, to be with you… and did we not do so? I think we even gave you the thousand anyway, so she could get settled, didn't we, Mr. Chalupa?" He abruptly turned from him and returned to the front of the room. Stanis had sat back down in the meanwhile.

"You Germans, did you want to stay in Germany? How about you Italians? You Russians, you couldn't wait to join the food lines, could you… and I wouldn't want to leave out our Japanese or Chinese guests, would I? The point is, your passports and travel visas are worth more than any amount of money to most of you! That's what you get out of the race, a chance for a new life! You men and women—"

"Chow fah hai!" a male voice loudly cut through their thoughts.

Number One's face erupted into a mass of red. His blood was already up but he kept his temper. "You think you're the only one that speaks Chinese here? Stand up!" One again reached for a file and Number Six obliged. "Mr. Chu, or Number Fourteen, as we like to call you, thinks the women in the room are smelly, cheap cunts!" One glared at him, then threw his file to the floor. Number Fourteen stood there with his head bowed in disgrace.

"Evelyn Sharp, please stand up." One's voice was resonant and impressive.

She stood as tall and as erect as she could. She gave a little sneer in the direction of the Oriental.

"Number Twenty-six's file, please." Once again it was front and center. He opened it and began reading out loud. "You were a member of the famous WASPs. How many hours do you have in the air?"

"Over 3,000 hours, sir!"

"What type of aircraft have you flown?"

She grinned in the direction of the foolish man with his head down. "P-38s, P-47s, BF-13, P-51s, A-24, B-25s, and even a VC-78, Number One, sir!"

"Did you and your group go to the same flight school as the male cadets?"

"Yes, sir!"

"Under the same conditions and requirements?"

"Yes, sir!"

He closed her file and handed it back. "You may be seated, thank you. Oh, by the way, how many women were killed in action while you were a member of the WASPs?"

Her face saddened a bit as she answered, "Thirty-eight."

"Number Fourteen… raise your head!" One could see a raw hurt glittering in his dark eyes. "You could fly a fighter in the morning and return in a bomber that night… could you? I think not!"

He did not answer. His brows drew together in an apologizing expression.

"Amy Johnston, please stand." The Chinese pilot was still standing but his back was bowing more with every word. One was given her file. "You've already made this trip before, haven't you?"

She kept the left side of her face turned towards the group. "Yes, Number One, in a Gypsy Moth in 1930, a little over 11,000 miles solo."

"You also were a pilot for the RAF from '39 through the end of the war. I see here that you women of the Air Transport Auxiliary were not allowed to engage the enemy." She didn't answer. "Can you explain how the aircraft you were flying got credit for five victories but you got officially none? That means your plane was an ace but you were not!"

"I got tired of being shot down!" She tried to smile but a grin was the best she could manage.

"Thank you." He glanced back over to where the Chinese pilot was shrinking. "Katya Yegorova, please stand." Number Six tried to hand him her file. "I don't need a file on her!"

Viktor was yelling and whistling over in one of the corners. She looked at him and signaled him to shut up.

"How long were you in the Soviet Air Force?"

"The whole war... since the pigs invaded Poland!"

"Senior Lieutenant, how many victories do you have?"

"Twelve unassisted and eight assisted."

"Enough said!" He walked up to the Oriental and said, "Anything else you got on your mind? No... I didn't think so! Sit down!"

He walked back to the front of the room. "As you might have already concluded, your hatreds, prejudices, and dislikes will be a part of this race. It was meant to be that way. During your combat days, I'm sure you asked yourselves many times, who's the best? This race will find that out!"

One turned to Two and whispered something to him, then returned to the group. "Before I go on, there's one more thing I don't want to forget. You will be immediately disqualified if you interfere with anyone involved with the running of this vessel or not following rules on the flight deck. Is that clear? You will be restricted to the second deck, where you are now, up to the sickbay. You are not to go any further aft than sickbay. You may go on the hangar deck but do not interfere with any of the maintenance people or flight personnel. The flight deck is okay as long as there's no operation going on. Stay in officer country! In with your stack of information are maps of the ship, with outlines of the different decks. You have your own Pantry, Lounge, and wardroom. The Ready rooms are where you will be taking classes. While I'm at it, in your information you will find conversion sheets, from metric to American systems, all measurements of distances, all aircraft manuals, a booklet of acronyms used by the navy—everything you will need to succeed. You will be quartered in alphabetical order but the women, even though quartered with the men, will use the heads in sickbay. If you use another, you do so at your own risk. Is that clear, ladies?"

"What is a head?" Katya asked.

One smiled, "Toilette, privy, bathroom. Showers are also there, and the nurses in sickbay will have all your female needs."

"I've got a need!" The Italian flyer grabbed his crotch and pumped the air.

One's smile became stone hard. "Everything onboard is permitted, as long as it's consensual. Got it?"

"I'm not sleeping with any niggers!"

The voice that shouted out the words of disapproval definitely had a Southern drawl to it.

Katya's interest became sharp and attentive.

One looked around the room for the speaker; it had to be one of the Americans. But then one of the Germans stood and said, "We all know these blackies are an inferior race!"

"Mr. Nolder… yes. I'm surprised I haven't heard from you yet, you being in a class of your own, so to speak. So, you think the Negro is not up to par with the mighty German race?"

"Mr. Yokes, please stand." Two handed the file to One. "You flew Mustangs, P-51s. Did you fly with any white men?"

As he tried to stand at attention, his 6' 2" 195-pound body was shaking from his effort to hold his temper. "No, only colored!"

Katya became mystified; it was the Africans that had scared the people on the train. There are no police in black; she was semi-relieved. But why do they hate and fear them so? She never read anything about any war between the Americans and the Africans. And why would a goddamn German dislike them? Those words, nigger, spear-throwers, or fruit-eaters used by the German and the people on the train must be derogatory. The look on their faces when they spoke of them gave her the chills. The black ones she had seen on her trip were nothing but kind and cheerful. She wondered why some of them could walk and work with everyone else, but some had to be segregated to separate cars on the train. Even here it seemed that way, it didn't make any sense.

"So, all your squadron's credits would have to be by Negro flyers?"

"Yes, Number One." His anger was bringing him to the point of tears, and sweat had appeared on his brow.

The anger in the room was palpable and his own temper was rising. "Do you know the loss rate of the bomber groups you were supporting before your outfit took over the job?"

"On an average... three bombers a mission, sir."

"And afterwards?"

He snapped his head from the front of the room to the back, to glare at the German. "None. We shot all those krout bastards down!"

"How long did your group keep a zero loss of bombers?"

His eyes still fixed on the Nazi's blues he answered, "Till the end of the war!"

"In what theaters were you operating?"

"Sicily, Italy, France, then Germany."

"Do you yourself have any victories?"

"Seven, with two probable."

"Please be seated." He felt good inside; a small warm spot grew in his chest. *Now to this German,* he thought.

"Mr. Nolder, weren't the Olympics held in Berlin in 1936?"

Nolder was sucking on a cigarette and pretending not to care what was being said when the question was asked. "Yes, I attended." A smug expression was still on his face as he took another puff.

"Didn't your Fuehrer make a point to have at least one German in every event?"

The grin that had been on his face was melting into a frown. "I think so."

"Didn't a Negro gentleman named Jesse Owens tromp the living shit out of the German so-called superiority? Winning I think at least four gold medals?" Before he could come up with some kind of answer, One turned to Mr. Yokes and asked, "In your victories, what type of aircraft did you shoot down?"

Yokes replied with a smile, "Messerschmitt 109s."

With a slight turn of his head and an arching of his brows, One asked, "Mr. Nolder... who's inferior now!"

"I have one hundred and one victories. I don't have to answer to any of this blackies so-called seven with probable! He's lucky he didn't come up against me!" He flung his cigarette to the floor. "I received the Iron Cross!"

One grinned, for the German had taken the bait. "Let's take a look at your so-called victories!" He turned the pages of the file, then stopped and looked up at the German. "Let's see, there were 59 WWI vintage bi-planes, all outdated even then… they were shot down by you in the first three days over Poland. You in a ME 109 with four times the air speed, six times the munitions, and a surprise attack. No combat training by the Poles, and you had been training for almost a year, with that Dog Pack technique; what was that, three or four to one, was it not? Tell me, how did you divvy up the victories among the pack?" He didn't wait for the German to answer, as he watched Nolder puffing his cigarette rather rapidly. "It says here you destroyed thirty-one planes on the ground. Were those aircraft counted with your other victories? Oh, I'm sorry, the answer is right here, yes, they were," he said with a grin. "Next, there were two observation balloons—I hope they were large balloons—three observation Pipers, and one glider… come on… a goddamn glider?" He was enjoying this to no end. He didn't like the smugness of the Germans. "That seems to leave only five air combat victories over equal or superior aircraft. Again, I ask, who's inferior?" He gave the file back to Number Six. Nolder was pretending he wasn't listening and lighting another cigarette.

"Listen, I'm not judging any of you. We all have to do things distasteful in war… it's the nature of the beast. Do yourselves a favor and look upon this race the same way. It's a race for warriors! I'm going to turn you over to Number Two. He will be running the show from here on in."

Two took up One's place. "I'm Number Two, the flight official and operation official, like your squadron leaders used to be. We have a ten-day sailing to Hawaii. In that time, you will be given classes on how to land and take off on a carrier. That will take up the first two days. Some of you know this already, but you'll take the courses anyway. You're at least a little rusty.

"Then you will get to fly in each of the aircraft you'll be racing in. Classes in the mornings, then you'll be tested and graded and then given maneuvers in the afternoon. The maneuvers are all the same for every plane. The grading on both the classroom and the flying will be by these men here in black. The best nine scores fly in the race. Simple."

The pilot from Japan raised his hand and stood. "Why don't we just practice in the planes we're going to race in? It's apparent we will be flying in the aircraft we all flew in during the war. That's why you brought us together, isn't it? A second match-up?"

"You're mistaken, and you're correct. Each day of the race there will be a drawing to see which aircraft you'll be flying that day. So, you'd better learn as much as you can about all of them. You'll never know until one hour ahead which one is yours for that day.

"By the way, third prize is $25,000. Second is $50,000. First prize is $150,000; the rest get $1,000 for every leg completed and a ticket back to wherever they wish to go. The flyers not picked will get a ticket on arrival in Honolulu. The exact rules will be given to the chosen nine." It seemed easy to the group. Two saw no signs of confusion, no murmuring of discontentment.

"Now, I need you to pick up your stack of information; your berthing number will be on top, then proceed to your cabins and dress, no civilian anything. Everyone's the same for this trip. Make sure the number on your suits matches your number on the information sheet, along with your name. Using the wrong number could cost you the race!

"When you're finished, return here and be seated by your number on these chairs. They will be numbered by the time you get back. Oh, if there's anyone who doesn't like the berthing arrangements, he or she is welcome to spend the nights sleeping here in these chairs for the next twenty days. Or I could arrange for the helicopter to take you back to Alameda? No takers for a helicopter ride, I see. Well then, see you back here in an hour."

The group rose and headed for the tables. On top of each stack of manuals and such were the flyer's name, number, and a map to their cabin with its number. The stack was a little heavy and awkward to carry but everyone managed. The women seemed to gather around each other, hoping to be berthed together; they lingered to the rear to be the last.

"What number are you?" asked Amy.

"Number Thirty," replied Katya.

"That leaves me out, I'm Sixteen." Amy didn't look unhappy though.

Katya glanced towards the other woman, who looked a bit confused. "I'm sorry, I don't remember your name."

"Evelyn Sharp... I know my husband's not going to like this situation."

"So, don't tell him! You heard Number One, it has to be consensual, so don't say yes. By the way, what's your number?"

"Twenty-five!" Her voice quivered slightly.

"Good, we'll be somewhat close. We'll look out for each other, okay?" The other two women nodded their heads in agreement. Katya was trying to help the other two gals; she had been rooming with men for over three years. In the war you slept in the first empty bed you could find, next to a man or not, and most men only talked a good game anyway. When it came right down to it, they were kittens.

"After we get dressed, let's meet in the sickbay. We have to find where we piss anyway. I don't mind sleeping with a man in the room but pissing, I need a little privacy." Katya noticed that Amy didn't seem to be bothered by the arrangements at all. Maybe she liked men... but something felt weird about her.

CHAPTER THREE

THE NARROW PASSAGEWAYS WERE CROWDED with flyers trying to read their maps, carry their things, and find their quarters. The deck was riddled with manuals and booklets that had been dropped in their quest. The noise echoed endlessly throughout the ship; everything being metal seemed to intensify the volume. The bulkheads, the doors, even the goddamn floor was all the same color (gray), which made every room and closet look the same. There was also a chill in the air and the bulkheads felt cold to the touch. Number One had positioned his men in black at different junctions so they could assist the flyers.

With about two-thirds of her materials still intact, Katya finally found her quarters. She entered to find a very well-built, 6' 2" man just pulling his new flight suit over his well-rounded ass.

"Don't you wear underwear?" she asked.

He seemed to shrink into his flight suit. "Oh, pardon me... I'm sorry... I didn't mean to..."

Standing in the middle of the doorway watching him button up his flight suit, she could tell he was nervous and more than a little embarrassed. Little points of perspiration were creeping up on his forehead while he fought with the buttons. "Men... with their big hands." She walked over to the dresser and laid her things down on its top, then strolled over to the large man. He still had the two top buttons to go. With a motherly look she said, "Here, let me help you." She took his immense hands and gently lowered them to his side, like you would a child's. "There, that's not all that hard, if you stay calm." She smiled and tilted her head to one side.

He looked like he was going to cry. His face was wrinkled up and the sweat started to flow like tears. He wasn't old; actually, he was very young, maybe his late twenties. But the fear on his face aged him twenty years. "Please, ma'am, tell me you're not my roommate!"

She took a half-step back in shock. Anger overtook her and with a scornful tone said, "I got the fungus or something?" She looked down at herself, then at the bottom of her shoes. "I stepped in dog shit, or maybe some cow manure?" She looked back up at him; there was something definitely wrong with the man. "Are you all right? You look ill." Her disposition turned from anger to sympathy and concern.

"I'm going to have to sleep for three weeks out there in one of those Godforsaken chairs." His eyes lowered and he turned toward his bunk and his things.

Katya knew the problem was the sleeping arrangements, so she put her hands on her hips and regained her sober stance. "You got plans on raping me or something? Or maybe you think I'm going to try to rape you?" She walked closer to his retreating backside. "I have to admit, you do have a nice ass, but I don't think it's going to keep my nipples erect all night. Stop this nonsense and pick a drawer, top or bottom?"

He turned quickly around, gracefully for a big man. "Please, ma'am, don't talk that way. Someone might hear you."

She slammed her hand on top of the dresser. "Fuck someone! Listen, I say what I please and I'm not a ma'am, my name is Katya. Now pick a goddamn drawer!" She'd be damned if she would put up with all this white against black, male against female shit. It made no sense to her. Anyway, all men lie. They're all the same; all fools just trying to get their dicks rubbed.

His shoulders fell, he slumped over a bit and his head turned slightly down. "I just don't want any trouble, ma'am."

She put her hands back on her hips and regained that motherly look. "What'd I tell you about that ma'am shit?" She then pointed to the dresser with a scowl.

Yokes picked up his things and walked over to the dresser. He opened the bottom drawer and put his things neatly in.

Katya smiled. "Good. Since you got to pick which drawer you wanted first, I get first pick on the bunks. I choose the bottom." She flew over to it and threw herself in the middle of her mattress. "By the way, what's your name again?"

A very large smile split his face and the perspiration had dried up. "Yokes." The extra years that were there only minutes ago vanished as he relaxed and shook his head. "I think I'm going to like you, Katya!"

She returned his smile with a little giggle. "With a man your size, there's never any doubt which side I'm on. I'd better hurry and get dressed or we'll be late." Hopping up from the bunk, she soared over to the metal closet. She opened it and took out one of her suits. "Number Forty, my lucky number. And I've always loved blue!" She turned to him and raised her shoulders and eyebrows. "I see you're Forty-one." She then unzipped the side of her slacks.

"Wait!" He held his hands forward like he was pushing something. "I'll go right outside the door." He picked up his shoes, then turned his head so as not to see anything showing as he hurriedly passed her for the door.

A puzzled expression overtook her. "Don't worry, Yokes... I wear underwear!" She started laughing as he shut the door. "Men!"

Viktor was busy looking at the numbers outside the cabins: 226, 228, 230... it must be on this side. He moved further and further back till he could see only a dead end in front of him. He was being followed by one of the Orientals, only a few steps behind. He had turned several times to smile at him but didn't say anything. *Finally,* he thought, as he opened the door and walked in. "There's prison cells larger than this!" The smell of new paint lingered in the air. It was dark, and only the light from the passageway dimly lit the room. It had no porthole to the outside. The lights startled him as they came on and he turned quickly back to the door.

The Oriental was standing there with his hand on the light switch. "That's better, isn't it?" The yellow-skinned man was short, maybe 5' 4". The bundle he was carrying looked to outweigh him. He was dressed in military garb, camouflage in the green patterns, but he definitely didn't look like a soldier, more like a child pretending to be. He took a couple of steps and put his bundle down on the lower bunk. "Is that all right with you?" His voice was low, very manly; it surprised Viktor. "My name is Sadaaki Akamatsu." He spoke so fast Viktor couldn't tell where the first name ended and the last began. The small man recognized Viktor's confusion. "Just call me Sake," he said with a smile.

Until he smiled, the man didn't show any expression at all. The Orientals with their blank faces; they do it to confound people, Viktor thought. He had never seen an Oriental before but he had read about them, the same with the African. "Are you Chinese, maybe?"

"No, Japanese!"

Viktor was amazed by the way in which this Oriental spoke English, like he had just come from Yale or Harvard. He had no Japanese accent at all and there was no bowing. Viktor thought all slant-eyes bowed. "I'm Russian, from Moscow."

"A fine country, now that it leaves Japanese islands to Japan. Your Czar had to learn that lesson the hard way. Aren't you called comrades or Soviets now?"

Viktor got stiff, slightly insulted. "That was a long time ago. We don't have Czars anymore, not like some of us who need Imperial leadership, we Russians rule ourselves now!"

Sake smiled and extended his hand in friendship, "*Touché*, friend!"

In a room down the hall, another two roommates wandered the room putting their things away, not saying a word to each other and both liking it that way. They would occasionally glance around to see what the other was doing. After she arranged her drawer and put some personal things on the bottom bunk to claim it, Amy went to the closet and brought out a blue suit with a number Twenty-three in bold, white lettering on it. She wondered how Number One could know so much about all of them. The suit was exactly her size, the shoes within a half-size; for a woman, not too bad. Even the bra and panties were right. All that information that he knew at the first meeting, those files, were huge. He really tore that German a new asshole, she thought as she grinned. She glanced over to where the old man was standing. *He couldn't hurt a fly; he's so old. How could he have flown in the war? Maybe he's an ace from the first war? His skin is so weathered, and those bags under his eyes… they are beautiful, black eyes, though.* But he still reminded her of a hound dog. All she knew was that he wasn't English and definitely not from the US. Americans couldn't keep their mouths shut for more than five seconds. *He also doesn't have that arrogant look of a German or a Finn.* She'd have to ask around. She gathered her clothes and left for the sickbay to change.

Pinche puta! How the hell did that bitch expect an old man like him to climb up to that bunk? Females, they're all the same, me, me, me. He slammed his things into the drawers. His name was Angel Diego Harrazabal, but that didn't mean he could fly! If he had her ass back in Barcelona, he'd teach her some manners. He was appreciated there; the name Harrazabal was treated with *respecto*. He was a fucking hero in two wars; the Spanish Civil War and with the Germans on the Russian front. He was Spain's greatest ace! Now he was stuck with an ugly, white as a bed sheet, flat-chested woman with her tongue cut out. Wait a minute, Diego! That might not be bad luck at all… a mute woman?

He turned to his own metal locker and removed the blue suit. "Fucking Twenty-two." What kind of number is that for a man like him? Whatever happened to number one? After he put the suit on he sat and put on his new shoes. He stood and looked down at himself. "Not too bad, it'll do."

Amy walked back into the room with her civilian clothes in her arms. She saw Diego sitting on her bed reading one of the manuals. He took his glasses off and cleaned them on her pillowcase. "You're going to have a hard time getting up on that bunk, aren't you?"

He put his glasses back on and glared at her. *She can talk… I knew my luck wouldn't last!*

She gave him a smirk and then reached behind him for the things she had laid there earlier. Her gloved hand brushed his arm and he moved to one side. She picked up a picture, put it on the top bunk pillow, then walked to the laundry sack hanging on the door. She filled it with the clothes that were in her arms, then turned back to him. "Since you already soiled the pillowcase on the lower, I'll take the upper." Amy was starting to feel at ease with this man. She wouldn't have to worry about being hit on and he was quiet enough. Hopefully, he didn't snore. The arrangements would suit her just fine. She walked over to the pile of dirty clothes that were lying on the floor and looked down at them. "I'm not your maid, either. Please pick up after yourself."

He smiled and then nodded his head in agreement. He was grateful for her concession. She wasn't that bad after all; a little pale, but not that bad. He could never get a good look at her face, she was constantly moving. He rose, picked up the dirty laundry and put it in his bag. As he turned, he saw her burying a small black bag under the clothes in her drawer. *Private stuff,* he thought. "I hope you don't snore!" She turned slightly towards him and they both smiled at each other.

"Let me tell you a joke," Mike said.

"We don't have time for this, you guys," Dufresne popped up.

"It'll only take a minute." Mike was holding onto Matt and Mel's arms.

"Okay... okay, but hurry up. It's too crowded in here, I can't breathe," Mel said.

"How do you know the most popular man in a nudist camp?" Mike was grinning from ear to ear.

The three men answered in harmony. "I don't know... how?"

"It's the man that can carry two cups of coffee and a dozen donuts!"

Dufresne didn't really get it but laughed anyway. "Now, let's go!"

"No, no wait, the joke's not over. How do you know the most popular woman in the nudist camp?"

Once again, "We don't know!" the group sang out.

"The woman that can eat the last donut!" Mike started laughing uncontrollably; he thought it was the best joke ever.

Mel and Matt just got up, without the slightest grin, and headed for the door. Dufresne followed. Once outside and down the passageway a bit, Mel said, "That was quite funny. I'll have to remember that one."

"You going to show me around when we get you back home?" Matt said to Mel.

"You'll love Brisbane… it's nice in the summer."

"I hate to tell you, Mel old man, but it's almost October."

Mel smiled as he ducked his head through a passageway. "That's just the start of summer down under."

As they passed some others going the wrong way, Mike turned halfway. "All we have to do is get our asses in the race. If not, it's back to Alabama." Mike and Matt had been naval pilots so they knew their way around the ship. So was Mel, but his duty was on British vessels so they were a little different. The Frenchman was a follower. They left the fo'c's'le berthing and went aft, then down a ladder to the second deck, where the wardroom was filling fast. The small group gathered in the back of the room waiting for orders. The murmuring in the room grew with every new contestant's entry. Different groups started to form. Europeans of, shall we say, the Axis point of view, were front and to the right. The Allies were to the left, and in the middle were the Orientals. They simply stood alone like they didn't want anything to do with either clan. They seemed to be a little leery about sitting. They didn't know each other's names and wouldn't know if they would be split up by the alphabetical system. Smoke was filling the air. Matt noticed them nervously puffing on their cigarettes or pipes.

With all that was going on in the room, his thoughts drifted back to Katya. Her face was the loveliest he had ever seen. He had noticed she had a little quiver to her bottom lip when she was angry and a twinkle in her eyes when she seemed happy. On the train, when he was watching her daydream, she looked like an angel. Her hair gleamed gold with every beam of light that shone through the window of the moving train. Unlike the women he was accustomed to, she had a natural beauty that he liked very much. She listened well, too—or pretended to. He hoped she wasn't kidding about being his partner. If only he wasn't such a klutz about starting relationships with women.

Number One looked at his watch and then glanced over to Number Two. "It's time." He walked to the front of the room. "Please be seated." Katya and Yokes walked into the room just as the request to be seated was announced. "Your numbers have been put on the chairs. Please sit in these assigned seats from now on." Rumbling sounds were everywhere as the flyers looked for their seats.

Once the group was seated, there were more murmurings, some in disapproval. The group gawked from side to side, investigating their new neighbors. "Your attention please! Please! The rest of the day and night is to get acquainted. The Pantry will be open for mess at 18:00 hours. Breakfast is at 07:00 hours and lunch will be at 12:00 hours. The lounge is open from 19:00 hours to 22:00 hours. It's up to you if you wake up with a hangover!"

A Chinese pilot stood. With real confusion in his voice, "You're going to feed us three times in one day, every day?" he asked with a sidelong glance of utter disbelief.

"Yes, three squares a day." One grinned, knowing the man was honestly shocked with the eating arrangements. He probably never ate that much in his whole life.

"Are you sure you can get the planes off the deck, with us weighing a ton?"

"Number Twenty-one, you don't look like you have had any trouble getting off!"

"But, One, sir, that kind of getting off is not what we're talking about!" The room erupted into laughter, including the ladies.

After a few chuckles, One said. "Okay, okay, settle down. Let me finish. Tomorrow we'll be training on landing and taking off on the carrier. We will be using the Hellcat all day and the Sea-fire the next. You are all required to attend classes and pattern flying. If you miss class, you will automatically be sent home in Honolulu, even if you were a carrier flyer in the past... is that understood?" One looked over the room for someone to disapprove. "Okay then!"

He reached behind him to a table, picked up three booklets, then turned back to the flyers. "If you're smart, you'll give these three manuals a looking-over tonight. This one is the manual for the Hellcat; this one is the conversion table and without it, you pilots not familiar with our way of measuring things are going to have trouble. This last one is on the Delta and Charlie patterns needed to take off and to land. I want only the best in this race, the very best, so do your homework. I don't like burials at sea."

One looked over to Two. "Anything else for now?" Two shook his head. "Oh, by the way," One glanced down at his watch. "If you like, you've got time before mess to go up on the flight deck and watch us go under the Golden Gate Bridge."

For some curious, unknown reason, Matt instinctively turned and looked at Katya to find her staring back at him with that twinkle in her eyes. She shook her head. He smiled back, knowing her meaning. Number Nineteen, the Frenchman, slapped Matt on the leg. "Good work, you old dog!" He turned and also smiled at Katya.

Katya stood and waited for Matt to cross the room. He had to fight his way through the others headed out the narrow passageways. Like a little girl, she trembled with anticipation.

Yokes rubbed the back of her neck. "Loose, girl... stay loose." He smiled and gave her a wink, then withdrew to the passageway.

Matt extended his hand and gently pulled her towards him. "You don't want to miss this!" He noticed how soft her hand felt and massaged it slightly, and didn't turn it loose though it would have been easier to navigate the passageways. When they reached the ladder to go up, he put her in front and was pleasantly surprised at the view swaying from side to side in front of him. She was slender but not frail, he liked that... matter of fact... he liked all of her more and more.

When they walked through the hangar deck, he noticed that the other fellas enjoyed the view also. She looked good in blue! When they reached the last ladder, he got in front and on the last few steps he lifted her, mainly to show off his own strength but partly to feel her weight. He couldn't believe that he had touched a woman this much and she was still smiling. This was a first for him. Twenty-eight and his mother was the only woman he had ever kissed. Maybe, just maybe, this would be the one.

When they stepped out on the Flight Deck, they looked up to witness the sky on fire. The reds had merged with the oranges, some pink had filtered through the massive clouds, and there were yellows with streams of pure white. Jagged and sharp edges of the vapors formed demons straight from hell, and other clouds formed gigantic mountains of flame. They were surrounding each other in an endless decoupage of lights. It looked as if the heavens were at war. It took their breath away.

To the left was San Francisco, to the right, Oakland. They had just gone under the Bay Bridge, which Katya had mistaken for the Golden Gate. The moon shone over Oakland's skyline but San Francisco still looked to be on fire. They passed a small island right under the bridge and then they saw it. Its huge, arching cables with pillars standing so erect, it looked as if it was holding up the heavens. The sun suddenly got softer and the sky gave up its heat to a beseeching calm. The hues that gave off so much heat turned cooler as the sun faded into the horizon. It was the moon's time to reign. The waves were gentle as they passed under man's greatest technology. The wind was soft, with a slight scent of heather coming from the hillsides. They started walking from the front of the ship to the rear. The two of them wanted the moon, its blue softness and its romantic flickering. Almost all the other spectators had gone below decks; their stomachs were more in tune with food than with moonlight.

She heard him breathing, not loud, but in a smooth and steady way. She reached behind him and tucked her head into his side as they walked. The stars matched the twinkle coming from the houses that lay over the hillside and the city lit up the blackness of the starlit night with its peaks of fluorescent beams. The ship swayed slightly now, like it was waltzing with the waves. The moon took on a blue tint, and Katya swore it winked at her. Matt was building up his courage. He knew what the next step was but he didn't know if he could pull it off. He'd been to this point so many times before with girls and always flubbed it. He didn't want to look a fool again. His spit was hard to swallow and his blood pressure was gaining strength. He could feel his face tighten but the slow and constant rubbing of her hand on his back made him feel at ease. They stopped and turned to face each other. The moon's light reflected in her eyes as she looked up at him. He could only make out the outline of her face in the moonlight. This made things easier for him; she could not see the nervousness that was overtaking his face.

He looked down towards the water and saw the outline of the net that lined the deck. "Shall we sit?" he said in a dignified manner that was not his way at all. He prided himself in being a down-home boy. He felt he was starting to blow it, trying to become something he wasn't. As he helped her to sit on the edge of the deck, he heard her humming something. It was a light tune; the sounds of the waves were accompanying her mellow voice. He knew the tune but couldn't place it. "That's lovely," he said in a whisper.

"That's why I learned English and Italian at university. Their music is so mellow and soft. Their music has feeling to it; even if you don't know the words, it gives you chills to hear a love song sung by Sinatra or Como. I like Dean Martin, too. His Italian songs give me goose bumps. Of course, I like to swing to Benny Goodman or Dorsey, but my favorites are still the love songs. We used to pick up the American radio signal at night. The women flyers would huddle around the radio and dream that Como was singing just to us. I would translate his words of love to the other girls; after a while, there was no need to translate." A brisk wind blew on their backs and Kat pressed closer to Matt. He took out his left arm from his jacket and pulled it around her. He blew warmth on her hands and then tucked them into a pocket to keep them warm.

"Is this strange to you, Kat?" his soothing voice probed.

She sighed and then turned her chin upwards. "Strange... yes. At my age, very strange. But would I change places with anyone right now? No! I deserve a little romance, even if it lasts only one night."

The underlying sensuality of her words captivated him. He didn't know where the question came from or why he asked it, it just popped into his head like someone else was doing the thinking and talking for him. "Kat... what are you looking to get out of life?"

She took her head off of his chest and took a small lean backwards. She took hold of both his hands and kissed them. "You'll laugh."

His brow centered with confusion. "No, I won't... please!" The words still seemed to come from a movie plot or some romance novel he had read in the past, but he was glad he had said them anyway. They seemed important to her and in a small way, their future might rely on them.

She lowered her head and put his hands to her forehead. "Tenderness... a soft touch... a low and loving voice, gentleness in a man's eyes and a heart big enough for me to live in forever." She waited for him to say something but heard only the waves passing by the hull of the ship. "I missed out on my time for love. The war took it away from me and replaced it with hate and misery. I'm tired of fighting. I just want to love and be loved." She let his hands go and raised her eyes to meet his. She saw something she thought she would never see. A small tear was falling from his cheek. A star's glimmer reflected in its moisture. Her tears joined his and they made shooting stars as they kissed tenderly, oh, so tenderly.

The two of them sat out on the deck for several hours, necking, touching, and talking of love, like a couple of teenagers. She told him of her childhood back in Russia and the one love she had lost during the war. Matt told of Tampa life with its beaches, warm weather, and great people. She was just going to love his mother.

She asked him why the Americans disliked Africans. She was pleased to find out that all white people didn't dislike them and they weren't Africans, but Negroes or colored folk. His family didn't consider any race different from any other, and being more liberal than the rest of the South, had generally progressed past most of the bigotry and prejudice of that earlier period. Matt wasn't too happy with Kat's quartering, though; not because Yokes was a Negro, but because he was a man. Matt had noticed Yokes rubbing Kat's neck and the smile she had given him. He was surprised to feel a little twinge of jealousy.

They also talked about their business plans and how serious he was about making her a partner. For some reason, she wasn't too worried about the partnership. She never had money before, so losing it or jeopardizing her funds didn't bother her. She wasn't out to make money, just to fly and be happy.

They missed supper altogether but neither was hungry. Matt

didn't want to say goodnight but Kat made him. "You want to win the race, don't you? Then you got to get your sleep. Anyway… looks like I'm a prisoner. I've got nowhere to run."

Matt walked her to her quarters and gave her a last kiss goodnight. "By the way, who's your roommate?" He already knew the answer by the seating assignments but wanted to know how a Russian female would respond to such sleeping arrangements.

"Yokes," she said.

"Big Yokes?" His smile widened.

"Yes, Big Yokes. And we're good friends, so you better watch out or I'll sic 'im on you! Now go to bed, you idiot!"

Yokes listened from his bunk. He watched her as she shut the door, then leaned against it for several seconds, then smiled as she wandered over to her bunk.

"I think he's a nice guy, don't you?" said Yokes.

"Terrific!"

"I laid out your pajamas on the bed. I'll turn towards the bulkhead. Good night, Missy."

"Good night, Big Yokes."

CHAPTER FOUR

THE SIREN, A FOGHORN- TYPE device, sounded that it was 06:00 hours and time to rise and meet the new day. The two companions in Berth 226 simultaneously jumped to their feet, Yokes almost landing on Kat. They found themselves standing at attention; the military life was hard to forget. Kat had only put on her pajama top and Yokes only slept in his skivvies, so both were a little embarrassed the first morning. "I guess this sleeping arrangement will take some getting used to," Kat said, her eyes still half-shut from only a couple hours of sleep.

"Do you want me to stand guard while you shower and fix yourself up, Missy?"

She dropped her head and glared at him from the top of her eyes. "I don't like that Missy shit but I do like Kat... Kat does mean feline, doesn't it?" Matt had called her that all night and she liked being compared to a cat.

Yokes, wearing an approving grin, said, "Yes, it does!"

She smiled as she stared at the ceiling. "Someone called me that last night, I think I like it... Kat!"

"I wonder who?" replied a mocking Yokes. He purposely started admiring Kat's shapely legs, knowing she would react soon.

"They're better looking than yours!" She smiled as she reached for the bottoms of her pajamas. The drawer slid open and she hurriedly picked out underwear and then went to the closet for a fresh uniform. "I'm dying of hunger. I hope they have plenty to eat on this ship!" She turned to him. He was still standing in his skivvies watching her, his stomach hung over the elastic band a little. "Looks to me like you could miss a few meals there, Big Yokes!"

He immediately sucked in his belly and said dryly, "I'm in perfect flight condition."

"I'll see you at mess."

He smiled at her as she left the room for the sickbay.

"One right turn, down the first ladder, then right again, then aft and you're there." She remembered the map well.

There were two nurses and a doctor in the sickbay when Kat arrived. "I'm here for a shower and to get fixed up a bit."

"Right this way." One of the nurses escorted her to a far head, where there were three shower stalls, three toilets, and a number of sinks with mirrors over them. "We've been instructed to give you these." She handed Kat a box with a comb, a brush, toothpaste and toothbrush, rubber bands, and bobby pins. The feminine napkins came in their own little box. There was also another silver box; something special, she thought. Perfume. Chanel, it read. As she entered the stall and pulled the shower curtain closed she asked, "Have the other women been down yet?"

"The American likes to shower at night," replied the Aussie nurse. "We were told there were three of you though. We haven't seen the Brit yet."

"Is this where I come every day to wash up?" she asked, rinsing the hand soap from her hair.

"All males, including the doctors, are to keep clear of these heads. They are for the nurses and you women flyers. You are so lucky to be able to fly. I'd give anything to fly."

"Could you hand me that towel, please?" She reached through the plastic for the towel. "Is that why you like aircraft carriers?"

The nurse closed her eyes as if to dream. "Yes, the men and the planes. They both can give you such a thrill... can't they?"

She stopped drying her hair and lifted her brow as she said, "Yes... and in the same place, too!" Kat stepped out and started to get dressed. "You ought to learn how to fly when you get back home." She tied the last shoestring and gathered her dirty clothes. "Thank you very much for your help. See you later, I hope." She found her way back to 226 and deposited her clothes into the bag that was hung on the back of the door. She walked over to the dresser and picked up a picture that was there. A young woman and a child were sitting in what looked like a front yard. Their smiles were not contrived or posed but large and truly happy. The woman wore a rose-colored dress that complimented her fawn-colored complexion well. She was holding a baby; the ribbons in her hair left the impression it was a girl. They looked to be very happy; must be Yokes' family, "Lucky guy!" She put the picture back down just as her stomach made a hideous sound. "This won't do, got to eat something before I faint away."

When she entered the wardroom she saw Matt, the Frenchman, and the American, Evelyn, sitting at one of the tables. Their trays were full of food and they were busy eating. The room was about two-thirds full, and the other third were in line in the Pantry. Matt motioned Kat to where the end of the line was; her stomach took over and she got there hurriedly. Kat spotted Amy about five persons in front of her. She turned and smiled. Kat asked if she would like to join her at Matt's table. Amy agreed.

As Rudy approached the server, who had a giant slab of ham ready to slap on his tray, he gestured that he didn't want the meat. He slid by to the next server who was throwing hot cakes, butter, and syrup.

"That's all we need… a goddamn Jew!" The contemptuous words flowed out of the Romanian's mouth and silenced the room.

The German eyed Rudy straight on. "They're everywhere, like goddamn locusts!" Werner turned inward to his Romanian counterpart. "Don't worry… I won't let him crucify you!" His lips twisted into a cynical smile.

Rudy's face became a marble effigy of contempt as he threw his tray at the two Nazis and brazenly approached them. "Leap froggy! Make your move!" Rudy had sweat from his anger and fire streaming in his eyes. "I'll squash you like a toad, you Nazi bastards!" Every muscle was tense and at the ready. "I've been paying you assholes back for years now for what you did to my people. With every fascist plane in flames, my joy increased." His fists clenched to white, his trembling body and contorted smile left no doubt that this man was not to be reckoned with, at least not right now.

The two Nazis stood frozen like ice sculptures, their trays wavering slightly in their hands and the food mixing together to form an ugly texture.

The room was still hushed when Number Two spoke. "Are we through now with the religious hour? How about a sermon from the Baptist, or maybe the Catholics. We got some Buddhists? Think we should light some incense?" Everyone turned to him as he spoke. "Get your faces fed so we can get on with it!" The room exploded with a fury of eating and drinking. The three men silently backed off from one another, their faces twisted in bitter resentment.

Rudy left the wardroom steaming mad. The German and the Romanian laughed it off, trying to restrain their newfound fear. They weren't accustomed to Jews standing up for themselves. They brushed the food from their clothes and then continued through the line. Werner turned slightly and leaned towards his friend and whispered, "I think we ought to keep our opinions to ourselves. We're outnumbered here." The Romanian nodded his head in reply.

Kat was upset with this entire male ego crap. She'd lived with it all her military life. Men with their… know-it-all attitudes. I'm a better flyer than anyone else and I've screwed more women than any three men, my dick's longer than yours! All of it was nothing but horse dung and lies. She had learned to recognize and ignore most of it. The Rose had taught them that women could compete as equals right alongside the best of them.

Her stomach rumbled for some sustenance and the smells of breakfast lured her on. The young man behind the steam tray offered her a slab of ham. Kat pushed her tray forward to receive it. The mess cook put the piece of meat on her tray—it covered almost two-thirds of it—and then turned to the next person in line. In the middle of placing the meat on the next tray, he stopped and looked at Kat. Her tray was still extended. "Do you want more?" he asked.

"Yes, please!"

"How many do you want?" he asked, grinning in disbelief.

She widened her eyes and tilted her head. "One more will do!"

The cook turned to the next server in line and grinned at him. "Hope you got enough hash for this beauty."

As Kat moved to the next server she asked, "What is hash?"

"Corned beef and potatoes," he replied.

"Yes, I'll have that!"

The eggs came next; they were scrambled. The server raised his eyelids in surprise. Her tray was overfilled with ham and hash and some toast she had picked up at the beginning of the line. "Some eggs, ma'am?"

She looked around and then frowned. "Do you not have any regular raw eggs?"

The cook became bewildered. "I could get you some if you wish."

She smiled at the young man. "Yes, please."

He leaned forward and in a soft voice asked, "How many, ma'am?"

She leaned towards him and whispered, "Two would do just fine." While she was waiting for the cook to return with her raw eggs, she sampled the pink meat. Licking her fingers, she turned to find some of the flyers in line staring at her curiously. She grinned and said, "I've never had anything but gruel for breakfast before. I've never even seen meat in the mornings before that train ride. You got to bless these here Americans!"

"Here you go, ma'am, two raw eggs. You sure you don't want me to fry them up for you?"

She shook her head. "And ruin my dessert?" She took a pen from her uniform and punched a hole in the fat end of the egg, then a larger one at the smaller end. With her finger over one of the holes, she started to suck the egg from its shell, alternating her finger with the sucking. "Delicious!" she said as she finished it off. The cook's mate looked like he was going to get sick. Kat looked at him, shrugged her shoulders, and got back in line, where she picked up three cartons of milk. She looked back to the table where Matt was sitting. Yokes and Amy had joined the group and were waving her over.

As she made her way to the table, she saw Matt push Yokes on the shoulder; they were laughing and kidding around.

"You sure you got enough food there, Missy... I mean, Kat?" Yokes was still laughing when Kat arrived at the table.

"You assholes are telling jokes or something? Better be clean ones. You do have ladies sitting here." Evelyn was smiling, but Amy was stone cold. The brawling between the German and Rudy had apparently upset her.

"They've been okay. They're just talking about back home, and wouldn't you know, they're both Southern boys," said Evelyn. "Come sit by me and Amy. We've got a lot to talk about." As Kat reluctantly took a seat between Amy and Evelyn (she was hoping to be sitting next to Matt), her eyes never left Matt's face. That boyish grin was still there, along with those sparkling teeth and that simple twinkle was still in his eyes. Evelyn looked at Kat's tray. "You do know they serve lunch onboard?" Evelyn touched Kat's hand to get her attention.

Kat didn't hear her the first time. "Yes... pardon me... I didn't hear you!"

The two women looked past Kat and to each other. Kat was ignoring them and they smiled at one another. They knew what that look on Kat's face meant. At the same time they turned to Matt, to find the same look on his face.

Mike was loudly telling another joke to one of the Chinese flyers when he passed Matt's chair. The Oriental apparently wasn't getting the joke and strolled off shaking his head. "Mattie, old buddy, how's it hang-in'?" His Southern drawl was sickeningly thick. Matt didn't answer; he was too busy watching Kat watching him, over a piece of meat. Mike became upset with Matt's lack of attention. He leaned both hands on the table and stared right at Kat. "How does it feel, little lady?"

Kat, surprised by the question, replied, "How does what feel?" Her woman's intuition overtook her. Her eyes narrowed; she just knew there was going to be trouble. She clenched her steak knife and leaned forward.

His voice hardened ruthlessly. "To sleep with a nigger?" His last word barely got out of his mouth when he felt the pain. The bones in his jaw cracked and his teeth rattled in his mouth. He felt himself falling backwards onto another table. As his back hit the table, he lost his breath and his eyesight grew dimmer and dimmer till only blackness surrounded him.

His stare drilled into everyone. "Goddamn it!" Matt shouted, his fist and arm still in the air from the uppercut he had landed on Mike's jaw. He found himself standing over Mike's body as it crashed down on the table next to theirs. The legs gave way, leaving the occupants sitting in a circle looking down to the floor at Mike's already bruising and bloodied mouth. Mike wasn't moving; he was out like a light, with the food lying all around him. "I'm tired of this!" Matt growled. "You so-called brave warriors." The contempt in his voice was evident as he scanned the room for someone else that might have something to say. "You all make me sick!" He eased up a bit as there were no replies. "You condone rudeness to women? Religion is a joke to most of you! Rights and freedom mean nothing... but it's going to! You brave little men with big mouths can defend yourselves but I'm here to tell you, you keep your mouths and hands off these women or I'll put you all in sickbay for a long goddamn time! I will not tell you again!" Matt's sweaty and reddened face had every muscle tightened to the ready as the proof of his words. A few seconds passed and as the echo of his speech died down, the room started to empty. Some gave a thumb up as they passed, others just looked nervous.

Number Two had already left the wardroom. Brevan walked over to where Mike was laying. He looked at an Englishman and one of the Russians. "Get him to sickbay." The two pilots picked him up (Mike was beginning to come to and was moaning now). They helped him to his feet and down the gangway to sickbay. Number Three turned to Matt. "Noble speech... but watch your six!" Expressionless, he turned and walked through the mess that was on the floor. "Let's get this place cleaned up!"

Matt slowly turned back to Kat, who was now casually eating her hash, seemingly unconcerned with Matt's actions of a few seconds ago. "What the"

With a mouthful of hash, she tried to smile and talk at the same time. "It's your fault… you shouldn't have starved me last night." Inside she was filled with pride and respect but she would be damned if she was going to fall all over him for saving her reputation. She would save that gesture for later.

Yokes stood from his chair and extended his hand. "Thanks, friend!" They locked hands and shook rapidly.

Kat swallowed hard, then stood. "I thought you were defending my honor?"

The two men started laughing. Yokes pulled her to him and the three left with Kat describing Matt's blow with aroused vigor.

Amy, still sitting with a cold-hearted glare, followed the Germans as they left.

"See you later, Amy." Evelyn stuffed the last bite of toast into her mouth as she got up to leave.

The admiral stood on the landing portion of the flight deck and watched the first rays of sunlight creep up on the horizon. The ship moved easily through the calm seas. The air was brisk, but not quite cold; his choice of a light jacket had been a good one. He had not had a good night; his memories and thoughts had made him restless, giving him pause about the game. His wife's voice kept haunting him. Every time he would close his eyes and fall off to sleep, she would appear and tell him to think it over. What good would it do? she would ask. Would it change anything? Yes, it would, he thought. It would make things right in his heart.

He started to walk the length of the deck and when he reached mid-ship, the port elevator started up. The flight crews were bringing up the planes for today's lessons, Number One observed. The sun was in full strength now and the blue of the Hellcats gleamed in the morning air. The aircraft's skin looked tight from their newness. He continued his stroll past the two Sikorskies that were tied down forward so as not to be in the way of the work crews. He finally stopped about fifteen feet from the end of the deck. The wind had picked up, and the sounds from the engines brought back days better forgotten.

He thought of his son sitting in a cockpit, on a flight deck similar to this one, waiting for the sun and his Wildcat to warm up to operational temperatures. He watched the roll and pitch of the deck as it cut through the waves. His imagination heard the intercom on the deck shouting, "Turn into the wind." He looked up to a now empty Pri-Fly and saw shadows of the past signaling for takeoffs. The ghosts on the deck had the Wildcats throttling up, waiting for the flight officer to signal go like hell! Then they were being launched past him into the vast blue of the skies. He raised his arms and dashed to the center of the flight deck. "No… don't go… Mikey, don't go!" Tears appeared on his face and he started to grit his teeth. As some of the crew watched him, the voices faded and the roar of the engines took their place.

The wardroom was almost to capacity. At the front of the room were Brevan, Number Two, and some flight personnel. There were also charts and specifications on the Hellcat and a small movie screen. "Please take your seats." Brevan's request was a stern one and the room came to order quickly. "First, all orders will be given in English. So from now on think, breathe, eat, even shit English. Second, when flying, you will be addressed by flight control by your aircraft's number. It will be displayed front and center of all canopies, for those who can't remember their numbers. Also, all operations learned in the next two days will apply to all landings and takeoffs, both on the carrier and on ground landing strips. Any detouring from these procedures, without an emergency, will result in disqualification. Is that clear to everyone?" He looked around the room for someone that seemed to be in doubt. "Okay then!"

He turned to the chart and then quickly turned back. "Oh, by the way, don't miss a class the next two days, they're mandatory." Brevan looked to the middle of the group to find Mike nursing his jaw. He turned back to the table that was in front of a large chart. "Do you all have your materials? If not, come up to the table and see if they are here. We found these in the passageways yesterday. They will have your number on the inside if they're yours." As the room scampered to the table, Brevan walked over to Number Two, to go over last-minute thoughts.

"Now that we all have our required reading materials, let's start. All flyers will be using the Hellcat today. I assume by your files that you all can fly efficiently. So, for most of you, this is just a recap. I also hope that you all didn't stay up all night smooching on the flight deck or fighting about some last-minute religious differences or maybe the sleeping arrangements. I hope some of you are taking this race seriously. But, we'll find that out soon enough."

"The Hellcat." He pointed to an illustration hanging from the bulkhead. "Please follow me in your manuals. The F6F-3 uses a Pratt & Whitney R-2800-10. Its takeoff horsepower is 2000. Its max weight at normal load is 11,424 pounds. Max speed at sea level is 303 mph, 376 mph at 23,400 feet, and its normal cruising speed is 168 mph. Service ceiling is 38,100 feet. Her max range is 645 miles at 177 mph. Internal fuel capacity is 250 gallons. The rest of her dimensions are there in the manuals. One thing I can tell you from my experience flying the Hellcat in the war is, it's the most rugged and stable aircraft in the world. It can fly through anything and get your asses back on the deck." He smiled at the group and they responded with some laughter.

"It also has a heavy stick, which is good for landing on a moving deck. It's hard to overfly the plane." Brevan looked to Number Two and raised his finger for one more minute. "Takeoff distance is 265 feet. It will take off at 250 feet in a pinch. Respect its muscle! Do not exceed 440 knots, even in a dive. Maximum permissible speed for unlimited use of ailerons is 260 knots. Don't lower landing gear above 135 knots. This is not the plane a lot of you are accustomed to. It will flat-out kick butt. One other thing… it's a quirk of mine. Do not dogfight with a Zero! It has muscle but not much agility." His words and grin penetrated the room.

"One last thing; the Hellcat costs the navy $35,000 each. You can judge for yourself how mad Number One's going to be if you put one in the water or crush one on landing. Carry your manuals with you when you fly. Now, Number Two will take over and instruct you on flight procedures."

"Thank you, Number Three." Number Two brought the pattern manual with him to the front of the room. "First, let me acquaint you with the flyer's most important personnel. These guys get your ass off the deck and back on it in one piece. You will trust them implicitly! When in doubt, do exactly what they tell you or signal you to do. They know more than you do!" He motioned at one of the crew to step forward. "Purple; I hope everyone noticed this man is wearing a purple vest. Please nod your heads so I know there are no colorblind pilots here." He looked over the room and smiled. "Good!" He looked back at the young crewman. "Purple means Aviation Fuels, nickname, Grapes. Blue are plane handlers and elevator operators." He touched the crewman with a blue vest. He then moved down the line to the end. "Green are the next in line; maintenance personnel, ground support troubleshooters (GST) and helicopter landing signal personnel (LSE).

"Did you see the titties on that Aussie nurse when we came onboard? I'd like to wrap my lips around one of those," the Italian whispered.

"I wonder if she likes her nipples bit," the Chinese flyer replied, pretending to be listening intently to Number Two.

"I bet she does. They all like a little nibble now and then." The Italian became wary when Number Two quit talking and searched the room.

Number Two suddenly headed for the back of the room and stopped next to the Italian and the Chinese pilots. He slapped his metal leg with the pointer he was carrying. "Let me tell you something, fellas. My leg hurts like hell when I have to hurry after a couple of assholes that are not paying attention, especially if they've never taken off from a carrier before. It makes me cranky and out of sorts. You don't mind listening up now, do you? You fucking bastards!" His last words sent spit across both men's faces. As he straightened up and limped slightly back to the front of the room, he rendered a situation to the group. "What happens when a pilot is standing off, in his pattern, waiting to land, with low fuel, but can't land because some son of a bitch has the deck on fire because he didn't pay attention?" He turned back to the two men wiping their faces. "Everyone after them goes swimming or becomes barracuda morsels. Listen, gentlemen; there's no other place to go but into the ocean, and that's not a sure thing either. Sometimes hitting the waves is like hitting a three-story building. Get my meaning? So, let's get with the program!" He took a deep breath and sighed.

"Yellow are aircraft handling officers. Red are ordnance, but more important are crash and salvage crew. These guys are going to be the ones to pick your sorry asses out of a crash. They might even save your life. Next is Brown. They're air wing captains. They get your ass off the deck but for most of you, White will be your favorite color. He's the LSO, the landing signal officer." He turned to the men in line. "That will be all, except you, Lieutenant. Please stay one more minute."

As the flight crew filed out, Number Two said, "These men are here to see to it that you live to fly again and again." Number Two walked over to the lieutenant and talked face-to-face with him. The lieutenant shook his head and picked up some paddles. "The LSO is going to illustrate what you'd see from the LSO platform on landing. You'll see it again when we view the film later. By the way, he's the meatball."

The lieutenant laughed and then became serious. "This is too high." He raised both paddles. "This is too low." He lowered both paddles. "Left wing too high, now right wing too high." He tilted the paddles from side to side. "If you've been good little boys and girls, this is the signal to hit the deck and grab a cable. If you've been bad, you'll get this motion; that's a wave-off, climb and try again."

"Thanks," said Number Two.

"One other thing; no matter what you think or what your instincts tell you, trust me! I won't let you down."

"Thanks again!" Number Two watched as the LSO walked out. "Are there any question so far?"

A Finn raised his hand and asked, "If we find ourselves in the water, what next?"

"During all takeoffs and landings, there will be two Sikorsky helicopters aloft at all times."

An American pilot was next to ask, "What the hell is a helicopter, Sikorsky or otherwise?"

Number Two replied with a grin, "They're like an airplane with an egg beater on top. You'll see one flying in the film and you can view two of them on the flight deck later. They can hover overhead and drop a cable into the water and lift you out. You'll be schooled in rescue on one of the ten days, but they're only good within a hundred miles of the ship. After that, we have a Vought OS2U-3- Kingfisher. It will follow the contestants each leg and pick up anyone in need. After that, you'd better just pray to your God… because your ass is on the nearest shark's menu. Let's take a break, smoking lamp is lit."

The room went easy; some went to the heads, others to the coffee pots. The cigarette lighters struck everywhere; in no time, the wardroom was filled with heavy smoke. Kat and Matt escaped to the hangar deck and made plans to meet later.

Viktor was joking in the middle of the room. "I can't swim. How are they going to pull my ass out of the water if I can't swim?" He was saying it jokingly, but deep down it wasn't funny.

After about ten minutes, Number Two asked everybody to take his or her seat. It took about five more minutes to comply. "Quiet down." He reached for another paper. "Get your view of the ship out. It looks like this." He held up the paper. "The first page shows the Island Structure. Look to Number 10 on your illustrations. This is the Pri-Fly. It's where the Air Boss is located. It's the same as a tower on land. Note that 11 is radar, and 4 is the navigation bridge. Now look to the flight deck; 7 is the landing area, and 10 is the landing centerline. You notice it stops halfway; there are restricting cables halfway. Six uprights to stop you if you forget to catch one of the eleven cross cables that stop you safely. This is what the little hooks on the ass end of the aircraft are supposed to engage. By the way, does everyone see the number 22 painted at the end of the runway? Always takeoff and land in that direction. It will always be into the wind. There will be no exceptions; it's a one-way deck." He noticed a little confusion in the group and smiled. "You will have the chance to go up to the flight deck and check out everything we've spoken to here before you fly."

"Now to the fun part; takeoffs." A devilish smirk formed on his face. "Everything's the same, with some exceptions; two-thirds flap configuration, cowl flaps half open, then apply power to 30 inches MAP, or manifold pressure. Release brakes and advance throttle to takeoff power. Directional control should be maintained with rudder and minimum use of brakes. The use of brakes aboard ship will affect acceleration to flying airspeed. The air captains will time your takeoff. When released, rotate the nose-wheel from the runway at about 80 kts, IAS, also known as indicated airspeed, to establish a takeoff attitude. At about 85 kts IAS, the aircraft will be flown off. You all got that?"

"Yeah, yeah, we got it. That's all old stuff!"

He was surprised the takeoff wasn't bothering anyone; they all appeared to take it in stride, an everyday event.

"Okay now, let's get to these patterns. Delta is your takeoff pattern; now follow me carefully." He turned the page of his booklet. "Once your aircraft is in position and the air wing captain takes you under control, he'll have you throttle up to his rpm recommendation. He can tell just from the sound of the engines the right rpms. He also watches the pitch of the ship, so he can release you right at the moment you'll be pointed upward at the end of the runway. Keep your eyes on the wing captain, not the horizon. Your view is distorted, his is not."

"Didn't we just go through this?" a Brit said.

"I'm sorry, but that's the way the lesson's laid out!" With a frown that stiffened the group, Number Two said, "You don't mind, do you?" With the silence, he turned back to his manual. "When he turns you lose, release all brakes and pull your stick back quickly but gently. No sweat! Once airborne, you will then take a 45-degree right climbing turn until you're clear of Charlie pattern. This should take about two minutes. Climb until you reach 1,000 feet, then take intervals to join Delta. Maintain a 1,500 yard oval around the carrier. Make 15-degree banks at each turn. Now speeds; after takeoff, throttle up to 140 kts. Once in Delta, slow to and maintain 130 kts.

"When entering Charlie—or landing, for those who can't keep the two separate—slow to upwind) 100 kts or downwind 85 kts. Then when you reach the paddle approach, slow to 83 kts. Sounds really simple, right? Well, it's not over yet. Once you've dropped to 350 feet on your approach, commence your landing checklist. Do I have to go over this list? Okay, after completing your checklist, bank 15 degrees, call the meatball, and give your fuel in pounds to flight command. Flight command will then adjust the arresting cables for your aircraft." He stopped and looked intently at the pilots. "Important subject here… give the right call on your fuel. Those cables can tear you right out of your harnesses if not adjusted correctly. Also, calling the meatball means you see and can decipher the LSO on the fantail of the ship. Do yourself a favor and don't fuck around with these two calls. Once done, drop to one hundred feet and obey the LSO. You'll be in his command only about 15 to 20 seconds.

"There are a couple more things. The aircraft on a carrier never take off and land at the same time. Nine planes will take off, complete their maneuvers, then land. Then the next nine will repeat the same. During the race we can take-off aircraft every twenty-seven seconds, landings about every three minutes. If you are given a wave-off, you will climb back and merge into Delta pattern and wait for instructions. The only exception is in an emergency, which you will declare to the air boss in the primary flight control. Such emergencies may be low fuel, low or no oil pressure, or a hydraulic problem. This situation will put you in the front of the line." He threw the manual on the table. "Anyone cutting in line to make a hot date or a quick head call, will answer to me."

Number Two pointed to one of the mates standing by the light switch. "In a minute, will you turn the lights out?" The seaman nodded his head. "I want you to watch this film on landings and takeoffs. It gives you a pilot's view of what's going on. You'll also hear their thoughts as they go through the procedures. It covers everything we've talked about here today and a little more. After the film, you'll be free to go topside to look over everything. Then you'll have some lunch and then we fly. Okay, lights please."

The cigarette smoke almost obstructed the view of the film but it did show the pilots what Number Two was talking about in detail. When the film was over and the lights came back on, there was a mad dash for topside to get a birds-eye view of this Hellcat.

CHAPTER FIVE

FOR THE FIRST TIME SINCE she'd been onboard, a plane was more important than Matt. She couldn't wait to sit in one of the most famous of all warbirds, but her need to get to the deck was being hampered by Evelyn. She was having trouble getting through the doorways with her leather pillows. She needed them in the cockpits to raise her up so she could see out of the canopies. Kat grabbed one of them as she forced herself through the opening to the flight deck. Once outside the mist smacked her in the face. It was a warm and gentle spray and it felt good on her cheeks; it helped clear the smoke from her eyes.

She handed Evelyn her pillow and gave her thumbs up. She turned aft, then she saw it. She looked right past the others to the last one on the right. She rushed towards the sky-blue stallion. The other pilots had stopped at the closer planes but she bypassed them all to admire this one. It beckoned to her, its muscles bulging at its seams. She felt like it was hers and hers alone, like a lost lover found. It seemed like a lifetime since she'd flown, about a year now. Washing dishes and peeling potatoes was not her idea of a military career, so she had resigned from the air force.

She climbed the small ladder to the cockpit. She noticed moisture between her legs from her excitement as she climbed to the top. Her breathing was labored and short, like meeting a lover and anticipating the night. "My God, it's beautiful!" She stroked the instruments like one would touch the strings of a Stradivarius. She kissed the top of the canopy as she climbed in. Little surges flitted throughout her body and her hands trembled from excitement. As the stick fell between her legs, she caressed it with a lover's touch, kneading its length and then squeezing its handle. "You're mine, baby... all mine!" She got out her manual and compared it to the console in front of her. She smiled as she tried one lever after another, a toggle switch and then a dial. A group had gathered at the bottom of the ladder.

"Come on, Kat, share the wealth!"

Kat had to be crowbarred out, but eventually she gave up and went down the ladder, bitching all the way. The plane had but one marking, and that was of a large eight painted on its tail. One through nine was painted on each of the planes. She reached into her pocket and brought out a tube of lipstick and drew a heart on one of the propellers, then patted it and said, "You're all mine." She then went aft to check out the other topics that were mentioned in the lesson. Every once in a while, she would glance back at eight and smile.

The two Sikorskies and the Kingfisher were tied down near the edge, to give room, she supposed. A crewman was speaking on the flying capabilities of the Rotor-rotor machine, but Kat was more interested in its looks. "This goddamn thing flies? No goddamn way." The crewman grinned, nodded his head, then signaled the Pri-Fly and then an announcement came over the intercom. "All pilots gather at mid-ship on the operation of a helicopter."

The group formed around the machine and a small lecture was given. The group was told to stand back of the blades, and some flying maneuvers would take place.

The helicopter's blades started rotating and the current of air it caused made all that were wearing covers hold them or lose them overboard. The helicopter rose straight up and tilted to one side and then gained about three hundred feet. It then turned and dove straight for the waves. Then, like a gull, it hovered about twenty feet above the white tips of the water. "Rescue time is about three minutes," said one of the crew left behind.

"Hell," one of the pilots muttered. "This man's navy is getting too fast for me!"

"You won't think that if your ass is in the water!" Kat grinned at the pilot.

The Sikorsky lifted and returned to its landing circle as gentle as you please.

The Kingfisher was strapped down a little forward. It looked a lot like the Hellcat but had a rear compartment. Its giant pontoon ran its full length, with smaller floats on both wings. It had a tail wheel and two landing wheels off the main float. It looked odd at best; ugly at worst. But the pilots were glad it was there.

The pilots were still talking about the helicopter when they spotted the six restraining cables crossing the deck about mid-ship. "You don't want to run into these if you don't have to," said Mel. "You could break your neck if they're anything like the ones on the *Implacable*. Even if you caught a cable on the deck, it better be one of the first ones or your ass will be thrown into one of the goddamn restriction cables that sends the plane's nose down and your ass praying to the heavens. The Aussies were always kidding the Brits about their carriers. We used to tell them they had to bend over at least once to the Queen."

"Do you think we'll have that problem on this ship?" It was one of the Chinese pilots who asked the question but it was the whole group that was waiting for the answer.

"American carriers are superior. They give you a lot more room and their planes are better, also."

"What did you fly, Mel?" Andre seemed a little worried, not having the experience of carrier flying. His voice had a little tremor to it and the group picked up on it.

"I flew Sea-fires, a great plane against a Zero." Mel's face became a little blushed when he noticed Sake was listening intensely.

Sake replied in a soft and controlled voice, "The Sea-fires are a fine plane but have no long-range capacity. They can't stay in the fight long enough."

"Maybe not, old friend, but while they're there… it was pure hell, wasn't it?" Mel's blush was replaced by a foul grin.

"Let's go to the rear or aft or the fantail. I can't remember which term to use." Kat was eager to defuse the moment. "I want to see where the LSO stands. I want to make sure I'm looking in the right spot."

"Don't trip over these cables, guys. They're so goddamn thick and long," said Stanis.

The Italian grabbed his crotch. "That reminds me of something growing in my pants."

"Better get down to sickbay really quick... you do know that hemorrhoids grow real fast, and if they're already thick and long, you could be in some real trouble."

The laughter could be heard all over the flight deck. Geno just stood there with a smirk on his face, shaking his head. Kat came up to him and gave him a pat on the cheek. "You remind me of someone, he's just as full of shit as you are." She turned and looked about the deck. "I don't see him."

"See who?" asked Masayuki curiously.

"Viktor!"

"I think he's down in sickbay with some kind of back problem." The Spaniard's voice seemed distressed. "I think I'll be visiting the doctor soon myself. My back is killing me also."

An announcement came over the intercom. "Mess is being served for the next hour."

Kat looked for Matt and found him talking to Rudy near the exit to the lower decks. As she approached, she said, "Bet you're hungry." Rudy didn't know if she was talking to him or Matt.

With some delight on his face, he said, "Hope there's something kosher to eat down there. I'm losing weight like a madman eating nothing but salad and bread for lunch."

Kat took him by the arm. "Come with me. I'll see to it that your ass gets fed, and not with sauerkraut either, if you know what I mean. I've got an in with the mess cook. Anything I want, I get. Can you eat raw eggs?" she asked Rudy.

Matt's mouth went sour and so did Rudy's. "Raw eggs... who the hell eats raw eggs?"

Kat stopped and put her hands on her hips. "You got a problem with someone that enjoys eggs, raw or not?" Before he could answer, "Some people just don't have good taste." *In women, surely, but taste in food… no way,* she thought. "In Europe the people eat raw eggs like they eat candy here."

Matt turned to Rudy and gave him a high eyebrow. "I'd rather eat salad but it's your stomach."

"Men," she said, her head shaking from side to side as she turned and led the way to the ward pantry.

Once there, they got in line behind Lo Chu and Andrea. "Macaroni and cheese and hamburgers. How about that, Rudy?" said Matt.

Rudy was busy spying around for the Nazis. He found them sitting with each other in the corner of the wardroom. They simply taunted him with smiles.

Matt nudged Rudy. "You're going to starve if you don't let it go!"

Kat wasn't paying any attention to Rudy. She was too busy gazing at all the dishes that were available. "There's no pig in any of this, is there?" Kat looked to Matt for an answer.

"No pigs at all. Now chow down, Rudy."

The cook's mate smiled as Kat came through the line. "Would you like some more eggs, ma'am?"

With the same sour face from before, Matt said, "If she's sucking raw eggs again, I'm going on a diet."

Kat shrugged her shoulders and asked the cook, "Do you have a better class of people to dine with around here or do I have to put up with this kind of barbarism?"

"Okay, okay, suck eggs if you want to, but I'm having a hamburger with the works. How about you, Rudy?" Matt was ready to chow down.

"I'll have the same," he said, shading his face from Kat's glare.

Yokes appeared with an empty plate in his hands. "Can I cut in line? I just want one more burger."

Kat could not imagine Yokes eating just one sandwich at a time. "Just one? How many have you already eaten, big guy?" she asked.

"Three!"

"How many?" Her eyes widened in disbelief.

"Okay, four."

Her forehead lowered and she peered into his eyes. "I've already seen that belly hanging from those skivvies of yours. You're not going to fit in the cockpit if you don't quit feeding your face. Does your wife let you eat this much?

"No. She's always on me to lose weight." His bottom lip was hanging a little.

"Give me that plate! Now go up on deck and run around or something. I think I'll put in a call to your wife and tell her you're going to be a blimp when you get back home. Now go on, get the hell out of here!"

He smiled at her and then turned to leave. She blew a kiss to him and he smiled his widest smile.

"I wouldn't talk about how much folks eat around here if I were you. According to my observation this morning, it looked like you can put it away pretty good yourself." Matt was ready for some sarcasm as he finished his little speech.

"I work it off though," she said as she faced the food.

Matt raised his brows and widened his eyes. "When do you find the time? Classes in the day, flying till sunset. There's not much time for working out."

She tilted her head to one side. "At night... I do all my workouts at night."

After last night's necking and fondling, Matt was feeling secure with his manhood; maybe a little too secure for his own good. Regardless, he decided to push a little to see how far he could go, him being so irresistible to women and all. What could he lose? "How about working out with me tonight?"

She didn't answer. Instead, she continued in the line, placing her tray out at every station whether she wanted that food or not. Matt felt the tension and tried to talk to her but she turned a deaf ear to him. As she reached the end of the line, she made for a full table, where she pushed her way in. Matt was left standing with his tray in hand. Kat wondered if she should say something or would her silence speak for her. She decided the latter and started eating. Rudy came by and together he and Matt sat at another table. The men at Kat's table said nothing; apparently, they had been in a similar situation with a woman and knew when to keep their mouths closed. The room grew thick from the silence and then an announcement came over the intercom. "All pilots will proceed to the wardroom with all documents needed for flight. Ten minutes, ladies and gentlemen."

Kat stood, then got in line to scrape her tray. Matt fell in behind her and tried again to apologize. Kat smiled to herself as she observed that he hadn't eaten a thing, but still stayed silent. As she headed for the wardroom, Matt pulled her into one of the ready rooms and closed the door.

"Please, I just want to talk to you one minute."

She could hold her silence no more. "I thought you were more of a man than that, Matt. You think I'm that easy, or some kind of Russian slut, maybe a whore? You offered your dick to me in front of other men; you humiliated me!" She stopped and waited for his reaction. He couldn't even look at her. "You acted like a schoolboy on his first date. I should have known your tears last night were all a fake. You were laughing at me all the time." She was on the verge of tears herself, she was so angry. "Let me tell you something; this is one piece of *peechka* you'll never get!" Kat started to leave but he held out his hands to stop her.

He looked at her and his eyes started to well up. "I've never been ashamed of myself till now. I'm so sorry." He gently held her face with his hands and sighed. "You're right. I did act like a kid. I will never embarrass you again, ever. I am the slut or bastard or whatever you please. Give me another chance, I'll make it right, so help me God!"

"I told you last night you didn't have to love me. Right now, friends are good enough. So, think with your head and not your dick from now on." She stepped back and extended her hand. "Deal?"

"Friends… good friends." Matt took her hand and kissed it tenderly. As he looked back into her eyes, he could tell that her anger was gone.

The moment had passed and all was forgiven. "Let's go fly!" She pulled him by the hand out the door and down the gangway to the wardroom.

Two was standing at the front of the room like he was posing. "The experienced naval pilots will take off first. The rest of you, pay attention and learn from these pilots. The list of pilots and their flight sequence is posted on the board as you leave for the flight deck. Make sure you get your headgear and life vest before your flight time. One other thing; all the aircraft have been fitted with the same radios so they'll all read the same. Good flying and stay dry!" Two turned and left for the Pri-Fly.

A scramble for the flight list erupted. Matt muscled his way through the crowd and found that he was in the first nine to fly. Kat and Yokes were in the last. He had been dragging Kat behind him all the time. "Just watch me, it's easy, no problem." Kat didn't seem worried at all, she was eager for the skies.

They picked up their gear and headed for the flight deck. The nine planes were already warming up on the flight line. Matt looked to see what number plane he had, then kissed Kat and headed off for the plane. He was the second to take off; Mike was the first.

The air captain stood at the ready alongside Mike's plane. He gave Mike the rev-up signal, then when it sounded right, he gestured him to hold those rpms. The captain watched the pitch of the ship and then when the ship's pitch was down, he signaled Mike to go like hell. By the time Mike reached the end of the runway, the pitch of the ship was facing upward for maximum loft. Mike's takeoff was letter perfect and the other pilots cheered. Matt was next, and like Mike, was another success. There were no real problems with any of the first nine to take off. The others watched as they got into the Delta pattern and circled the ship. Kat and Yokes watched the number two plane cruise slowly around.

"You like this guy, don't you?" Yokes never took his eyes off Matt's plane. "I mean, you really like this guy?" He dropped his head to find Kat still following Matt's plane.

"Do you think it's too soon?" Her head was still pointed upwards but she was paying more attention to Yokes than the flyers in the sky.

"Soon... that all depends on how you define soon. I fell in love with Georgina in about five seconds." A chuckle was in his voice. Some may say that's soon, but I've heard it can take up to, maybe even six or seven minutes to fall head over heels, and I wouldn't say that was too soon… would you?" He regained his fix on Matt's aircraft.

"How do you tell that it's not a one-way thing?" She didn't take her eyes off the skies but took hold of his arm.

He patted her hand gently. "Now that's what can take some time."

After about an hour of circling, the first aircraft was called to land. It lowered into Charlie pattern, then into an approach pattern. To the pilots on deck it looked like the aircraft was going too slow and would not make the cables. They were wrong; the plane gently sat itself down right between number four and five cables and stopped way short of the restraining wall. Many cheers and whistles came from the observers. Matt was still aloft; they were not landing in order. This puzzled Kat a little but as she watched Matt fly, she thought there must be some reason for it and her concerns faded. Her mind drifted back to Matt and the ready room; was the argument earlier somewhat her fault? He had admitted he was not accustomed to women speaking so abruptly and with such vulgarity. Men, yes… but these frail females over here, what else could he think? Talk like a tramp and maybe you are one, bitch? She slapped her leg with her hand. Of course… he was acting just like a man. Those male juices always get them into trouble sooner or later. Maybe she should start thinking more feminine and use maneuvering more than commanding. That meant giving up some control, but it might be worth it. She would make a point to talk with some of the other females onboard. She would have to develop a technique of her own. Kat smiled as the number two plane was called upon to land.

Matt maneuvered the Hellcat like it was part of his own body, a slight sway here, a short dip there, almost like a waltz against the blue sky. Then, like laying a newborn in a crib, the plane touched down. Matt climbed out like it was an everyday event, shook a few hands, and then ran over to Kat and Yokes. He grabbed her and kissed her to the shouts and whistles of the crews. He stopped in a panic, his face went pale and then he said, "Me kissing you in public doesn't embarrass you, does it?"

"Don't be foolish. Everyone onboard has us married already."

She didn't know where that last comment came from but then again, maybe she did! She waited for his response but he just smiled and hugged her again.

Two goddamn days, she thought. *All it takes is some kissing and feeling, one small fight, a little flying and you got them hooked. The world works in mysterious ways. Boy, do I love this country!*

The three of them sat and watched the others taking off and landing. Evelyn and Amy seemed to do just fine. The Spaniard had trouble keeping his speed down on his approach but managed to get the plane on the deck in one piece. The difference from the first group's flying abilities to this group was obvious. The skills learned in the navy were going to be an advantage in the race. The pilots caught on to this early. There was a sense of concern growing on deck; $150,000 was a lot of money to lose. Different groups started to form, each trying to learn the techniques of the others. This wasn't fun and games anymore. There would be a price for not paying attention to your enemy's strengths and weaknesses, one that these men weren't accustomed to paying.

As the last of the group landed, Matt turned to Kat. "You're up!" She had a hard time waiting for her aircraft to be positioned for takeoff. She had to wait for one of the Sikorskies to be refueled. Evelyn came over to wish her well. "A piece of rye," she said, giggling.

Matt straightened her headgear before he slapped her on the ass as she turned for the plane. Twisting around halfway, she pointed a finger at him with a smile on her face.

"That's for that marriage crack. If I wanted to get married, I don't need a whole crew to ask for me."

Yokes would go first, then her and then the Frenchman. He would bring up the rear. There were only the three of them left. She hadn't noticed the pitch of the ship before, since the seas were calm. But sitting there in the cockpit looking down the runway, she watched the whitecaps appear and disappear with a rhythmic motion that calmed her. She saw smoke come from Yokes' manifold as he lifted off the deck. He took off right over the white arrow and banked smoothly.

She throttled up to get in position and then her eyes were on the wing captain. His arm was straight up in the air and he was bent over, almost kneeling. The flag he held was circling round and round, motioning to bring up your rpms. She wondered if she had missed anything on her checklist but it was too late now.

The vibrations enhanced the thrill, and the volume of the noise sent goose bumps through her body. She squeezed her legs together slightly; those urges to pee were growing. Then, like striking a tennis ball, the captain lowered the flag and off she went. The power of the aircraft took her breath away. No Yak ever felt like this. She climbed from 85 knots to 140 knots in a matter of seconds. She raised the landing gear and started trimming the aircraft. She then checked all cockpit instruments and finally turned off the auxiliary fuel pump. She entered Delta pattern with Yokes about five hundred yards in front of her. She screamed for joy and massaged the stick again. "You beautiful thing!" As she made her first bank, she caught sight of the Frenchman entering Delta.

Her love for flying re-entered her soul and she started to giggle like a schoolgirl. It was one of the first times flying that she didn't have to look to her six for an enemy sighting her in for the kill. She felt odd but for the first time, really free. Looking downward and not seeing anything but blue took the giggle out of her. It was her first time flying over water and it seemed bizarre not to see mountains, lakes, and rivers below. She used to navigate by the towns and she would follow the railway tracks back to her base. It was also hard to judge her altitudes. She kept checking with her altimeter. There was nothing to compare to on the ground but little whitecaps and she could barely see them. She thought that she had better do some work on that radio mapping when she got back to the ship. She could easily get lost out there on her own.

A voice over the radio brought her back to her situation. The air boss was giving commands to the Frenchman to start his descent and begin his landing checks. As Kat made another bank, she watched him lower from behind her and begin his descent into Charlie pattern. The ship looked much smaller up here. "We're supposed to land on that little thing?" Kat started to worry a little. The fields she was accustomed to landing on were acres wide and long, not this toy ship. By the next turn she saw the Frenchman safely on deck. *If that French wimp can do it, I can!* she thought.

Unexpectedly, she noticed an emergency light and buzzer and it startled her for a second. She checked her gauges to find a low oil pressure warning light on. She tapped the gauge to free it. No such luck. "Flight command, I'm declaring an emergency!" She began to shake as the fearful images built in her mind.

"Your aircraft number please!" replied the air boss calmly.

Kat looked to the windshield and found her number. "Eight... my aircraft number is eight!" She hoped that heart on the prop would bring her luck.

"What is your emergency, Number Eight?"

"I have a low oil pressure light and buzzer!"

"What is the oil pressure now?"

She looked to see the gauge drop to zero. "It just dropped to zero, repeat, no oil pressure!" More than a little concern could be picked up in her voice.

"What is your temperature and manifold pressure?"

"Manifold is thirty-eight and my temperature is one hundred and forty degrees Celsius and they're both climbing!" Now her concern was replaced with fear; a calm fear, but fear nevertheless.

"Affirmative!" the radio crackled.

"What the fuck is *affirmative*?" Sweat appeared on her brow and she noticed some smoke coming from her exhaust.

"It means OK, we copy you, understand?"

"Clear the decks!" The announcement surprised the crews. "Stand by all emergency personnel, prepare all conflag stations, lock all fire division doors." The voice over the intercom was straightforward and stern. It took about five seconds before the crew jumped into action. The Aussies had learned their manuals well and their personnel manned the appropriate stations in a hurry. The pilots on deck were quickly escorted down to the hangar deck.

"I wonder who's in trouble," one of the Brits said to the group of pilots that were watching and listening to the deck above.

"Does it matter?" the Romanian said to his friend the German.

"A Blackie or a cunt, one less opponent to deal with. Does it

really matter which one? They're both inferior to either one of us."
The group rapidly divided into two parts.

The Brit hesitated, measuring him for a moment. "You're lucky
Matt's not here or you'd get what that other asshole got."

Werner bristled and started towards the Brit. "You want to try,
you British piece of shit!"

Viktor slowly approached the Kraut and got right into his face.
"If Katya gets hurt… I'm going to kill you!" He took a deep breath
followed by several even-measured gasps.

Mel jumped between the two groups. "Get the fuck down to the
wardroom and take your friends with you. The smell of you bothers
me!" He threw the words at him like stones.

The air boss proceeded by the book. "Number Eight, on your
next pass, drop to Charlie pattern. Get your checklist ready, we're
going to go through it together. Remember one thing… this aircraft
can land with or without power. So, if the aircraft stalls, stay with us."

"Affiritight, or affirmorite… what the hell! Okay, I understand!"

"Okay, here we go! Once you drop to three hundred fifty feet,
open your cabin hood."

"Okay, I've opened it! The temperature is rising to critical! Did
you copy that?"

"Just listen to me and do what I tell you! Mixture control to
auto rich and then put the propeller to 2,350 rpms. Bring your
supercharger to neutral… have you done that?"

"Just hurry the fuck up!" Her voice sounded hurried and a little
panicky.

"Cowl flaps to half-open, oil cooler flaps open." A dead silence
fell over the radio. "Lower your wing flaps now and extend your
arresting hook. Now, Katya, here comes the tricky part. Don't lower
your landing gear till you call the meatball and are with the LSO.
You'll need your landing gear up if you stall before that and have to
try a landing in the water. If you get a wave-off, retract your landing
gear first and you will then try a landing in the water, understood?"

Seemingly a lifetime went by before she spoke. "I understand!
I'm turning into approach, I'm calling the meatball, my fuel is half
and I'm lowering landing gear!" She listened for the gear to lock into

place and watched the indication light glow. Her fear left her now and her mind raced with all the possibilities of what could happen. She started to remember another time her plane was in trouble and she was going down. It was over the Donetsk region. On fire and losing altitude fast, she opened the hood and bailed out. But now she didn't have enough altitude. She would hit the water before her parachute would open.

"Good luck!" returned the voice of flight command.

All she could hear now was the sputtering and missing of her engine. Tiny speckles of oil started to fill the windshield. Okay, flagman, do your job! "A little right, no, too much, get back on line, you bitch… there, that's it, you got it… No, no, too low, make up your mind, too low, too low. I must be losing speed. I'm not going to make it! Nose up. Get it uppppp!"

Matt had avoided the roundup of the other flyers and was hiding in one of the gun sponson's that were still on the flight deck. He could see and hear everything that was taking place. "Come on, baby… get your ass down here to Papa!" He wasn't much into praying, but this time was an exception. He watched as she lowered and banked into her approach pattern but he noticed her landing gear was not down and the aircraft was smoking badly. That could only mean one thing, trouble! He moved aft along the outside of the gunnels so he could see the LSO. With every move of the LSO, he tried to relay his message to her. "Come on, Kat… up a little, get up, more, more. Goddamn it!" Heavy smoke was pouring out of her exhaust. "More power, baby, burn the son of a bitch up if you have to." His face grew red and his eyes burned as he bellowed out his words to the skies.

The sudden stop from the restraining cables almost threw her through the windshield. She frantically started turning everything off, from fear of fire, whether it was warranted or not.

"Get that pilot out of there and get that aircraft to the Hangar Deck and check it out. Move it!" The LSO was standing there looking up at Kat with a huge grin on his face. He turned to another crewman. "Move it! We still got another aircraft up there!" Saluting her, he returned to his station.

A relieved Matt decided to go to the hangar deck via the elevator. He didn't want her to see the fear on his face. It gave him time to return to his calm and collected self.

Two was the first to greet her as she stepped down on the deck. "One hell of a flyer! You do your gender proud!" He watched her standing there; she was trying to come to attention but her legs would have no part of it. "Go below, your friends are waiting for you. By the way, tell the barman to open a bottle of vodka early. You look like you could use a drink."

"Yes, Number Two." A drink did sound good.

The crew started to take the aircraft below but Kat stopped them. She went to the front of the plane and looked for the mark she had made earlier. It was a bit smudged and dirty but the heart was still there. "Thanks, Number Eight. I knew I loved you best!" She kissed the propeller, then turned to see Two smiling at her. Smiling back, she passed him for the officer's lounge.

Matt found her on the Hangar Deck, the oil from the engine leak had blackened her face and she was wiping it with a rag she got from one of the flight mechanics. "What the hell happened to you? You look a mess!" His pretense of ignorance was pretty good.

"What the hell do you mean I'm a mess? Not five minutes ago I was almost squid food!"

He tried to look shocked. "Did you have some kind of trouble with your landing?"

Her eyes widened and her volume increased to a screech as she threw the oily rag at him. "Trouble... a little trouble he says!" Looking at an innocent crewman she bellowed, "My goddamn engine quit on me, oil flying everywhere, the engine so hot you could bake pumpernickel on it, and by the way, where the hell were you?" Kat was speaking so fast that her accent started to get really thick and even she had difficulty pronouncing her next words.

Matt raised his shoulders along with his forehead. "I had to take a piss really bad. I've been in the head for the last ten or fifteen minutes. I didn't know anything was wrong. I thought with all your battle experience there wouldn't be any problem that you couldn't take care of." He let out a long, audible breath.

Her mouth opened wide and a gush of air escaped. "Pissing... you were shaking your pole while I was knocking on death's door? I had to piss at least a dozen times up there but do you see any piss on me?"

He slid over to her and took her in his arms. She was still arguing with him but no one could decipher her words, for he held her deep into his chest. Some that passed seemed curious at the two standing there mid-deck. Matt smiled and caressed her hair while Kat's muffled speech was going on and on. He knew it was good for her to relieve the pressure.

"Are you all right?" said Yokes as he hit the bottom of the ladder. "I heard everything over the radio."

Matt had turned her loose and she was calmer now as she walked towards him. "I kept thinking up there that thank God it's me in trouble and not that big-bellied Yokes. You'd never get your ass out of that plane."

He waved his hand at her and said, "Okay, but that was one hell of some good flying, Missy. You sure got your wings on straight!"

One of the Aussie doctors had come up to see if Katya was all right. "How you doing?" he said as he approached her. "Let me see your eyes."

"I'm all right, Doctor, really."

The doctor used his fingers to open Kat's eyes wide. "Looks to me like you got some oil behind your eyelids. Better come down to the sickbay and I'll rinse them out for you. You'll need to shower and change clothes anyway." The doctor turned halfway to Matt and handed him some tablets. "This will help with that nervous stomach of yours."

Matt tried to look innocent. "What are you talking about?"

The doctor looked a little puzzled. "You are Matthew Drew, are you not? The pilot that not more than ten minutes ago was puking his guts out all over the officer's head? I heard it's a real mess down there!"

"Thanks for the pills, Doc." Matt's face went flushed.

"You don't have this nervous stomach often, do you?" The doctor seemed a little concerned.

Matt looked to the ceiling and frowned. "No, it was my first time. Thanks again, Doc, I'll catch you later, if you know what I mean."

Yokes started laughing and then leaned down and whispered into Kat's ear, "Love comes quicker than you think." He rose up and winked at her.

"Pissing, hey!" She gazed at Matt with a whimsical smile.

He grabbed her and hugged her hard. "If you do that again, they'll have to put <u>me</u> in sickbay." He let her go and then took one of the pills the doctor gave him. Kat reached in and took one too, so did Yokes. The threesome then walked to the ladder that led down.

"Hurry up, I got to pee!" Kat laughed as she said it.

At the bottom of the ladder, Kat went one way and the guys went another. She reached her quarters and picked up some clean clothes, soap, and her hairbrush. She laid her headgear on her bunk. Through the reflection of her goggles, she viewed the mess the oil had made of her. "Hope I can get this shit out of my hair." She turned and headed for the sickbay, clothes in hand.

Once there, she passed a man lying on his stomach on one of the operating tables, with his head turned away from her. One of the nurses was massaging his back. She noticed a red mark on the man's right shoulder. As she got closer, the mark turned into a lip print, made from a very red lipstick. Kat gawked at the nurse; her lipstick was a little smudged. For some reason, the man's backside looked real familiar. She stopped. The nurse looked guilty about something and stopped her stroking. Kat smiled at her, then in a loud and military manner shouted, "Attention, Lieutenant Budanova!"

Viktor sprang to his feet without much effort and with no sign of any back trouble. He'd had his eyes closed for a long time and it took several seconds to adjust them. "<u>Sir</u>!" The shock of discovery hit him full force.

The nurse in her whites started to look worried. Kat winked at her.

"Still got that mole on your ass, I see." The towel had fallen off Viktor as he stood to attention.

Viktor regained his senses and his towel and then looked down at Katya. "*Eezveeneete*!"

"Sorry my ass. I was wondering where the hell you were!" Katya turned to the nurse. "Has he been here long?"

She held up three fingers.

"Viktor, three hours?" She returned to the nurse. "You've been stroking him for three goddamn hours? Those fingers of yours must be something special." Katya turned Viktor by the arm. "Your lips look special too!"

"He told me his back was bothering him."

"So, you had to rub it for three hours and then kiss it all better?"

The nurse simply dropped her head.

"It's all my fault, Katya! I was attracted to this nurse, she's so pretty and everything."

"And built very nice too, I see." She wasn't mad at Viktor, just concerned about the orders not to fraternize with the Australians. They might both get into trouble. She leaned over the table to ask the nurse, "I take it you like this little boy that has to come up with an ailment to get the attentions of a woman."

She smiled. "Don't all men?"

Katya grinned and nodded her head. "Before you guys start rubbing anything else, you better check this situation out with Number One and her superior. Okay?"

Viktor beamed as he turned to the nurse. "I'll take care of it right away!"

"Now get the hell out of here while I take a shower. I don't want you to see any of my moles." She walked to the showers. "I hope there's plenty of hot water. I'll need lots to get this oil off."

Matt and Yokes waited for Kat in the wardroom. They sat and started talking over a Coca-Cola. "You do know Kat likes you a lot," said Matt to Yokes.

Yokes chuckled, "Not as much as she loves you!"

"Love!"

Yokes stopped his chuckle and became serious. "I don't think she even knows it yet herself. She might have an inkling, most women do. But this Southern boy knows it when I see it."

"Man, I hope so!"

Yokes' serious expression turned into a hard and adamant one. "You wouldn't hurt her, would you? I'd be real upset if you did."

Matt seemed shocked as his jaw dropped open. Yokes' words actually offended him. "I would never hurt her... but it has been just a short time. How do you know when it's right?"

Yokes squeezed his arm. "Your heart will tell you. It's the only way you can get to love, through the heart. Your mind will deceive you and lead you astray and maybe even into denial. So will logic. They're both the enemy of love. True love is always spontaneous. Sometimes it takes a little time to recognize the spontaneity but sooner or later, love grabs you and like the ladies say, you're hooked! Just go with it. If what you have with Missy isn't true love, it will come out soon enough and you can both go on your own way. Right now, I think she's looking for affection more than love and you, too. Let her fix the boundaries and stay within them, then you'll never feel you have to say I'm sorry."

Matt grinned with a look of thanks. "What makes you so smart, Big Yokes?"

"Philosophy, old boy. In college I was a philosophy major, and also studied human development. No laughing now!" Yokes suddenly became solemn. "I've already been there. I remember, and I feel glad to be that lucky; but don't tell that to any women I know." They both just sat there staring at each other for several minutes. "Here she comes, my new partner." Matt rose to his feet as Kat walked into the room.

"Still fifty-fifty?" she replied.

"You bet!" He smiled and held out a hand to her.

"Partner, what's this partner stuff? I think I heard something about it." Yokes was grinning as he spoke.

"I told you, didn't I? We're partners after the race; half interest in some fat airboat airlines on some kind of island, somewhere where it's hot. Tell him all about it, I can't remember." She sat down between the guys and helped herself to Yokes' Coca-Cola.

Matt started to get excited again. "Do you know what a seaplane is?"

"Are you talking about a PBY?"

"Exactly, a small version of a PBY. It's called a Grumman Goose."

"I know that aircraft. I flew in one over England on the way to Sicily, a fine aircraft."

Matt took a deep breath. "That makes this explanation so much easier. Okay, we fly cargo and passengers from Tampa or Miami back and forth—"

"To the Caribbean Islands?" Yokes interrupted.

Matt's face lit up. "That's right! All over the Caribbean and the Gulf States. We'll make a fortune in a couple of years, and I have made a deal with the navy to purchase one."

Kat's eyes started to twinkle. "How about instead of half, we go with a third?"

For a moment Matt looked perplexed. His face was kind of washed out, then he looked over to Yokes and so did Kat. "Yes, yes, a good idea! What about it, Yokes?"

Kat slapped Yokes on the hand. "Come on, give us an answer, we don't have all day you know!"

"What are you talking about?" Matt's confusion was nothing compared to Yokes'.

"Partners, Yokes, three of a kind. We'll make a great team, you being from the South and everything." Matt was very happy with Kat's decision to take on Yokes as their partner.

"What do I have to do?"

"We've pledged that if we win any prize money, it goes towards the partnership. No matter how much each donates, the shares will be equal. We need somewhere around $60,000 for the plane, plus expenses. I've got the customers already lined up and ready to go. The way I see it, all we have to do is get one of us into the finals and we're sure to win close to, if not all of, the money we need."

"Sounds good to me." The three of them shook hands to seal the deal. "Georgina will like being a partner's wife!" They all started laughing.

"Let's go have a drink on it. Number Two opened the bar early for me. I guess you guys could come too!" Opening the bar early attracted a crowd. Most of the pilots were congratulating Kat on her landing. Some wouldn't say so but were obviously disappointed she made it. Matt and Yokes were busy talking over the best flight plans to Barbados, then Jamaica. Cuba was a gold mine, and don't leave out the Bahamas. Matt was also discussing the move of Yokes' family from Mobil to Tampa. Georgina and the kids would stay in Matt's family's guesthouse till they got going and could buy their own place. His mother loved children, and he knew she would be happy to have them.

"What if we're not one of the finalists?" Yokes spoke in a soft and low tone.

Matt looked surprised at the big man's question. He raised his shoulders and hands. "I'm the best... you and Kat are tied for second-best." He turned and stared at her concerned expression. "Don't worry, at least one of us will make it. That means we all make it, right?"

Mike was sitting across the room observing the two men talking about their plans for the future. He manipulated his jaw, trying to ease the pain a little. "Nigger-lover and a fucking black bastard, that's a pair for ya! I wonder whose ass-fucking who?" The smirk on his face made his thoughts obvious.

Werner was also observing the Americana glaring at the two other Americana's. This could be helpful, he thought. A little jealousy and prejudices with some anger... this could go a long way.

"What you said in the hangar deck was shit. You Nazis are always spewing crap!" Geno was upset with the German's words from earlier in the day. He didn't want to get in the middle of this fight. "You might find yourself all fucked up if you don't watch your mouth!"

Werner stopped his observation of the Americana's to answer the Italian's accusation. "What the hell are you here for?" He threw his cigarette in the ashtray. "All you *guineas* are so stupid. You can't fight... you can't even think for yourself. All you can do is screw and drink wine! You'd screw everything and everybody, including the sheep and dogs; you conquered the world by fucking your way across the known world."

The Italian stiffened. "You Germans did so much better? I think not. The Germans sure acted stupid at Nuremberg when the Americans had your Nazi asses on trial. 'I only did what I was told to do, Your Honor… please don't hurt me! The orders all came from the Fuehrer. We weren't allowed to think for ourselves.' Sure you didn't, you bloodthirsty fucks!" He forced himself to settle down.

"Look, you grease ball! The money, we're all here for the money. The less we have playing the game, the better chance I'll get my hands on some of it." Werner stood and lit another cigarette, then blew the smoke into Geno's face. "Let me tell you something; you get in my way, and I'll scrape you off the frying pan and throw you right into the trash with the rest of the meatballs!"

"Go to hell!" the Italian replied.

CHAPTER SIX

THE SIREN ANNOUNCED THE NEXT day in the same loud and irritating way, but this time there was no jumping to attention but instead a slow and thought-out plan to get their feet on the deck. Yokes' feet dangled over the side of the bunk while his normal yawning and scratching took place. Kate got up, turned on the lights, and started stretching in the middle of the room. They looked at each other but didn't say a word. She moved to the sink and glared into the mirror, trying to keep her eyes open. She just smacked her lips, shook her head, then lowered herself onto her elbows and draped herself over the sink. "My mouth feels like a goddamn desert, full of sand. Do you think Mattie has any more of those pills the doctor gave him?" She turned from her view of the sink to find Yokes swinging his legs and smiling that mitigating grin of his.

"Little too much to drink last night, did we?"

She turned her face back to the sink. "I don't need this right now, Yokes."

He jumped down from the bunk with a somewhat graceful stance. He had to use a little agility, more than he was accustomed to using. "What you need is some cold water running down your face." He strolled over to the cabinet, opened her drawer and took out the things she would need. He then went to the closet and pulled out a new uniform. "Here… now get your sweet baby ass to the showers and get squared away." He gave her a feigned look of indignity. "I'm ashamed to be associated with someone that can't even hold their liquor. I just hope my reputation's not shot all to hell now."

"Does your wife put up with this every morning, you dressing her and all?" She tried to frown at him but her head ached too much. Instead she pushed herself off the rim of the sink and grabbed the new clothes. That's when she noticed she was still in her old uniform. She had slept in it. She took the clothes and turned her blood-shot eyes up to him. "Stick it in your ass!" Yokes started laughing as she turned and went out the door.

As the door closed, Yokes' shoulders lowered and he sighed. "Damn, I wonder if there's any aspirin in here." He put both hands to his head and looked through his own things, then Missy's. He found a bottle in her drawer. He didn't know what it said, being in Russian, but it looked like aspirin. He took two and went to the sink, cupped his hand under the water, then shot both water and pills down his throat. He caught his reflection in the mirror. "Not look-in' good, old boy!" He grabbed his pants and put them on, then snatched up his shaving gear and headed for the showers. He tried to imagine the relief from the water running over his face.

All the sinks were taken, so Yokes went to the head. The guys in the head were not that loud and he could hear individual conversations. The babes in Paris were better than the broads in Roma, or the gals in London were all too skinny and flat-chested. The one thing they all seemed to agree on was all women should have a nice rack on them but they couldn't decide if 38Cs or 38Ds were the right set of knockers. "It all depends how big your mouth is!" The laughter filled the room. The man's brogue was thick.

Yokes chuckled and then from under the stall door he watched as his gear hit the deck. The man's brogue grew sharp and loud, "*Fuck away, Gerry*! That sink has been taken already. The guy's in the loo, drop-in' some crap!" There was anger in the Irishman's voice. More gear fell to the deck. Yokes pulled up his pants and opened the stall door to find three Germans and the Romanian trying to stare down the Irishman. Of course, if they had known any Irishmen, they would have realized that it was an impossible task.

"Is there a problem here?" Yokes could take at least two of the

Germans and he knew the reputation of the Irish for fighting, so he felt confident in the situation. There was nothing but silence from the Germans as they turned and just stared at him. Their leader was not there and they didn't know what to do now that there were two opponents.

"Sorry, Blackie," came a voice from behind Yokes.

Yokes turned slowly; he recognized the accent. Two or three other guys had encircled Werner.

"It was an accident, we apologize… profusely!" Werner's sickening smirk was almost worse than the conflict over the gear and the sink.

The Irishman looked down at the gear that was lying on the deck. "Accident, aye!" As he raised his head, his own smirk matched the Germans'. "Looks to me like the only accident around here was when your mothers didn't wipe between their legs after fuckin'!" He found a perverse pleasure in the challenge.

The five men's muscles twitched and flexed from anticipation. Yokes and the Irishman waited for their move. Werner's smirk turned into a large smile. "Pick their things up, you clods." The other men's faces went blank and then their frowns showed their unwillingness to follow Werner's orders. "I said it was an accident, so pick their things up and get out of here! We'll clean up later!" Werner half-ass saluted Yokes and the Irishman as he turned and left. The others picked up the gear and threw it into one of the sinks. There were some small cheers of encouragement from the rest of the guys in the head as the Krauts filed out.

Once outside, the five men gathered. Werner, with a stone face, turned to his companions. "Stop… don't say a word, Dumitrn. *Bitte,* we're friends, *freund,* we'll get them in our good time, not theirs. Just like in the war, we have superior genes. Our mental capacity is greater by far. We don't do the wrong thing at the wrong time."

"Werner, entschuldigen sie bitte!" Dumitrn lowered his head.

"You don't have to apologize, Dumitrn, just show your superior intellect next time and think things out. We want their money now, not their blood! It will give all of us a new start in South America.

Learn from these inferiors! We fight them on other fronts now, understand?" The men nodded their heads.

"I hope you'll be know in', Yank. Which of these things are yours?"

"Just take one of each." Yokes extended his massive hand. "My name is Yokes, what's yours?"

The red nose and sly grin of the Irishman preceded his handshake. "I be know in' you already, Yank! Everyone knows you and that Mattie boy. What an uppercut that Mattie has. Wish I had that punch back in County Cork." As he let Yokes' hand go free, he said, "I be Drummell Kenair, the biggest braggart in all of Ireland and the best-looking', too!"

Yokes chuckled a little. "Glad to meet you, Kenair!"

"Just call me Drum, but don't try to beat me." He held up his fists in a fighting stance.

"Not me... I'm not that stupid!"

The two of them started washing up. Yokes headed for the showers and couldn't wait to lather up, while Drum soaped up and started scrubbing his face.

"I hope I didn't get Viktor in any trouble yesterday?" The nurse's question startled Kat, for she asked it just as she was leaving the shower with a towel over her head.

Kat stopped and uncovered her face, then smiled at the nurse she had met earlier. "Don't worry about Viktor, or any other man on this ship. They're always in some kind of trouble, mostly women trouble. He can handle himself in most situations." Kat noticed the nurse's face, it had a kind of glow to it and her eyes twinkled brightly. "No... you're not in love with that Kremlin sex maniac?"

The nurse lowered her head. "I think so."

"What the hell is with this ship? Some kind of love curse onboard?" She walked over to her clothes. "Take your time, think it out, and keep your panties on." As she tugged at the uniform, she smiled at the nurse. "I'm really not the one to talk to you about this love stuff. I'm in the same situation as you."

The nurse appeared surprised. Her face went blank; she slightly turned her head, then smiled and said. "Righty-O!"

The prolonged anticipation was almost unbearable. "Yeah, my panties get wet every time I look at him. Just be careful, honey; try not to get too hurt if it doesn't work out. Viktor is an all right guy." She had to stop herself; this was the first time she had to look at Viktor as a man instead of the prank-filled, girl-chasing fella she always knew. "Listen, love, Viktor is my best friend, and he won't hurt you on purpose. Underneath all the jokes, he does have a kind heart. I've seen it many times back home."

The nurse smiled with anticipation of their next meeting. She considered the news on Viktor good. "Jolly right then!"

Katya recognized the expression on the nurse's face. "He hasn't been hardened by the war and that's good, but you still have to be careful. He is a young buck and thinks most of the time with his pecker." She winked at the nurse but she was somewhere else as she turned back to the sickbay.

Breakfast had ended quickly and without any incidents, which indicated to most the seriousness of the upcoming day's training. No one wanted what happened to Kat to happen to him or her but if so, they needed to be able to work it out like she did.

"Please be seated." One indicated a little fatigue. The scotch had flowed freely at his table last night. "It came to my attention that there have been some medical procedures that have taken up too much of at least one of the nurse's time. This will end immediately, understood?" He looked straight at Viktor. "Do your back problems after hours." He took a breath in and blew it out slowly. "The rule is that you can't go into the crew's area but there's nothing that states they can't come into yours as long as you remain gentlemen!" He glanced at some paperwork he was holding.

"Now back down to business. We're flying the Sea-fires today, pay attention; they're different than the Hellcats in many ways. But the main reason I'm up here now is to congratulate you pilots on a fine day of training yesterday. There were several incidents that could have led to some real bad situations. I'm glad I picked you pilots, you are the best!"

Number Two took the podium. "The Hellcats have muscle and speed; the Sea-fires have agility and maneuverability. But this can be a setback when it comes to landing on a carrier. Watch your crosswinds, your dead air, and your speed when landing. I've seen Sea-fires that were not powered enough drop twenty feet in the last hundred yards of landing, or the crosswinds take them completely off course in the same time. Stand by for a lot of wave-offs today, so keep your hands on the throttles. Even you American pilots that think you're so goddamn hot better be thinking all the time up there."

He glanced over the room. "I take it everyone spent the night doing their homework?" He stood and stared at the group for several more minutes. "Today the English and Australians will show us how it's done. They've flown the Sea-fires before." He noticed a hand go up in the middle of the group and nodded his head and grinned. "Yes, I'm sorry. We wouldn't want to leave out the Irish, would we? They fly them too. Is that all right, Mr. Kenair—I mean, Number 28?" His attention went back to the assembly. "People, you were the best yesterday, be the best today!"

He turned to Brevan and said, "All flight assignments are posted on the wall. Good luck, let's go!"

The Jap and Chin flyers seemed happier today. The aircraft used this morning met their requirements; they were more like a Zero. Surprisingly, the Chinese and the Japanese pilots were getting along fairly well. They gathered together on ship and kept their conversations to one another. They'd been warring for centuries but had united against the Americans and Europeans in this race.

The flight deck had a different sound to it today, a higher pitch. The Hellcats had a deep roar to them but the Sea-fires seemed to scream at the skies. The Blue Jackets and Airedales were on the job; every move was orchestrated like a ballet. The Americans were teaching the Aussies well. The music of the engines moved them from place to place with perfect precision and timing. The orders and signals illustrated their play. Then the word came: "First pilots, to your planes!" The intercom screeched out the orders with the stage already set. The nine pilots rushed to the aircraft while the others watched. They all took notice of the wind, the pitch of the carrier, the cloud formations, and how the gulls glided on the back of the currents.

The first to take off was Mel; his ship rose quickly, much quicker than the Hellcat and with less deck. The group of pilots looked at each other, for they knew what the problem was. Mel's craft teetered from side to side in the big wind but he handled it well. They were hoping the wind would die down a bit for his landing and for their takeoffs. His Seafire climbed apparently straight up into the air, to their amazement. The pilots smiled as they watched him attack the clouds. His rate of climb was so great that most thought he overshot the ceiling for this exercise. The Nazis and Fascists stood erect, like statues, with frowns on their faces, for they'd seen this kind of maneuverability before over the English Channel and in Italy.

The Frenchman was next. His plane's left wing tip lowered as he reached the end of the runway and almost struck the deck. "The crosswinds are murder!" The spectators' comments were mostly under their breath; they didn't want to show any fear. The group cringed as the Frenchman cleared the deck.

Kenair's plane was buffeting back and forth as it waited to take off. The captain tried to maneuver the ship for a better takeoff angle into the wind. "You get hit with it as soon as you clear the island," he explained.

The wind grabbed Andre, and he too soared upward and joined Mel. "This is not going to be an easy day flying!" someone from the rear of the group said.

The other flyers were glad they sent up the experienced pilots first. This aircraft could be tricky, especially in this kind of wind. They learned from the others and found themselves liking the Seafires once they got them in the air, though landing in the crosswinds was much more difficult than taking off in one. Trying to stay in the groove was quite a task, but they got the job done. Sometimes it took several wave-offs and some low fuel gauges to succeed, but their pride got them up, then back down in one piece.

Even the Germans smiled as they landed and were excited over the aircraft. Maybe they were just happy to be back on the deck. They all were true glamour boys, no greenhorns or ninety-day wonders here. They had passed the first test and were ready for the next.

Now there was time for some fun. There was to be a movie tonight, and later some music and dancing with the Aussie nurses; and maybe even Katya and Evelyn could shake a leg. Amy was not to be seen after flying. She stayed to herself in her quarters, talking to the Spaniard all night. He too was a recluse.

One had a huge cake made to celebrate everyone's successes in the carrier takeoffs and landings. The pilots had invited the whole flight crew to the party. The wardroom was overflowing with Airedales and Aussie Zoom-Pigeons. The flight guys were not allowed to drink, so the pilots brought out all their stashes. Coca-Cola, Nehi, and Nesbitt filled most glasses. Goo-Goo Clusters, Snickers, Baby Ruth, and of course, Hershey's, crammed their hands. There was even some Cadbury and Swiss chocolate there.

The word around the pilots was that the next eight days were going to be a pleasure cruise. But the Germans didn't see it that way; neither did the Orientals. They retired to their own little groups to study the next phase of the contest. The others were all in deep conversations over which baseball team would be in the World Series. Most favored the Yankees, but some hung onto the notion that the Brooklyn Dodgers would also be there. With the pitching skills of Branca, Casey, and Lombardi, who could think anything different?

Some, mostly the college guys, were into college football. There was almost a fistfight over which was better, Navy or Notre Dame. With the Heisman being won by Glenn Davis, a Notre Dame student, in 1946, the year before, who could doubt the better team? A giant of a man from Texas settled the matter of which colleges were better; his vote was for the Longhorns.

The Europeans were engrossed in their own sports. Soccer was the main topic with them. They couldn't wait to get the World Cup up and running again. Lucchini and Dufresne were reliving the 1938 Quarter Finals. With all the French and Italian cuss words they were using, one could not interpret which side had won. The men and women were happy, and for the first time since their departures, they felt at ease.

The announcement was given that the movie would start in a few minutes, so they should get their seats or plan on standing. Kat was with Matt and Yokes. They weren't discussing sports but PBYs and the air currents over the Gulf. Kat had to pull Matt from his deliberations with Yokes. "Come on, I want to get a good seat for the cinema!" She pulled and pushed both men to the ladder that led to the hangar deck that was set up for the film. It was a little chilly as they found seats, so Kat pulled Matt's arm around her neck and then looked at Yokes. "It's just for some warmth. Don't get any notions."

"Sure... I've never been to a movie with a girl before." Yokes smiled back at her.

Matt was too busy rubbing her arm to notice Yokes' grin.

"I love the cinema; I've been to them at least twenty times. I wonder which one it is. I hope it's one of Clark Gable's!" She was blissfully happy, fully alive.

"Gable... speaking Russian... that's not possible!" Matt frowned down at her.

"I hear it's a new one, just came out," Yokes said.

"We see Gable and Bogart in Russia, the Italian stars too. But I like Ginger Rogers best. Hush now, it's starting!"

The projector started rolling and the lights on the Hangar Deck dimmed. The sound was a little scratchy but cleared up soon. The title suddenly appeared on the wall. The lion roared as the MGM symbol came on the screen. *Easy to Wed* was the title and it starred, Lucille Ball, Esther Williams, and Van Johnson. The credits rolled on for several minutes, then as the opening scene took place, Kat cried out in shock. She turned to Matt with a wide-open mouth and started to stutter but the words wouldn't come, just a moaning sound.

"Please, we're trying to watch the movie!" someone in the dark said.

Matt grew concerned and took her hand. "Are you all right? Are you sick or something? Do you want to leave?"

Her hand was trembling. "You didn't tell me you were a cinema star!" She started shaking and fidgeting in her seat. "I'm in love with a goddamn cinema star." As Lucille Ball and Esther Williams came on the screen she thought, he couldn't love me! Look at those beautiful women he gets to work with, kiss, and who knows what else? She started crying; she couldn't help it.

He looked to the screen and found Van Johnson and Esther Williams in an embrace and kissing. "Baby, let me take you to sickbay."

"Baby... how many sex symbols have you called baby?" She tore away from his arms.

"Please! Shut the Sam-hill up!"

"What in God's name are you talking about?" Matt was more than confused. He leaned over and whispered, "Let's go."

She whispered back, "Why didn't you tell me?"

"Tell you what?"

"That you're a cinema star!"

Yokes burst out laughing.

"I hear this is a comedy but it hasn't gotten funny yet, buddy!" The voices in the audience encouraged Yokes to shut the hell up and watch the show.

"Is that not you up there on the screen?" Kat didn't really want to hear the answer.

"Stop laughing and tell her, Yokes!"

"No, Missy. Matt looks like Van Johnson, but that's all."

She stopped crying, hugged Matt and then kissed him hard, to the whistles and cheers of the other guys. "Are you sure? That Johnson guy sure looks like you, freckles and all!"

"Would I need money for an airplane if I were him?"

She kissed him again. "Be quiet now, I want to watch the cinema." She wrapped her hands around his arm and snuggled up against it.

Matt turned to Yokes. "Women!"

The dancing was just getting underway as the threesome walked in. The four Aussie nurses and Evelyn were picking partners for the next dance. Kat tried to get Matt out on the floor but he wouldn't have it. So, Yokes was elected to be the next Fred Astaire. One of the guys put on a swing tune and the let-down-your-hair time began. The six couples did pretty well. Since Kat had to learn by watching the other gals and following Yokes' lead it went slower for her, but she picked up most of the moves real fast. The other guys were lined up on the sides, waiting for their turn. They were clapping and shouting encouragement to the couples on the floor. When the song ended, Yokes joined Matt at the bar. He was panting and wiping sweat off his forehead with a handkerchief. The guys next in line devoured all the girls. The ladies seemed to like it. At least they were laughing as they tried to catch their breath.

"She's one hell of a girl, Mr. Johnson, old boy. You better get her while the get tin's good!"

Matt held up a fist. "Watch that Johnson crap. I don't want to go through that again." He turned to the bartender. "Give me another beer, will ya? You want something?"

Yokes looked at the bartender. "Give me one too."

After about four or five more dances, Kat needed a rest and begged off on the next go-around. The guys left standing were disappointed, but she promised to return after she caught her breath. She had never been the center of attention before and she liked it. "Order me one of those, will ya?" she said, almost stumbling to the bar.

"I thought you were a vodka woman," said Matt.

"My legs can barely hold me up now. No vodka tonight!"

Yokes smiled as he said, "You're looking good out there. I didn't know they knew how to jitterbug back in Russia. You were sure cook-in' with gas!"

"I don't know what I was cooking with but my legs are sure fried!" She took a drink from her beer and then noticed Viktor and the nurse leaving together. The guys begged her to stay but she told them she needed a rest. Kat wondered what kind of rest she was going to get. Maybe she'd have a talk with Viktor… or maybe she'd just mind her own business.

"What time is it?" Yokes asked Matt.

Matt looked down at his watch. "Eleven… a little after eleven."

"I think I'll pick up my schedule for the next eight days and then turn in." Yokes turned to Kat. "Do you want me to pick yours up when I get mine? How about you, Mattie boy?"

They both replied, "Thanks."

"See you two in the morning. Don't take too long saying goodnight; they start keeping score starting tomorrow." He patted her on the head, then turned and left.

"I think we got a good partner in that guy, don't you?"

Kat wrapped her arm around Matt's waist and they headed for the flight deck and their little hideaway off the fantail.

The fog was so thick they had trouble finding their place, but eventually they did. The night was silent and the dew was almost syrupy on the deck and on the railings. They slipped several times on their journey aft but Matt's strength always caught them in time. The ship pretended to be sitting still, not moving at all. The foghorn suddenly blasted over the deck and into the blanket of white. It startled Kat and she clung tightly to Matt's arm. He enjoyed being her protector, either from the fog or any man or woman, if need be.

They finally found their hideaway and climbed down. Once there, every other thing was left behind, only the two of them and their growing affection.

He held her tightly. "I think I love you, Kat!"

She had always been a little too straightforward for her own good, but Matt's love was too important. "I think I love you too, but let's take it day by day." She kissed him and then gazed into his eyes. "Make love to me for the moment; let's create our own passion minute after minute and with no regrets. For only time will tell us the truth!" She stroked his face and then kissed his lips tenderly.

His fire built into yearning and all tenderness burst into passion. His hands that once were lightly around her waist and gently caressing the back of her hair now engulfed her breasts and thrust at her thighs. He tore at her clothing like a madman. They both breathed uncontrollably, and the sounds of their passion drifted out over the silent whiteness of the night and then echoed back to incite more of the same.

He laid her down and opened her uniform to expose her naked breasts; she looked mystified at him but did not resist. Then suddenly words came back to him; her words, the first words. *"I need tenderness... I need some gentle hands to caress me, some soft words of love."* Her words rang in his head. He removed his hand from her thighs and looked at it through the shadows, the trembling of passion still present in it, and he became ashamed. The lust in him turned into compassion and tenderness.

Her eyes sparkled as he slowly lowered his head to her breast. He kneaded and then kissed each one gently and suckled on them while her moans filled his ears. She spread her legs and he massaged her mound with affectionate strokes. He left her breast to open-mouth her lips. Their tongues danced with each other to the rhythm of their breathing. She held him tight, with all her might. They both whispered words of love to one another. Then she said to him, "If you want to take me... it's—"

He stopped her in mid-sentence. "You don't have to tell me when it's right. We'll both know when... and this isn't it. Anyway, I believe in saving the best for last." His gentle words brought joy to her heart and he could tell that he had done the right thing.

CHAPTER SEVEN

"WOULD SOMEONE PLEASE BREAK THAT goddamn siren?" Mel was not in a good mood this morning. Evelyn had kept him up most of the night showing pictures and neurotically talking endlessly about her dear husband and her three glorious children, to his dismay.

"My family always wakes up to the smell of fresh-brewed coffee and hot cakes on the grill." Some of the photos fell onto the floor. Her face turned into a sad and lonesome portrait of a woman wishing she was somewhere else as she fumbled with the photos that had fallen.

"Don't start, Evelyn!" This housewife was killing him, all this home sweet home crap.

She moved the blanket off of her legs. "Turn your head like a gentleman so I can get up and get dressed." She too was exhausted from talking most of the night but it was the only way she knew to keep certain subjects off a man's mind. Don't give him a chance to think. This technique had worked with her husband and ex-boyfriends in the past.

"Evelyn, don't take all day, I'm starving!"

"I'll be just a minute," she said as she picked up and then piled the photos once more on her bunk.

"Do all American housewives chatter like you do and are they always so prim and proper? I don't know of one Aussie wife that speaks to her hubby like she's on a radio skit or something."

She turned to find that Mel hadn't turned towards the wall

and had been watching her in her flannels all the time. "You're no gentleman, Mr. Shaw!"

"Maybe not… but don't you think flannel in the tropics… is a little strange?"

After a moment she smiled and dropped her pretense. "I'm sorry, I was just a little nervous and scared about going on this trip, and especially sleeping in the same room with a strange man. When I'm nervous, I talk a lot. My husband would not understand these arrangements!" She lowered her eyes and head to the floor. "But that's nothing new; he doesn't understand much about me anyway. He threatened to leave me if I came on this trip, but he sure hurried to the bank with the thousand dollars that was in that envelope."

"Why are you still nervous? It's been three days and I haven't molested you yet." As Mel lowered himself to the deck he asked, "What's his problem? Can't get a good night's sleep with four blabbering women in the house, I bet." Then he thought, *Why are the women bunked with the men? Must be the Americans' way of equality.* He'd heard that they're high on that kind of stuff.

As she raised her head, some tiny tears started to form in her eyes and she stiffened her arms at her sides. Her voice became abrupt and as stiff as her arms. "I'm a pilot… I fly aircraft… I was trained right along with the men. We did everything they did, and better! I could fly rings around most of them!"

Mel arched his eyebrows in puzzlement. "I've seen you fly, so what's the problem?"

Her face grew red and her fists clenched to white. "It's not fair, it's just not fair! In one day… one goddamn day!" She put her hand over her mouth. "I'm sorry, I don't normally use the Lord's name in vain, but I can't help it! All the training, all the flying, all the women that died getting those planes to the frontline departure stations, and they just throw us away in one day! We had dreams, too! I'm an aviator, trained and qualified." She walked over to the sink and took some toilet paper and wiped her eyes. "I tried to get a job with the airlines as a pilot. Do you know what they asked me after reading my résumé? How many trays do I think I could carry down an aisle at one time, while they ogled over my shape, then my legs! I wonder how many men's legs they looked at with those peering eyes. I even tried to get a crop dusting job out in-the-middle-of-nowhere, Texas; I guess they figured the chemicals would ruin my nails. The farmer just looked at me like I was some kind of freak."

Mel strolled over to her and gave her a hug. "That's tough going; I never realized you women had to go through that kind of crap."

She leaned back and stared him straight into his eyes. "That husband of mine, do you know what he said to me? 'You don't want to take the jobs away from the men coming home, do you?'" She buried her face into Mel's chest.

He patted her on the back and said, "Fuck 'em all. Come on, let's get ourselves dressed and squared away, then go win us a future!"

She lifted her head up, smiled, and then nodded as she wiped the moisture from his chest with her sleeves. "Get out of here so I can dress in peace, and watch your language!" She grinned at him as he turned from her.

He grabbed some underwear, his toothbrush and a razor, then turned to leave.

"Thanks for letting me vent." She then waved him out the door. She smiled to herself in the mirror, took her flannel pajamas off and threw them on the bed. *They are a bit warm,* she thought. She had showered the night before, so she just had to brush her teeth and put on a clean bra, socks, and uniform. After she gargled with some water, she stood admiring her nicely rounded breasts; *perky… that's what they are, perky.*

The door made a squeaky sound and she turned briskly towards it. She saw one of the Oriental pilots grinning at her through a crack in the door. She dove for the bed and covered her bare chest with the pajamas that were lying there. She lay there for several moments in the piles of photos, watching the door and not breathing so she could hear better. She wondered if she should scream. *No… I'm a big girl, I can handle this.* She recalled times from her past when the guys on the bases would try to catch a peek, but this wasn't one of the guys. This was the enemy, and she had heard what they did to captured nurses and female civilians. Her heart started to pound rapidly and she felt a small drop of sweat run down her back. She looked around the room for some kind of weapon. There, on the dresser, was a pair of scissors.

Without taking her eyes off the door, she sprinted over and picked them up. Holding them like a knife, she turned back to the door that was now closed. She thought, *Get your uniform on and get the hell out of here and go to where you can get help.* She didn't waste time with the bra and socks; she just put on the flight suit and went to the door. She put her ear against it and listened for a few seconds. The deck was cold on her bare feet but that was okay.

She opened the door, looked left and then right and when the coast was clear, she flew down the passageway like a salt on his way to battle stations. As she passed the men's head, she saw Matt out of the corner of her eye. She grabbed the railing to slow herself down and then pulled herself into the head.

The men knew something was wrong just by looking at her. "Evelyn, what's wrong?" Andrea and Stanis were the first to her side. She was breathing heavily.

Matt asked her again, "What's wrong?"

"There's a peeping Tom at my quarters! Just a few minutes ago I saw—"

Mel rushed over to Matt. "I was there only moments ago. The asshole must still be there or close by!"

"On this ship he could be anywhere by now." Matt's face was still lathered as he turned to Evelyn. "Did he touch you or hurt you?"

Evelyn's fear had greatly diminished and she felt safe now. "No, just looking and smiling, that's all. It's probably nothing. Just some guy trying to remember what it looked like."

Geno asked, "Do you know who it was?"

"All I know is he was Oriental… but the Orientals all look the same to me, especially through a crack in the door."

Mel looked around the head and spotted Sake and Lo Chu. They were standing by their sinks and had been for several minutes. "That leaves three suspects," he said.

Sake walked to the front of the head. "Would there be this much commotion if the guy was an American or a white Anglo-Saxon? You pin up half-naked women all over your ships." The room went silent in thought. "I will take care of this matter, and promise it will not happen again!"

Mel looked to Evelyn. "Will that be all right?"

Evelyn smiled. "Sure... I'm being too childish. It's probably nothing, just guys being guys. I'm sorry I made such a fuss."

Mel turned back to Sake. "Since she agreed, it will be all right. Just see that it doesn't happen again."

Now that the emergency was over, the guys noticed that at least half of them were naked as Jaybirds and giving Evelyn a really good show. They scrambled for towels and clothing to cover themselves. She snickered as she put her hands over her eyes and left the head.

"I'll walk you back to our quarters and stand guard while you get squared away," Mel said.

"Thanks, Aussie." The thought that a man—even if it was only an Asian man—took pleasure in looking at her filled her insides with a sort of glow. She wasn't too proud of the feeling, but at thirty-eight, she couldn't get a rise out of her own husband or any other man for almost three years now. Banking and making money was all he thought about. He had virtually raised the children all by himself to be prim and proper. She was always off flying somewhere.

She smiled as she realized why she had come on this adventure. Like the others before, it broke the boredom of her life. The earlier incident had made her feel younger, or maybe she just liked being noticed, even if voyeurism was a little dirty. Maybe a little dirt was what she needed? She felt good, knowing that most of the guys would protect her if she really needed it. Maybe she would throw away those flannels.

When they reached the cabin, Evelyn turned and looked into Mel's eyes deeply, and in an almost seductive voice said, "I can take it... from here."

It took longer than normal for breakfast. This did not make Number One or Two very happy. The pilots sauntered into the wardroom slow and lazy-like.

One peered out over the room. "I see some of you guys are getting a little salty since the first two days went so well." His soft, genteel voice turned hard and vociferous. "That attitude will end right now, <u>understand</u>? Starting today, we're flying the aircraft that will be used in the race. There are nine of them, and if one of you hotshots puts one in the drink, there will be only eight contestants. If you destroy all of them, you will all be fucked, <u>get it</u>?" He momentarily looked over to Two and when he returned, he noticed a greater sense of awareness and attention. "That's better. Now, back to the aircraft."

He opened a folder and took a quick look at it. "There will be a Zero, a Yak-7, a Sea-hurricane, Sea-fire, Hellcat, a Corsair, Polikarpov, Messerschmitt, and lastly, a Macchi."

"Some of these planes don't fly off of aircraft carriers!" Viktor's voice cracked from his surprise at the aircraft chosen. "Some aircraft seem to be not adequate, sir."

One looked at Viktor. "Glad to see you're on the ball. There are three that had to be modified for carrier use."

"I see four!" Werner was up to his self-appointed brilliant self again. "Polikarpovs, Yaks, and Macchis are all strictly ground takeoff and landing aircraft, and the Germans never built a Messerschmitt to fly off a carrier." The smug expression by Werner almost incited Number One to anger.

"I'm sorry to see that your intelligence is not up to your reputation." One's smile faded into a harsh glare. "Germany did design and build a carrier Messerschmitt. The BF 109 T, or Traeger, was built to fly off of the carrier *Graf Zeppelin* but the ship was destroyed before it could be used. Her aircraft were already built before the sinking, but most of them were eventually converted back into regular 109s." He smiled back at Werner. "There will be schooling every morning for the ignorant!"

He started pacing up and down the front of the wardroom. "There will be classes every morning to familiarize you with the traits of the aircraft you will be flying that day. I know you all will be doing your groundwork at night so you'll be up to par, won't you?" His smirk once again turned harsh. "Let me get to the grading. First, classroom tests will be given and graded. Then you will be graded on your takeoffs and landings, and then there will be ten maneuvers you will perform and be graded on in each aircraft. The maneuvers will be the same for each aircraft and are straight and level flight, timed climbs, timed descent, then your three turns; 30-degree, 45-degree, and 90-degree, all timed. Furthermore, there will be your demonstrated stalls, S-turns, chandelles, lazy eights, spins, and lastly, your pattern flying. These grades will be added to your test scores, which will give you your grade for that day. This will be added to the previous day, and so on. It's simple. The ones with the best scores fly in the race, the rest go home or wherever they want to go. You all have been given your daily assignment sheets, so you know what aircraft you're flying on what day."

"Sir, may I ask a question?" Stanis asked.

"Sure, go ahead."

"On my third day it shows search and rescue. What's that?"

One smiled. "I'm glad you asked that. You've already been checked out on the Hellcat. You won't fly it again till the racing starts, so there's been a day set aside to practice rescue missions with the helicopters and the Kingfisher." Two and the black-uniformed instructors stood ready at the front of the room. "Are there any more general questions?" He waited a few seconds, then said, "Good, now look to your schedules and go to your appropriate ready rooms. Your instructors will take over from there."

One turned to Number Two. "I'm going up to the Pri-Fly. See you later." The room became busy with pilots rushing to different ready rooms.

"Where's your first lesson, Yokes?" asked Kat.

Yokes looked at Kat's schedule. "Same as you. What the hell is a Macchi- folgore?"

She grinned at him. "Who knows? It sounds Italian to me, but I guess it could also be Spanish."

"I wonder what Matt's got going?" Yokes scanned the crowd for him.

Matt looked for Kat and when he found her he grabbed her from behind, startling her.

"Is that gentleman-like?" she barked.

"Can I have one of those squeeze toys?" Rudy asked jokingly.

Matt quickly turned and glared at him.

Rudy raised his hands and smiled as he retreated.

Matt put her down, spun her around, and wanted to kiss her but thought better of it. He asked her instead, "What the hell is a Poli—Polikar—Povikarpov, anyway?" "That's got to be Russian."

"It's a small fighter; maneuvers well, but not much on range," Kat said.

"What do you have coming up?" Matt asked her.

"Same as me, some goddamn Folgore or Macchi; sounds like spaghetti to me," replied Yokes.

"I like Italian food; it's spicy, like someone I know!" Matt squeezed Kat's hand.

"Full of meatballs… like someone I know!" She rubbed Matt's arm vigorously and giggled.

"See you guys on the flight deck later." Matt turned and headed for Ready Room Four.

Yokes looked down at Kat. "We better get our asses in gear." They left side by side and down the passageway.

Mike was standing by one of the braces for the bulkhead, his right cheek still bruised from Matt's blow. He observed the friendship between the three flyers and his face turned sour.

Werner walked up to him and whispered, "Disgusting, isn't it?" Then offered Mike a cigarette. He took it, and Werner lit it for him. Mike took a puff and blew the smoke out slowly.

"Yeah… it is pretty disgusting."

"I've heard there are nationalities that promote threesomes… sounds sick to me, taking two men to satisfy one woman. Especially since the Blackies are supposed to be so well-endowed." Werner took a puff of his own cigarette, then turned and joined his friends.

"Good morning. I'm Number Seven, and we'll be talking about the Corsair today. You should already know the fact sheets on the aircraft if you've done your studies. I'm here to familiarize you with certain characteristics of the aircraft. First, it has more power than the Hellcat you've flown. I know, it's hard to believe, but it does, and with more maneuverability, greater climbing speeds, and most important, better range. It will almost keep up with a Zero as far as agility. The main fault of the aircraft is its angle of takeoff and landing. The pilot can't see over the fuselage and its huge engine. You almost have to take off and land on your instruments alone, even more so on land bases. Remember, there's no LSO to help you there."

In another ready room the instructor announced, "My favorite fighter." The instructor pointed to the aircraft's picture hanging from the bulkhead. "I've flown most of them. I know, the Spitfires got most of the glory in the Battle of Britain, but I'm here to tell you that the Hurricanes put more of a shit on the Germans than any Spitfire. The Sea Hurricane can be classed with any other carrier aircraft."

"Are you sure you're not a little partial, Sir Edward, since you were a Hurricane squadron leader yourself?" Kenair said for a laugh.

Eight just smiled at Kenair, "Righty-O, chappy! Nevertheless, we put plenty of those Jerrys in bitter dirt."

"That's sticking it to 'em, sir!" said Kenair.

The Axis members that were in the room just sat stone-faced and quiet.

The morning classes were getting pretty dull. The pilots were familiar with almost all the aircraft. Either they had actually flown the aircraft or they flew against them. Many times, they would remember wishing they had such aircraft, or on the other hand, they recalled that they were happy they weren't flying that piece of crap as they flamed it. The sessions had turned into reminiscing and storytelling. Each pilot was relating a mission or two and of course, how he singlehandedly won the war with each kill. The tempers and resentments were piling up high and were oozing from each of the ready rooms like syrup over hot cakes. The arguments from each room mixed with each other, then echoed along the second deck, eventually overtaking the entire passageway with their yelling and shouting.

The hard part to learn was flying off the carrier, and since they had mastered that little detail, the rest was chicken soup. They thought they knew it all; but when it came to written tests, it was a different story. The instructors ultimately got things settled down and gave them the tests. It turned out that seventy-eight was the highest grade given out of the entire test. The pilots were anxious to get to the ready line and fly these machines. To hell with all this bookwork; you could see this attitude in their faces as they looked at their finished test scores. For more than a few of them, school days had been over for years and some, decades.

The roar on the flight deck was mixed today as the Airedales and the Aussie Zoom Pigeons rolled out the collection of beauties. All the planes were cleaned up and painted as ordered. All the pilots were lined up alongside of them on the flight line. Due to the arguments below, the flyers stayed within their own groups as they watched the aircraft being prepared. Most of the pilots stood stunned as others pointed to certain aircraft. The flight crews gaped at them, then stammered within themselves for a reason for the unaccustomed delay. Could there be something wrong with the planes, or was it something they had or hadn't done?

The flight captains started examining their aircraft. Everything seemed all right to them. The planes looked all in order. On both sides of each plane's tail was a number painted in bold white, as ordered. Their fuselages were painted with the signatures of certain flyers that had flown the aircraft in the war, again as ordered. The LSO looked up to the Pri-Fly where One was watching and waiting. These signatures were known to most of the flyers, and One knew that. He also knew that old hatreds would start to grow.

With reminiscing still on their minds in the ready rooms, old recollections filled the air and it became thick with tension. One pilot never could have identified another pilot with their headgear on and with just a quick glance, but they burned the image of their enemy's planes deep in their mind. Squadron leaders even encouraged rewards and bounties for some enemy planes.

"Was that Macchi yours?" asked Andrea.

Geno was standing next to Andrea when he asked the question. "Yes, it was. It's almost an exact replica."

"I was flying a P-47 Thunderbolt out of Alto Airbase in Corsica when on the return lap I ran across a Macchi. It was just like this one; yellow nose, white stripe around its belly, with a black stallion in the middle of it and the number ninety-two. The plane was all alone, hunting, so I dove on it. You must have seen me coming, for at the last minute you pulled up and got on my six. A real fine move… you flew well. I thought my ass was gone!"

"Thanks. What happened then?" Lucchini asked. Both men never looked at each other, they just stared at the plane as they spoke.

"My wingman blew you out of the sky. I watched you dive to a lower altitude, your plane breaking up and smoking all the way. My wingman and I were both low on fuel so we left you to your fate and returned to our base."

Lucchini thought for a moment. "So that's what happened! All I can remember is waking up in a field hospital in Sicily." The Italian's throat grew dry as he forced the words out.

"Look, Kat, my old plane!" Matt was so excited. "Good old *Jap Seeker*!" He looked down at her and saw her crying. "What's wrong, Kat?"

She ignored Matt as she stared at the Yak-7, the large red star on its fuselage and the number forty-four painted next to the star. She looked long at the bright-white lily that was painted on the nose. "The Nazis thought it was a rose, so they called her the Rose of Stalingrad."

"What did you say, Kat?" It was hard to hear over the engines.

Her face suddenly went from remorse to extreme hardness. Her tears didn't cease but her face reddened, and her eyes went black from squinting and complete focus on the plane she saw next. She dropped her headgear on the deck and her hands started to shake as she slowly moved closer towards the aircraft. She started to mutter, then shout with uncontrolled fury. The closer she got to the yellow-nosed plane, the angrier she got. She touched the Messerschmitt's wing and then went back to the black forward leading arrow that was painted on its fuselage and then back to the iron cross insignia on its flanks. She struck the plane with her fist and then turned to the crowd of airmen standing watching her. Drool escaped from her mouth as she cursed to herself. Her eyes looked like a banshee on the prowl and her hair blew fiercely from the crosswinds. Her mind flew back to that day of her greatest sorrow of the war. She strained for the likeness of that Nazi son of a bitch. The group of Germans watched her with smiles on their faces. As she got closer, she examined each, then walked straight up to Werner. "They missed something, didn't they? You son of a bitch!"

Matt realized that Kat wasn't sick when she turned from the plane and approached the Germans. He could see the anger in her face. He and Yokes watched curiously as she found her way to the men. Matt was one of the first to fly; so, Yokes told him he would take care of things and proceeded to Katya's side.

Werner lit another cigarette and then casually looked at the Messerschmitt once more. "Yes, they did, little one. My black cross and red star insignia are missing." He smiled at her once more. "Thanks for pointing it out."

Her face turned monstrous and gruesome. Her sneer alone would have frightened most men. The deepness of her voice rivaled even the guards of hell. "Do you remember this?" She raised her arm, then her finger.

"I'm surprised you know that lewd and vulgar gesture, little one. I wasn't surprised the first time you gave me that signal of affection, but now that you're supposed to be a lady, I'm a little shocked!" Of course, he was lying.

"Stand by to be shocked again, you Nazi bastard." She spit into his face with the fury of a hundred hatreds and then stood staring in defiance. "I'm going to kill you!" Her tone was sinister.

Werner wiped his face with his hand and then bent down to within inches of her face and whispered, "The war's over... how do you think you can accomplish that?"

"How about I break your fucking neck!" Yokes startled the German. As he rose, Yokes got right in his face and leered at him.

Werner moved aside of Yokes, then said, "Your friend... the Rose, was shot down fair and square, little one."

Her erect body stiffened even more. "You forget I was there! You call fair, a half-dozen to one?" She took a small step towards him. "None of you were good enough to fight her one on one and you knew it. She flamed every one of you Nazis that was put up against her. You couldn't deal with that so you simply ganged up and used your pack method to get her."

"Listen, if you can have more than one partner, so can we!" Werner scoffed at her.

For a split-second the anger fell from her face and was replaced with quandary. "I don't know what the hell you're talking about but I do know you're a dead man! I don't know how I'm going to do it yet, but you're a walking dead man... understand, *Adolph*?" She left the Germans puffing on their cigarettes and mocking her. She walked back to her gear and Matt. Someone knew too much here, she thought. "Things are going to get real nasty around here, and soon!" She felt the screams of frustration at the back of her throat and it would be hard to remain coherent when so close to that bastard.

As Matt looked into Kat's eyes, he felt something out of the normal was happening. It was like a play or a novel was being written and they were the characters. "It feels funny to me too, babe." Matt looked up to the glass command center and saw One scanning down.

Yokes backed out of the group of Nazis and joined Matt and Kat. "Don't ever get that mad at me, Missy."

The flight crews were even more flustered by what had just happened. One had been watching from the command center on the island and could imagine the subject matter spoken between Kat and Werner, since he apparently had set it up.

"This is Number One." The announcement came over the intercom loud and firmly. "This is a race for warriors, ladies and gentlemen. This much, I figured you would have already figured out on your own." A few moments went by and the flyers looked at each other, not knowing exactly what was going on. "First pilots to your aircraft!" again the intercom rang out. Nine pilots rapidly sprang into action and leapt into the cockpits of their planes, to the pleasure of their flight captains.

"Watch her till I get back down!" Matt screamed over the engine noise as he started to run towards the Zero.

Yokes stood tall at her side. "No problem here, just kick some ass!"

Kat just stood there, still shaking a bit. Her tears had dried up but her anger still remained. *Calm down,* she thought. *Don't let them get to you.* She strained for a way to inflict her revenge and then all of a sudden, it came to her. What do they want more than anything right now? I'll kill their dreams, their hopes, and their ambitions. Beat them in the air, win the race, and make sure they don't win a penny. Money is power to them, so take it all away, even if it means helping others to finish ahead of them. She turned to Werner and they enjoyed the volleying of sneers and facial decays.

Yokes glanced down at her. "Why are you smiling, Missy?"

She removed her sneer and her face went calm as she breathed a large sigh. Her expression was like someone has just figured something out and was pleased with their conclusion. She did not answer, but looked away to the pilots taking off.

"Everything clear on this Polikarpov?"

She looked up at him and grinned. "Just call it an I-16 and watch your airspeed. This little toy can get out of hand really quick." She watched the sky as all the pilots were in the pattern now. The two of them spotted the ME 109 fall into the landing pattern. "Who's the first to fly the Messerschmitt?"

Yokes glanced at the schedule. "Looks like Rudy."

"He's coming in too steep. The crosswinds are going to catch him."

"He looks all right to me."

"Watch," she said positively.

They could see the LSO trying desperately to get him back on proper course. Then the wave-off came and it came again. Rudy ignored it and came in anyway. His speed and angle were wrong and he missed the cables, bouncing right over them. His brakes smoked as they tried to slow the plane down. The 109 yawed to the right and just before hitting the barrier it straightened out, then the barrier engulfed the aircraft. The plane stood straight up, nose down and tail up. The propellers were broken off like toothpicks, and Rudy was almost ripped from his harness.

"You goddamn fool!" Katya didn't move when the other pilots rushed to Rudy's aid; neither did Werner. Katya felt a little uneasy being alone when Werner came over to her.

"I like it when pilots make it personal. It enhances the game, just like your friend did back on the Russian Front. She and I tangled many times, with both of us scoring hits. She was good, very good. But she was a little too aggressive, didn't figure the odds well. It's going to be a pleasure competing against you."

Katya didn't say a word to the German, just stood there with a mocking sneer on her face. He did make some sense, she thought, as he went back to his returning comrades.

The Airedales were already on the plane with foam. The crash and salvage crews were busy pulling Rudy's ass out of the cockpit. He was smiling, with his arms up in victory, when the LSO came up to him. "You're lucky you're not still in the military or I would have your ass locked up and throw away the key, you fuckin' asshole!"

"Number Twenty-one, come to the Pri-Fly at once." Everyone knew what that announcement meant. "Aircraft handlers, clear the decks for future landings." Everything was put back into order in record time. The damaged 109 was lowered to the hangar deck and the barrier re-strung.

"Are you as stupid as you look?" were the first words Rudy heard as he stumbled into the Pri-Fly.

"No, Number One."

One turned to watch the next pilot landing. "Then it has to be anything German you hate. Even a goddamn German aircraft. How about German chocolate, German sweaters, sausages, beer?" He turned to see the embarrassment on Rudy's face. "Are you here to compete or to avenge yourself on the whole German race?" His straight glance seemed to be accusing him coldly.

Rudy's face turned stone-like, cold and ashen. "Maybe a little of both."

One turned away from him and smiled. "If the 109 can be repaired, you're still in the race. If not, you're out." He turned back around to study him. "If the plane can't be repaired, I'd watch my ass around here. There's going to be a lot of guys that are going to blame you for one less spot in the race." He looked to find little concern on Rudy's face.

"Now get the hell out of here. You fuckin' asshole. What the hell were you thinking? All of us have had a wave-off. There's nothing wrong with that." The Brit was speaking for the whole room.

Rudy just stood there in the wardroom and took his punishment. "It won't happen again."

Dumitrn was so upset he was beside himself with anger. "I tell you right now, if there's any more of this kind of shit going on, I'm going to put a boot in someone's ass. I don't care who it is, either."

The room acknowledged the Romanian's thoughts and agreed with his appraisal of the situation. They could all suffer from one man's stupidity.

The Romanian approached Rudy. "You're the luckiest Jew I've ever seen. If that plane can't be repaired, I'll have you for lunch." His eyes glowed with a savage inner fire.

Rudy's face suddenly erupted into fury. "That's right; you Nazis are good with ovens, aren't you!"

"Enough." Harrazabal stepped into the middle of the room. "We've all been stupid at one time or another. For some of us, being here might be one of those times. Relax, put on some music, have a drink, and think of something different than flying."

The flyers wanted to relax. It was their time, so the suggestion was welcomed. Some laughter and telling of jokes started up. They began milling around, but the day's topics and memories kept them segregated. The Orientals seemed immune from bringing up of the past. They were never joyful with each other's company, nor anyone else's, but appeared to tolerate their differences. Games such as acey-deucy and checkers became the topics of the night. The bar opened, and soon almost everyone had a drink in their hand.

Evelyn was sitting with Matt, Kat, and Yokes. The threesome was in heavy controversy on which of them was going to work the office while the other two were piloting to Cuba or St. Thomas. "Just because I've got better legs, don't get any ideas that you guys are going to leave me on the ground."

Yokes pointed a finger in the air. "We'll make Georgina the office personnel, okay?"

The remaining partners smiled and nodded their heads in agreement.

A feeling that someone or something was observing her bothered Evelyn; she scanned the room. Mel sauntered over and took a seat next to her. She felt better; Mel must have been the one she sensed. The hair on the back of her neck relaxed.

Mel looked at her. "Am I going to get some sleep tonight?"

The threesome stopped dead in mid-conversation. They weren't going to miss this.

Evelyn smiled slyly at the group. "It's not what you are thinking. It's just that Mel here isn't interested in my home life... that's all."

"So that means I'm not going to have to listen to how Margie got straight A's in school for the fifteenth time?"

"Don't be rude, Mr. Shaw." She gave him a half-smile.

A large poker game started up in the center of the room. "We got room for two more suckers." Stanis just happened to be the big winner from the night before.

Matt looked over to Yokes. "How about it, are you game?"

"Got to study; that I-16 gave me some trouble today; I don't need any problems tomorrow."

"How about you, Mel, you game?"

"Sure, I've got a couple of pounds I could lose."

Matt got up and kissed Kat on the cheek. "You don't mind, do you?" She shook her head. Matt and Mel left for the table.

"Missy and I are going to our quarters to study. Would you like me to walk you to yours?"

Evelyn's feelings of being watched were still with her but she declined Yokes' offer. "I'll be just fine." She watched the two of them leave, then noticed McGuire almost stalking them. Maybe this was what she was feeling? She didn't worry much about Yokes, he could take care of himself... of that there was no doubt.

Mike McGuire had followed the two down the passageway and she listened for any disturbances as she made her way to her quarters. Once there, she gathered her underwear, shampoo, soap, and her hairbrush, then headed for the sickbay to shower. She felt there was more privacy at night, rather than in the mornings when the men showered.

The passageways were quiet, and she didn't pass anyone on her way to sickbay. She searched for those feelings she had before but they were gone. She felt a little relieved, but she hoped there would be a nurse on duty when she got to sickbay anyway.

The lights were out in the rear of the sickbay when she arrived and there was no one on duty. She looked for the light switch and the intercoms, just in case, thinking it might be safer to shower in the shadows. A person could see outward into the light but could not be seen in the darkness of the rear of the room. Laying her things on one of the tables, she then started to undress, listening intently for the sound of anyone approaching, stopping two or three times and leaning an ear to the still air. Little taps and squeaks sent chills up her spine more than once, but she shook them off with logic. *A moving city makes little noises from time to time, you big baby.* As she took her panties off and laid them on the table, she reached in through the curtain and felt for the water knobs. Suddenly, a hand grabbed her arm and pulled her into the shower stall. When she tried to scream a hand covered her mouth. She could not see the person attacking her but he was not tall and smelled like fish.

"Don't make a sound, you white bitch." The man twisted her head to one side. "I'll break your pretty white neck if you make a sound." The man's other hand turned on the water, supposedly to cover any sounds from the stall. "You American bitches like your sex rough... yes... we've heard all about your kinky inclinations." His hand wandered down to her breasts and massaged each of them. The running water made a slight squeaking sound as he touched her. Her fear sent tremors down her spine and she gritted her teeth with every move of his hand. He slipped his hand down her wet body to her thighs, where he forced her to spread them a little. A small whimper escaped her throat as his rhythm increased. His fingers stroked her roughly and she started to breathe erratically. "You like that, don't you?" the voice chuckled sinisterly.

Through her tears, she pondered what to say. *Do and say anything to keep him from hurting you,* she thought.

"I'm going to take my hand off your mouth; make a sound and I'll still kill you, understand?"

She nodded, crimson with resentment and humiliation.

"Don't look at my face; just turn around and get on your knees."

Halfway down she heard someone come into the room and prayed that they noticed the clothing on the table or heard the shower running.

"Is anyone here?" the doctor said.

The rapist realizing the water was on, pulled her up and whispered, "Answer him." He loosened his grip on her so she could turn and answer.

Her heart throbbed uncontrollably from her fright and she gathered all her driving force and courage. "Yesses." She pulled away and ran towards the light, choking and gasping as she yelled for help.

The startled doctor flinched away from the naked woman running in his direction.

The rapist hurriedly escaped through a rear passageway in the room.

Evelyn bypassed the shadow of the doctor and grabbed the intercom and screamed, "Help! I need help in the sickbay! Please, someone help me! Hurry… please hurry!" With the water in her lungs and the sure terror of the rape, she collapsed against the bulkhead.

The doctor regained his senses and went over to Evelyn, covering her with a blanket. "You're all right, I'm here, you're all right now." He joined her and held her close, both of them on the floor, trying to calm each other down. She was shaking and sobbing.

"My husband told me not to come." Over and over, the same words came to her.

The whole ship heard her on the intercom and came running. The passageways were soon clogged with personnel trying to help. Mel was one of the first to arrive. As soon as he saw her on the floor with the doctor, he knew what had happened. To save her anymore embarrassment he said, "Give her to me." Mel picked her up then carried her, fighting the crowded passageway, back to her bed and the safety of her quarters. "You'll be all right, love."

"Yes." She turned her head towards him and with saddened eyes said, "He didn't get the chance to hurt me, but I think he would have." She sat hovered in one corner of her bunk. Her hair was still wet and she shivered. She didn't know whether to cry or be happy for her rescue, her rescuer breathing heavily, trying to regain his breath.

Kat came storming into the room. "Are you all right, Evelyn?" her stance at the ready.

Matt was still at the sickbay. "Who the hell was it? I'll break his fucking neck." Matt was clearly in a fury, as was everybody else.

"I don't know but he was small, and he's definitely soaking wet. He ran out through the rear passageway. It was too dark to see him clearly." The doctor pointed to the rear exit.

Matt turned to the guys in the passageway. "Find him. He's small and wet, probably an Oriental." Matt suddenly thought of Kat. He jumped to his feet and ran to her cabin; it was empty. There was all kinds of confusion and disbelief onboard with the search for the rapist. A notice came across on the intercom: "We have him, on the flight deck, aft."

"Stay with her, please," Mel said to Katya.

With a smile from both the women, Mel leapt to his feet and flew out the door. When he got to the flight deck, it was almost full to capacity. All the crew and all the pilots had surrounded the Japanese flyer on the fantail. Mel muscled his way through the crowd till he was within just a couple of feet of Nakase.

Nakase stood defiantly at the edge of the fantail. "I've broken no laws. We're in international waters. There are no laws to break out here," the Jap said with a smirk.

"Yes, there is." Number One stood like a statue in the mist. The breeze was blowing his white hair forward onto his brow, his eyes blazing and the clouds of fog swirling around his body like the arm of judgment from on high had come. Armed security men were at his side as the crowd gave them room.

"You can lock me up, but you will have to set me free at the next port of call." The sneer from the Jap was irritating. "She wanted it, anyway; women like her enjoy the rough stuff. I just brought a little pleasure to her life."

Mel glanced over to Sake, his body quivering from anger. "I thought you personally guaranteed the safety of the women. I guess the word of a Jap isn't worth much." The quivering stopped and his body stiffened in readiness.

One asked Sake, "What would be the penalty for rape in Japan?"

Sake never looked at One; his eyes were still fixed on Mel. "Raping an American woman... nothing... nothing would be done at all." Sake grabbed and then pulled out a .45-caliber pistol from the security man's holster, then turned to face Nakase. "But to dishonor my word is to die." He fired three rounds into Nakase; his chest opened, and huge amounts of blood instantly burst forward. The momentum of the rounds forced Nakase back and eventually off the end of the deck and into the open sea. The look on Nakase's face was that of disbelief and shock.

Sake turned to Mel and bowed. "Will that be satisfactory?"

One took the pistol from him, then with a smile, simply turned and walked away. The security men followed behind him.

Sake and Mel's eyes had not left each other. Mel bowed slightly and without a word spoken, left to attend Evelyn.

This kind of justice was commonplace during the war, swift and final. Sake was left alone on the flight deck as the crowd disbursed. The mist rose with the new breeze. He walked to the edge and stood tormented as he gazed at the splattered blood left on the deck. Then he turned and looked down at the wake of the ship as the sun started to creep up. His stomach started swirling and a feeling of falling almost overtook him, like Nakase was beckoning him. He asked himself, is it worth it?

The next three days proceeded at a somewhat normal pace. There were no more killings or rapes, but there were new tensions. The scores were posted every morning and the flyers at the rear of the list seemed to be getting jealous of the frontrunners. Evelyn had resigned herself to go back home and was no longer in the competition. Her heart was heavy; she had wished to compete and make a life for herself in aviation when she returned to the States. But her mind would not be on flying now; the hands of that sick man would linger for some time.

CHAPTER EIGHT

FROM THE FLAG PLATFORM, ONE watched the weather team in their morning ritual of sending up balloons and collecting their findings. Moisture had settled on the flight deck from the night's fog, but now the morning air was almost stale from lack of a breeze and the newfound heat. That meant the ship was getting close to the tropics.

He cast an eye to the white wake of the ship and reflected on the past few days as he looked down and watched the crews raising the aircraft for today's lessons. He almost felt shame when he remembered the decision Sake was forced to make regarding Nakase, for he'd known Nakase was wanted by the Military Police for an alleged rape in Tokyo when he picked him. However, the warmth he felt deep inside as he observed Sake's agony lifted him to new heights. His hatred built each day for him, and he fantasized on how he could make this man's life more difficult and anguished.

"Sir, can I have a word with you?" Two's voice was not urgent but there was something in it that was not right.

"Of course, Number Two."

Two pulled out some papers from a briefcase. "I need to discuss these scores. Numbers Eight and Nine tell me that you've been changing Sadaaki Akamatsu's scores. You always have him number one on the list. You know he's no better than twentieth or maybe even twenty-fifth. So, what's up?"

One became irked by Two's cool, aloof manner. He turned and entered the island and climbed the ladder to the Pri-Fly.

Two followed him, confused with the admiral's behavior. He persisted with returning impatience. "Sir?"

"Just keep him on the list. He will always be number one on the list. Do you understand?" he replied with heavy irony.

Two's face became a little flushed. "That's not right, sir. It's not fair, either. What about those other guys down there?"

The look on the admiral's face confused Two even more. His normal calm and direct expression suddenly erupted into a fierce and contemptuous mask. He had never seen this look before on him.

"Are you hard of hearing or don't you understand English?" One stopped and took a deep breath to calm himself. "Please, John, just make him number one always."

"Yes, sir." As he turned and walked down the ladders of the island, he couldn't help but wonder what was going on. There must be some reason behind it. He walked over to the bulletin board and posted the scores of the previous days. A small crowd gathered to read the scoring.

The first nine on the list read Akamatsu, Drew, Nolder, Yokes, Encionin, McGuire, Shaw, Chalupa, and Lucchini. Then Kenair, Chu, and Yegorova were in tenth through twelfth place. "That no-good Jap is still in the lead. I can fly bananas around that asshole." Chu was not happy either. Sake was leading, and he was still on the cuff at eleventh.

"Maybe you ought to take some flying lessons, old chap." Kenair's little comment didn't go over to well with Chu and Kenair knew it.

After the day's lessons were over, the flyers seemed tired. Tension and frustration filled the air like smoke from a forest fire, almost choking them, and definitely clouding their view of things. Scheming and plotting took place widely throughout the ship. Pilots were looking for advantages anywhere they could find them, and they knew they were running out of time. They crowded each other in the skies and did a little crowding onboard the ship, also. The joyful leisure cruise they thought it would be had now turned out to be a fight for their lives, if not their futures. Sides were being taken everywhere, with defections galore. No one trusted anyone, even with his or her own kind. The feelings onboard seemed to be derived or planned out somehow, by someone or something. Forgotten hatreds and dislikes were being manipulated and heightened, but by whom?

When not flying the pilots were now drinking, and they drank a lot, which brought on bitching and excuses for their bad performances that day. The nurses no longer came to the wardroom at night to dance and have a good time. They knew there would probably be a fight. The pilots complained about everything; the food was not good enough or the weather played tricks on them today.

"That goddamn limy asshole in the front of the pattern today, she stalled her plane too soon and jammed up the rest of us." The flight deck was filled with such comments.

"I wish that son of a bitch would crash and burn so we could at least get back on deck right." The excuses were mounting up pretty high. They were also getting tired of the same thing day after day. The repetition of the same pattern flying every day left them bored and frustrated. Not having obstacles to prove their flying abilities was taking its toll. These were fighter pilots, not Sunday Piper Cub trainees on a weekend flying lesson. They hated most of the aircraft that wasn't their own; they could not maneuver the other aircraft like they could the ones they were accustomed to. The scoring was so minuscule that only a few half or quarters of a point where the difference between first and last. This also suggested they were derived. No one had ever used fractional scoring before and this bewildered all the men, including the instructors. The men's anxiety and disappointments came out in the open. It finally came down to threats, then ethnic slurs, then religious condemnations. A man's skin tone or accent became a reason for a verbal, if not physical, altercation.

One had to finally have security present in the wardroom at night. He had the pilots serve themselves meals or go hungry. They were taking out their frustrations on the cooks. He also enforced a curfew of ten o'clock, and eventually closed the bar. One appeared to be content with the new arrangements and feelings onboard but that was nonsense—or was it?

Kat lay on her bunk studying for the next day. As a woman, she had not been caught up in the egos of the men. What happened to Evelyn had made all of the guys more respectful towards the women onboard. Of course, this respect could be because Kat and Amy hadn't been in contention for the top spots yet. Kat's friendship with Drew and Yokes, and a little bit with Mel, weren't worth a broken jaw. The ship, as big as it was, had become smaller and smaller every day. The same faces, fake smiles, sneers, and especially their demeanors made them grow irritated with every glance or every captured word. She felt like one of the children in the Mother Goose rhyme, *Old Woman in the Shoe*.

An Aussie seaman poked his head into Kat's quarters. "Ma'am, have you seen Mr. Budanova?"

Katya laid her manual down and looked at the seaman. "No, matter of fact, I haven't seen him for a couple of days."

"Sorry to bother you, ma'am." The young man turned and walked to the next cabin and she heard him ask the same question.

Kat thought, *What is Viktor up to? I better go find out.* She got up and headed for the wardroom, hoping to find Matt or Yokes playing cards or something. She spotted Kenair playing chess with Chu. The wardroom was only about a third full, and no Matt or Yokes. She wandered over to the game and asked Kenair if he'd seen Viktor. He raised his eyebrow and got a funny look on his face, then blurted out, "No." He recognized whom he was talking to and then sheepishly returned back to his game.

"Checkmate," said the Chinaman with a very large smile.

The Irishman's face turned beet red and his cheeks blew outward like little balloons ready to pop. "Damn the gods. You be an evil one, yellow man. You must ride with the *Pookadoos* to get this good at chess. I... me thinks this be the third time you've pummeled me, with me own shillelagh!" He snapped his head back to Kat with an expression like, if it hadn't been for your interruption, I would have won. But he smiled nevertheless. "What did you say, my queen of the bogs?"

"I was looking for Viktor." She knew he was upset with her.

"Yes, the Bolshevik lover boy of the year." Kat's look stopped all his comedic tendencies. "I apologize, lass." His reddened cheeks diminished to little pink circles and a red-tipped nose. "Come, I'll take you." He nodded a goodbye to Chu as he stood to leave. He took her by the arm and headed for the far passageway. "We could get into trouble if we get caught." He raised an eyebrow to her. "You know we're not supposed to be in the crew's areas."

"I knew it. He's with that nurse, isn't he?"

"Maybe not." He gave her a wink.

They went down the ladder to the second deck and then aft, past the sickbay and the laundry into the enlisted men's area. Their dark-blue flight suits made them stand out from the navy uniforms that surrounded them. Kenair stopped at the ship's store for some tobacco for his pipe. Katya didn't like it. She felt so out of place, but she waited quietly. He turned to her. "A good excuse if we're caught." The enlisted men seemed appalled to see a woman in their area. She picked up some soft murmurs and subdued complaining from the men as she passed. This was men's country, and women were normally not allowed. Even female officers were restricted down here.

The passageway opened up into the CPO mess and pantry, where she saw Viktor sitting with some other men at a table. She looked around for the nurse but she was nowhere to be seen. She glanced back at Viktor; he hadn't seen her yet. The men at the table stopped their conversation and stared at her. The whole room grew silent.

Viktor turned her way and frowned. "Katya... what are you doing here?"

Katya returned the frown with extra vigor. "What the hell are *you* doing here? Are you in civilian clothes? Do you want to be shot as a spy? Where is your uniform, you crazy peccadillo?"

Viktor smiled. "There's no war on anymore, Katya. Nobody's going to shoot anyone. I just need to be able to walk around down here and talk to these Australians. When I'm dressed like they are, the security men leave me alone."

"Get your ass back in uniform and go to the wardroom and we'll talk."

"Yes, Katya, I'll be there in a moment."

She turned to the Irishman and glared at him. "Get me out of here."

Kenair bowed and motioned with his arm. "This way, my lady."

She looked over the room. "Sorry for the intrusion, men." She was glad to be leaving this area. Not out of fear, but respect for the men's privacy. She didn't like her own privacy invaded, and she'd be damned if she would do the same to these men.

The wait was not long in the wardroom. Viktor showed up in the right uniform and with head lowered, slithering over to where Katya was sitting all alone. "Take a seat." Her tone was stern and low-pitched.

As he sat, he folded his hands in front of him. "I know where I want to go after the race."

Fire seemed to flicker from her eyes. "After the race... what race? You mean the one you're going to be kicked out of for violating the rules?" A grave look came to her face like he had been sentenced to death. "Viktor... these pilots are just waiting to get you knocked off the list. They would take your place in a second. Don't you understand?"

Viktor smiled and reached for her hand, took it, and softly stroked its smooth whiteness. He looked into her eyes. "I love you, Katya... like an older sister... or a best friend. And even a mother at times. You are the bravest person I've ever known and I envy you in most ways. But I think it's time that I work out my own life."

He spoke to her of far-off places and as her mind and heart listened, she felt warmth inside; somehow, she understood him. She always had. His words seemed true and with conviction. She was glad to see him grow to be a strong man, a happy man.

"Your nurse friend, is she from this place?"

"Brisbane... yes. She tells me it's the most beautiful place on earth and it never snows. Remember the blizzards we used to endure in Moscow, the mud for miles in the spring?"

135

"The summers were nice though." She knew what he was talking about and she too had no inclination to return home.

"The enlisted men I've talked to tell me that Australia is filled with nothing but foreigners. Except for some kind of tribal group, all are from somewhere else. I'll fit right in."

"They're called Aborigines, and don't ask me how I know that. I must have picked it up somewhere; at university, probably." She watched as his face softened to boyish again, looking for approval. "Does the woman love you, and do you love her?"

"I think I love her, but love her or not, this new land will be my future home." She looked like she understood. "Katya, I didn't come here to race. I came to escape from everything back there. The food lines were larger now than during the war in some places, while of course the politicians and the generals feed like pigs." He directed his attentions to a far table. "I'm surprised that the Pollock over there even talks to either one of us. To him, we're no different than the Nazis." He looked back at Katya, then lowered his head in remorse. "The Soviets have enslaved the whole of Eastern Europe, and what for? Europe is nothing but piles of rubble and devastation. There's no need for Russian tanks in the streets of Budapest or Prague. I don't want to be thought of as a Soviet. I'm a Russian, and always will be. Both you and I fought for the freedom of our people; you for the whole war. You lost so much… everything, right?" He lifted his head and showed his reddened eyes. "So, I'm grabbing the ring from this merry-go-round and I'm making the best of it. I will never be ashamed again." He used all his strength to hold back his tears.

She gazed back at him and as she did, she realized he'd become a stranger, one with morals and convictions, but most of all, truth. The joker had fled into the night and a new man sat across from her and she smiled. Her ears had never heard so much seriousness spewing from Viktor's lips before and he had never made more sense. Along with her fondness for him, there was now a pride for him that would never fade. Strength had come to him, along with happiness. Most of the happiness she figured came from the woman, and she was glad of that.

She had always given him advice, but what could she say now?

"I agree with everything you've just said and I'm proud of you; but use some sense now, Viktor. Would not some money help with your plans? I'm sure the young lady hasn't got too many objections to some rubles in her pocket? Money in a new world could only help."

"Yes, you're right." He grinned at her with that boyish look again.

She knew the childlike expression on his face would soon disappear, maybe never to return, and she would miss it. All mothers do… even appointed ones. "So, get your ass up, get ready, and fly the hell out of those other guys."

"You're right, Mother dear." His smile widened to full face.

His words touched her heart and the earlier warmth returned. "If you need some seclusion with your nurse friend, borrow my room, Yokes will understand."

"Thanks, Katya. I owe you a lot." He patted her on the hand and then stood and left through the near passageway.

It was almost 21:00 hours when Matt and Yokes came into the wardroom. Katya was still sitting at the table, drinking a soda. She and Kenair were having an argument. They were shouting from across the room on the correct procedures for playing chess. Katya, using her Russian, was verbally winning the day. What he couldn't understand, he couldn't argue. The two of them walked up to her. "We've got the day's results and it's looking really good. It looks like at least two of us will be in the race, and if you could get your sweet behind in gear, it could be all three of us," said the massive black man.

She dropped her head but not her eyes. Her glare was glassy, like when she shot it at Matt. Her stare was more telling than Yokes' words. "Don't you guys worry your poor little tallywackers off. I'll be there when I need to be there." She sat back and took a big drink of her soda. "I'm not sure I want to put out the effort racing. You guys seem to have everything going straight ahead. The money's in the bag, and that means I can take it easy and let you guys do all the work." She tilted back on the two back legs of the chair. "I'm an equal partner either way… am I not?"

"Listen, smarty pants, the testing is not over yet, and only a few decimals divide the top nine. With you moving up to number eleven, you could be there tomorrow or the next day, so keep on it. Our future depends on it!" Matt's voice appeared a little harsh.

"I don't know about you, but I'm going to marry a millionaire." She stuck her nose high in the air and gave him a profile.

"Sure, but it will take me a couple of years to become one of those," Matt replied abruptly.

She froze, and the balancing of the chair froze with her. Matt's last sentence sent numbness throughout her body. After a few seconds, she managed to gleam at Yokes.

He just shook his head, shrugged his shoulders and whispered to her, "I'm married; I've already been through this."

Matt, unconcerned with the topic, turned back to her and kissed her on the forehead. "I'm turning in early so I can study. See you in the morning." He turned nonchalantly and left.

"Did you hear him?" Her lips started to quiver and her eyes welled up as she spoke to Yokes. "Was that a proposal?" She slammed the chair back to the floor and with her mouth gaping open, uttered an ungodly groan.

Yokes didn't know what to say. "I don't know, but it sounds more subconscious to me."

"I've got to go to my room." She stood then left, waving her arms and talking to herself. "That man drives me nuts. What a thing to say to a girl! You shouldn't lead a woman on like that, building their hopes up, then just walk away like you just ordered a cup of coffee to go." The passageway echoed her voice for several minutes as she made her way to her quarters. The men in the wardroom looked at each other and figured it was just a female thing and didn't get in her way.

"How about some cribbage?"

The voice took Yokes by surprise. He turned his head to find Gershwin standing there with a cribbage board in his hand.

Rudy smiled down at him. "Do you know how to play?"

"Yeah… sure." He glanced at his wristwatch. "I guess we got time for at least one game."

Rudy sat across from Yokes and laid out the board. "White or black?"

Yokes was still concerned about the time.

"What color pegs do you want, black or white?"

Rudy's abruptness brought his thoughts back to the table. "Whites have always been luckiest for me."

"That's good. I like the black ones myself." Rudy dealt the first hand out and looked at his cards, then as he threw down his crib hand, he asked, "You're pretty high on the list, aren't you?"

"Yeah, third or fourth. But I don't know if I'll be able to stay there." Yokes glanced over the top of the cards at him. He got the feeling Rudy was trying to say or maybe ask him something, but didn't want to come right out and do so.

"I'm almost out of the running. I think I moved up to eighteenth today. At that rate, there's not much chance in me making it to the finals."

Yokes threw his two cards on top of the crib pile. "Don't give up, Gershwin. Some asshole may get airsick and move you right up. I hear we have rescue training tomorrow; maybe someone we don't like will drown."

Rudy looked away from his cards and smiled. He seemed to be somewhere else, in deep thought.

"Is it your crib or mine?" asked Yokes.

He slipped back to the present. "I dealt. I think that makes it my first crib."

The two men played for over an hour. It turned out to be fun for both of them, but Rudy kept fading in and out of deep thought. He could have won the game but he was too preoccupied with something else to concentrate much on the cards.

"Fifteen two, fifteen four, and a double run for twelve. I win, Gershwin."

Rudy stood and smiled at him. "Good game, Yokes, thanks for playing with me. I appreciate it more than you know." He left the cards on the table and walked out and down the passageway.

That man was definitely weird, thought Yokes. *Maybe that's why he's so behind in his flying. He has always got his mind somewhere else.*

He put the cards back in their box and then noticed that he was the only one remaining. The ship had been turned down for the night, and the harsh metal walls made him feel a little cold. All unnecessary lighting had been shut off and the rest dimmed, and only the sounds of the engine could be heard. He looked at his watch again. "Damn. It's almost 2300 hours. I got to get my fat ass to bed." He quickly stood and hurried towards the hatch.

A shadow of a figure was standing at the other end of the darkened passageway. "Big Guy. Hurry!" the figure shouted. "Yegorova needs you on the hangar deck, she's in trouble!"

"What's the matter, is she hurt?" That earlier sense of coolness abruptly turned into a shiver that shot up his spine.

The shadow replied, "I don't know... I was just sent to get you. Hurry!" The figure in the passageway turned and disappeared down one of the ladders.

Yokes' legs instinctively started moving. His hurried pace shortened and as he passed the ladder he looked down, but saw nothing but darkness. All he could think about was the time Evelyn's voice rang over the intercom and her cries for help. He could only imagine and fear the worst, but he kept thinking over and over that if they laid a hand on Missy, he'd break their fucking backs.

When he got halfway up the ladder to the hangar deck, he realized something. No one called Katya by her last name, and no one with any sense would refer to him as Big Guy. A feeling hit him deep in the middle of his chest. Something was wrong with this whole scenario. He slowly raised his head so he could look along the hangar deck, his hand gripping the railing firmly. It was dark, with a single light shining down from the bulkhead. He thought, if there was something wrong with Missy, there would be some kind of commotion going on and there would be people on the deck. There was nothing but darkness and silence, and his sweat dripping into his eyes. Even though his feelings told him this was bogus, he could not take the chance that Missy was hurt and she might be at the far end of the deck.

As he took the last step onto the deck, he yelled, "Missy... can you hear me? Are you all right, Missy?" Yokes walked towards the light and to the far end of the deck. It was like crossing a football field. The light made a circle about eight or nine feet across, and once in it, he had trouble seeing out beyond it. "Missy... answer me!"

Yokes heard someone walking towards him. First, he saw some shoes, then legs, then finally a whole person stood in front of him. The downward light shaded his features and made him look devilish. "How you doing, Darkie... had any watermelon lately?" Mike had a glare on his face. His mouth was turned downward and his cheeks were raised to make his eyes squint. "No watermelons? Too bad. I know how you niggers love melons." He stopped his glaring, tilted his head and stuck out his bottom lip. "You've had to compromise your taste a little, haven't you? No watermelon available, so I guess some nice, young white ass would have to do."

Yokes' fists became rock hard as he clenched them, and some of his sweat rolled off his face and onto his shirt. His eyes were fixed on Mike, registering his every move, down to the twitch in his left eye. Yokes' expression had become as evil and frightening as Mike's was previously.

"I bet you sweat like that when you're fucking dear old Katya, don't you?" Mike's demon look turned into a large smile that covered his whole face.

Yokes lowered his shoulders and tightened up his biceps. The anger in his face showed that hell was coming for Mike and he was its messenger. With each of Mike's words, Yokes was uttering side sounds and grumbling in a deep, godforsaken, animal-like growl. "I'm going to hurt you, McGuire, really bad, so you better start praying to your Maker cuz you'll be see-in' him real soon." Yokes took a half-step towards him, then stopped.

Mike started laughing, louder and louder, then abruptly went dead silent. "I want you to meet some of my new friends."

Yokes straightened up and turned his head from side to side. The darkness was unexpectedly filled with silhouettes and shadows. They moved to all sides of him, yelling and heckling him, while Mike stood firm in the light. Yokes faced him and he watched Mike as he salivated over the potential massacre. "Seems a little bit funny; you're now friends with these guys, and only a few months ago they were the assholes. I guess there's not much difference between white sheets and hoods and swastikas."

Mike frowned at hearing Yokes' words but then a befuddled look took its place. "I wonder who's going to meet their Maker now." Mike started laughing again. The hangar echoed his terrible delight; over and over again the devil's victory cry bounced off the bulkheads and stabbed at Yokes' ears.

A pipe struck Yokes at the back of his neck and then a whirling chain came around and hit him firmly across his head. Blood was sent to the deck, and Yokes watched it hit as he followed it down. He was on all fours when a blow to his face came from out of nowhere. He could taste the leather from the assailant's shoe as he felt his jaw dislocate. Another blow, and another. He grabbed hold of Mike's leg and tried to force him to the ground but there was so much blood in his eyes he couldn't see. He lay there in the light, half-unconscious, trying to gain any strength to fight back but it was no use. All his blurred vision could see was the smirk on Mike's face as he stood over him.

"He wasn't that tough, just a big buck, nothing else." The gang of men snickered and jeered at him as he lay silent and motionless in his own blood. Yokes' right arm was lying between a wheel choke and a toolbox. Mike lifted his foot and came down on Yokes's forearm, breaking it in several places. The splintered bones protruded through the skin hideously. "One less contestant, I bet." Mike's voice reeked of evil.

Yokes drifted in and out of consciousness for hours. He lay there on the cold steel deck until a security man found him. Yokes endured his pain with the memories of home and family, and the new life he was going to have with Missy and Matt. His wife's voice called to him through the darkness and he heard the laughter of children playing. Flickers of light played tricks with his blood-soaked eyes. Flashes of his dear Georgina stroking and comforting him and telling him it was all right. "I'm sorry, baby."

He came to lying on an operating table in the sickbay, with a doctor and nurses and a goddamn huge blinding light beaming down at him. The doctors and nurses kept asking questions. Can you feel this... can you feel that? A thought suddenly raced through his mind. "Missy... where's Missy?" He tried to get up from the table but the medical staff pushed him back down.

"Strap him down. I can't work with him moving like this." The nurses then strapped him down.

Someone banging on her door awakened Katya. She tried to clear the sleep from her eyes but that constant goddamn banging was infuriating her. The book that was lying on her chest fell to the floor and she noticed Yokes didn't turn off the light she left on for him. "Okay... okay, we're up. Quit that goddamn banging!" She turned her attention to the upper bunk. "Yokes, get your ass up, it's morning." The handle on the door wiggled back and forth. "That's the last time I leave the light on for you. I hope you break your big toe in the dark next time." She looked at the handle again and then like a bomb going off, pieces of wood were being flung at her as the door broke open. "Yokes!" she screamed.

Matt came through the door like a madman. He scared her half to death and she was confused. "What?"

"They got Yokes. The bastards beat the hell out of him."

"What bastards?"

"I don't know what bastards, just some bastards." His face was already reddened with the glow of his fury.

"Where is he?"

"He's in sickbay." He frowned at her and asked, "Why did you lock your door if Yokes wasn't here yet?"

"I didn't lock the door. I've never locked it."

Matt was lost in deep thought. "Yokes's beating was planned, then. They figured to keep you out of the way by locking you up here."

"Screw plans. Take me to Yokes."

He took her by the hand and off they went to the sickbay.

"Is he going to die? How bad is he?" Her words were coming too fast. With the pace they were moving through the passageway, she had trouble talking and breathing at the same time.

"I don't know, Kat, I just got a glimpse of him as they took him into surgery. He didn't look good though."

"Surgery? He's going under the knife? What did they do, try to kill him?"

They ran into a crowd as they got close to sickbay. They fought their way through to the hatchway that led into sickbay. A security man was on duty at the entrance and he stopped them. "We need to talk to a doctor about Yokes," Katya said, trying to catch her breath at the same time.

"Sorry, the doctor said no one but medical personnel."

Katya thought quickly on her feet. "I'm a specialist... I treat Mississippians, you know... black people. Now let me through or I'll have your Australian ass for breakfast."

Since she was dressed only in the tops of her pajamas and not in the uniform of the other people, he figured she was telling the truth and he let her in. After she passed him, he watched her fine-looking legs enter the sickbay. He looked at Matt and said, "Strange but good-looking doctors we have around here, don't we?"

Matt just shook his head and smiled.

Kat softly and quietly moved towards the table that held Yokes. She saw Evelyn lying on a bed in another part of the sickbay and smiled at her. Evelyn returned the smile. From across the room, she could hear metal instruments and glass containers being used. The doctor was bent over Yokes ordering calm but stern instructions. His voice sounded deep at times and frustrated as he worked as fast as he could. She remembered the hundreds of times she was in the field hospitals during the war and could tell by the way the medical team moved around the surgical theater as to their competence. She felt good about this close-knit crew.

As she moved closer, she could see the bloody gauze and surgical compresses that were being thrown on the deck after their use. She watched one after another being discarded and her mind wandered to the worst. She was feeling queasy as her nose picked up the smells of damaged flesh, blood, and alcohol. The light from above seemed abnormally harsh, and she could tell that it bothered Yokes' eyes. He was constantly trying to shade them with his hand, which irritated both the doctor and the nurses trying to do their jobs. He was stripped naked and had a tube coming from his nose and one going into his arm. He was moaning something, and one of the nurses was trying to figure out his words. The other nurse was cleaning him up with alcohol.

"He's asking for me," Kat whispered to the nurse. "I'm Missy." She moved to his side and he looked up at her with his one good eye. She held his hand and he relaxed at her touch.

The doctor saw Yokes' reaction to Kat. "Will you stay?" he asked.

Kat nodded. She stroked his hair with her hand. His face was beaten badly. The different shades of purple and blues mixed grisly with the black of his complexion and the dried blood from his open wounds. His right eye was completely closed and bruised. Scratches and cuts were everywhere; her fingers glided past the place on his head that was already stitched. "How you feeling, Big Guy?" There was healing in her voice.

The doctor turned to her. "He doesn't feel a thing, but I don't think he can understand you with the drugs I've given him. I have to get this arm prepped for surgery. It's the worst break I've ever seen."

Kat looked down to the arm and the sight of it almost made her vomit. She tried with all her power not to cry, and only a single tear escaped. She thought, *No-good sons a bitches! They'll pay; I'll make sure they pay, Big Guy.* She looked back to his eyes and was happy that he was completely unconscious now. She softly touched his shoulder. "Sleep, friend. Sleep long and hard." She walked to the foot of the bed and motioned one of the nurses to her. Viktor's girlfriend approached her. "Anything, anything at all that he needs, you make sure he gets, okay?"

She smiled and nodded, then returned to her duties.

Kat headed for the doorway out and saw Matt. As she reached him, she noticed Number One was standing beside him. Kat walked straight up to him, "You planned this. I don't know why or how but this is your game we're playing, isn't it?" A look of pure disgust came over her face. In a flash, she realized what was happening and her thoughts almost took her breath away. "You didn't pick us for our flying abilities or our accomplishments, did you… that's what you said." The two of them stood firmly face-to-face. "You hand-picked us for one reason only. We couldn't say no, none of us could afford to say no. Either law or governments were after us, or maybe to get our wives out of occupied nations and to freedom, like Stanis? How about helping to inject a little revenge? That's not beyond your scope. And let's not forget the money. We all need money, don't we, Number One? But the best, the very best one of all is our futures. We couldn't turn down new futures, could we?"

She turned towards Matt, "The simple promise of eating every day, maybe even more than once, like they do in America. Working and developing our skills to create a new life for us. You promised us dreams… and nobody could turn down dreams, could they, Number One?" She glared at him, but he returned nothing but emptiness.

His face was void of all expression; there was no anger or confusion, just a blank, lifeless look. He did not speak to her, just stood erect and tall. The group that surrounded them grew weary waiting for his answer to her accusations. They finally dispersed to their quarters, leaving Matt and Katya staring down the admiral. The sound of the white curtain being drawn around Yokes so the doctor could start work on him broke the tension. The three looked back at each other. "I'm telling you this; if I find out you did this to him just for your amusement…" No more words would come from her. Threats were useless on this man, and she knew it.

"I need a new roommate and I chose him, and I don't give a rat's ass if you like it or not. He's the only one I can trust around here, next to that man on the table in there." Katya's tone was definite, and as Matt took hold of her arm, Number One finally spoke.

"You forgot something, didn't you? Love and tenderness. I knew what you were looking for, didn't I? It wasn't a future or a past, just a touch of understanding and kindness." He tilted his head in Matt's direction. "You too, Matthew… flying and romance. Or was I wrong in thinking this is what you wanted to acquire?" Finally, a grin worked its way to his mouth. "You're right, Katya. I am a black-hearted bastard, but even the worst bloodthirsty pirate has his day." He turned and left the opposite way of the couple. He did not turn around, but Katya and Matt heard his words echoing off the bulkheads. "Even the best of plans sometimes goes astray."

CHAPTER NINE

THE MORNING SUN BROKE THROUGH the clouds with its normal punctuality, but this morning was more humid and warmer than the others had been. Maybe it was not just the weather that made the ship sticky and uncomfortable. There would be no flights today, and below deck, more than tension and heat was in the air. The Aussie and the American crewmen alike were not accustomed to killings, rapes, and beatings like those that had been taking place the last few days. Number One had to speak to the Aussie captain to ease his mind about going on with the competitions. In the captain's mind, this was becoming a war, not a race.

The wardroom pantry was empty. It was breakfast time, and the food was laid out as ordered but the pilots were nowhere to be seen. A few were wandering the passageways, sticking their heads in and out of cabins, and some were walking the flight deck, taking in what little breeze there was. The pilots in the hangar mingled with the idle flight crews and talked about what had taken place there the night before.

The young Aussies especially were a little worried about what was going on. Most of them were not in the war, and this voyage was their first sea duty. The ones that had seen some limited action had picked it up on the tail end of the fighting. Though they told lies about their bravery during the war, they too were a little leery. The pilots tried to calm them down, telling them that in two more days, they'd be rid of most of them.

"I'm going to kill the bastards that did that to Yokes." Matt and Kat walked the flight deck as they talked. Kat was trying to settle him down but it hadn't worked all night, no matter how she tried.

"What good will it do? You know it's the Germans and probably that bastard Mike. So, you run the risk of getting your ass thrown out of the race or ending up like the big guy, for what… to kick their asses? You know they intertwine like snakes in a hole. You can't beat them all at one time. That's what makes them so arrogant and cocky; they never leave the hole alone. They know no one onboard is going to stop them. It's like someone wants all this turmoil and friction. I feel the same way you do, but use your good sense. The only way to beat these pieces of shit is to take away their futures, their plans. Make our plans succeed and win all the goddamn money!" She stopped and turned him to her, then narrowed her eyebrows. "Leave them standing there at the end of the race with their fingers stuck up their asses."

"Okay, it's a deal. No rough stuff till the race is over. Then I'm going to kill them." He laughed, then picked her up and kissed her.

Evelyn noticed he was moving in his bed. "How are you feeling, Yokes?"

It was hard for him to speak with the pain in his jaw but he managed. "Not too bad, considering I'm supposed to be half-dead." He tried to smile but couldn't accomplish it. "How are you doing? I'm sorry about what happened to you. No woman should have to go through that."

"Thanks. Most men don't understand. At least I don't think they do." She smiled smoothly, betraying nothing of her torment.

"Nonsense… real men understand. They understand too well. To a married man, it's his greatest fear." He was getting angry at the topic and started thrashing around and trying to lift his arm. The pain forced him to relax to his normal demeanor. "Damn… those assholes sure did a really good job on my arm and it was my good one, too."

"If you don't calm down and quit trying to move that arm, I'm going to put you back to sleep." Nurse Rose stood at the end of his bed with her hands on her hips and a scowl on her face.

"Okay, okay. Not another shot, I'll be good and just lay here."

Nurse Rose smiled at him, then at Evelyn. "Are you okay today?" she asked as she walked to the side of Evelyn's bed.

"Fine. I think I should go back to my quarters now."

"Aren't you a little afraid?"

"No. The rest of these men are good guys. They wouldn't hurt me; just like they're not going to hurt you." She tried to show her confidence with a smile.

"I guess you could ask Number One if it's okay."

Matt and Kat walked into the room. "How's it going, Big Guy?" Kat asked.

"I'd like to say you're looking good… but…" Matt smiled at Yokes and took his hand.

"You're just jealous of my gorgeous features. But do me a favor and keep the mirrors far away." Yokes was kidding, but serious at the same time.

Yokes glanced over to Nurse Rose. "I'll be good, I won't move a thing. Okay?"

Nurse Rose smiled at him, then at Kat and Matt, then left.

"We talked to the doctor and he said everything but that arm should be all right soon, maybe in a week or so."

"That sounds good; but it's going to take me out of the race, isn't it." He looked downhearted and apologetic. "What about our partnership? I'm not going to be able to contribute, and that's not fair to you two." He looked back up at them with a frown and a tear clustering in his eye. "You guys go on and do your thing without me, it is okay." He turned his head slightly, trying to hide some of his emotions. "Back home this kind of thing happens all the time to us Negroes. We're kind of used to it."

Matt pretended to be angry. "Shut up. I don't want to hear that kind of crap again. The deal was and still is: no matter who gets the chance to win, we all are partners. It's even steven across the board. Even if none of us make a dime here, we're still partners. You got that?"

Kat rubbed Matt's back. "That's the way I feel, too." Her expression softened quickly. "There's one piece of good news. With you out of my way, it looks like I'm in the tenth spot, with ninth just around the corner."

"Look, guys, I've been laying here thinking how lucky I am, two good friends, and both of you whiter than Sunday sheets blow-in' in the wind." He looked at Kat. "Matt here can tell you that's a pure miracle where we come from. Negroes befriending whites and vice-versa. It's truly God's will. I'll make it up to you when I get on my feet, I swear. Thanks, guys."

Evelyn, overhearing the conversation, thought even back home, friendships like that would be rare. She leaned over her bed and smiled at the group. "You guys are very fortunate to have each other. Go show them how it's done."

"Thanks, Evelyn," said Kat.

Matt looked at his watch. "We've got to get moving. We don't want any points taken off for being late."

Kat bent over and kissed Yokes on the cheek. "We'll see you later, Big Guy."

Yokes looked over Kat's head. "Watch your back, Matt, and Missy's too. If they can do this to me, they can do it to you if you're not careful."

Matt nodded his head and winked back at him. "Right."

"All pilots to the wardroom… repeat… all pilots to the wardroom." The announcement rang throughout the ship and reverberated out to sea. The crewmen watched as the pilots took their sweet time in obeying the orders. This was something else they were not accustomed to.

The wardroom filled slowly and the look on Number One's

face showed contempt with every minute that went by. The room finally filled and quieted down. One looked at his watch, then up at the aviators. "I've noticed a lack of intensity lately." His voice was adamant and determined. "I hope some of you brought passage to wherever you plan on going to after your little trial here is over." His face grew dark red, almost purple, and his eyes and nostrils twitched from some kind of nervous problem. He suddenly threw the papers he had in his hands at the assembly sitting in front of him. "You fucking assholes! I didn't pay good money for a bunch of quitters. I went through a lot of trouble getting your sorry asses out of the shit you people were in. This is my payoff! I didn't bring you here to win a race… I brought you here to compete and compete you will, to the last minute, or it's a long walk home. You fucks forget I have your papers, and I'm just about ready to have one hell of a bonfire!" He stood like a marble statue, his eyes fixed on the men in their seats. A brazen look emerged from his being and no one was moving a muscle. "Am I understood?" He relaxed a bit and moved to one side. "As a reward for your understanding and cooperation in this matter, the bar and curfew restrictions will be lifted. Also, for those of you not picked for the race, there are accommodations awaiting you in Honolulu while you wait for the transportation to your final destinations. So, there are really no losers, are there?" He walked back to the center of the room. "By the way, my records show only six of you are completely out of the running and there will be no more postings. That seems to have been a mistake. You all know who the ones on the fence are. Anyway, who knows, there might be some kind of act of God that would overtake some of the leaders; who can tell?"

From his expression, it was obvious that Two was tired with Number One's speech and interrupted, "May I proceed, One?"

"Yes."

Two looked to the papers in his hands. "Rescue drills are the day's agenda. Everyone will participate, no exceptions. And you will be graded on today's exercises." He pointed at the guys. "Nolder, Encionin, and Budanova, you will be our first victims. You three get your bathing suits on and report to the flight deck. The crews on the helicopters are waiting for you."

Encionin stood and asked, "What the hell are we going to be doing?"

"Drowning," replied Number Two.

The three men got up and went to get their suits on. The rest of the group sat and snickered at them. Matt and Kat looked at each other, then whispered simultaneously, "Think that act of God might happen sooner rather than later?"

"Chu, you will be the first rescued by the Kingfisher. Go and get your suit on and report to the hangar deck. You're going by boat first. The rest of you are going to observe the procedures either by boat or helicopter. At the end of the day, there will be a test. So, no fucking around when you're supposed to be observing."

He looked back to his paperwork. "Eleven through Twenty-three are to go to the flight deck. Twenty-four and beyond are to go to the hangar deck. Instructors will be there to direct you to the exercises. Class dismissed."

Matt turned to Kat. "Watch out for yourself. You know what happens when they split us up."

"I'll be careful, but its daylight. Those serpents only come out in the shadows of darkness. I should be all right." She moved his chin with her hand. "Don't you get goaded into anything, you hear?"

"Yeah, yeah." Matt spotted Mel leaving the room.

"Be careful, love." He kissed Kat, then hurriedly pursued Mel. "Mel… Mel, old buddy." The Australian stopped when he heard his name. "Do me a favor and watch out for Katya for me, will-ya? I can't be in two places at the same time."

Mel smiled at him. "She's as safe as a babe in arms… no problem, Matt." He put his arm around Matt's neck and said, "I'm sorry about Yokes. Those fucking cowards. How they didn't get killed in the war is some kind of miracle."

"You got that." Matt headed up the ladder that led to the flight deck. "Thanks, buddy, I'll see you when we switch, okay?"

Mel looked for Katya and found her gabbing with Geno about

some cinema star she liked. "Looks like I'm your babysitter, for at least today."

"Matt's idea?" She was actually happy to have someone watching her back.

From the hangar deck, Chu was lowered to a boat where he was dressed out in a life jacket, given an orange canister of dye, and a red flare. The ship came to an easy halt and became dead in the water. The pilots that were to observe the rescue were lined up at the fantail. They could see the small boat with Chu and the crew standing off the starboard side, just to the rear. They could hear the Kingfisher circling above.

The instructor told them that once they were in the water to inflate their vest and release the dye into the water. They were to only pull their flares if it was at night, foggy, and/or overcast. They saw Chu in the water and the boat left him. It only took a few minutes for the dye to make a five-foot circle around him.

Next, the Kingfisher made a pass over him and tilted its wings at him. This was to show the rescued flyer that he was spotted by the plane, the instructor announced. The Kingfisher came in low and hovered over the water. It took him about three hundred feet to come to a stop. The pilot planned it just right and was only about fifty feet away from Chu. He swam quickly to the plane, where he used the foot holes to climb up into the rear slot. The plane then throttled up and in about six hundred feet escaped the waves' grip and took to the air. The instructor turned to the pilots. "That's a perfect rescue."

He gathered the pilots close in. "You guys are lucky the water will be warm, so there's no chance of hypothermia. There is one problem… a Kingfisher can only rescue one pilot at a time, so keep your planes in the air till you at least get close." He looked to his notes. "Okay, who's next?"

When both the Sikorskies were operational, the noise was

deafening. The instructors waited for the helicopters to be loaded and took off before they gave their little lecture. The port side was lined with the rest of the pilots. The instructor informed the pilots that the same procedure was carried out in both rescue schemes, using the dye in daylight and flares when the sighting might be obscured by overcast fog or lack of sunlight. The helicopters hovered about ten feet from the top of the highest wave. They saw one of the pilots jump into the water, then another and another. They saw them release the dye as the helicopters flew back to the flight deck. The group seemed a little puzzled as the machines settled down on the deck.

One pilot asked, "Why didn't they just pick them back up?"

The instructor smiled, then said, "Number One thought these guys needed a little soaking and some exercise treading water. Maybe it'll get some of the crap out of them and make all our lives a little easier." He signaled for the helicopter to go get them. The group watched as the helicopters hovered once more over the three. They watched as lifelines were lowered to them one at a time and they were lifted up to safety. "Remember… the Sikorskies can only operate in a hundred-mile radius." Each one of the pilots were tested in the water, with mixed results.

Dinner couldn't have come at a better time. Being wet and pulled upward by your own body weight most of the day brought one thought to mind. Everyone was starving, and couldn't wait to get at the food. The morning meal they'd all missed was what their evening meal was. The Europeans and the Orientals didn't seem to mind eggs and shit on a shingle for dinner. Some others did complain, but to deaf ears. Since there were no more postings of scores, the atmosphere was more pleasant and almost cheerful, especially when the bar opened. There appeared to be no early-to-bed and study people tonight. Instead, they were thinking about sore muscles and water-logged brains.

The German group and their friends appeared overly confident this evening, to what purpose, no one knew. But as their strength returned to them, so did their bad natures. The liquor flowed freely most of the night, and so did the laughter and gaiety, which was rare in this group. They sang songs of the Fatherland and of course, beautiful women. Sometimes two or three songs were being sung at the same time, each from different tongues. The rest of the room was at ease since most of the tensions on ship came from these men, and since they were happy, everyone else could relax and be happy too.

Kat even got Matt on the dance floor; of course it was a slow one from Peggy Lee, which she'd picked out herself, hoping Matt would get the message. The song was "I'm Glad I Waited for You" and was a big hit with both the guys and gals onboard. Kat was pleasantly surprised when Amy walked into the room and took a seat with Evelyn and Mel. She never left her room after meals until late in the evening, then she wandered the decks in and out of unoccupied quarters and the shadows. Some say they heard her laughing and talking to the darkness, but she didn't look happy now. She looked more inquisitive, like she was looking for something or someone. Kat noticed Diego watching her. He moved to a far corner of the room and sat alone. "Ouch... damn." A pain shot up from her foot.

"I'm sorry, Kat, I get all tied up in the words of that song and forget to watch where I'm stepping."

Her heart swelled and the pain in her foot vanished with his words. "It's all right, *boobblia*."

He liked the sound of the word. She made it sound sexy. "What does that mean?"

She smiled a girlish grin, also very sexy. "It's like honeybun, or stud muffin, something like that."

"Good. Just don't tell anyone else." He bent down and kissed her and then walked her over to the table.

"Looks like Matt there is going to take up dancing when he gets back home." Rudy started to laugh.

"Looks like Rudy's trying to become a comedian." Matt turned his thumb downward as he passed him.

Kat saw Amy and straight behind her, she also saw Diego, still eyeing her. An uneasy feeling overcame her, and she wondered if she should say something to Matt or Amy.

A fast song was playing from the jukebox and two of the Germans got up to swing dance. They were so drunk they could barely stand. They eventually fell to the floor and in a heap of laughter tried to get back up, but to no avail. Some buddies came to their rescue and picked them up. Werner waved for them to be taken to their quarters. A parade of drunken pilots jammed the passageway as they left. Werner said goodnight to Dumitrn, who decided to stay for one more drink. The rest of the pilots took their cue from the Germans and started to leave also. Diego was one of the last ones to leave, which left Dumitrn and Amy and a few crewmen that were cleaning up.

"I want to see Yokes before I turn in, okay?" Kat picked up Matt's hand and they took off for sickbay. They found him in good spirits; Evelyn had just gotten there and was joking with him; they both were laughing.

"Hey, guys, I've got good news. The doctor said that maybe tomorrow I could get a cast put on this arm so I can get up and walk around a little… good news, ha?"

"You're not going to walk down these dark passageways at night, are you? You'll scare everyone right off the ship looking the way you do, and especially in the dark. Someone might take you for Frankenstein," Matt joked.

"Shut up, you're so good-looking. I think Yokes looks better than you do. At least he doesn't have all those little brown spots all over his face." She smiled at him, then stroked his face gently with her palm. "You know I didn't mean it?"

He frowned at her, then smiled those teeth at her. He turned to the bed and asked, "Seriously, how you doing?"

"Good, really good. I just look bad. As soon as the swelling goes down, I'll look a whole lot better."

"Is it all right if we don't stay long? I'm tired as hell," Matt said, feigning exhaustion.

"Get the hell out of here. I'm tired myself, and I want to hear the end of Evelyn's joke anyway."

"Good night, Big Guy," said Kat softly.

They turned and started down the hallway. "What's this crap about you're so tired? I know why you want to get me back to the cabin, you're not fooling anyone around here." Her vixen look made its point.

Matt just raised his eyebrows and smiled.

Dumitrn looked over to Amy with glassy eyes. She was staring intensely back at him but in his condition, nothing bothered him. He took his last swallow of Schnapps and tried to get up; he stumbled against the table, but managed to get to his feet. The lights were being turned out throughout the ship. The sounds of life were becoming less and less as the ship's engines overtook them. The rhythmic beating of the huge machines sort of hypnotized one, especially drunkards.

Dumitrn tried to walk and fight off sleep at the same time. He bounced off the bulkheads from side to side as he made his way to his cabin. The lights were sparse, and only lit up the intersections in the passageways. He passed no one as he took a wrong turn and climbed the ladder to the hangar deck instead of down to his quarters. As he followed the sound of the engines, he saw the same light that shone there the night before and fear engulfed him. Looking around for an escape from the darkness but in his stupor not finding one, he floundered towards the light that was gleaming in the middle of the deck. He knew too well there was no safety there, but the darkness was worse than any terror from the light. He started to scream for help, like a woman in panic. The high pitch of his voice slammed against the bulkheads and returned a deafening screech, but no one answered. Tears ran out of his watering eyes and his dulled face had spit flowing from his lips. Flashes from the night before came to his intoxicated mind and he pleaded openly of his innocence. "Werner made me do it!" As the last word spouted from his mouth, he passed out in the middle of the light.

Quietly, like mist coming over a hillside, Amy stood over him. Her motions were silent but her eyes blazed with hatred. In her hand was a black velvet bag, and as she stared down at the passed-out

Romanian, she formed a hideous grin of pure delight, untied the bag, and took something out. They clamored against each other in the bag. She held one of them in her hand and inspected it, and as it hit the light, it shined and glimmered. A long, silver, and well-polished dagger was in her hand. The hilt was carved with the skull and cross bones with a swastika on its face. The blade was a good nine to ten inches long. It was one of the Gestapo knives, one of their favorite devices for use when they tortured innocent people for the fun of it.

She knelt and laid the bag on the deck as she turned him over so he was facing her. It pained her to smile but she did so. "It's too bad you're not awake for what's going to happen to you." Her voice was calm and straightforward as she whispered the words, English dryness in every syllable. There was no regret, no shame, no remorse, only hatred and disgust for the Nazi and his kind. Honestly believing he deserved to die, she raised the dagger to strike.

"It won't make you feel better." A voice came out of the darkness and startled her.

She froze for a second, her arm still in the air over him, the dagger still pointing to his chest.

"Killing never helps, I know." The voice was calm and direct, like God on high.

She was trying to fight off the feeling that gripped her. Her hand started to shake and her tears fell onto Dumitrn. "I haven't cried since the day my husband left me." She lowered the dagger to her lap and turned to the blackness. "It's you... isn't it, Diego?"

Diego walked into the light and knelt next to her. His tight expression relaxed into a smile.

"I laid in that hospital for six weeks before my husband got the nerve to see me." Her voice quivered as the tears fell on the blade. "I heard him talking to the doctors. What kind of life would he have with a monster like me? When I opened my eyes, all I saw at the end of the bed was pity in his eyes. I died right there in that hospital and my life ended. So why should he live? My torment couldn't be my husband's fault, so it had to be theirs."

Diego put his arm around her and spoke in an undertone. "I'm a paid killer, a born taker of life. I've been made a hero for doing it well, and I know it won't soften your pain." He reached for her chin and raised it to face him. "Come walk with me and we'll talk." He took the dagger and the black bag from her. They stood and both looked down at the drunken piece of shit that lay before them. "I wonder if he knows how lucky he really is." Diego's own disgust for him showed through in his words.

They climbed to the flight deck, where they found the moon was as large as a giant balloon searching for a rider to sail the skies. The warm breeze settled on Amy's hair and she tried to hold it down.

"Let your hair fly with the moon. I'm the only one here, so free yourself this one time and dance with the wind." Diego's words were like a song to her.

She raised her arms like a child that was pretending to fly as she ran against the zephyr and let its power overtake her. The simple childhood pleasure of her clothes rustling against her skin and the mist splattering on her open face renewed her newfound happiness. Her mind began to fly with the stars. Her breath came hard and fast and she felt lightheaded as tears of joy ran across her cheeks. Her giggling had embraced the sounds of the splashing of the waves and became music to her ears. She had reached the far end of the deck when she stopped and looked around. The figure of the old man stood like a beacon in the wilderness, a steeple of faith and the strength she had forgotten from long ago. With every step she took back to him she wondered how she could make this moment last. There was always someone for everyone; could he be her savior?

"Feel better now?" His smile showed even in the darkness of the night. "Let the hate go. Let it return to the darkness where it came from and set yourself free of it." His voice was velvet-edged and strong.

The wind still blowing from behind her grew calm and a hush overtook the ship. The mystery in his eyes beckoned to her irresistibly. "Are you a wizard or magician, or were you just sent from heaven?"

The fire that was once in her eyes had vanished and he was pleased. "No, neither… I just know pain when I see it. It's an old friend of mine." He took her hands and started to remove her gloves. She resisted a little, then complied.

She felt her heart bound as his touch seemed mystical. "Do your magic again." She watched him throw the gloves into the sea, then he took her hands and gently kissed each finger, like a father making a wound all better for his child.

He lifted his head from her hands and the moon shone in his eyes. "I have a story to tell you. Will you listen?"

Tears of joy ran down her marred face and she nodded her head.

He looked to the helicopters and motioned her to one of them. Once there, he helped her to the doorway of the machine and they sat in the back of it. The wind had picked back up and started to mingle once more with her hair. The moon's light appeared even brighter and bluer. Little sparkles of light danced off her eyes from time to time and her breathing seemed rhythmic, subtle, and in tune with the roll of the ship. She caught her reflection in the window and found her ugliness had vanished. The moon and the wind had set her free, and she recognized that it was the hatred that was so repulsive.

Diego was having trouble getting started. He had never spoken of such things before. He stared out over the water and seemed to travel back in time. "Your scars are deep, and most are on the outside. My wounds are inside, thrashing at my heart and my guts. I gave up everything to be a hero, the greatest flyer in Spain's history." He turned to her. "The greatest killer, I mean." His face took on the likeness of a skeleton. All life seemed to have drained from him in the seconds it took to speak his words. Grief and self-loathing replaced his manly features. All forms of pretense willowed away to sorrow and repentance. He reached into his pocket and pulled out some photos, then gave one to Amy. "She's beautiful, isn't she?"

"Yes, very." The moon's light showed a young woman and a man playing with children.

He looked down at the next photo. "This is the one I look at every day." He handed it to her.

She gazed at it in disbelief. The picture showed the same woman with a scar running down the entire left side of her face. Amy snapped her head back to Diego's sorrowful gaze. "Did you do this?" Amy's face showed horror at the thought.

"In a way… yes." He hung his head. "I was part of it; part of the whole Franco fiasco." The photos started to tremble. "Of course, I didn't have to see it up close." He turned to her once more, hoping for understanding. "I was the number one ace in Spain. They put medals on my chest and wrote of me in the newspapers, the foremost soldier of the war. My self-pride overcame everything, even my family. My father saw what Franco was… a pure dictator, and savage. He and my family arranged to leave Spain for Mexico, but I wouldn't listen. I was a hero, an important man in Franco's eyes. In reprisal, they did that to my sister-in law." He took back the photo. "I loved the flying, but did I see the senseless killings? No… I was too much of a national hero to care about some child's mother being tortured by Franco's soldiers, even if it was my own blood."

His lips trembled and his eyes grew dull. "Then the Germans came with their superior killing machines and made it even easier to mow down the bodies. The war broke out, and again I wallowed in the stench. The Russians, this time; made it a little bit harder to slaughter. They fought back. But again, I reveled in my talent for killing. Once again the newspapers proclaimed me a hero." The telling of his story was getting to him. He almost choked on every word. The pain shone through and his eyes welled up but it seemed he had no more tears to shed. "Franco was a coward. When the war looked like the Allies were going to win, he brokered a deal with the Americans to save his ass. That's when I knew it was all for nothing."

"What happened to the woman?" Surprisingly, Amy's voice didn't hold any animosity towards Diego.

He became hopeful from her tone. "She went to Mexico; my whole family escaped there." He held out another picture. "Acapulco… my father brought them there and started a new life. The hotel has a little café and bar. My two brothers run the business now that my father has passed away. We write often now that the war is over." New life came to his face when he spoke of Acapulco and his brothers.

"It looks beautiful! The cliffs look high and steep… and what

161

is that place at the top?" Diego's brutal story fled from her reason; there was no more room for hatred or judgment, only her sanity.

Her words were calm and gentle, he thought. Should he dare ask? "It's your and my future."

His words stunned her. "What?"

He could not look at her and he stumbled with the words. "I'm not good at this kind of thing. Please don't interrupt till I'm through or I won't be able to get it out." He took a deep breath and then sighed. "I want you to come with me, to Acapulco, I mean, to live. But not to start over; to finish your life with someone as scarred as you." Only the rush of the wind broke the silence. "I don't promise to love you. I don't think I can love… my heart is too black and decayed. I do promise to be your companion and hopefully, you mine. I will ask nothing of you and I will take care of you, protect you and respect you, no matter what happens."

He looked to find a reaction from her but found only astonishment. "My brothers are holding my share of the business, and that house at the top of the cliffs." He thought he hadn't handled it right and his blundering saddened him. "I knew you didn't come on this voyage to race, but revenge is not the way. There's no future in it. I, too, didn't come to race. I am fleeing my own name; the sound of it sickens me. That's why I use Diego instead of Angel, and that's why Mexico is my morality; not that brutality I left in Spain. No one but my loved ones know me there and I can live like a decent man."

It took a while for his words to sink in. She stretched her mind for a reason to say no, but then she grinned and kissed his hand. "Yes, magician, I'll go with you, and I'll try to be a good companion to you. But no promises on either side. One day at a time and for us, that's a lifetime." His grateful expression matched hers and they huddled together watching the moon's flight across the sky. Neither had any fears about the other. Warm contentment was creeping into their hearts as their pasts faded away.

CHAPTER TEN

THE FINAL DAY HAD ARRIVED, and again the morning meal went uneaten. The pilots were all over the ship waiting anxiously for the last day's instructions. There had been no postings for the last two days, so all were confident of success. There was no more time for conniving or maneuverings, so the atmosphere was like that of the first day, fairly loose. The soakings of the previous day left most of the tensions out with the bounding waves.

Yokes was sitting on the side of his bed talking to Evelyn when Matt and Kat walked in. "Hey… come and sign my cast, the doctor just put it on." It was still painful to smile but he managed a grin.

Kat looked worried as she approached him. "What the hell are you doing up?"

Yokes looked for help from Kat's scolding manner. "The doctor told me to move around. It helps the muscles get back in shape quicker." He boyishly pointed to the next bed. "Ask Evelyn, she'll tell you."

"Looking like you do, I hope 'in shape' comes soon." The ladies in the room stared sternly at Matt. They did not appreciate his idea of funny, but Yokes didn't mind.

Kat didn't like the way Yokes' eye looked. She touched around it with gentle fingers, trying to gauge its swollen hardness. "That doesn't look good, Big Guy. I wonder what your wife's going to say when she sees that shiner."

"Probably to keep his hands off the women's skirts, I bet," Matt said, still hoping for a laugh.

"You're still not funny there, freckle face." The derisive look Matt was getting from him shut him up fast.

"How'd you guys do yesterday?" asked Evelyn.

"I felt like I was bait at the end of a fishing line," replied Matt, a little miffed.

Kat pointed a finger at him and said, "Now that's funny, *boobblia*!"

"*Boobblia*… what the hell is a *boobblia*?" asked Yokes curiously.

Matt's annoyance was evident. "It's a goddamn pet name she gave me. You know, all women have to give their men pet names," Matt said, faking disgust.

Kat purposely kept her attention directed on Yokes by examining his cast. "*Their* men… that's the first I've heard that you're my man." She sent a small grin in Yokes' direction. "I've been looking around, and Rudy's looking really good these days." She turned and smiled a smarmy smile at him.

"A lovers' quarrel already?" Evelyn grinned at Kat and Matt.

"Sign this thing and get the hell out of here. You don't want to be late the last day, do you?"

"See you later, buddy." After Matt signed the cast he hurried to the wardroom, with Kat bringing up the rear.

Most of the flyers had been on the flight deck inspecting the aircraft. They overly stressed with the Airedales that perfection was needed today, no fuck-ups. The air was filled with the scent of land and they knew they were close to Hawaii and for some, the end of an adventure they would never forget. The others would have their dreams fulfilled and their futures set. But everyone would have new beginnings or endings. Either one would bring happiness to most of them.

"All pilots to the wardroom… repeat… all pilots to the wardroom." The sound of the bellowing intercom sent quivers down a lot of the men's backs. The wardroom already seemed full when the announcement came.

Number One stood at the front of the room. He looked fairly

pleased but still stern. "I'm here to tell you nothing." A couple of puzzled looks were seen in the group. "You already know what's expected of you. Believe me when I tell you that most of you are still in the running, so do your best. I will release the winners tonight. That's all."

"Pilots to the flight deck," said Two.

As the room emptied out, Two asked One, "Will you be in the Pri-Fly?"

"No… I have some business to do, I'll see you later." He was wearing an old flight jacket from the *Lexington*.

"Can I go back to my quarter's tonight, Doctor? I'm feeling really good and I'm no longer afraid," asked Evelyn.

"I think it will be all right, as long as you're not still afraid of sharing quarters with a man."

"Mel." She laughed. "He's my knight in shining armor. I trust him more than my own father."

"Okay then." The doctor turned to leave but found Number One standing in the hatchway listening to them. "Sir."

"It's okay; I want to talk to these two."

The doctor left down the passageway. One walked over and sat on the foot of Evelyn's bed. "Good morning… it pleases me to hear you're doing fine, and you too, Yokes." In his arms he had two documents and a book. He pulled out the top paper and laid it on her bed.

"Thank you for your concern, Number One. I want you to know I don't hold you responsible for what happened to me. It could have happened in my own shower, back home."

"Nonsense, but thank you anyway." He stared into her eyes for the longest time trying to find something there, a strength maybe. "Your home back in California is as safe as a baby in its crib. The people there are moral and God-fearing men and women. Take your husband. He just doesn't understand the new ways of things… most men don't."

"Sir?" She looked confused.

"They don't understand that a woman can be independent and self-fulfilling and at the same time a loving and caring wife and mother. It's the times, and believe it or not, the times are a-changing." His words started to flow like a river, smooth and forceful, and he saw that she was starting to understand his meaning. "Women in the future will stand next to men, not behind or in front, but side by side in every way." He looked like he was remembering someone or something. "During this war, women have proved their salt and they have announced their ambitions and they won't be set back. Women have more power than they could ever imagine; they just have to learn how to use it. Go back home and gather all like you and teach your husband and all of them your worth."

Her heart was so full and pleased that someone finally understood her feelings that a tear fell from her cheek. "How do you know all this about me?"

"I know all about you. I know all about everyone onboard this ship and the reasons they're here. It's why I picked you, so you could learn and then go back and teach. Over the years you've made only one mistake. Don't show men, teach them." He moved the paper so she could read it.

"You're kidding?" Her mouth was agape and tears fell freely.

"You'll be stationed out of Hamilton Air Base in California with the rank of captain. Your duties will be a flight school instructor."

"It's signed by the Secretary of Defense!" She wiped away the tears so she could read the rest.

"You'll be the first woman in the Air National Guard. So, sign and get the hell out of here, Captain Sharp, I've got other things to do." His rough voice was just a pretense and she knew it.

Her hand could barely hold the pen it shook so badly. "Thank you, sir."

"Go up to the radio shack. I've arranged for you to talk to your husband over ship to shore."

She kissed him and then crumpled the document to her chest. "God bless you, Number One."

"I hope he will," he said in a hush. Smiling he watched her, still in her pajamas, leap for the hatchway and to the radio shack. His smile faded as he turned to Yokes.

"That was a nice thing to do, sir," said Yokes.

His expression became sad as he looked at Yokes. His eyes were dim and almost lifeless. He tried to speak several times but his words stuck in his throat. "Do you know why they did this to you?" he said softly.

The sadness of the admiral's face reflected his own. "I'm a no-account nigger." He lowered his eyes from the admiral's.

"You couldn't be more wrong." The voice that was soft before now became haughty and loud. His face was full of life and a fire rose in his eyes. "Don't ever use that word again… ever." His words echoed off the bulkheads like sirens pleading for attention.

Yokes raised his eyes to see a determined and fearless gaze on the admiral's face. He, on the other hand, seemed flustered; a white man telling him not to use derogatory words about coloreds anymore?

"They took you out because you're the best." His temper rose with each word. "They could see from your flying they couldn't compete with you… so you had to go." Several moments passed with the two men gazing at each other. One's face gradually cooled and became paternal. He stood and looked down on Yokes. "Did you hear what I said to Sharp? It goes the same for you. I picked you for your strength, both in body and in your compassion. When you go back home, teach them with deeds, and not with anger or self-righteousness. Teach your own kind to stand straight and on their own two feet. Don't let prejudice and bigotry defeat you in your goals. Humans will get away with whatever they're allowed to get away with and your own kind are no different. Find your leaders, no matter what race they may be, and help them to find the way."

Yokes suddenly felt like he was in church and being preached to by God himself. "I don't understand."

The admiral relaxed and put his hand on Yokes' shoulder. "This partnership you have with Drew and Yegorova; that's the way. Show the people back home that your enterprise can work. Colored with white on equal basis, the way it should be, and one day, will be. It all starts with people like you, and it will grow and grow till the word *nigger* is wiped off the tongues of even the most hardened bigots. The spokesmen of such words will have to hide in shame from the rest of us. Do you understand now?"

167

Yokes' good eye started to water. "I think so, sir." He had never heard these kinds of words spoken before, not even from his own kind. He thought, *God does move in mysterious ways.*

"You've made a good start already; got yourself educated and made a fine name for yourself in the military. Your whole group did. Now take what you've learned and teach others." He loosened his grip on the paper in his hand. "Here, take this, sign it, and have your partners witness it." He threw the document on the bed and extended his hand. "Please, let me shake the hand of the best." They exchanged handshakes and looks of appreciation and then One turned for the hatchway out. Once there, he stopped and turned back around. "By the way, stay onboard all the way to Australia and here, you'll probably want to study this. It might help to know how to fly what you're signing for." He threw the manual on the bed and then left laughing.

Yokes was in shock, but picked up the manual and read its cover. *The Complete Operating Manual for the C-47 Transport.* He shook his head in disbelief. "Devil be damned!"

The day's exercises went by in record time, to the relief of everyone onboard. Honolulu was now in sight off the port side about twelve miles. Its scent of flowers enhanced the air, and the crew watched as Diamond Head kissed the billowing clouds that surrounded it. The decks were now clear of all aircraft and the ship's engines moaned softly in a slow tempo. The ship stood nearly still, just enough speed to maneuver. A small pilot boat from Pearl came alongside and a naval officer came onboard with a satchel of documents for Number One.

The announcement came quickly and sharp. "All pilots to the wardroom. Repeat…" There was no need to repeat the order, all the pilots were already there or lingering nearby.

When Numbers One and Two walked in, the pilots were all seated and very attentive. "Okay, before we get started, has everyone turned in their travel request?" He looked around the room for a response. A hand came up in the rear and then Viktor spoke.

"What if Australia is where we wish to go?"

"If Australia or anywhere in the South Pacific is your destination, stay onboard, but there will be no flying." He looked once again to the group. "Anything else?" The room became quiet as a church during Mass. "After I read the list, do yourself a favor and stay near the wardroom. The top nine will be taken to Number Three Ready Room and the official rules will be given to them. There might be a chance that some of the pilots will not fly under those rules and will want to back out of the race. In that case, the next in line will be picked... understood?" The room started to erupt with whispers and suppositions. "Okay... okay, let's get on with it. As your number is called, please go to Ready Room Three."

He took a deep breath, then spoke. "Eleven, Twenty, Thirty-nine..."

Please pick me.

I got to be in the race.

My whole future depends on it.

I've got it in the bag. No problem.

One hundred fifty thousand American dollars.

The room was filled with expressions of hope. Some seemed smug and sure while others were sweating from the tension.

"Number Eighteen, Thirty-seven, Twenty-eight, Twenty-two, Thirty-one, and finally, Twenty-one. The rest of you, please stand by."

Katya's heart froze as she saw Matt's smile. Thoughts raced in her head; with her not being picked, it meant they would be separated by thousands of miles. And what of their future? Was it also thousands of miles away? *He made no promises to you; one day at a time. Those were your own words. So be happy for him.* She grinned nervously.

He glanced over to her as the guys were congratulating him. It was then that he realized she didn't make it and he could see the doubt in her eyes. He slowly walked towards her, a large smile on his face, kind of cocky.

"I knew you'd get picked, you're such a flying fool." She strained to hold back her disappointment as he went to hold her. She said, "I'm sorry, I've failed you."

He laughed loudly, almost a belly laugh.

She pushed him away in anger. "You cold-hearted bastard!" she screamed.

"That's my Kat… feisty as ever." He looked down at her, still smiling, and for a moment, he studied her intently. "Will you marry me?" His face became reconciled and hopeful.

She went limp in his arms but her eyes regained their twinkle and her lips their smile. "*Boobblia*. Oh yes. Yes."

"Number Eighteen, let's go, the race is waiting." Number Two smiled as he watched the two kiss and then face each other.

"I've already thought of what might happen and I've talked to Yokes. You'll go with him to Tampa and I'll win the money and join you two there, so quit worrying."

"I never worried a second." She lowered her eyes slightly.

"Sure you didn't." He kissed her again, then turned and ran through the passageway.

Amy had been watching the scene between Matt and Kat and her heart grew light as she watched Diego leave for the ready room. The magic man would not desert her, he gave his word. Her thoughts drifted to the night on the deck and the truth that was in his eyes and she smiled. "Looks like you finally hooked him," she said to Katya.

"Damn, there is a God." She was trembling, and her words came fast and furious. Kat started dancing little steps like a child that had to go to the bathroom and was holding it. She went over to Amy and hugged her. "I'm going to be a wife… a goddamn permanent bed-fellow. Love, cherish, and obey… all that crap. Wish me luck, Amy." As she looked into Amy's eyes, she became a little confused at what she saw. She held up her pace, slowed her words and took a deep breath and deliberately let it out. "What's happened?" She noticed that she was looking at Amy's full face. "The smile… it becomes you."

Their eyes focused on one another. "I know where I'm going now, and it's not to hell." She reached out and hugged Kat once more. "I'm so happy for you."

The room filled quickly, with the pilots seated in a single row. None of them spoke. Some were still priding themselves on their success in being picked; others seemed not to care. Werner simply puffed on a cigarette, as usual. The two leaders were talking to each other when they walked into the room. Number One went to a table that was in the front, his back was to them.

"Sir, may I have a word?" Diego said nervously as he stood.

Before One even turned around, he said, "I already know, Diego." He turned and with a paper in his hand, approached him. "I know, Diego… I knew it from the beginning." He gave the papers to Diego. "I've acquired a freighter to Acapulco for you and your friend. It's longer, but that will give you more time to get acquainted."

Diego looked almost teary-eyed as he stared at One. "Thank you, sir."

Number One seemed overly happy to see Diego fall out of the competition, to the surprise of the others. The men sat there wondering about the purpose of One's conversation with Diego. They had an idea that there was going to be one less pilot to worry about. They wondered who would be picked to replace him.

"I want you to know, I think your father would have been proud of you for finally getting out." One started to get a little emotional. "Good luck… and please send in Number Forty."

As Diego passed the others, still looking surprised and confused, "You fool," Werner said.

"What are you doing?" came from another. Their comments had undertones of glee, for they had witnessed Diego's abilities with an aircraft and felt better for themselves with his departure. He just tipped his head to them and ambled through the hatch.

Amy and Kat were talking about married life when Diego came walking in the room. They stopped and gazed at him; Katya for one reason, and Amy for quite another. "Number Forty… pronto, you're needed in Ready Room Three." All the time he was speaking, he never took his eyes off Amy. They were talking to each other with every flicker and glimmer of their eyes. One thing was sure; they both had become very happy.

Kat went flying out of the room without saying a word, and Diego slowly sauntered over to Amy.

"Who's Forty? Damn it, who's Number Forty?" the Frenchman was yelling.

"Are you fucking blind? *She's* Forty," said Brevan.

"He's sending us by ship," said Diego in a calm and steady voice as he handed her the tickets.

"That's good, it gives us more time." She smiled and moved her hair from her eyes.

"That's what One said." He gently brushed her cheek.

Katya came gliding into the room and stopped short of knocking Number Two down. "I'm sorry, sir, very sorry. I'm just a little excited."

"Hear the rules before you get too excited," explained Number One. "Please, sit there next to Matthew. Encionin, please give your seat to her."

"Is this part of the rules… the pussies get favoritism?" sneered Werner.

"Shut up and move your ass. Everyone keep quiet till I'm finished, then it will be your time to bitch."

Katya gave a quick smile in Matt's direction, then sat at attention with her face expressionless, looking straight ahead at One.

"First, from now on you will use your names; only the instructors will be addressed to by numbers. Second, all rules currently in place will remain except for five miles out and five miles in." He sensed a little confusion. "It means once you're five miles out, there are no rules till you get within five miles of landing, understand?" He watched the smiles and nods of the pilots.

"One more thing about rules. Here on this ship, all of you are under my rules and discipline. On the land bases you will be under US military laws, and as some of you know, that can be very strict. So, while you are on land, you will not be able to leave the billeting area. There will be no drinking, fighting, sexual aggravation, and no contact with the natives. You will be perfect ladies and gentlemen at all times. The penalties will be as follows for every infraction, small or large: All moneys will be forfeited. All traveling papers confiscated and you will be left there, wherever that might be. Some of you guys can tell the others about the South Pacific paradises you fought the Japanese for. Once back on this ship, you'll be under the same rules as always." Everyone seemed to understand.

"Okay… now to the actual rules of the race. Every morning, there will be a drawing for aircraft. How you finished the day prior will set the order in which you are assigned for the draw. First place gets the first pick, second gets the second plane drawn, and so on. Each morning's draw will probably be different. You will then be given weather, longitude, and latitude of destination, with an initial heading from the ship or ground base position. You will have access to photos so you can log any landmarks you may feel necessary. You will then do your own flight plan with range computations, fuel usage, and wind compensations. Remember… there will be ten legs and all aircraft can, under the right flying and calculations, make each leg. Some of these planes will have to fly at very low speeds to make the range. You will know right from the beginning of that leg that you will be in last place and lucky to make the leg at all. So be on your toes and remember what you've learned in the classes." The room became quite serious as they remembered some of what they had learned about these aircraft.

"First place, ten points… second, eight, third, six… and all others will receive one point. Before I forget… and if I'm repeating myself, then good. You must finish all legs to bring in the prize money. Even if you accumulate a winning score before the last leg, you still must fly it. If you don't successfully achieve a leg, no matter what your point accumulations are, you will not win the prize money.

"Radio frequencies are the same in either direction. There will be a C-47 with Number Two and his staff at all land bases. He will fly from island to island. As you fly to the carrier, he will be flying to the new land base, the same with the carrier. The prize money you already know, and for each leg, there will be a thousand-dollar bonus. If there is mechanical or any damage to the aircraft that makes it impossible to fly the next leg, the pilot that used that aircraft the day before will be eliminated from the competition but will be given credit for finishing that part of the leg. If a pilot does not touch down on the runway of either land or sea, the pilot will not be given credit for that leg. So, in other words, if you're going to crash, crash it on the runway." The room chuckled airily.

"I want you all to think about this next subject seriously. Now is the time to back out if anything bothers you. There are others that are ready to take your place. There are no rules once you're airborne and five miles out. You want to fuck with one another, that's your business. But let me tell you now. Each aircraft will be loaded with munitions once and once only." Their faces went stone-like and their thoughts filled the room to its limit. Matt looked over to Kat and raised his eyebrows.

"You mean we're supposed to shoot at one another?" Geno's words broke up as he spoke them.

"No... I'm not saying that at all."

"What kind of race is this?" Mel looked down the line to Matt and shrugged his shoulders.

"It's a race for warriors... how many times do I have to tell you people that? Do you think I would send out warriors without their swords? Think about it!" His face grew red from anger. He couldn't understand their objections. "If you don't want to use the munitions, don't use them... it's that simple."

Werner stood and took another puff of the fag in his mouth, his ash falling to the deck. "Munitions will be loaded only once, what is that?"

One smiled. "The aircraft will be loaded at the beginning of the race and not reloaded after that. So, if you use up the ammunition early, you won't have any at the end. Get the message, Mr. Werner?"

Kat noticed Number One's befitting attitude now that Werner had asked his question. Why was he doing this? What would he gain? Her thoughts tore at her. He was covering up something, but what? It didn't matter, she was still used to fighting and so were the others. Then she thought, to get Werner in her sights might be worth it all.

With a smooth and unsuspecting look on his face, Number One asked, "Is there anyone that wants out?" A dead silence overtook the small room. "Good." He pulled a small bag open and stuck his hand into it. "Since there are no winners right off, this will be the order tomorrow." He pulled the names and announced their order.

Kat was third or fourth, she was not paying attention. She was still worried about the rules. She caught Werner looking in her direction and he smiled when he spied her noticing. She thought, *This could and probably would become more than just a race, and she felt One knew it, but what reason did he have?* She knew he wasn't telling the whole truth. Sake walked in front of her as he left. He was calm enough; live bullets didn't seem to bother him a bit. *The Oriental mind*, she thought.

"Let's go down and tell Yokes the good news before we have to go," said Matt.

"Sure, let's go." She glanced at One as she left with Matt. He didn't see her gawking but he looked content enough.

They rushed into the sickbay to find an empty bed. "Where the hell is he?" asked Matt. They looked around but saw nothing, and then out of the blue, Kat heard singing.

"Over there." She pointed as the two of them walked to the far side of the sickbay. An opera was being sung to the splatter of water on the shower curtain. The tempo of the piece raised as the pitch grew out of the singer's range. A clearing of his voice brought the vocal range back into focus.

"Hey, Big Guy, you missed your calling. That sounded pretty good to me!" They both started laughing.

Yokes poked his head out of the shower. A yellow towel was wrapped around his cast. "Never mind, you two, do I have some great news for you!"

"We have some news for you, too."

"Go back to my room. I'll be there in one minute."

"Okay," said Kat, then pulled Matt by the arm.

"I think he sang pretty good," Matt said as she pushed him down on the bed next to Yokes'.

"Look, guys, there on the table, isn't it great?" Yokes pointed to the table, then threw himself onto the bed.

"Be careful, Big Guy, you're supposed to be injured."

"I don't think he's hurt at all, he's just faking those cuts and bruises." Matt smiled as he said it.

"Never mind me. Look at the papers!" he yelled.

"It's some kind of ownership documents, for a C-47, whatever that is." Kat looked a bit confused.

"Did you say C-47 transport?" Matt's jaw hit the ground.

"Yes. The new owner is Lovie Hewing Yokes."

"Your name is Lovie? You're kidding… goddamn Lovie Yokes? No wonder you go by your last name. I don't believe it!" Matt was almost hysterical from laughter.

Kat saw the embarrassment on Yokes' face. "I think it's a fine name. I read once that a Great Russian hero was once named Lovie." She saw the disbelieving looks coming from the guys. "We pronounce it differently though." She smiled back at the two.

Matt suddenly became serious. "Are you sure it's a C-47?"

"Yep, it sure is. We got a business, partner!" Yokes extended his hand and the three clenched each other's hands and shook together.

"It's a plane, isn't it? What kind?" Kat was excited but wanted to know why.

"Yes, it's a plane, a huge plane. Cargo or passengers, whatever we want or need it to be. There are at least twenty airstrips in the Caribbean. We're going to be rich; one in the water and one on land. We'll have all the bases covered." Matt's enthusiasm took a sudden turn. "Where did you get it laying here in sickbay?"

"Number One gave it to me. He said that I was the best flyer of all of you guys and that I should have the plane to go back home and teach the people there how to work together. He's really a swell guy. He helped out Evelyn, too."

One was a mass of contradictions in Kat's mind. Was he a good man or a demon looking for prey? She would have to watch him closely after this. "I'm so glad for you, Big Guy."

"I'm a real partner now." His chin rose a little.

"Damn right you are. Now all we have to do is win the operating capital." Matt's heart was light and full of happiness; not for just himself, but for all three of them.

"That's not a problem now that both of us are in the race. It's a piece of cheese," gleamed Kat.

"You mean a piece of cake?" Matt snickered.

"Just because you're going to be my husband, don't think you can speak for me, you bastard."

"Kat… you're going to have to watch your language when you get home. My mother's not going to understand all this bastard this and bastard that." He grinned and lowered his head.

"He did it?" said Yokes. "I knew he had the guts, but I didn't think he had the brains. I'm so happy for you guys. Are you going to wait till you get back home?"

"If I can keep her off of me," Matt said with a snicker.

Kat swung at him, missing, of course. "You think you're some kind of gift from the gods. I bet your talley-wacker isn't as big as this pencil here."

"Never mind how big it is, you're just going to have to wait."

"In a church?" Yokes asked.

"What religion are you, Kat?"

She appeared a little nervous. "I don't have one. I don't think I believe in one. Does that make a difference?"

"Not at all. Maybe to the Southern Baptists back home, but not to me. I love you no matter what you are." Matt's voice sang out crisp and clear.

"Georgia and I got hitched by the Justice of the Peace."

"That sounds beautiful. I want to be married by a judge and for peace." Kat's face was engulfed by a large smile. "Will you stand up for me, Yokes?" She became a little sad. "My father cannot, he was killed in the war." Her voice trembled as she spoke.

Yokes looked at Matt. "I'll stand for both of you if you want."

"There's nothing I would like better."

"Is everything in order? Is there anything else you need?" One seemed to be in a hurry to get the ship underway.

"I think I have everything but one." Two wanted to ask a question.

"What is it?"

"Why? You told me at the beginning that you would tell me. I think now is the time. I won't be seeing you again till Australia, so please tell me now."

The admiral wandered to his desk and opened a drawer. He pulled out the photo that was on his wall back in Alameda. He threw it on the desk, along with a folder.

"The picture of the Zero, you showed it to me earlier." Two appeared confused.

"That picture was taken December 7, 1941, at Pearl. You know my wife had passed away, but did you know how she died?"

"No… I figured that was your business. You never talked about her, so I never asked."

His eyes darkened with emotion. "She was found in the rubble about three weeks after the bombing. Apparently, she was at the hospital at the time of the attack. It was hit with a five hundred pounder and completely destroyed." His voice cracked from time to time. "I was in England at the time coordinating with MI-6. I had just taken the promotion and arrived there only a few days earlier." He lowered his eyes to the picture of his wife that was on the desk. "She was so happy for me that I was made an admiral and head of Naval Intelligence." He picked her picture up and his hand started to tremble. "I called for days trying to reach someone in Honolulu but the chaos was tremendous. I finally dropped everything and made my way back, just in time for her burial."

He stopped talking, sat down at his desk, lit a cigarette and took a puff. "I tried in every way I could to get a combat mission but was denied every time. I was told I was too important. I insisted that I be transferred to the Pacific Theater and to COMPAC. That, happily, was granted." He hesitated once more and put the cigarette out in the ashtray. His eyes welled up and his face grew ashen. He pointed to the file that lay next to the photo. "After Pearl, I lived my life by reading combat reports every day. I read thousands of them. With each one my heart broke a little more, with each pilot shot down or missing." With watery eyes, he looked up at Norris. "You know my son, Michael?"

"Yes, we met several times. Once on the *Lexington*, I think."

"That's his file, a very complete and thorough one. His flight commander took extreme measures to gather all the details of the incident."

Norris started to read the report. It stated that Michael's plane had been shot up and he had to bail out. His flight commander stayed with him as he drifted down in his parachute and radioed Sea Rescue. The commander was out of ammo so he could do nothing but observe Captain Garrett descending into the water. The next thing the commander observed was a Zero returning for the kill. The Zero made two passes at the parachute, the second time around cutting Garrett's body in two. From the waist down, his body fell into the sea. The commander took special notice of the plane's markings and were described there in the files. He stopped reading and looked up at the admiral, then at the photo. "It's the same plane, isn't it?"

"Yes, the same aircraft that bombed Pearl and maybe killed my wife, killed my son." His face went from pale to fiery red. He was trying in every way he knew to hold his anger in.

Two looked at the picture again and saw the name that was written on it; Sadaaki Akamatsu. "Why haven't you killed him yet? I would have," he said with quiet emphasis. Two suddenly remembered. "Yes, that's why that Bearcat's onboard." There was no judgment in his eyes or in his tone. "Do you think you're good enough?"

One leaned forward and lowered his voice. "If not, my pain ends either way."

"I'm sorry for your loss. I don't know what I would do without my family."

One quickly and without any apparent effort became calm, and all signs of his grief disappeared. "When you get to Sydney, wait for Yokes. He's taking you and some others back with him. I've given him the C-47. Take the same route back as you took getting there. Once you get to Honolulu, dial this number; there's a surprise waiting for you. Keep it safe, don't lose the number." He handed him a small card. "Any money that's left, you keep it. You deserve it."

His business-like manner confused Two. "Where will you be?"

"Probably at the bottom of the ocean; if not, maybe in jail, once the authorities find out about the race." He stood to shake hands. "Don't say anything to Sake, save that pleasure for me, okay?"

"Yes, sir." Two's remorse was immense. The story of his friend having his life torn away from him was almost too much to handle.

It was around five o'clock when the final helicopter took off with the last of the pilots that were not chosen. They were headed for the naval base and then on to different hotels where they'd wait for their departures. The remaining nine, along with Brevan and Two and his crew, waited on the flight deck. The nine fighters were warming up and the helicopter was running, waiting to be boarded.

One gave the order and the pilots manned their planes. Two and his crew boarded the helicopter and took off for Hickman Field. The planes started to taxi into position, then takeoff, and follow Two to the field. One watched from the flight deck as the last planes left and disappeared over Oahu.

His mind drifted back to before the war. He was fishing in almost this exact spot. The mahi-mahi were not biting that day, but he didn't care. The sun shone like a giant yellow ball and played games with the clouds, ducking in and out, then shooting its rays down to the green of the hills. The clouds followed just behind and their dark rain showers raced to see which one would get to the land first. The fragrance of hibiscus was everywhere, like sheets of music painting the landscape with their scents. His boat rocked in the waves like Neptune himself was trying to put him to sleep. His boat was like a giant baby's cradle. The waters were so clear he could spy the bottom at twenty or thirty feet. He knew this was heaven, and so did she.

His wife had picked this piece of heaven to be together and live forever. He could see her even now, standing on the porch, waiting for him to climb the pathway to the house. Anxious for his return, his son would run towards him with eager intent. She had visited here as a child and was glad she could return and call it home. The only place better on earth, he thought, was in his beloved's arms. His whole life was her, and still is.

He signaled the captain to set sail for sea. As the sounds of the ship's engines conquered the still air, he motioned to the flight captain. The elevator glided swiftly upwards, bringing to the surface a beautiful sight. The dark blue of its skin shone in the evening light and its newness and sharp features outlined a killing machine for the ages. The crew stood in awe of its massive design.

One of the younger Airedales asked, "What kind is it?"

Another just gazed at it and replied, "Bearcat."

One put on his headgear and then walked over to the aircraft. He stroked its flawless texture as he made his way down the wing. The vibrations seemed to call to him that she was eager and ready to fly. He looked back to the island as they left. "I must see its beauty one more time," he said, then climbed into the cockpit. The power felt good to the old man's hand and his throttle hand felt young again as it pushed the lever forward.

With the speed of the gods, he lifted off the deck and into the blue of the evening skies. The plane banked right and climbed to three thousand feet. He could see Pearl and Diamond Head and the sheer cliffs that overlooked both of them. He gazed across the harbor to the hill that lay to the west, and the road that bent its way upward to his house at the top. He remembered the time he took Michael up to see the islands from the air; he must have been ten, maybe eleven? They both enjoyed the sight of Joanna waving at them as they flew above the house. 'Look, there's Mom!' He could hear the boy's words like they had just been spoken and saw the sheer glee at the sight of his mother.

Slipping the Bearcat to the left, he went down to the beaches at Waikiki, his son's favorite surfing spot; not for the waves, but the female tourists. The waters faded from dark blue to green, then back to shades of blue again as he passed over the breakwaters. Looking upward, he spied a giant thunderhead about ten thousand feet up. He throttled to the maximum and pointed the nose straight up to attack its billowing whiteness. The plane held him deep into his seat as the speed increased to its limit. It took but a short time to pierce the cloud's outer formation. With nothing but white mist all around him, he felt like heaven had taken him and for a split-second, he wished it were so.

The sun abruptly struck his eyes and he had to shade them from the glare. Leveling off, he became a little lightheaded. "I need some oxygen, better put on my mask." His altimeter read thirty thousand feet. "Haven't been this high in years." All the islands were visible from here, or at least most of them. Out to sea, he even spotted the carrier steaming straight and true. He felt good, like after the hard workouts he used to have back at the base. "Pretty good shape for an old fart. Better get this old ass back on the deck." As he headed back to the carrier, he wondered, *Am I good enough?*

CHAPTER ELEVEN

"WHY DO WE HAVE TO wait till we get to Tampa?" Her eyes were twinkling in the morning sun as she spoke.

Matt's frown stopped any more conversation on the subject. "I told you, when it's right, we'll both know it, and until we're married, it's not the right time."

Kat started pouting. Her lower lip extended far out from the upper and her eyebrows formed two arches as she slung her arms to her sides in disapproval. "You're no fun."

"Fun or not, what if I get killed in this race and you're all knocked up... and what then?" His words appeared strong and final. "It's the right way or no way, understand, Kat?"

His lecture angered her but at the same time, pleased her. "Okay, okay... you don't have to be such a bastard about it." Her doe eyes welled up on the verge of crying. She loved testing his respect for her. It was one of the things that drew him to her.

"I'm sorry, but you've got to be reasonable. Do you know how hard it is for me to wait?"

"I'd like to know how hard it is," she said, grinning.

His scolding look only lasted a few seconds and then that great smile overtook his fatherly expression. "Be patient... I'll take care of everything." He then kissed her on the head, to her dismay, and walked out of the billet and over to Number Two's quarters. He knocked on the door and with permission, walked in. "Sir, I've got a problem and I hope you can help me with it."

"You want to marry Katya," he said without even thinking about it.

"Yes… but—"

"A blind man could see it. You and she have been walking around like high school sweethearts since you came onboard. Do you think it's the right time, though? One or both of you could get hurt in this race."

"I know, but there's no stopping her. I just have to do the right thing here, it's the way I was brought up."

"What do you need?" He stopped and looked skyward. "That was stupid. You need a church or an authority to say the words and make it legal, right?"

"I only have one problem; we both want Yokes at the ceremony."

Two smiled. "That actually makes it even easier. Since Yokes can't get off the ship, you'll have to be married by the captain." He walked over to a map that was laid on a desk. He spent some time examining it, then gazed up at Matt. "Can you wait three more days?"

Matt smiled eagerly. "Yes, sir."

"I'll get the authorities to issue the license at our first land base, then the captain can marry you the next day onboard the carrier. Will that be okay?"

"Goddamn, that will be terrific!"

Two's face became firm. "Look, Matt, on the serious side. Some of your competitors are going to figure this is a team match if you two marry, if they don't think so already. So, watch your six and watch Katya's six, too." He suddenly got a shit-eating grin on his face. "Why not? Since they'll think it already, why not form a team and be each other's wingman?"

"Sounds like a good idea to me," Matt said. "Maybe Mel and Drum could do the same, and only race between themselves in the last twenty or thirty miles of the legs. Thank you, sir. I appreciate your help."

"I'll contact One and tell him of our plans. I'm sure it will be fine with him."

"Thank you again, sir." Matt turned and left. He whistled as he made his way back to the billet. His heart was light and he felt really good about himself.

"Where did you go?" Kat inquired.

Matt showed her a half-grin and crossed his arms. "That's my affair. It's a secret."

"Starting to have secrets already and we're not even married yet?"

"We're nagging and not even married yet?" His return stopped her cold. "You'll just have to wait. It'll be worth it."

Her mood changed from demanding to pleading. "Please, *boobblia*, tell me the secret, please, please?" Her whimpering was soft and affectionate.

With an adamant tone, he said, "You'll just have to wait."

Since her begging didn't work, she thought to use the direct and stern route. "Okay, since you won't tell me… you're cut off." Once she realized what she had said, she eased up and began laughing. "Please, tell me."

"You'll know in three days. Now quit bothering me. We only have another three hours till we take off and I want to talk with you about something, but I need to talk to the other guys, too. Let's go round them up." He enjoyed the attention and affection this secret was giving him but there were several important issues that had to be discussed.

He found Mel and Drum eating breakfast. Drum was eating everything in sight and drinking glass after glass of milk. "You guys sure you want to eat and drink just before flight time?" Matt asked.

"What the hell are you talking about, Mattie old boy?" Drum seemed impervious to the notion of getting rid of his breakfast in flight.

"What if an urge comes over you to take a dump in the middle of the Pacific Ocean? Kind of hard to pull over and drop your pants, don't you think? Unless you and your plane can walk on water." Kat was trying very hard to hold in her laughter.

The look on Drum's face was worth a million bucks. "I didn't think about that. I'm used to only flying for two or three hours over the Channel. Never had that problem there." He put his knife and fork down and gazed back at the three that were staring at him.

Matt lowered himself on his elbows and spoke in a low voice. "Look, guys, I figure we're going to have to look out for each other in this race, with bullets probably flying around sooner or later, so here's what I have in mind. We form a partnership and protect each other's sixes till we get within twenty or thirty miles, and then everyone for themselves. What do you think?"

"What about Rudy?" Having Rudy on the team troubled Mel. "He's not here to race, he's here to kill Nazis."

"Let's see how the bloke takes it. If he's out for nothing but revenge he can fuck away." Drum's green eyes sparkled as he spoke.

"Agreed then," said Matt.

"Agreed." said the rest of the group.

Werner gawked at the group hovered at one end of the room and wondered what their conversation was about.

The Bearcat was warming up on the flight line. The seas were a little rough, and the pitch of the ship was quite high. One looked up to the Pri-Fly and saw the indicator for the wind. Thirty knots. He smiled as the mist and the wind blew his hair as he put on the headgear. The small flight crew stood ready for the two planes to take off. A Hellcat was in position behind the Bearcat. Only these two aircraft would be used today. Number One wanted to get some experience behind the stick of the Bearcat, so he and Number Four would fly some combat maneuvers this morning. Number One walked over to Four. "You get on my six first and I'll try to shake you, then you try to shake me, okay?"

Number Four nodded his head. "Got it." He then walked to his plane and climbed in.

Number One did the same. "Bearcat to flight boss, ready for takeoff."

The reply came quickly. "Bearcat... okay for takeoff." One looked down to the flight captain holding his flag. He signaled the Bearcat to rev up its engines to maximum, then lowered the flag for takeoff. The Bearcat didn't even need half the deck to lift off and bank to the east. Number One climbed to and maintained Delta, while Number Four took off and then joined him in the pattern. "You feel like bust-in' some clouds today, Four?"

His response came over the radio, "You show me the way and I'll be right up your ass."

The Bearcat took a forty-five-degree bank and dropped five hundred feet, then throttled up and climbed to twenty thousand, with the Hellcat right on his tail.

"You can do better than that, Admiral." The radio screamed venom at him.

"Just getting warmed up." He slipped into a dive and spun three or four times, then pulled up and banked the plane back to level flight. He was clocking about two hundred sixty knots when he suddenly pulled straight up and climbed into a cloud cover at about three hundred knots.

"Nice... very nice, Admiral."

The poison that was in the radio before had diluted into mere buttermilk. The admiral grinned as he saw his reflection in the canopy. He appeared younger, like the last time he saw Michael.

Number Four keyed his mic. "Okay Admiral... it's your turn to stay on my ass. I'm at fifteen thousand, on a heading of 019, waiting to take you for a ride."

"On my way," the confident One replied. He came out of the clouds to find the Hellcat cruising right on course about five thousand feet below him. He maneuvered to within about fifty feet of the Hellcat's tail. "Surprise!" He started to laugh, for he knew what was coming up.

In a winking of an eye, the Hellcat was banking and climbing, then spun three times and dove a thousand feet. The Bearcat was left still spinning and the admiral lightheaded from the Gs' as the Hellcat climbed to the Bearcat's six.

"Not good, Admiral." Number Four's voice was tentative.

Embarrassed by how quickly Number Four maneuvered him out of position, he answered, "That's why we're up here, for me to learn. I start my lessons tomorrow... okay?"

"Carrier to aircraft... come in."

"Bearcat to carrier... go ahead."

"Enter Delta and proceed to landing vectors... we need the flight deck cleared to receive aircraft drills."

"Bearcat to carrier… Roger." Number One looked over to Number Four and pointed to the carrier. "The victors are always first."

"Ten-four, One." Both aircraft entered Delta, the Bearcat following the Hellcat.

"I wonder who's going to win the first leg," Yokes said, his mouth full of biscuit.

"You're spitting crumbs all over your bed." Nurse Rose brushed the morsels off the blanket.

Viktor picked up a fork full of eggs and threw them down his throat. "It all depends on what plane you're stuck with. I hope Katya gets that Zero. It's got a range like a Howitzer and will give her a good edge."

"I just hope Matt or Missy don't get into that Polik… Polak… that goddamn I-16. The Kingfisher could beat your ass to the ship." Yokes continued stuffing his face with his breakfast.

"I wonder how many miles they have to travel today. I know they're going to have them leave later so the carrier would be further out."

Yokes frowned at Viktor, showing some doubt in his figuring. "How do you know all this?"

"Brains, my boy… all brains. The LSO isn't on duty till five and he has to be early, doesn't he? So, the takeoff time must be just around noon or one o'clock. That makes it in about two or three hours, I figure. They'll have to fly maybe close to five hundred miles today."

"Then I hope Missy or Matt do get that Polikarpov or whatever it's called. That little bastard can go like hell if it doesn't have to worry about fuel."

"Faster than the Corsair or the Hurricane?" Nurse Rose asked.

Both men stopped dead in their tracks and gazed at her. "You know about fighter aircraft?" Viktor's surprise was obvious.

"Sure… my brother flew P-51s from India to Burma." She looked a little annoyed that the boys were surprised at her knowledge. "You don't think I wouldn't study up on airplanes and pilots after dating one of you, do you? All you guys talk about are your gorgeous planes and women's bodies. I'm not the type to be left out of any conversations, so I put some time in at the ship's library reading up on airplanes. I already know about women's bodies."

The two men looked at each other and shrugged their shoulders. Nurse Rose just kept making beds in the ward while the guys finished their late breakfast.

Two opened the door to the flight room where all the pilots were gathered. "It's almost noon… I'll be picking the order of your planes at that time. Please line up in the order you were chosen onboard ship." The room quickly became alive with bodies lining up.

"What number am I?" asked Kat.

"You're number four, right behind Werner," Matt replied. He was ninth in line and brought up the rear. He hoped Kat got picked for a powerful plane like the Zero or the Corsair, then no one would bother her on this leg. He could watch out for himself, but it was better that she was safe.

Werner rotated his head slightly backwards. "Am I going to have trouble with you?" he said, almost in a whisper.

"A little scared, are we?" she said in a loud and boisterous tone.

After Werner caught Dumitrn's eye, he turned back around and didn't say a word.

"Okay… before I choose numbers, you all know the procedures, or you should know them. Once you get your number you will have one hour to plot your course, do a flight check on your aircraft, and be ready to take off on time. Weather is there on the table, along with the map and the longitude and latitude and your initial heading. There are also photos on the wall of some checkpoints; there aren't many, some small quays and sand bars. I'd list them anyway in my flight plan.

"One caution: allow at least twenty miles for maneuvering once you find the carrier. This would be a good thing to do no matter where you're flying. Fuel is critical, probably the most crucial, so do your fuel consumption math well. The carrier's radar will pick you up about eighty miles out and correct your course if needed. Do yourselves a favor and do what they tell you. Your call sign is Nine ball, the ship's is Gray lady, and on the land bases it is Rocky." He gazed at the men and woman in line. "Believe it or not… I wish you all luck." He glanced at his watch. "It's time."

One of his crew held out a bag with slips of paper in it. Number Two put his hand into it and pulled out the first number. "Two." He handed the slip to Sake. "Five." Dumitrn was very pleased.

Save a good one for her… please save just one. Matt's mind raced with every number picked as he prayed to his God.

Kat kept looking backward at him with crossed fingers, smiling and throwing kisses at him, obviously not a care in the world.

"Number one." Number Two saw Matt fidgeting at the end of the line, then he smiled at Werner and handed him the slip.

The goddamn Zero is gone, goddamn it… goddamn it! What's left? The Hurricane… yes that will do… give her the Hurricane, damn it… please!

Two looked to Matt as he picked the next number. He looked down at it, then up at Matt. "Seven… Katya, you get seven." He handed it to her without taking his eyes off of Matt.

Matt lowered his head and eyes to the floor. He didn't pay any more attention to the drawing. When it was his turn, the Messerschmitt was the choice for him.

Kat was already at the maps making her computations when the worried Matt came up behind her.

"What are you going to do? That I-16 is the worst draw you could have gotten," he said in a dull and troubled voice.

"Nonsense… if you've got to have it… better to have it on a short leg. My arithmetic shows the carrier is only five hundred thirty miles away from base. That means I can cruise the I-16 at about two hundred forty miles an hour and with reserves, there's no problem making it along with the best of them. What did you draw?"

"The 109." Matt relaxed a bit, knowing Kat would be fine.

"You're going to have more trouble than I will. Those Messerschmitt's have the damnedest time flying straight and level.

You'll be massaging that stick all the way. Now quit talking to me… I've got things to do."

He smiled at her back as she turned once again to the maps, then started his own figuring.

Werner left the field third and promptly turned onto the initial heading and trimmed his aircraft. He adjusted his speed and heading to the figures he had calculated from the charts. He was hoping the aircraft in front of him hadn't compensated for the twenty-mile-an-hour crosswinds coming in from the southeast. This would put them about thirty miles off course by the time they reached the ship's radar. He was uneasy flying over nothing but water, something he had never done before. But if the Americans could do it, so could he.

He could not see the aircraft in front of him but saw their contrails. It looked like at least one of them was veering off to the northeast; not a large mistake, but maybe enough. He hoped his own calculations were right. He didn't like looking the fool.

It had been almost two hours and the rush of the air and the hum of the engines were all he could hear, and it almost soothed him to sleep more than once. The trip was becoming boring; nothing to look at, no buildings, mountains, and not even cloud formations to play with. Then he noticed his airspeed; he had let it drop to one hundred eighty knots. "Must be a headwind, and a strong one."

Then, out of nowhere, the I-16 flew past, about two thousand feet below him and moving fast. He checked his airspeed again; it should have been two hundred six knots, but how long had he been at the lower speed, he didn't know. Then he checked his fuel gauge. "I don't dare increase speed." Could his calculations be off, or was she burning up all her fuel and going to drop into the ocean just miles from the carrier? He looked at his flight plan and then his watch. One hour thirty-five minutes; that put him three hundred nine miles out. But at the lower speed. Was that right? "She's right… goddamn it… that Russian bitch is right." He lowered his nose and followed her trail. Katya's aircraft was out of sight by now and as he dropped to a thousand feet, the Corsair powered by him. "Fuck. I can't outrun that Corsair." He looked behind him and saw three little dots, and they were getting bigger with each second that went by. He pushed the Hurricane to its limits, but so was everybody else. Most of the aircraft were moving close to three hundred knots, then over the radio they heard, "Gray lady to Nine ball... Gray lady to Nine ball, leader respond."

Geno in the Corsair replied, "Number Six to Gray lady... come in."

"Number Six, we have you seventy miles out. Come to course 194 degrees. All planes maintain positions at the five-mile point. Will contact you then... over."

Geno looked starboard and saw the Zero gaining on him. He put the throttle all the way forward and turned to the new heading. He was screaming through the skies, but so was the Zero. He noticed some black smoke coming from the Zero and smiled and started to pull away. "Arrivederci, ciao." He was feeling good about the situation.

A shadow appeared on the water just below him. He glanced back to see Katya in the I-16 barely keeping up.

"Salve, ciao," came from Katya's plane. She could see the wake from the ship now and she knew the five-mile marker would be coming up soon. She also knew she couldn't overtake the Corsair but she was struggling to beat the Zero.

"Gray lady to leader... you have reached the five-mile marker. All aircraft maintain positions and enter Delta pattern. All aircraft acknowledge."

"Number Six... *Grazie mille.*"

"Gray lady to leader... English at all times."

"Yes, Gray lady."

"Number one... I'm here, mate."

"Number seven... Roger." There was some disappointment in Katya's voice but if she had to get beat out, Mel would have been her choice.

"You don't know how to figure crap, they're already here!" Yokes wanted to be dressed when his friends arrived but Viktor's data was a little off. As the ship was coming to stations, Yokes hurried with his pants. Nurse Rose was on one leg and Viktor the other. "My shirt, it's over there. Forget the shoes... one of them might be first and I don't want to miss that!" They helped him down the passageway and up the ladders to the flight deck, his cast banging on everything it could but that didn't matter. The threesome made it to the flight deck and scoured the skies for the planes. They were all in the Delta pattern by that time and they didn't know who had won that leg. "Who's flying what?" Yokes asked an Airedale.

"I don't know, but I think they're going to land in the positions they finished in."

Number One came through a hatchway onto the flight deck and saw Yokes and company standing there. He walked up to Yokes. "Get your ass back to sickbay, right now, and stay there till the doctor releases you." A suggestion of annoyance hovered in his eyes.

Yokes was going to complain but decided not to and simply turned and headed back down to sickbay. He motioned Viktor to stay and he did. Nurse Rose helped him back down the ladder.

Number One leaned his head towards Viktor. "She's in the money, third... she did well. So did Matt. I'll send them right down, now go tell him the news."

Viktor smiled at the admiral. "Yes, sir."

Yokes could barely sit on his bed as he waited for the two of them to come. They burst into the room, followed by the admiral. "Third and in that stubby ride, I can't believe it. You are the best!" He dragged her over to him and kissed her. He looked up at Matt. "How'd you do, guy?"

"I made it, that's about it." Matt's small grin showed his frustration.

"It counts, doesn't it? Those German's can't make a decent airplane anyway." Yokes was just happy to see them. He didn't much care how they did, just wanted them to get back in one piece. "You never know when that one point might come in handy. And we've got two thousand for the bank; not bad for a day's work."

The admiral was enjoying the reunion from the back of the room but was pressed for time. "Can I interrupt a minute?"

"Yes, sir!" barked Matt.

"I had a talk with Number Two today and the arrangements you made, Matt, will be all right with me." One shook Katya's hand, to her surprise. "Best wishes, Katya." He turned and started to file out of the room. He stopped short and motioned Matt to him. The two men went out into the passageway. "Take this… it's the only thing I have left that belonged to my wife. I'm sure she would like it used in this instance." He handed Matt a ring. It was a simple gold band with a heart carved on its face. "It will make me feel good seeing it on Katya." He closed Matt's hand around the ring, then left down the passageway.

Matt was lost for words and almost in tears. He put the ring in his pocket and re-entered the sickbay.

Her woman's intuition and female instinct took over. A look of veneration enveloped her face. "What arrangements, and what am I being wished well for?"

"I'll tell you when we're alone." Matt tried to avoid the question.

Her face turned blush and her eyes narrowed. "I want to know now."

"You're going to spoil the surprise, now stop and I'll tell you later!"

Her face drooped and she began to pout.

"All right… if you must know and ruin the surprise… we're getting married by the captain next time we come onboard. Two is getting the paperwork together at our next island base, and we'll bring them back here and the captain will say the words, okay?"

Her face lit up like a Christmas tree and she started yelling all over the sickbay. "Yokes… you can stand up for us!"

"That's great news, you guys!" He pulled off the covers and yelled for Nurse Rose. "Rose… I need to speak to that quack of a doctor. I need out of here and back into some decent clothes by their wedding. Get that doctor, quick!"

CHAPTER TWELVE

RUDY CAME INTO THE HEAD yawning and rubbing his head, trying to wake up. This five o'clock wake-up was getting old fast. He carried his gear over to one of the sinks and laid it down. He heard one of the toilets flush and then heard it flush again. He thought, someone's got the shits or a big hangover, and he was glad it wasn't him. Just then, Drum came out of the stall. He could barely walk; his legs seemed to be cramping or they were asleep or something. "What's the matter with you?"

He waddled over to the sink next to Rudy's and leaned on it. "That goddamn Katya, she put the ki*bosh* on me yesterday. I think she's a Gypsy or a daughter of a banshee."

Rudy stood there, still half-asleep and rubbing his eyes. "She did what?"

"The goddamn *kibosh*," he yelled. He could see that Rudy didn't understand. "I'll explain. Just before we took off yesterday Katya, the *she-wolf* that she is, reminded me about eating and drinking problems when flying."

"What problems... like don't eat salami or you'll get airsick, something like that?" Rudy was still quite confused.

"No. The problem is how you get rid of it in flight."

"Oh... that problem." Rudy put his hands on his hips and grinned.

"It wasn't more than five minutes after I took off that I had to take a piss. All I could see was her laughing... and then after about an hour, I couldn't even keep my mind on flying. My stomach started to roll around and cramp, and then pressure started to build up. I had to keep my asshole puckered for the rest of the time. She put the *kibosh* on me all right. I think she's got a little Irish in her."

"So why are you sitting on the john so long this morning?"

"I've been in here all night and I haven't eaten a goddamn thing. I'll be damned if I'm going to lose this race because I shit me pants in the air!"

Rudy started laughing. "I bet you've got a toilet seat ring tattooed on your ass."

Drum's face went beet red as he rubbed his rear end. "Shut your gob."

"I wonder if we'll take off late today," Kat said over a plate of eggs.

Matt took a bite of biscuit, then quickly swallowed it. "I doubt it. We're flying to a land base today. I just hope we get some good picks and the leg is not enormous."

She felt his anxiety. "Long or short, it makes no difference to me. I just want to get to wherever it is and get that piece of paper in my hand." She winked across the table to an equally eager Matt.

"You'll care if you draw that I-16 again or that Macchi; those twelve cylinders are hell on fuel," noted Mel.

Kat put her fork down and took her eyes off of Matt to turn her attention to Mel. "The odds of me getting that Polikarpov again are slight, don't you think? The Macchi, if you trim it out right, is not that bad."

"You mean it takes a woman's touch to teach the Italians their stuff?" Mel said with a smirk.

With a blank expression on her face, she retorted, "It takes a woman to teach any man, of any nationality, anything." A grin came to her lips.

A mortified Mel uttered his amends. "Sorry I opened my flam-in' mouth."

Matt got Kat's attention once more, to Mel's delight. "I've got something to do before flight time. I'll see you in the ready room when it's time, okay?"

Her genteel look told him it was okay, as she nodded her head and mumbled something over a bite of rye. She blew him a kiss as he stood to leave.

Matt walked into the sickbay with an almost forced jubilance. "How you doing, old buddy? Back in uniform I see. Looks better than those pajamas they had you in. The blue, it goes good with that cast." He grinned.

Yokes could tell right off that something was wrong. "Come out with it, what's wrong?" He motioned Matt to sit.

Matt was surprised he could see through him and catch on so fast. He couldn't look at him. The words were hard to say, so he sat, folded his hands, then gazed at the floor as he spoke. "I don't know where this feeling's coming from or why, but I think of you as more than just a friend, more like a brother. Somehow, I trust you, and I believe what you tell me. I need a favor, and it's a big one." He turned his eyes from the floor and stared deeply into Yokes' eyes. "I need you to take Katya to Tampa if something happens to me." He looked for an affirmation, a sign that he could trust. "Will you do that?"

Yokes didn't answer. His eyes said all the words, his bruised and scarred face showed understanding and feeling for the two. "Don't worry, she's my friend too, and I would do anything for a brother."

He turned back to the floor and his voice lowered to a whisper. "I love her so much and worry about her. The things she's told me about her homeland—dogs shouldn't live there. The second we're married, she becomes a US citizen, and even if I'm dead, America will welcome her. She'll need some help getting started, and my mother will do that."

Yokes frowned and tensed up. "What's this dead talk? I won't have it."

Matt stood slowly. "Face it, Yokes. They've got real bullets in those planes out there, and half of those guys would rather see both

Kat and me dead. Money says a lot and killing means nothing to them; they've been doing it for years now." He turned away towards the bulkhead. "I've even thought of quitting." He stood for several seconds in the silence of the room, then slowly turned to face Yokes again. "What would you think if we both quit?" Tears were rising in his eyes and he forced himself to keep them in.

Yokes stayed silent for a few more seconds while he thought. "You're the president of our company. You call the shots. But do you think you can?"

"I don't know what I'd do if she got hurt, or worse."

Yokes stood and put an arm around him. "The same as my Georgina will; you'll take her with you always."

"But how can a madman go on?" He wiped the wetness from his eyes. "Here... this is a letter to my mother. She'll welcome and love Kat." He stared at the envelope. "It would be nice to see the two women I love together."

"It will be nice," corrected Yokes with a stare.

He smiled at him. "Well, we've got to fly at least two more times to even get married; we'll talk again then, okay?"

As Katya walked into her quarters, she picked up a photograph of her mother that was perched on the dresser and started talking to it. She straightened out the faded and torn photo as she spoke. "Mama, I'm getting married soon, and to a real nice gentleman. He's everything you told me to look for in a man. Papa would like and approve of him too, I think. He's tall, with lots of muscles, and intelligent, too. And he loves me, Mama, and I love him. He's strong but has a gentle hand. I don't think he would ever beat me, unless I really deserved it. He's not Russian, but is American." She tenderly stroked the outline of her mother's face. "Remember when Papa would show me America on the map, and we would dream of the streets of gold and bread like cake? I would give up all the gold in the world to be Matt's woman." She hesitated a moment while thinking. "By the way, your new son-in-law's name is Matthew Drew... Mrs. Matthew Drew... it's a fine name, isn't it, Mama?"

She heard rustling from outside in the passageway. "I've got to go now, Mama. Kiss Papa and tell him I love him, and tell him not to pinch the lady angels' behinds. We wouldn't want him to lose his wings now, would we? Goodbye, I love you both." She put the picture back down on the dresser and walked over to the porthole for a breath of air and waited for the announcement that she knew was coming soon.

Her mind drifted backwards towards home, then suddenly, something touched her like a strong breeze stroking her hair but it was more; it also touched her heart. She gazed at the sky and watched a dark cloud pass by. "I feel you, Mikhail; I'm glad you've come. I wanted to tell you about him. Has Mother told you? He's a lot like you were; mild and comforting in a lot of ways, with your touch and your voice of velvet. Though he's opposite of you, too, a warrior with fists of granite, not healing hands like yours. He's light and you were dark, but I'm lucky to have loved both of you." A tear surrounded her eyelids then fell to her cheek. "You'll always be my love... my first love." A voice entered her thoughts; she felt it more than heard it. "No, my tears aren't from sadness, but out of joy. I know you will be happy for me and watch over me. I'll always love you, Mikhail, and you will be with me always."

"Do all the aircraft check out all right, chief? The Zero was smoking badly yesterday on its landing." Number One looked at the aircraft that were lined up in the hangar deck, all shined and polished and apparently ready to go. Their mechanical crews stood by each plane with pride in a job well done.

"The Zero had a weak ring in the sixth cylinder, it was repaired overnight. All the aircraft were checked out and all are ready to fly."

Number One smiled a look of achievement at the crews. "Good job, Chief. Are the Aussie mechanics coming along all right?"

"They're great; they know much about the different aircraft already."

"Keep it up, Chief." He nodded to the chief and then headed for the command center and the morning's briefings. Once there, he was approached by the weather commander and informed about some potential bad weather in the future. "When will it get here?" asked Number One.

"It looks like two days from now. Singapore is reporting gale winds and two to three inches of rain in the last thirty-six hours." The commander looked concerned as he examined his charts.

"We will alter our plans if need be. Keep the captain informed of the storm's progress."

"Aye, aye… Number One," he sighed with relief.

The three men huddled together around a table in the wardroom. "They've made some kind of pact. They stay together in the first two-thirds of the leg, then it seems it's all for one in the last quarter. I think they're afraid we're going to shoot them out of the sky." Dumitrn snickered as he gave his report to Werner.

"If you could win that way… why don't you?" Werner was suggesting bringing out the old Nazi dog pack way of flying; of course with him on the outside, flying solo. With the other pilots worrying about the Nazis, he might be able to slip away and win some of the legs. How could he get his comrades to go along with the plan? Simply put, one wins all wins; but Werner would change the rules at the end, of course. "So, what about this… even if you don't fire on them, we could nudge or harass them a little… maybe… you think? Keep their minds on saving their miserable asses and let me win the legs." He saw some doubt in their eyes. "Who cares who wins if we all share equally at the end?"

"Sounds good to me," Geno chirped zealously. *Say anything, just keep them on your side for now, the German thought.*

Dumitrn raised his eyebrow. "Sounds real familiar to me." He peered into Werner's eyes. "The dog pack, like during the war?"

"Just like the war." Werner smiled at his comrades.

"All pilots to the ready room… repeat… all pilots to the ready room." This was the signal they all wanted to hear. The ship's crews all sprang into action and the carrier quickly became a hive of people rushing to their stations.

Geno took a fast glimpse at Werner as he got up to leave. Not having the courage to say so at their little war meeting, he whispered, "*Vaffanculo*." He's not giving up his first-place money to any *Tedesco spocro* he thought as he led the group out the passageway.

Number One looked around the room. "Is everyone here?"

"Looks like nine to me," said Drum.

"Please get in line in the order of finishing yesterday, thank you. All the materials you'll need are there on the table and hanging from the wall." He looked to his watch. "Okay, it's time."

He put his hand into the bag and pulled out number five for Geno. He rushed to the table with a grin on his face. Next was Mel; he drew the Sea-fire. He shrugged his shoulders and proceeded to the map table to do his figuring.

"Did Geno get the Hellcat?"

"Yeah, the lucky stiff, two good picks in a row." Drum was annoyed that Geno was so lucky.

Matt wasn't as jittery as he was yesterday. He was certain that Kat couldn't be unlucky two days in a row.

Number One's hand once again hit the bottom of the bag. He pulled the slip of paper out and read it. His face became like stone, cold and gray, then his eyes lowered. "Kat, I don't believe it, but you've drawn the I-16 again."

"Bullshit... that's not fair... she had it yesterday!" Rudy was more upset than either Matt or Kat. "Give it to one of those assholes." He pointed in the direction of Dumitrn.

"Fuck off, Jew-boy." Dumitrn was in no mood for Rudy's tempting.

Rudy's face reddened as he glared his disdain at the Nazi but didn't say another word.

"You do understand it's the pick of the draw, don't you, Katya?" Number One's voice seemed apologetic.

"Yes, One." She held out her hand, then took the slip of paper and went over to the table.

Quit... we could quit right now. Who needs that blood money anyway? Yokes and I can find another way. He watched her slow walk to the table, never looking up at him. *She'd be a sitting duck again and I won't have it.* Matt prepared to tell Number One of his decision when he was handed the number one slip.

One smiled at him. "You've drawn the Zero… that's good for this leg." He directed Matt's eyes over to Katya. "You get extra flying time in the Zero."

In a state of confusion, Matt made his way over to Kat.

She looked up at him with a worried look on her face. "I figure six hundred thirty-five miles. With a tail wind"—which she knew was non-existent— "somewhere around eight or eight and a half hours, at seventy-five knots and at a hundred feet altitude."

"That's barely flying. You can't stay in a cockpit for that long, no one can. You'll be at least two hours behind everyone else. I won't have it. I'll stay back with you." His fear turned to anger and he stalked the group for potential threats.

"Nonsense, you've drawn the best plane for this leg. The Zero has the greatest range of all. We can get the ten points out of this!" She brushed the hair from his eyes and stroked his face. "Do you think any of these bastards are going to fly at a snail's pace just to take my ass out of the race? I probably won't make it anyway and they know that, so I'm not worried about them in the slightest." Her look of distress turned quickly into stern determination. "So, shut up, *boobblia,* and quit worrying about me. Go, go take first place."

She seemed to analyze the situation quite well, leaving him in a stupor. Logic was with her; but he would still linger around at the start to make sure she was dead last and wouldn't be bothered before he made his move.

Brevan walked up to Katya. "What kind of speed do you think you'll be doing?" He knew the score, and was certain he would be doing his job today.

She looked up at him. "Looks like about seventy-five knots and eight hours."

He smiled; he thought the figures were very conservative. "Stay on the initial heading till I catch up at least, then I'll keep you company the rest of the way in the Kingfisher." He wanted her to know he would be there for her.

"Thanks, Brevan."

"Has anyone heard of this Wake Island? It looks real small to me." Drum wasn't too good at navigation, and figured to follow the leader till the island was in sight, then go like hell.

"It's small all right, just north of the Marshalls," said Matt.

"Who's got the Corsair?" Drum looked around for an acknowledgment.

Sake raised his arm halfway.

"You're off, what, fourth? Looks like I'm on your ass this flight." Drum smiled as he pretended to figure out his flight plan.

The planes lined up in order on the flight deck and prepared to take off. Mel signaled there was something wrong and was pulled off to the side as the others took off. "What's wrong?"

"Oil pressure, low oil pressure!" Mel shouted to the flight captain. He looked to see Katya taxiing into position for takeoff, then powering up and she left the deck clean. He shouted back to the captain, "The oil pressure looks fine now… let's go!" He took off and lingered over Katya for a few minutes. He checked out the skies for intruders, then out of the blue, the Zero dove on him. "Hold it, Matt… I'm just making sure she gets off okay."

"Thanks, Mel… I didn't know it was you!" Matt barked out over the radio.

"You boys want to get your asses back into the race and get the hell out of my way?" Kat was happy that they stayed behind but there was a race to win.

Dumitrn was listening like the others to the radio chatter between Matt and Mel. "Those idiots… losing precious time worrying about some *schlampe*." He had seen better schlampes in the whorehouses of Munich than this Katya.

The stick felt stiff in Dumitrn's hands. The Yak was not handling the headwinds well and he wished he had the Hellcat back. He looked to his flight plan; one hundred twenty knots at fifteen hundred feet should put him right on target in about five and a half hours, with some six gallons to work with. "Now… let's find someone to play with." He looked down and caught the Messerschmitt cruising about five hundred feet below. "The Jew-boy... who could be better?" He slowly throttled forward and took a bead on the tail of Rudy's plane. "How about a foot, or maybe a couple of inches, from his ass?"

Just at the last minute he noticed Rudy turn and see him dive on him. "Just a small burst, to rile the crucifier." Before Rudy could bank away, Dumitrn sent about fifty rounds screaming just behind the Messerschmitt's six. The radio sang out with Dumitrn's laughter.

"I'm going to blow you out of the sky, you bastard!" Rudy throttled up and got on the Yak's tail. They maneuvered for position for about twenty minutes, not firing on each other, just maintaining a killing zone. Their altitude was way over five thousand feet and the rest of the pack, including Katya, was in front of both of them by now.

The radio clicked open once more with the calm and direct voice of Brevan. "I suggest you boys get your asses back in the race. Neither one of you can afford to be shot or forced down right now. In case you haven't noticed, I'm in front of you, which leaves no one to drag your miserable carcasses out of the water."

The two broke off hostilities and struggled to get back on the right heading. The two planes flew side by side, with both pilots giving hand gestures to one another.

Rudy gazed at his fuel gauge. "Damn... I've got to refigure my range. Where's the manual on this piece of shit... damn it, I've left it behind." He looked to his flight plan, then back to the gauge. "I'm flying at one hundred twenty-five knots. I better get my ass to about ninety and drop to five hundred feet. Damn, I was stupid!" He looked over to see the Yak copying his moves. "I've got to fly this leg looking at him all the way; must be my punishment."

"That didn't turn out as planned." Dumitrn countered every move Rudy performed with the same. He figured if Rudy could make it, so could he. No more of this fooling around; it's not worth it. And where in the hell is that *dago*? The dog pack was one thing, solo fighting was another. And he'd be the first to tell Werner.

The leaders were comfortably cruising at their prescribed speeds. The Corsair had about a five hundred-foot lead on Matt in the Zero, with Geno's Hellcat about two hundred behind him. The Hurricane was lazily cruising just in sight of the leaders. Katya had picked up a trail of heavy smoke. "Seven to One… come in." Her voice held more than a little concern.

"One here… go ahead."

"Who's smoking up there?" she asked.

Matt looked around and found none of the aircraft that he could see were smoking. "Nothing up here, must be someone in the middle."

"Nine to Brevan," the radio sang.

Brevan answered the radio. "Brevan to Nine… what's wrong?"

"I'm heating up and dropping a little oil pressure. It looks like I'm smoking, too." Werner's voice was calm and straightforward. Brevan could imagine him puffing on one of his cigarettes as he spoke.

"Are you declaring an emergency?"

"No… just keeping the curious folks in the rear informed… Nine out."

Katya was relieved that the trouble was not with Matt's plane. She was concerned about herself, though; she was using too much fuel. Only two hundred miles out and her fuel gauge read between two-thirds and half. That's not good. She refigured her position and range. She lowered her altitude to fifty feet and slowed to sixty-five knots; without this headwind, she'd fall out of the sky. "That'll make it nine and a half hours… I wonder if that's a record." She was worried, extremely worried.

"What's the problem, Seven?" Brevan already knew and he was saddened by the forced move.

"It's the only way, Brevan." She looked over to him.

Matt's throat went dry when he heard the message coming over the radio. "Brevan… what's the matter?" The radio was silent. "One to Brevan… come in." Matt's voice had terror written all over it.

"Brevan to One… Seven has to proceed at a lower speed. This headwind is sucking her fuel like a sponge."

"God… I knew it… Son of a bitch!" He flexed his hand

around the stick like a stranglehold. "Brevan, are you with her?" His accelerated heartbeat left him a little lightheaded.

"We're a team all the way." Brevan tilted his wings at her.

Katya looked up at Brevan and the Kingfisher and gave a thumb up. "Thanks, Brevan."

"You stay with her... Brevan, did you hear me?"

"He won't leave her, lad." Drum's words brought some comfort to him.

"Shut up now, Matt... I've got figuring to do." Katya turned off her radio.

The hours passed slowly but in the fifth hour, the leaders caught a glimpse of a cloud formation, usually seen above landmasses. Most of their fuel gauges were reading close to empty, so they hoped this was it. Then the radios sang with the words, "Rocky to Nine ball... repeat... Rocky to Nine ball. We have you seventy-five miles out. Leader, correct course to 240 zero degrees. Will re-contact at the five-mile marker." The four leaders accelerated towards the cloud cover. Matt took the lead on the new heading, with Geno right on his tail. They both looked back to find the Corsair has sputtered or flooded out or worse, ran out of fuel. But then the Corsair kicked into gear and came on hard. The remaining minutes were tense. After what seemed only a few seconds, the radio sounded again. "Leaders, maintain your positions and enter Delta pattern."

Matt had won, but was in a hurry to get on the ground. Katya had not turned her radio back on and Matt was going mad not being able to talk to her. He had tried many times but with no success. He requested to be the first to land and it was granted. The minute he was down, he demanded to be refueled so he could go back for Kat. His request was denied, so he waited at the runway with Number Two.

All but the Macchi and the I-16 were in and on the ground. The pilots were celebrating finishing this long leg at a makeshift bar that had been set up for them. The no drinking rule had been lifted for an hour or two. Matt continued to try to contact Kat but with no success. Brevan kept him and Number Two posted on their progress. Matt had been on the ground now for an hour and a half and was going insane. "We've got one of them. He's out about sixty miles and off course about twenty degrees." The radar crew was happy with the find.

Number Two and Matt knew it was not Kat. It must be the Macchi limping in.

"Correct his course and bring him in," ordered Number Two to the radar crew.

The news brought the other pilots out to see the landing. They cheered and hollered when they saw the smoking Macchi approaching the field. In the midst of their reverie, they heard the engine die. As they watched the smoking ceased, and all they could see or hear were the wind and the sky. They held their breath and some hoped for the best.

"I think it would be fitting if he got just to the edge of the field before he crashed into a ball of flames." Rudy didn't look right or left as he spoke the words but he prepared himself for combat.

Dumitrn pretended he didn't hear the Jew but all knew that wasn't so. He glanced over to Geno, who was drinking a beer, and just shrugged. He returned his attention to Werner's plane. The crosswinds were bad and made the plane buffet to and fro. Werner, being the pilot that he was, just made the strip and fishtailed to a stop halfway down the field. Dumitrn and some of the other pilots rushed to congratulate him on a fine landing. They fought their way through the mechanics that were eager to get to the problems with this aircraft.

Matt and Rudy stayed at the radar shack, Matt out of concern for Kat, Rudy for his own reasons. "Any sign yet?" asked Matt as he glanced at his watch.

"I'm sorry," replied the radar technician.

Matt turned to Number Two. "Contact Brevan... I need to know something. It's been over eight hours now."

Two pointed to the radioman and nodded.

"Brevan here." The crackle of the radio seemed haunting.

"What's your status?" asked Number Two.

"Nearly out of fuel myself. I think we're about eighty or ninety miles out. I don't know how she's standing up to this. She still has her radio off but she waves every once in a while. That planes got to be on nothing but fumes."

"I got 'em! I got 'em! Come right to 239er, you're only fifty miles out." The radar tech looked down at the two men standing on the runway. "They must be flying so low we couldn't pick them up."

Two looked through his binoculars and spotted them on the horizon. "They're right there!" He pointed to show Matt the spot.

"Come on, baby… come on, baby. Just a little further, a little more, get some height. If it conks out on you at that height, you won't make it. Tell Brevan to get more altitude, he needs more altitude!"

"Rocky to Nine ball, we suggest more altitude."

"Roger that."

Matt grabbed the binoculars and watched the Kingfisher start to climb. "Follow him, baby… come on, follow him up." She wasn't climbing with the Kingfisher. "Goddamn it. Turn on your goddamn radio, you mule."

"*Boobblia*, are you there?"

Matt tore the radio from the operator's hand. "Yes, baby, I'm here."

"I love you… you're my sweet *boobblia*."

"Shut the fuck up and climb. Get that goddamn plane's ass in the air. Climb with Brevan, you'll need every inch. Do you hear me? Go! Go! Go!" Her plane climbed ever so slightly.

Brevan was in front of her and higher when his engine stalled and quit. His float seemed to give him a little extra lift and he barely made the field. Kat was still a mile out but her engine was still pulling, but she was still too low. All of a sudden she powered up, full throttle.

"No… no… what are you doing? Damn!" He wanted to turn away. Just the thought of her crashing brought narrowness to his eyes and a quiver to his jaw.

"Smartest dame I've ever seen." Number Two looked to the

end of the runway as Kat's wheels touched down, with her engine still running.

All, including Werner and his gang, were there to praise Katya's flying. Geno handed her a beer as she climbed out of the cockpit. She took a drink, then looked for Matt. He had bit his lower lip, trying to hold back his emotions. The cheers and the howling muffled Matt's words to her but she understood and kissed him deeply, and for them it seemed to last forever.

Brevan walked up to Number Two. "That was a close one, much too close. Do you think we should shorten the legs a little?"

Number Two looked to the two kissing, then back to Brevan. "Then what do you say to Katya; we only push the limit for you? I don't think so. We'll leave it like it is."

"I got to go take a piss, see you later for a beer, okay?" Brevan waddled over to one of the barracks.

Two waited for the crowd to thin before approaching the couple. They all wanted to know how she did it, in case they got the unlucky pick, but she was not telling. Two held a piece of paper in his hand as he made eye contact with Kat. She pushed Matt off and ran straight for him.

"Yes, Two… you have something for me. Can I have it? Is it the license? Can I have it now… please, pretty please?"

"How could you run over here after all that time in the plane?" He shook his head in amazement. "Of course you can have it." He handed her the document of marriage.

Kat read the document. "By the authority of the US territory known as Wake Island, this license of marriage is binding and lawful, signed this day. Look, *boobblia*, we got it! Thank you, sir."

"All we have to do now is get back to the ship. And if you get saddled with that Polikarpov again, we're staying and growing old together right here."

CHAPTER THIRTEEN

A KNOCK CAME AT THE door. The admiral awakened and turned on the lamp next to his bunk. As he pulled the covers off him he glanced over to the clock and became annoyed. "Yes… come in," he said in a staunch voice.

The lieutenant looked a bit leery about awakening the admiral. "Sorry to disrupt you, sir, but you did want to be kept informed about the approaching storm."

"Yes, is there a problem?"

"I think there might be, sir." The lieutenant handed him a report.

"Tell the commander I'll be right there."

"Yes, sir." The officer turned and quickly left.

The admiral read the message. "Piss." He stood and started to dress.

The admiral entered the command center and approached the weather team. "What's it looking like, Commander?"

"It doesn't look good, sir." He handed him some radio dispatches from Saipan and some other islands in the Marianas. "Looks like we've got about ten hours, then all hell's going to break loose. Twenty-foot waves, forty to fifty mph winds with torrential rains. An early monsoon, if you ask me."

"Okay, what are our options?" The admiral started examining the charts with the commander.

"It's 03:30 now. If we can steam towards Wake and shorten the leg, and if they can get off the ground by 05:00, I think they can make it back to the ship. You can decide what else to do then." The commander took out a compass and started figuring and plotting the new positions.

"Okay, do it. Figure the new heading and position and then relay it to Number Two as soon as you can." The commander started his pencil moving, so the admiral walked out of the command center and onto the bridge, where the captain was sitting, sipping coffee. "We got a problem, Rupert."

"I know. I've taken the liberty and turned us towards Wake. I can knock off about two hundred miles for your flyers. But what are you going to do with them once you get them? I saw their landing prowess in the first ten days. Some barely made it, even on a perfect deck. I hope you know what you're doing."

"So, do I, Rupert… so do I."

"Sir, a message from the carrier." From his demeanor, you could tell that the radioman had read the message.

Number Two was busy with the mechanics trying to get the Macchi repaired. He took the paper but before he read the message he asked the chief, "How much longer?"

"About an hour," the chief replied, wiping his hands of excess grease.

Number Two started reading the words from the admiral. "Goddamn it… that's too damn close." He looked at his watch and then to the radioman. "Tell all the crews to prepare for takeoff in an hour and a half. The cooks should be up by now; tell them to throw something quick together, there's no time for a big meal. Get Brevan to wake up the pilots and get them to the main hall as soon as possible. Tell them I'll explain there, now hurry!" He just shook his head as he looked back at the chief.

The lights to the barracks came on, blinding everyone. "What the hell is this… it's only four!" Rudy covered his head with a blanket.

Brevan continued to hassle the pilots into getting up. "There's trouble and we need to start early, so get your asses up."

"We're not starting at noon, like before? This isn't right; a man needs his sleep." Drum was up late with a bottle of Jamison he'd smuggled from the bar.

"You'll get left behind if you don't make the time." He didn't make the rhyme on purpose but it did sound good. "Get your asses in the main hall in ten minutes."

"I wonder what's up." Kat looked over to Matt as she put on her shoes.

"Beats me." He and Kat had gone to bed early. She needed the rest after the day's attempt to stay in the air, so they weren't that bad off; not like some of the guys. "You ready?"

"Sure, let's go," Kat replied.

The two of them walked through the darkened pathways to the main hall. The rest of the base was quiet and dark. The stars shone brightly and the night was clear and crisp. The others follow behind, and just before they entered the hall they heard engines starting—their engines.

Once in the hall, they found army mess personnel pouring coffee and placing donuts and sweet rolls on the tables. Brevan was standing in the front of the hall talking to the chief about something. When he noticed the group of pilots falling in, he stopped his conversation with the chief. "Please be seated and help yourselves to coffee and goodies there on the tables."

Katya perceived something wrong with Number Two but couldn't put her finger on it. She shrugged it off and began sipping on a cup of coffee. She looked over to Matt and Mel as they gulped down their coffee. The room should have been noisy and bustling with questions of why and why nots, but instead it was quite somber.

Two took a glass cup and banged it on the table. "May I have your attention please?" He waited for the last word to be spoken. "I have a message from the carrier... a storm is coming our way and it's a big one. We have to move everything up to be able to reach the carrier before it hits. Most of you don't know what a South Pacific gale can be like. I can tell you... you don't want to be in it... ever. I've seen it tear the skin off the best aircraft made... believe me, the winds and rains can get that strong. It looks like the estimates are about eight hours from now, so if we get our asses in gear and get going, you should be onboard the carrier before it hits." The weather crew brought in the charts. "New headings have been figured as we speak, with the carrier steaming closer to you. This will make the leg shorter by about two hundred miles, so get there as soon as you can, but still watch your fuel. One other thing; you might want to knock off the dogfighting today and just get your ass to the ship."

One of the crewmen brought him the bag with the numbers in it. "Okay, let's get this out of the way. Line up like before, and after finishing your coffee and eats, figure out everything. By then you'll be able to check out your planes and get ready for takeoff." He stuck his hand in the bag and pulled out several slips. "Matt, here's yours, Geno, yours, Sake, here." He reached in for the last of them. "Dumitrn, this one's yours. Mel, it looks like number eight. Werner, you're the big winner today." The rest all smiled as they received their assigned aircraft, especially Katya. The worst seemed to be behind her now for she drew the Hellcat, her favorite.

She raised her eyebrows to Matt. "Looks like you'll be watching my six today." A convincing smirk showed her confidence. "And don't give me any of that worried crap. If any of these assholes try to pull some funny stuff with me, I'll blow them out of the skies, simple as that."

"Did I say a word? We all know you're a killer from way back… who would draw on you? You're the fastest gun in the west." His attempt to ease the moment was successful.

She smiled at his turned and enlightened face. "Just make sure you get there; no excuses for being late to my wedding."

His face became sober. "Enough fooling around. Fly straight and fast, okay?"

"Let's go." They stood together and left to inspect their planes.

The darkness filled the sky as they lined up in order. The lights from the field flickered along with the stars. The flashes from the exhausts lit up their fuselages and reflected off the propellers. The noise from the aircraft awakened the rest of the base and small lights were being turned on everywhere.

The first plane took off and then disappeared into the night.

The others followed in their order. Two looked at his watch, then turned to a radioman. "Signal the carrier that they're off at 05:30."

The chief walked up to Two. "Well, they're off. I wish them luck. I'm having my guys fall out for some sleep. Is that okay, sir?"

"No problem. By the way, good job, Chief." Two walked to his quarters to turn in. It'd been a good night's work and he rated the sleep. As he reached for the doorknob, the sun was making itself known with small rays of light shooting from the horizon and attacking the darkness. He smiled and stepped in, stretching and yawning.

Dumitrn was happy with his luck. Like Katya in the first leg, he had drawn the I-16 but similar to hers, this leg would also be short, and no problem with the fuel. As he cruised at about one hundred twenty knots, he looked out to a perfect blue morning with the sun shining brightly behind him. He glanced at the instrument panel, bright in the sun's rays. He didn't care too much for this aircraft. He remembered it from the war. It was somewhere near Stalingrad in the morning hours (it seemed to always be in the morning hours). His squadron ran across some Yaks and one I-16. His comrades took on the Yaks and he bore down on the Polikarpov. His opponent flew very well. He was never in his sights long enough to flame him; one of the few he had to let go. It had a yellow Star of David on its fuselage, almost daring the German pilots into combat. *God, I hate Jews. They're dirty, smelly creatures. The Fuerhor was right; they should be eliminated from the earth. For him to even be sitting in a plane that a Jew might have flown brought up thoughts of vomit and bile.*

His thoughts suddenly drifted back to a younger day. It was in the early thirties and he was just a boy of thirteen or fourteen. He was an honored member of the Hitler Youth Corps. He would roam the streets of Berlin with his fellow members looking for and keeping track of suspicious folks. They would report all unusual movements of listed peoples to the police, then when ordered by the police or the Party, they took part in the destruction of or damage to businesses owned by Jews. He remembered that his father did not approve of such things, though he seldom discussed the matter openly. His mother and father had Jew friends in the early years and this embarrassed him. His friends used to question him about his mother and father's dealings with them. His schooling contradicted his father's teachings. All were not equal; the German was the superior race, and all others should be subservient to the Nazi way of life.

He remembered the day he led the Gestapo to his house and opened the door for them. He waited outside on the street as they went inside and dragged his parents out. He straightened his armband as his friends looked on. They snapped to attention as the Gestapo officer came through the door. He was filled with pride as the officer looked down at him and spoke. "You'll go far as a Nazi, young man. Good job." He remembered feeling nothing for them as they screamed and struggled to get free. Enemies of the state, he thought, as his mother pulled at his arm, her tears falling on his swastika emblem. The crowd threw vegetables and fruit at them as they were pushed into a truck and hauled away. He participated in the ransacking of his own home. The mob threw all his parents' belongings out into the streets, where they fought over the pickings.

Rudy lurked about ten thousand feet. He was waiting for the sun and the Polikarpov. He had waited for this match-up to take out his revenge. He slowed the Corsair to a mere crawl and looked all the time for that flash of the I-16 far below. He knew that soon Dumitrn would be dead last, with no one to help him.

He started to imagine how the attack would be. First, he'd dive on the unsuspecting Nazi. The initial burst would do little damage to the plane but it would blow out both kneecaps of Dumitrn. His pain would be excruciating and he'd bleed badly. On the second pass, he'd take out the plane's rudder and most of the stabilizer. The Nazi would cry for help but there would be no help coming. The last pass would be done slowly; Rudy would come alongside and gaze at Dumitrn dying. He'd turn on the radio. "Die, you baby killing asshole… then go straight to hell!"

A flicker from below brought Rudy back to reality. He smiled as he pushed the throttle forward and the nose down. The first burst took out the I-16's right aileron and continued on to the cockpit. He saw blood spatter onto the windshield as he completed the pass.

215

He banked, then climbed for another pass. He got on the Nazi's six and prepared for another blast but held up. Something was wrong; he should be evading or at least trying to get into position to fire. The radio was dead, not a peep; there were no cries for help and no pleading for his life. The Polikarpov was just cruising at its normal speed; straight, and right on its heading. This was not the way it was supposed to be. He wanted him screaming in agony as he watched himself plummet into the open sea.

He cautiously approached Dumitrn's plane and as he pulled up even with Dumitrn, he saw him sitting behind the stick like he was asleep. The blood that surrounded the canopy was the sign that he was dead and the plane was flying itself. Rudy became enraged. "You fucking bastard… you went out too easily!" He slowed to get back on his six, then put the Polikarpov in his sights and blasted it into a ball of flames. He watched as the pieces fell into the waves below, then calmly turned back to the heading and throttled up to catch the rest of the pack. "One baby killer down, two to go."

Due to the navigational inadequacies in his flying, Drum was forced to follow behind Werner in the Hurricane. Katya was keeping Werner in front of her, just in case. Matt was flying her wing, a little high and to the right. They were out about two and a half hours when Brevan called for a radio check.

"One is here, old man," Drum sang out.

Mel was next, then Werner growled a reply.

"I'm getting hungry for some pizza," joked the comedic Italian.

"Sounds good to me, whatever it is!" shouted Kat as her stomach growled.

"Six here," was all Rudy said. The air went dead with static.

"Seven, come in… repeat… Seven, come in." Nothing but static was heard. "Has anybody got Dumitrn in their sights?"

"He's not up here with the leaders," radioed Katya.

"I'm in the middle of the pack with the Messerschmitt, and only the Macchi is in view. What plane is Seven?" Mel's voice sounded concerned.

"It's the I-16. His radio might be out, so keep an ear out for him. I'll keep my eyes open for him… out."

Rudy smiled as he caught up to the Messerschmitt and the Macchi. He started singing as he blew by them both, figuring he might as well take out the Italian if he could catch him.

Brevan had a feeling that something was up. He scanned the horizon, then down at the waves. He thought, those waves would swallow up any wreckage pretty fast, if there was any wreckage.

"Matt, do you see that in front of us?" Kat's voice suggested concern.

"Looks pretty damn black to me." The plane buffeted a little.

"Look at those waves down there. They look to be as large as a house; and those whitecaps—that means wind and lots of it." Drum had apparently seen this kind of sea before.

"How much further do you think?" Kat's concern had turned into fearfulness.

"I think at least another hour or so." Matt's voice wasn't sounding good either. "Brevan, come in."

"Brevan here… what's the problem?"

"Looks like a goddamn hurricane to me. I think you better kick that Kingfisher in the ass and get up here real soon or you're not going to make it."

"What about Number Seven? I still haven't seen him."

"Quit looking… you're not going to find him, he's sucking sea water." Rudy's revelation made it clear to everyone that Dumitrn was no longer in the race.

"Why didn't you tell me earlier, asshole?" The anger in Brevan's was apparent.

Rudy keyed his radio. "Because this pizza-eating fascist in front of me is about to join his Nazi brother in the deep six."

Geno never bothered to look behind him; he throttled up and banked to the right, barely missing Matt in the Yak. Geno used him as interference, and the Corsair didn't make the turn. He climbed, then took an 80-degree and fell right behind Rudy.

"Stop it, you fools… are you both blind? Can't you see that mass of weather in front of us?" Werner was screaming over the radio.

"All right… if the Jew agrees." Geno didn't really want to go up against the Corsair. If he didn't take him out the first pass, he would be in trouble.

"Another day, fascist." Rudy was staring at the biggest and the blackest clouds he had ever seen. Lightning was striking off in the distance and his ship started buffeting from the turbulence.

"How are we going to see the carrier in all that bloody shit?" Drum's voice had more than just a little concern to it.

"Brevan, we've hit the outer ridge of the storm and it's real hell. Push that throttle all the way and get your ass up here. Try calling the carrier and tell them there won't be any Delta pattern today. I think we should climb to five thousand feet so the radar can pick us up sooner, agreed?" Matt didn't wait for any replies, he pulled his stick backwards.

"I'm with you."

"Me too."

"Hell yeah," came over the radio.

The headwind had slowed the leaders so the others had caught up. They climbed as a group and formed a squadron-like formation, with Werner in the lead. The wind became furious and the turbulence dropped some aircraft twenty or thirty feet at a time. What had been day just moments before quickly became night from the dankness of the clouds. The clouds' black rain battered the planes like hammers on an anvil and the lightning scared the pilots. The wrath of God was upon them and they thought of hell. Small prayers filled the cockpits of every plane. "Gray lady to Nine ball… repeat… Gray lady to Nine ball, please come in."

Werner replied eagerly, "Leader to Gray lady… come in."

"Leader, turn to 216 degrees. All planes try to maintain one-mile distance for straight-in landings."

"Roger." The thought of being the first to land made Werner smile. He knew how to command and he did so. "All pilots, take note of your position, circle to maintain a mile, then come straight in on heading two one six. Listen up; when I go in, I'll relay information back on the conditions of the deck."

The carriers' radio crackled. "Leader, start your approach now… there will be no wave-off."

After about five minutes, Werner caught sight of the carrier and breathed a sigh of relief. Maybe a little too soon with that sigh, for he saw the deck rocking and pitching like a teeter-totter and the rain flooding the deck. He watched the crosswinds blow the rain 90 degrees to port and that was not good. He relayed back to the others, "Watch the crosswinds, it's to port. It feels like fifty mph winds, so come in heavy, then stall short. The decks are flooded, so your brakes are going to be almost useless. Well, here I go."

There was no more radio chatter for the longest time. The pilots were wondering if Werner made it. They couldn't wait any longer. The storm was battering them badly so Katya started her approach. The ship looked to her like it was on the back of a bucking bronco. She spotted the LSO; she could tell he was having trouble just standing but he did his best. It was pure luck that prevented her plane from turning over and dropping into the sea, but she made it. She had no time to radio Matt as the crews tossed her out of the cockpit and cleared the deck for another landing. She stood with Werner to watch the others land. The rain beat on her face and she looked up at him. "I never thought I'd be thanking you for anything, but thanks for the information." Her wet hair ran down her neck and onto her shoulders.

Suddenly, out of the downpour came Drum. The crosswinds caught the Zero and pulled it right to the edge of the deck, where it stopped just short. Drum was slammed into the side of the cockpit and was injured. He made it out and limped to the island and the waiting arms of Nurse Rose, holding a blanket. "I banged my knee." He was taken below to sickbay.

"I wonder who is next?" Werner asked without looking at her.

The Yak came in too fast and barely caught one of the last cables. The plane hit the barrier anyway and was put nose down in a hurry. The flight crew rushed to right the plane and tried to get the pilot out but he was unconscious. Kat started to move in the direction of Matt's plane but was held back by Werner. "You'll just be in the way, little one." The crews finally got him out and down the ladders to sickbay, with Kat in hot pursuit.

All but Rudy were onboard, a little bruised and battered from the storm, but they made it. The earlier trouble Rudy had with the landing of the Corsair made him leery of the runway. He had picked to be last in case there was trouble. He didn't want to jeopardize anyone else's life with a mistake of his own. His hands were shaky on the stick and his lips were dry. The winds were still tossing him from side to side like a child's rag doll. The ship was just moving too much, he thought. He looked to his fuel gauges for hope that he could maintain flight for a while longer, but no chance. It was a must go now, so he lowered his nose, put on full flaps, and lowered the landing gear. The wind tore at the gear as it lowered and made handling even more difficult.

He saw the LSO but like before, he figured to land this plane on his own. Just before he touched down a huge crosswind picked his right wing up and bounced the plane like a basketball on the deck, then threw the plane completely over and off the side of the ship. He never even made it to the cables. The flight crews could only watch as the Corsair was eaten up by the waves below and along with it, Rudy. The news passed through the ship quickly. Only Werner and Geno were pleased. Geno was more relieved than happy. Werner looked at it as one less competitor to deal with and one step closer to the money—and of course, it was only a Jew.

The sickbay was full with small injuries. They all looked like a bunch of drowned rats with a cut here and a bruise there. The whole ship had been shaken up from the storm. Matt and Drum were the most seriously hurt. There was a very large bump on Matt's forehead. Kat and Yokes looked on as Nurse Rose gave him a sedative so he could sleep.

Yokes started to get Matt out of his wet clothes. "I just get out and you check in." He handed Katya and Matt each a towel. Katya started drying her hair. Matt couldn't care less if he was wet, his head hurt too badly.

"This bed's pretty comfortable and I should know. It had a good-looking guy in it not long ago; maybe some of his good looks will rub off on you." Yokes was trying his hand at humor.

"Seems a little lumpy to me." Matt tried to smile but his head started pounding.

"Are you all right, Katya?" came a voice from the passageway.

Katya turned to see Viktor's grin as he emerged.

"Is my girl taking good care of you?" He walked over to Rose and gave her a kiss.

"Not now, I'm on duty." Nurse Rose pretended to be annoyed as she pushed his hands from her hips.

Katya gave him that motherly look, as usual. "I'm fine, just a little wet and tired, and very hungry." Kat was wiping the rain from Matt's chest, then softly stroked the lump on his head. "If you don't watch out, you're going to end up looking like the big guy here, and I dread what the wedding pictures will look like." She looked up at Yokes and noticed an improvement in his eye. "That eye's looking better today. I was afraid it might be permanent. I'm glad it hasn't ruined that big baby face of yours." She returned his grin. "We wouldn't want Georgina to have to look at that forever. And what would the kids say if they saw Santa Claus with a shiner like that? You'd be found out really quick." Everyone in the sickbay but Drum started to laugh.

Yokes stuck out his big bear claw of a hand. "Don't worry about me, the doc's given me roaming orders. No more sickbay." The roll of the ship took everyone by surprise as it suddenly pitched, then leaned sharply to one side. Everyone grabbed hold of something to steady themselves. The sounds coming from the hull put fear into each soul, no matter how much sea duty they'd had.

"This is not good." Viktor started sweating a little with each movement of the ship. "Why didn't the ship buck like this before?" Viktor had not been topside since the storm hit and didn't quite comprehend the severity of Mother Nature's anger.

"I've been in worse than this," Nurse Rose said. "You're just lucky you're on a carrier. The last time I rode one of these out, I was on a hospital ship a third the size of this one." She gazed at the light-ashen skin of Viktor, whose eyes were rolling around in the back of his head and she chuckled. "On that ship, you either looked like you were in a title fight or were as green as Viktor here."

He quickly looked around the room for somewhere to deposit his stomach. He tried to hold back that gush that he knew was eventually going to come. His mouth and throat filled with the first eruption. The group saw his predicament and pointed to the rear of the sickbay. He hurried as best he could but the ship wouldn't cooperate. As he moved towards the rear, the bulkheads and support beams seemed to block his every move to achieve relief. Vomit started to drip over his lower lip as he spotted the stall and entered and cradled the bowl. The vile music he was making made all that heard it a little queasy. They looked at each other, not wanting to show their amusement in case the same fate might strike them. Inside, however, they were totally enjoying Viktor's unique way of imitating the mating call of the sea lion.

"Nurse, over here." The doctor was examining Drum's knee.

Nurse Rose felt for Viktor but she composed herself and hurried to aid the doctor. She first helped him remove Drum's wet pants; there was no time for modesty as they almost ripped the trousers from his body. The ship was still buffeting badly, which made the doctor's job just that much more difficult. Katya and the two guys looked on as Drum's knee became exposed. It had only been an hour or so since it happened, but the knee had already turned black and blue and was badly swollen. The doctor touched it and found that it was very tender also. "I think you've cracked your kneecap." The doctor was slammed backwards by another impact from outside. Nurse Rose held Drum on the bed and reached across him for the doctor. With her help, he returned to the bedside to complete his examination. "The knee will have to be drained... there's too much fluid."

"It's okay, Doc... it's just a banged-up knee, and haven't I had worse bruises than that when I was a lad back home in Galway." He looked over to Nurse Rose. "You don't want the lassies to think I'm a *sissy boy*, do you?"

"I've got no time to argue with you. Just lay there while I get my instruments."

"You're not takin' me ass out of the race now." He frowned at the doctor defiantly.

"Don't be give-in' me any of your bloody crap, you Irish hooligan. I'll take me shillelagh and lather you good, I will."

Drum just sat there in shock. "What be happen-in' to your brogue, Doc?"

The doctor's harsh glare turned into a smile. "I be leave-in' it back in Ballyvaughn twenty years ago, along with me foolishness about lassies and sissy boys." His smile turned into a look of scorn once more. "It's ashamed you should be. Now sit there and shut your gob and let me do me cut-in'. By the way... you be want-in' a large or a small scar?"

Kat was amused with the Irishmen's stratagems. She was surprised that the doctor could hold his own with Drum, but being an Irishman himself made it easier. She looked down at Matt and found he was already half-asleep. She raised his hand to her lips and kissed it gently. "I'll see you tomorrow, my almost groom. Sleep well." She tightened the straps that held him in the bed, looked once more over to Drum, and winked. "You'll be just fine, take it easy." She turned around to Yokes. "Let's see if there's any pizza onboard. I'd like to try some of that. If there's going to be no spice in the bedroom tonight... might as well eat some."

"Have you ever tried pizza?" Yokes had never tried it but he saw it being made once in Little Rock. He wasn't too sure about any food that was thrown in the air just before you eat it. Fried chicken was more his style, especially the way Georgina fixed it.

"It's Italian, isn't it? At least Lucchini eats it... he said so when we were flying. Let's go find him and have him make us some." The two left Matt snoring heavily and proceeded to the galley.

"Have you got that report ready for me to go over?" One was eager to send Number Two the report of what happened today. He took the papers from the lieutenant and read the reports quickly. "Have these sent on to Two immediately. Have him proceed to Tarawa, and if all is right with the weather, we'll pick up the race there. That will keep us on schedule. We'll give credit to the pilots for the two legs we have to cancel."

"Sir, how do I list Dumitrn Encionin's death for the insurance company?"

"Why complicate things? List both Gershwin and Encionin's death as accidental. Why should their loved ones suffer because they were assholes? Pay the claims." He looked to the captain "South by southwest at your good time, Captain, at slow speed." He handed the captain the coordinates.

"The weather guys tell me we'll have two days of bad weather, then we can resume." He smiled at the captain. "Would you like a cup of coffee?"

The ward pantry was empty when Kat and Yokes entered. They noticed the pots and pans were all clanking around in the galley and making the weirdest music in the background, like chimpanzees beating on garbage cans. They walked over to the huge coffee pot and started pouring themselves a cup. "Doesn't look like it's mealtime around here." Katya took a sip of her coffee, then handed it to Yokes. "You go get us a seat and I'll scrounge up something to eat."

Yokes nodded his head, then headed for the wardroom. He put the coffees down, then saw a radio on one of the cabinets. He walked up to it and started dialing it in on a station.

"This is the number one news and music station of Honolulu, KJVE, and we'll be right back with the best jive, swing, and of course, the best in big band music in just a minute. But now the news and weather." The station was coming in clearly, so he turned it up to catch the weather report. Kat entered the room with a tray of goodies; a variety of meats and cheeses and breads were piled up high. "Over here, by the radio. I've got the news from Honolulu. The weather is coming up. Maybe they'll tell us how long this storm's going to last."

"When's the last time you remember the weathermen getting anything right?" She set the tray down and began layering the meats and cheeses on some rye.

Dots and dashes filled the background as the newscaster spoke. "Flash… the top story of the hour. A mainlander was killed last night outside a bar in downtown Honolulu. Witnesses say the man, identified as Michael McGuire, was brutally beaten in an altercation over the rights of Samoans to drink in the same bar as whites. The chief of police reports that he hasn't had an incident of racial hatred since the end of the war. He is putting out orders to all his people to keep a sharp eye out for any more such incidents on the islands. There are no suspects in the case. Now to weather."

"That is the asshole that was on the ship!" Katya looked over to see Yokes grinning evilly.

"Couldn't happen to a better asshole," he whispered.

She saw on his face the delight he was having over the news of Mike's death. It didn't fit well on such a gentle giant's kisser. As quickly as it came, the look faded and the real big guy was back. "Looks like two more days of bad weather. I wonder how they'll handle the race."

"I don't know, but two more goddamn days of waiting to get married will drive me mad. You know that with this weather and the small crew we have, they won't take the time off to marry me. They're going to make me wait. I just know it." She took a huge bite of her open-faced sandwich and muffled cuss words as she chewed.

"Who taught you how to make a sandwich? Here, give it to me. I'm surprised you can even swallow this dry, heavy mass of flesh and grain. Don't you know anything but rye? I'll be back in a minute." Yokes stood and headed for the galley.

"Don't take my food, you big bully. I'm starving to death."

"You're choking to death, you mean. Just wait a minute, I'll be right back."

Glad that something else had come up to take his mind off of the beating, she watched as he returned with a jar of mayonnaise and mustard and the old standby, catsup, on the side. He also brought vegetables; why, she didn't know. She had never seen these foods before and wondered just what they did for a sandwich.

"Here, let me make you a sandwich." He piled on ham and then Swiss cheese, a layer of lettuce, a slice of tomato, then swiped a large amount of the mayonnaise on one side of the white bread. He then put it together and cut it in half. He threw down a handful of some kind of wafers and announced, "Voila."

Katya didn't hesitate a second. She picked up one of the halves and took a big bite. "Damn. This is the best I've ever eaten, Big Guy. You can cook for me anytime." She started devouring the rest of the sandwich, then noticed the wafers and ate one. "This is very good too, what is it?"

"It's a potato chip."

"The same thing we make vodka out of?"

"Yeah."

"Russians are stupid. To hell with vodka, I like these better," she said as she threw a handful into her mouth.

"You should get more sleep, Admiral," the bridge officer said.

The admiral looked outside the bridge to the storm still bounding away. "By the look of it, I'll have all day to catch up on my sleep."

The officer simply nodded his head as a gust of wind hurled the sea against the window. "It's supposed to last another eighteen hours, so the weather guys said."

"That means it could last all week." The admiral smiled straight ahead, not looking at him.

"Well, you do know how their predictions go. Maybe half the time they're right." The officer gazed at the admiral's reflection in the window.

He turned from the storm and asked, "What time is it?"

He looked to the ship's clock. "It's 05:30, sir."

He reached for the door. "I think I'll go below for some coffee. Want me to send some up?"

"If you don't mind, sir." The officer was surprised but pleased with the thoughtfulness of the admiral.

The ship was still pitching, but not to the degree that it was earlier. The admiral didn't have any trouble getting below decks, even at his age. On his way he passed the command center, where he saw Brevan drinking coffee.

"Good morning, sir. It's a fine, bright morning, isn't it?"

"You're not funny, Brevan."

"Yes, sir, but my ass isn't in that Kingfisher, either, which makes it a fine morning, if you know what I mean."

He smiled in agreement. "Have you posted the scores yet?"

"No, sir. I wasn't sure if we were posting them, so I was going to check with you first."

"I don't see the necessity to keep them secret anymore."

"No problem, then, I have them right here."

He handed the list to the admiral. "Have you given each of them credit for the legs missed?"

"Yes, sir. Two points apiece, like you ordered."

"Go ahead and post them in the wardroom and send a list to the sickbay, too." He looked once more at the list before handing it back to Brevan. "Geno is leading with twenty-one points. Who would have dreamed that Werner would have let him get that far? I'm glad to see Katya is second; my money's on her. Who's your favorite?"

He smiled as he took the list from him. "I like Katya too, but Mel or Matt seem the better flyers."

"But don't count out experience, Brevan. Katya was blowing Germans out of the skies three years before these guys knew what a fighter was."

"You've got a point there, Admiral, but strength and endurance are with the guys."

"You forget who was waddling like a duck after that landing on Wake Island. Number Two told me all about it."

Brevan raised his eyebrows. "You got me there. I might have to re-think my position a bit." He grinned as the admiral turned away, then gave the list to a seaman. "Have these posted both in the wardroom and the sickbay."

"How's that cute little bump today?" asked an upbeat Yokes.

"What's with you? You look like you've just won a prize from a Cracker Jack box."

"Prize... you may call it a prize, but I would call it second place after halfway. Missy is in second place behind Geno. Isn't that great news?"

"No."

The abruptness of Matt's reply made Yokes freeze in mid-step and his face went blank. "What do you mean, no?"

Matt sat up and leaned on his elbow. "I've been lying here thinking. If she gets in the lead, these guys eventually are going to take her out." He threw a pillow to the end of the bed, which Yokes took and used to support him against the rail. "The money's not that important if it means her getting hurt." He tried to convey his meaning with his eyes. "You and I can find another way. I can't keep my mind on the race if I'm worrying about Kat all the time."

"Have you talked to her?"

He didn't have time to answer. Kat came into the sickbay with a flower in her hand. "Where did you get that?" he asked sternly.

"Never mind, it's not for you, grouchy." She walked over to Drum's bed and gave him the flower, to the amazement of the two sitting with their mouths open. "This is for you… I knew you would appreciate its beauty, you being a loving man, and a caring soul." She gave Drum a kiss on the forehead and asked how he was feeling, then glanced back over her shoulder to the envious Matt. His face reddened just a bit, to her liking. "I have to go now, Drum, there are other patients I have to visit. You take care now with that knee."

She turned around and approached the big guy, who was sitting at the bottom of the bed; she didn't even look at Matt. "That eye is looking really good and the cast… is it too tight? I can talk to the doctor about putting another one on you." She caught Matt out of the corner of her eye. His complexion has reddened even more, still to her delight.

"I'm fine, Missy… just fine." His eyes wandered over to Matt, he was hoping her eyes would follow.

"Oh… Mister Drew, I didn't see you lying there. How are you this fine morning? Well, I hope." Her playful grin was saying much more than her words.

"I hope you're here to comfort the wounded." She nodded.

"I am; all that are truly afflicted, of course, like this poor soul." She rubbed the arm of Yokes as she stared at Matt.

"What about my injuries?"

"You mean that little scratch on your head? Really… you're not trying to get sympathy for that little knock on the head, are you? I've seen children with bigger bumps playing soccer in their front yards. Aren't you being a little baby now?"

"I think it's time for me to leave. Catch you guys later." Yokes wanted no part of this game.

The two of them watched as Yokes walked out the passageway. They looked back at each other. "You over that grumpy stuff? I hope so… cuz if you're not, I'm going to have to give this big wet, tongue-playing kiss to the first guy that walks by."

"Okay, okay."

She leaned over and open-mouthed him so long he had to push her away to get a breath. "Damn, woman, don't you ever breathe?" They both started laughing. Drum was just about to say something when Nurse Rose walked over to his bed.

"The doctor wants an x-ray of that knee." She gave him a look and he just shrugged and went quietly. She pushed him in the wheelchair down the passageway.

"I'm glad he's gone. I want to talk to you, Kat."

"About what? I know, the wedding—" She started to say more but he interrupted.

"It's not the wedding, it's the race."

"What about the race? Did you hear… I'm in second place!" Her face was glowing with accomplishment.

He peered into her eyes and waited for her to calm down. "I want you to pull out of the race."

Her jaw dropped, as well as her spirits. "Do what?"

"Quit."

"You quit." Her confusion turned to anger. "If you need someone to quit the race, you do it. Have you forgotten I'm the one in second place?"

"You don't understand."

"No… you don't understand. Just because you're such a goddamn worrywart you can't fly, don't hang it on me."

"Now I'm an asshole for worrying about the woman I love."

229

"No… you're not. You're an asshole for asking me to quit. I never quit anything, especially flying."

He lowered his head and said nothing.

His silence tore at her. She was saddened by what she was about to say. "I think we'd better postpone the wedding till the race is over." She waited for a response. She prayed for him to speak, to tell her he loved her and everything was all right, but nothing. "I'm moving back in with Yokes. That way you can keep your mind on the race." She waited once again for him to look at her but he didn't. Her heart grew heavy with the thought of losing him, but what else could she do? She pulled the wedding license from her pocket and laid it on the bed, then quietly turned and left. The rest of the day she spent sitting at their special place on the flight deck in the rain. Crying was no longer an option. The wind and the rain tore at her but she didn't care. Her heartache was greater than anything Mother Nature could throw at her. She remembered when love was in this place. She looked to where she had lay and Matt had kissed and caressed her all night. That was real; she knew it was not an illusion or a dream. She prayed to all that was good that he would come to his senses.

The day after the storm was quiet. The crew and the pilots were getting antsy for some action when the news came. Tomorrow at six, the race would resume. Once more the ship came to life, getting everything ready for tomorrow. Katya and Matt avoided each other, both thinking it better for the other not to see or speak. Yokes was urged from both sides to watch out for the other, which he was happy to comply with. Breakfast with Matt, lunch with Katya, then back to Matt for dinner, then half the night talking about nothing but Matt with Katya. Yokes was glad the race was back on; at least the two could talk over the radio.

CHAPTER FOURTEEN

"PILOTS... TO YOUR PLANES." THE orders echoed over the flight deck and the flight crews eagerly awaited their pilots. Werner, in the Messerschmitt, was first in line for takeoff. He throttled up for takeoff and then left the deck trouble-free.

Katya took her position in the Sea-fire. As she revved up, she thought back to the last landing and hoped for good weather the rest of the race. The flight captain lowered his flag and the Sea-fire cleared the end of the deck.

Drum rolled the Macchi to a stop and started his takeoff sequences with little or no problem. He entered the skies quickly, along with the rest of the group. The flight crews cheered as the last plane climbed into the sky. Brevan waited a few minutes for his takeoff.

Sake took over the lead fairly soon. He was glad that most of the pilots preferred the Zero, there was great honor in that. He looked back at the rest of the group and started pulling away because of the range and speed of the Zero. He knew it was not the great power of the Zero that made it preferred over the other planes but its agility and its great range, something he was grateful for in the war. Knowing he could fight long periods of time and still have the fuel to get back to base or the carrier made him feel secure. There were a couple of drawbacks in the design, though. The builders put in agility and maneuverability but left out armament and a sealed fuel tank. This left the pilots vulnerable to bullets coming through the cockpit and fuel tanks. Those fears still stayed with him.

As he stretched his lead, he wandered back to the last dozen days. He had been glad to stay in the background and keep to himself. That way, he didn't get all tied up in the emotions of the race. Look at the situation with the Russian and the American; he wouldn't want to be in that American's position for anything.

A large cloud appeared in the distance and reminded him of home and the last time he saw it in one piece. There were hundreds of people in the streets, and the washerwomen were hanging out their laundry to dry. The fish-peddlers were singing their songs to entice a patron. The children played with yo-yos and pick up sticks. He could smell his wife and mother's cooking, and heard his grandfather telling stories to his father and his friends as they sipped sake.

The cloud that he watched grew larger and as it did, it brought with it a twinge of anger and pain. He had to look away from it. The mushroom shape brought tears to his eyes and memories of shame to his heart. As he accelerated past the cloud, he regained himself, only to remember the punishment he had to apply to Masayuki. One seemed to enjoy the execution. Why, he didn't know, but it still left a bad taste in his mouth. He thought, *Please, Buddha, help me cast away this shame, this dishonor. I will repent… I do repent.*

"Anyone up here got a headache powder?" Drum was joking with the others, but he did wish he had something for his knee.

"I'll take one too," chimed in Matt. A rare chatter on the radio; he usually was a serious flyer.

"Woo… the Sky god speaks." Mel's laughter was heard in each plane.

"All right, you guys, I've got a small headache, there's nothing wrong with that. All gods have a bad day now and then." He chuckled to himself.

"Some have more than one." Katya's retort was stern and went unanswered. She didn't know why she said it; her hurt was turning into anger, she thought. She was angry that Matt hadn't tried to make up, even though she had avoided him at all costs. He could have gone through Yokes and he knew that. This was his fault, entirely his fault. *What does he think I am, a baby? I can take care of myself. I have for years. I don't need him to tell me to quit the race. I'll do whatever*—her thoughts were interrupted by the radio.

"Who's buying me a pint when we get to this Tarawa place?" The radio was dead. "Don't all you lads speak up too fast now." Drum rubbed his aching leg. The pain had moved up his leg almost to his hip; he could barely climb into the cockpit today. The cramped quarters didn't help and stiffness was setting in, so he dreamt to relieve his pain.

He needed the money from these remaining two legs to complete his goals. The seven thousand dollars was just right for the makeover of his pub back in Enniskerry. The bar and floor were still sound enough but the tables and chairs would have to be replaced, sure enough. The Dublin *squires* and the good patrons of the town would never come down to an untidy place. Dublin men were used to the finer things in life, and he would only stock the best of drink. Jamison, Patty, Bell, and of course, the dew of the Irish countryside, Guinness—and maybe some Harp for the ladies.

He remembered when his father had to throw out big Red McFeirson. Not an easy task, mind ya, and the man being as big as an ox and a temper like a drunkard denied drink. The fight... be lasting almost three days, so the people of the town tells it. The whole countryside turned out for miles around, they did, some all the way from Knockasheena. Both men battered and bruised but not an inch would either give. Father O'Malley finally put a stop to it, after he lost three shillings to me mother. A bronze plaque memorializes the place, and even now the people talk of it. Me-father, God rest his soul, and Ol' Red McFeirson in the finest use of fisticuffs in all of Irish lore, so the tale goes in Enniskerry.

Katya abruptly throttled up and made a run at Sake. She was about two miles behind but was closing fast. She hoped everybody would stay off the radio so she could surprise the Zero. The Sea-fire was clocking almost two hundred fifty knots. She climbed to ten thousand feet; maybe at this height, he wouldn't even see her till it was too late. "I'll show him who needs watching over." She looked down and caught the Zero against the blue of the water. She checked her heading and then the fuel gauge. *It's going to be close, but here goes.*

She put the plane in a dive to pick up even more speed without using excess fuel. She figured she was about two hundred miles out, and it would take the Zero more than fifty miles to catch her; then it would be too late, the radar would have them. When she reached a thousand feet she was going over three hundred knots. She came out of the sun, and Sake never saw her take the lead.

The rest of the group started to bear down on the Zero, which Sake figured, and he throttled up just enough to keep them behind him.

"Go… girl."

"Kick ass!"

"You've got him."

"What a move!"

"Wish I thought of that."

All the chatter over the radio was confusing Sake. He took a head count and found one Sea-fire missing. He turned around and throttled all the way up. The Zero was screaming as it cut through the air. The temperature started to climb; he knew he needed altitude to cool the engine down but that took time, and he still couldn't see the Sea-fire.

"Rocky to Nine ball… repeat… Rocky to Nine ball."

The radio waves were overcome with cheers and congratulations. The group could still see the Zero and they knew they were still too far out for the radar to see them. The only other option was Katya. It was her that the radar saw and they then knew she had won the leg. "You better watch out for the little one, Matthew. She can out-fly you with a blindfold on." The cheers still came from the speakers. "You forget… she's flown against the best." Werner's words were meant to incite a little anger in Matt and it worked very well.

"You just look after your own six, Kraut, and leave the good flying to me and my woman."

"I hear she's anyone's woman these days. If you can't handle her, maybe I'll give her what she needs."

"And what's that, asshole?" He knew he shouldn't have said it, he played right into his hands.

"A real man's *schoodle*."

"Nine ball, watch your language, you're on open air," came a message from the carrier.

Katya was listening to Werner and Matt and she was saddened by the lack of chivalry on Matt's part. He didn't challenge Werner to a duel or fistfight for her honor or screamed and hollered profanities; no, just dead air. She had won this part of the race but her expression was one of quiet anguish.

"Try to get your ass out of this one, Admiral." The Hellcat bore down on the Bearcat's six. They both were traveling over three hundred knots.

The admiral took the plane and banked, and then a figure eight and came right up to position on the Hellcat. "How's that?"

"Damn, Admiral... you've come a long way in three days." He throttled back down and allowed the Bearcat to come up even with him. "You planning for the next war or something?" Four's words struck a nerve.

"No... just remembering the old days when I could fly rings around you rookies."

"I'm running short of fuel. I'm heading back to the ship. Same time tomorrow?" Four's voice sounded a little tired.

"Yes, and tomorrow you take the Bearcat and I'll use the Hellcat."

"That will be a pleasure, Admiral. I'm looking forward to it. I've never flown a Bearcat before."

"See you onboard. I'm going to cruise around a bit longer, it's so beautiful up here."

"Right."

He pulled up next to a thunderhead and watched as it changed shapes. The cloud reminded him of a day far in his past, the day

235

he met Joanna. She was so lovely sitting on the lawn, reading. The building's red bricks enhanced her hair and complexion, and the green of the grass complimented her soft, white dress. She took her eyes off the pages and saw him staring at her. "Yes?" she said.

He stuttered a bit, then asked, "What book are you reading? may I ask."

"*Love in the Clouds.*"

He walked up to her and took a seat on the grass next to her. "May I see it?"

"I think it might be too racy for a young man like you." She grinned after she spoke.

"I'm a man of the world… I go to Annapolis."

"No kidding. I thought all young men walked around in naval uniforms."

His face reddened and his eyes fell to the ground.

"I'm sorry I embarrassed you. Can I make it up by offering you some tea?"

His embarrassment faded at the prospect. "It would be an honor, ma'am." He helped her to her feet and she handed the book to him to carry.

"I'm glad to find that there's still a gentleman in 1905." They started walking, her hand on his arm, to her parents' house and the tea.

"I was so young." He smiled, then lowered the nose of the plane and headed back to the carrier.

As Number Four landed on the flight deck a crewman asked, "Why does that old man fly every day he can? They look like they're dogfighting all the time they're up."

"Old navy guys have a problem giving it up, I guess."

"I'm surprised he can even see the ship, he's so old. He better give it up before he slams into something hard, real hard."

The planes entered Delta pattern and came in without incident. Drum's plane almost went to the end of the runway before it came to a stop. He didn't taxi in like the rest, but stayed motionless at the end of the tarmac. Two saw it there but ignored it to greet the newlyweds. As Katya and Matt approached him, he held out his arms to Katya for a hug. "You look beautiful as a bride, even though those flight suits leave much to the imagination." Something was wrong, he could feel it. Matt was walking with Mel, and Katya's face looked like she'd just been in a fight. She walked right by him without saying a word or even looking at him. He felt stupid standing there with his arms open and everyone walking by. "What the hell is going on?" he asked Matt.

"It didn't happen," said Mel as he shrugged.

Matt kept staring at Werner as he followed the group to their quarters.

A crewman came up to Two. "What about him?" He pointed to the far end of the tarmac.

"Something must be wrong. Who's in the Macchi today?" He started walking towards the plane.

"It's Mr. Kenair, sir. The report we got this morning from the carrier said he's apparently got a bad leg."

"Is there any indication of a problem with the aircraft? Was it smoking at landing? Did he radio in anything?" He quickened his pace. "Get the army doctor over here, quick." He jumped onto the wing and looked through the canopy. Drum was sitting there, still strapped in and unconscious. Two turned and yelled for the ambulance to come over, then returned to the canopy and banged on it to awaken Drum.

Drum came to and gave a small salute to Number Two.

"Unlock your canopy."

Drum did what he was told and the hot, humid air soon hit him straight in the face. "Hello, sir. Fine evening we're having. Is the pub open yet?"

Two unbuckled him and tried to lift him out of the cockpit. Drum winced and moaned with pain.

"It's your leg, isn't it? Which one?"

Drum took hold of the bad leg and pulled it free. His face was red and sweaty. He pulled off his headgear and tossed it out onto the runway. A crewman took Two's place and then another got the other side as they lifted him out and onto a gurney. Once inside, the ambulance hurried towards the small med station.

Two examined the aircraft for bullet holes but found none. A sprained leg couldn't be the problem. Maybe he was drunk and he hadn't smelled it. *That's it, he was snockered. I'll have his ass for this,* he thought.

Two entered the room to find Matt and Werner arguing and the rest of the group enjoying the show.

Katya was sitting over in a corner enjoying the demonstration of male egotism. Say anything about anything but not a male's pecker or how he uses it, she thought.

"Shut up." The room immediately quieted down. "Does anyone know if Kenair is drunk or sick?"

Katya stood and said, "It's his knee. He hurt it in the storm when he landed. The doctor thinks it's a cracked kneecap. I watched him climb into his plane today and I'm surprised he made it. Is he all right?"

"We sent him over in the ambulance to the med station. The army doctor will look at it. I'll go over later and find out what's up. You guys take it easy." He turned his attention to the two who were arguing. "That means you two… understand? The next building over is the mess hall; eat anytime you want. The army is taking real good care of us, so help yourselves. The building opposite the mess hall is our quarters. First come, first served when it comes to picking your bunks." He started to walk through the door, then stopped. "Because of the argument I saw as I walked in, there will be no booze on this island tonight." The room erupted into moans and groans. "But there will be a movie outside the mess hall." He stepped through the doorway and the group listened to him walk away.

"Fine, assholes. Because of you, we go dry tonight. Thanks loads." Geno was upset with the no booze decision, but even more so in his flying today. It was the second time he didn't finish in the money.

Werner sneered at Geno. "Shut your *dago* mouth. All you Italians think of is wine and women."

Geno retorted, "And what were you thinking about up there today? Katya and your little *schoodle*."

Werner started at Geno but was held back by Sake. "Take your hands off of me, you yellow piss ant."

Sake used his judo and struck Werner in the throat, then threw him to the floor. "You have a bad habit of picking on people smaller than you. You should watch that, it may get you into trouble one day." Sake, calmly and without effort, picked up his headgear and strolled out the door.

Everyone stared at Werner lying on the floor gasping for air. Matt looked over to Kat. She turned from him. He picked his gear up and followed Sake. The rest of the group left for the mess hall; Katya was last. For once, she was not hungry, and she headed for the sleeping quarters. Werner was still on the floor as she stepped over him to leave.

When she arrived, she reconnoitered a position near the wall. At least she could turn away from him if he took the bunk next to hers. She would wait till he had eaten before she left to eat dinner. Maybe he'd come to his senses soon. The nights were cold and lonely without his arms to cuddle up in. Wishing she could do what he asked, she knew she couldn't. She didn't know how to quit. But was it worth losing him? What would life be if she did? She couldn't be subservient to him. Their lives together must be as equals. Her mind raced from doubt, to fear, and then back to her love for him. She could win the race and give him all his dreams, if only he would let her. "Mikhail... help me. Four more days of this; I wish it were all over."

Two picked up a cup of coffee and strolled over to where Matt was sitting. "What's up, Matthew? Eating all alone?" His smile was pretentious but effective.

"Yeah." He kept on eating.

"You want to tell me what happened?"

"It's private." he said bluntly.

"Private, aye? It wasn't private when you came to me and asked to arrange the paperwork so you could marry Katya. What makes it so private now?"

"I'm sorry, I didn't mean it that way." He put his fork down and turned in the direction of Two so he could speak softly. "She called it off. I asked her to quit the race and she refused."

"Good for Katya." The room took notice of the two men's conversation.

Matt frowned at him. "You can say that… she's not your wife and in the lead of a race of lunatics, with predators surrounding her at every turn waiting to get her in their sights and blow her out of the skies. To hell with winning… I want her, and in one piece, not a check. Maybe she'll come to her senses with me not around. I'm hoping she'll miss me more than the money."

"You're the biggest idiot I've ever seen. You know nothing about her or women… real women. She's not the little, frail, dainty thing you have back in Tampa, running around in bathing suits taunting young males into beating off behind the schoolhouse." He took a large breath and sighed. "You read her dossier; she's the best fighter pilot Russia had to give. That's why she's here. Russian men were looked at as inferior compared to her so they released her to come on this trip. That way it got rid of Katya and pleased their male pilots' egos. They needed her out of their system. So, you desert her now, too?" He shook his head in dismay. "I thought you were better than that, boy." He stood and crossed the room.

Matt pulled out the license from his shirt. "I am an idiot." He picked up his gear and headed out the door.

"Mr. Kenair, I have to ground you. I'm sorry, but that knee needs operating on and we don't have the facilities to perform it here. We're going to send you back to Pearl. The naval hospital there will fix you right up."

Panic like he'd never known before welled in his throat. "I need to complete one more leg… I have too."

"I'm sorry, but that'll be impossible. We'll keep you here for two more days, then it's off to Pearl."

"What if I sign a release or something?" Drum was desperate.

The doctor just shook his head as he left. Two passed the doctor as he came in for a visit.

"When I first saw you, I thought you were drunk. There was

going to be hell to pay. But I hear you're going back to Pearl to give the navy nurses a go around instead."

"Sir, I need this one leg. Can you do something so I can finish this one leg?"

"Why is it so important?"

"I've got it all worked out. Seven thousand dollars will re-make my family business back home. I don't want to let the family down and come up short."

"Nonsense, there's nothing too short about you. What you don't have in height, you have in integrity. Listen, One has authorized me, at my own discretion, to give some of the money that has not been set aside to pilots that have shown extraordinary flying skills during the race. And I believe that you qualify, Drum. On my way back to the States, I'll stop in and see you at Pearl and make sure you get the bonus, so quit worrying and start dreaming about those navy nurses."

He exhaled a long sigh of contentment. "May God bless yah, sir."

"Thanks. I've got to go now; the mechanics will be wondering where I am." He shook hands with Drum, then turned and left. He felt good as he pushed the door to the outside. He hoped both Matt and Drum would work things out.

Matt opened the door to the barracks. Kat was the only one there. She had fallen asleep. He softly approached her slumbering body and looked down at her soft, sensuous curves. He remembered the satin feel of her breasts and the velvety softness of her skin. The slim waist that flared into aptly rounded hips with long, supple legs. How could he have rolled the dice with such an angel? He would not lose her again, this he promised himself. Pushing stray tendrils of hair away from her cheek as he sat next to her, he then cupped her chin tenderly in his warm hand.

She leaned her head back and gazed into his eyes. "Matt."

"I think we should talk." His hand explored the soft lines of her back, her waist, and her hips.

"Talk later." Aroused now, she drew herself closer to him. She gasped as he lowered his body over hers. The involuntary tremors of arousal began and her eager response matched his. She drank in the sweetness of his kisses. They lay there for what seemed forever. A thousand kisses and a hundred strokes of love were spent till the moon gave way to the morning sun. They didn't talk much—they didn't have to. They were one now, and always would be.

The race was still there and they both would proceed eagerly, both trying to win. The scores were posted that morning and to no one's surprise, Katya was the leader with twenty-seven points. Matt and Mel were bringing up the rear with fifteen and thirteen points. All but Geno were pleased with the selections. He drew the Messerschmitt, Katya the Yak, and Matt finally drew the Hellcat. Now he could put some points on the board, he thought.

After about an hour out Mel was in the lead in the Hurricane, his favorite. Werner was in the Sea-fire, dogging Geno. Matt and Kat were saddened that they had to leave Drum behind but were glad to get rid of the Macchi. Now all the aircraft had about the same chance as any other—except the Zero, of course. Sake had drawn it again, which was good, since Werner had sworn revenge on him.

This leg was a short one and the speed showed it. Mel was screaming towards his first victory, with Matt in hot pursuit. This day was more relaxed. The pilots joked and chattered most of the way. Of course, Werner kept to himself. He had become the villain of the group. A title he didn't seem to mind.

"Gray lady to Nine ball… repeat… Gray lady to Nine ball. Have you eighty-five miles out. Leader turn to… 259er degrees. Pick you back up at the five-mile marker." The ship's crew all rushed to their stations. "Helicopters to your positions." The giant blades started to turn as the Sikorskies fired up their engines. The blasts of air from the blades lifting off caused the deck crews to hold onto their hats. "Gray lady to leader… have you at five miles. Enter Delta pattern and prepare for landings."

Mel won this leg of the race, to the joy of the Aussies onboard. They cheered and yelled as the announcement came over the intercom. The crews watched as the planes lined up in the Delta pattern. Mel was signaled to drop to Charlie and began the landing pattern. He did so quickly, but then radioed that his landing gear wouldn't lower. He was told to regain altitude and re-enter Delta.

The other aircraft took their turn and landed like pros. Mel was still struggling with the landing gear. The LSO noticed that the hook on the Hurricane had not lowered either. Mel was radioed the information, to his dismay. All aircraft had landed and the deck had been cleared. Mel kept circling and desperately tried everything he could think of to get the gear down. Brevan suddenly appeared on the horizon in the Kingfisher and was made aware of the situation. He stood off in case he would be needed for a rescue.

"I have no more fuel. I'm running on empty." There was fear in Mel's voice.

"All stop!" shouted the captain. "Tell him to put it in the water, we'll pick him up."

"You're going to have to ditch it in the water, Mel. Have you ditched before?"

"Yes… and I didn't like it."

"Open your canopy and pull your straps tight. As soon as you reach a glide path, cut your engines, neutral the propellers, and get out fast. Do you copy?"

"Yeah, I got it."

"Good luck. Gray lady out."

Everyone onboard was on the flight deck and lining the rails to watch Mel. He came around parallel with the ship and lowered to a few feet while the sounds of his engine became silent. As the crew watched, he skipped across the water three or four times and then came to rest on a gentle sea. The waves were small, and even Neptune would be pleased with the landing. Mel jumped out of the cockpit without any problems. The helicopters were right there, and one of them lowered a lifeline to him. The plane floated rather well and gave the rescue team plenty of time to do their jobs. Brevan watched from the air and when he saw everything was okay, he landed.

"That's a goddamn shame," said one of the Aussie crewmen. "We finally get first place and the goddamn plane took a dump on him. That's bullshit."

The whole crew cheered as the helicopter landed with Mel. "Are you all right?" asked One.

"Yes, sir. This puts me out of the race, doesn't it?" The look on his face was surreal. He knew the answer, but had to hear it for himself.

"Sorry, Mr. Shaw. Yes, it does."

"Well, I made some money anyway. Thanks for inviting me to come along." His look of loss turned into an expression of gratitude and a job well done.

The next three days would prove to be a little boring. There would be no more aircraft lost and no more fighting or quarreling between each other. Matt and Kat enjoyed the days of racing and the nights of lovemaking but they both had decided to wait to be married till the race was over and they were back in the States. The crew was taking bets now on who would become the overall winner. With one more day to go, Katya was in the lead with forty-two points. Matt was in second with thirty-seven. Geno was still holding onto third with a score of thirty-four. Werner had thirty-two, and Sake was last with twenty-six. They all knew the rules stated that you had to finish the race to win, no matter what score you had. Matt was getting nervous again.

CHAPTER FIFTEEN

"WILL EVERYTHING BE UP TO par by takeoff, Chief?" The hangar echoed the admiral's voice. Only he and a small tune-up crew were working this late.

The chief wiped his greasy hands on a rag. "What time is it, sir?" He looked to his wrist. "It is now 03:30."

"No problem. They'll be purring like kittens in a couple of hours." The chief sensed something was different with the admiral. He couldn't tell if it was enthusiasm, anticipation, or just the excitement of the final stretch of the race, but something was different. Whatever it was, it was something that hadn't been there before. He saw it in his eyes, in the way he snapped his words out, like a young ensign on his first combat mission. It worried him a little.

"Good... we wouldn't want anything going astray on the last day, would we?"

"No, sir." The chief went back to his work.

The admiral walked back to the fantail to watch the sunrise. He was surprised to find Sake also waiting for the sun's gentle radiance. The two men converged at the railing with simple nods of recognition. "How are you feeling today?" The admiral's voice was soft but cold, very cold.

With a touch of surprise Sake answered, "I feel fine... why do you ask?"

The admiral turned to face him and with a vacuous look said,

245

"Because I'm going to kill you today." His words were spoken softly, but mimicked his hostility.

Undisturbed, Sake replied, "I didn't think you had too much love for us Japanese."

"It's not the Japanese… it's you." His tempo and volume picked up a bit.

Sake scowled back at him but then hesitated a moment as he tried to think. "You're too old to have been in the war, and I know I've never met you before this trip, so why, may I ask, do you want to kill me?"

From his jacket, the admiral pulled a picture of the Japanese Zero he carried with him and handed it to Sake. "This was your plane, was it not?"

Sake frowned again. "Yes, it was… it was very lucky for me in the war. I had this same plane all the way till the very end. How did you get a picture of it, and why?"

The admiral was still surprisingly calm as he spoke. "To answer your first question, I was head of Naval Intelligence during the war." He waited for some kind of expression from Sake but none came. "The second answer is that you took part in the sneak attack on Pearl Harbor."

Sake was surprised but even more confused at the admiral's assertion. "You hate me for a military mission?"

A muscle flicked angrily in the admiral's jaw. "My wife died at Pearl Harbor." With that, his voice became rough and much louder.

A sudden pleasure overcame him, then faded to reason.

"Sir, I'm sorry that your wife was killed, but you do know as well as I that a simple airman doesn't determine targets in the military, nor judges them." His eyes tried to reason with the admiral.

The admiral took a deep breath and let it out slowly, trying to calm himself once more. "You're right." He looked out into the peach-colored sky as the sun's first rays began to penetrate the darkness of the night. "Do you remember where you were in September of 1943?"

The question stunned Sake a little. "I was on duty, on a carrier, in the Coral Sea."

The admiral slowly turned from the dawn. "You were also dogfighting with Wildcats. One morning you downed three. The fighting lasted a long time and both sides had to quit and retreat, but you and one other American had to fight it out, one last time." He grinned at him suspiciously. "At that time, we didn't know how to bring a Zero down and you flamed that last Wildcat, too." He took another deep breath so he could continue. "But unlike the others, this pilot was able to parachute out." He stared intensely at Sake's stone face. "His flight officer stayed to watch him glide slowly to the sea below. He observed the Zero's return, at which time the pilot commenced to machine-gun the falling pilot. The flight officer observed the severed body hit the water." His eyes started to well up. "That pilot was my son." His voice was thick and unsteady. He strained his emotions to continue. "The leader also had a remarkable memory of the markings on the Zero."

Sake grimaced at the photo but didn't say a word.

"You killed my family... and that's why I'm going to kill you," he said matter-of-factly. All emotion had drained from his words but just by saying them, he brought a numbness to his animosity.

Sake snapped his head erect and glared into the admiral's eyes. "Family? You accuse me of taking your family?" Rage was growing in Sake's voice and in his manner. Like the rising sun, his face turned red and his eyes sent a glare of fire towards the admiral. "Your wife was at the wrong place at the wrong time. I never fired upon civilians. Yes, some get hurt and even killed but you know that... that's war. Your son was a fighting man, during a war... soldiers get killed." He too took a deep breath to regain his composure. "I do apologize. It was not honorable the way I killed your son but I was young, and eager to do anything I could to help my country overthrow the Americans' self-righteousness." The admiral was staring at him with confusion and loathing.

Sake turned to him and said, "Don't be so sanctimonious. Can you say the Americans never bombed civilians or performed any atrocities? What about my family? With one bomb you took my mother and father, grandparents, my wife and two daughters... my whole life. Where was the military base at Nagasaki? If you were an Intelligence expert, you knew there were none." His voice cracked.

"The Japanese would not have given up without the A-bomb." The admiral's retort was automatic and without feeling. It was the military line at the time.

"If the United States was being invaded, would you give up?" The meaning rang through the deck like a siren and fell upon the admiral like a preacher's sermon.

Both men went silent and turned to the new morn. The breeze had picked up and the smell of the sea was everywhere. Both men pondered their words as tears ran from their eyes and then simultaneously they turned and without speaking a word, walked away.

"You better get up, lazy bones, or you'll miss all the action." Kat pushed and tugged at Matt to get up.

"Let's stay in bed all day, to hell with the race." He smiled at her as he teased.

"I'm going for a shower and you better be up when I get back." She shook a finger at him.

"I think I'll pretend to be a Jap sex maniac and jump you in the shower." He knew that wasn't funny and he shouldn't have said it before she could reply. "Okay… okay, that was shitty and I shouldn't have said it. I apologize."

That scolding look of hers was all over her face. "Just be ready when I get back. We're supposed to be having breakfast with Yokes and Mel, and I think even Viktor will be there." She grabbed a new uniform and some fresh underwear and headed for the sickbay and her shower.

"Get moving, dude. There's money to be won!" He too grabbed new clothes and started for the head.

They both arrived back at their quarters at the same time. Kat with wet hair that she'd rolled up in a towel and Matt with shaving cream still on his jaw. She threw the towel down and took a couple of strokes with a brush. "Come on… I'm starving."

"Didn't you ever eat in Russia?" He stood there, mouth wide open. "Where did you get such an appetite?"

"Never mind, body like a tree stump. Let's go eat."

Everyone was in the wardroom when they entered. The captain, all the officers, the chiefs, and even the LSO were smiling over in one corner. The crew had been pushed in and made room for. One got up to speak. "I wanted to thank all of you for a job well done. We've had some tough times to deal with but you came through them with flying colors. It's been a pleasure sailing with you." The room broke out in cheers and whistles.

"There they are, over there." Matt pointed to where Mel and Yokes were sitting.

"You go… I'm getting some food. You want me to get you some while I'm there?"

"Maybe a donut and some coffee." He walked up to the guys and took a seat. "You're looking good, Yokes. You wouldn't even know you were in a beef if it wasn't for the cast." He looked over to Mel and grinned. "I still have a hard time with what happened to you. It was pure bad luck, the plane's landing gear going south like that."

Mel grinned. "We all have our different roads to travel. We have to be able to change directions whenever good or bad hits. It's like when you get your initial heading on a mission, you always have to compensate. It's not where you start, it's where you end up." Mel took a sip of coffee to wash down his words.

"I didn't know you were such a philosopher, old man." Yokes was surprised by Mel's thoughts, but understood and agreed with them.

"Just a realist, Yokes. Anyway, I'm still ahead of the game. The money I've won will buy a new ram and some new lambs for next season. I'm doing fine."

"Look at that plate of food!" Yokes' eyes were bugging out.

"If you know what's good for you, you'll keep your mouth shut," Matt snickered.

"Don't worry about me, cat's got my tongue." Yokes snapped his mouth shut.

Katya coolly put her meal on the table. "You guys not eating?" She handed Matt a donut and his coffee. The silence between the guys was evident. "What?"

"Nothing... nothing at all." Matt changed the subject. "By the way, when do you guys leave the ship?"

"We're supposed to be on the flight deck by 13:00 tomorrow. The helicopters will take us ashore and I guess we'll meet at the Aussie air base." Yokes took out a small paper from his shirt. "I got a note that One wanted to speak to me later."

"Look at the time... we've got to go, Kat. Nice knowing you, Mel, good luck to you."

"I'm not half through yet." She slammed down her silverware. "That's why I'm hungry all the time. I never get a chance to finish a meal around here." She reached over the table and shook Mel's hand. "Good luck to you, Mel." She turned towards Yokes. "I'll see you tomorrow, Big Guy."

Viktor was coming in as they were leaving. "Viktor... wait, Matt, I want to talk to Viktor a minute."

"Sure... I'll meet you up on the flight deck. I'll bring your things."

"Thanks... baby."

He was halfway up the ladder before he realized that she had called him baby and it made him feel good.

"Viktor, I'm sorry I don't have much time, but if we don't see each other again, I want you to know, I love you. Like a sister to a brother. And here, it's Matt's mother's address so we can write and stay in touch." Tears started to form in her eyes. She stretched upward and kissed him on the cheek. "Take good care of that girl, she's the best thing that's ever happened to you." She turned quickly and ran up the ladder.

Yokes walked up to One. "You wanted to speak to me, sir?"

"Yes, here. I would appreciate if you would give this to Number Two for me, it's rather important."

"Yes, sir. No problem. But why not give it to him yourself? You'll see him tomorrow, just like me."

"I don't think so." His eyes were strange, dull and lifeless.

"Whatever you say, sir." He watched the old man pass through the passageway and up to the hangar deck.

"All pilots to the hangar deck… repeat… all pilots to the hangar deck."

There was no waiting for anyone to arrive. All were present and eager to get underway with the race. "Now, to the choosing." The bag was held for One to pick. He put his hand in and pulled out a slip. "Geno, you get the Hellcat." Geno was overjoyed. Number Four reached for the slip from One's hand to throw it away. Number One just shook his head negatively and put the slip in his pocket. "Katya, you get the Sea-fire." Again, he put the slip in his pocket. "Werner, what else, the Messerschmitt. Matt, you get the Yak. And that leaves the Zero to Sake." He didn't look at Sake; he didn't need to. They both felt the tension as he put the last slip in his pocket. "Your information is there on the table. You have one hour till takeoff. Good luck."

"Someone confirm my figures, I can't believe it." Geno was in shock; his mouth began to run uncontrollably with mumbles and murmurs.

"I have it at six hundred eighty miles." Kat was also shocked.

"At a snail's crawl you'd have a tough time making it!" Geno screamed.

Sake stayed calm and continued working the numbers. He looked at the weather report and smiled. A tail wind; *Finally*, he thought.

"You and I are just about the same; the Sea-fire and the Yak are pretty equal. Damn, it's a long way to go. Leave it to them to make the last leg the hardest. Well, good luck. I'll see you at the finish line—right behind me." Matt displayed a mischievous grin for Katya.

"Behind you, my ass." Kat smiled broadly at Matt as they left for their checkout on the flight deck.

Everything seemed to be a go, with Geno all ready for his

takeoff. Katya had taxied to the ready line. But Matt's engine stopped without warning. The crews rushed to find the problem. The chief pulled the engine panel and decided the problem was that both magnetos had shorted out. He yelled to a crewman to retrieve one from the hangar deck. As he waited, he pulled one of them to save time. Matt asked what the problem was and the chief told him that he was going to have to fly on a single magneto. Matt didn't like it, but agreed. Only one more plane to take off, and Matt would be disqualified if he couldn't make the ready line in time. The chief finally shut the panel and signaled Matt to fire it up. The engine kicked right over and Matt taxied to the line just in time but had lost four positions. He was last now, and did not have enough fuel to catch up. He took to the air with no more problems.

One came down and asked what the problem was. The chief filled One in and then One congratulated him on getting Matt into the air. The Bearcat was raised from the hangar deck and One put on his headgear and climbed in. He immediately took off in pursuit of the others.

Within an hour, a voice came over the radio. "You bastard!"

"That sounded like Geno," Matt sang out over the airways.

"Get off my ass, you Nazi bastard."

The sounds of machine guns were heard in the background. The other pilots didn't know what was going on and they chattered between themselves. Then suddenly, "Mayday. Mayday. I'm going down." The sound of a large blast was heard over the radio, then nothing but silence.

"Brevan to Werner, come in." He waited for the reply.

"Werner here."

"Don't waste my time… is Geno down… or is he gone?"

"He's gone to Michelangelo's heaven in the skies." There was a trace of laughter in his voice.

"Kat, keep an eye out for that bastard. The only way he can win is to blow you out of the sky." Matt's voice pierced the air with anger.

"I'm ready for him." Her tone almost sounded eager.

Another voice came over the radio, a mild and unfamiliar voice. "Do you want to keep this personal or not?"

Everyone looked around them for the voice. Then suddenly the Zero climbed rapidly. "Let's keep it private."

Matt saw the Zero and a Bearcat lining up for combat. "Where did that Bearcat come from and who's flying it?"

"I think it's Number One," radioed Brevan.

Matt watched the dogfight from below. The Zero got first advantage, then lost it in a smart move by the Bearcat. It fired burst after burst, hitting the Zero in multiple places. Small fragments fell from the Zero as it tried to outmaneuver the big cat. "Why the hell are they fighting? Number One's not even in the race... talk to me, Brevan."

"I think it's personal."

"Personal? How can it be personal?" Kat was also viewing the dogfight.

"I don't know, it's just what I heard. Just keep your asses racing. I'll watch out for them."

"Ten four, Brevan."

"You too, Kat."

"Right," she replied.

Brevan climbed a bit so he could see more clearly. The Zero did a figure eight and was on the six of the Bearcat. Its 20 mm cannon had blown a hole through the fuselage and hit the motor cowling. The admiral banked right to clear Sake's fire. They both maneuvered for several more minutes, neither gaining enough advantage to fire again effectively, though Sake fired many times without hitting the admiral. The admiral pulled into a cloudbank and Sake followed. Brevan lost sight of them.

After a minute or so, he radioed for them to answer, with no replies. Then out of the corner of his eye he spotted smoke. It was the admiral. He was coming out of the west at about twenty-five thousand feet. He suddenly started to dive and Brevan looked down. Sake was in the east at about five thousand feet. He must have seen the admiral, for he started to climb and throttle up. The two aircraft shrieked at each other like giant birds of prey, both howling tracers and rounds at each other. Like two dragons they sent burst after burst of fire from their throats. Each struck the other, each inflicting damage. Smoke and flames were coming from both planes, then the light from the tracers stopped illuminating the darkened clouds that played background to their theater. Brevan knew what they must have known; they were out of ammunition. The jousting didn't stop, however. Without any hesitation, they aimed their birds straight at each other and throttled up. Brevan had to look away at the last moment but he saw the fireball that was left from the collision. The warbirds were no more than small pieces of shiny metal floating down to the blue ocean below. The flames and smoke vanished into the darkened clouds that surrounded the tournament of warriors. He thought of olden days when honor and pride were settled this way. But who had won the day? Maybe both or... maybe neither.

"Brevan... what's going on? I saw a flash back there. This was not supposed to be!" Matt was confused by the entry of the admiral into the race. He didn't like surprises.

"Here's a little surprise for you, little one." The German's voice had a twinge of evil to it.

A blast of about forty rounds came screaming across Kat's right wing and over her canopy. She wasn't hit, but there was damage to the wing. She climbed and looked for Werner. He came out of the sun on his second pass but she was waiting for him. She throttled back and gave full flaps and he flew right by. The plane was buffeting badly from the flaps being down so she lifted them and accelerated to catch him. As she got him in her sights, she started to squeeze the trigger but nothing happened. She tried again, then again. He must have damaged the guns on that first pass. If she called for help, he would know her guns didn't work and would surely have her. *Stay on his ass*, was the only thing she could think of. But what of the fuel? They would both run out short of Sydney. She'd worry about that later. She banked and turned with every move he made. The two of them took up the whole sky with their moves and she stayed right on his tail.

"Nice flying, little one... but are you out of bullets? Or maybe you just can't pull the trigger anymore. The sight of blood is kind of scary for young children and little girls."

"I'm waiting to put one right between your eyes. I want to see you die, you Nazi son of a bitch!" Her anger almost got to her. She found herself trying to ram the German but came to her senses and backed off. But she got close enough to see the terror in his eyes as he looked behind him at her propellers snipping at his tail.

"You Germans do like chopped meat, don't you, Herr Nolder? I hear you like it raw… hamburger, I think you call it." She just couldn't help herself; she had to say something.

"I'll show you dead meat." Werner banked, then dove for the water. He was trying to out-power her and gain position.

"I'm losing it," she whispered to the thick cockpit air. "He'll get position on me and blow me out of the skies. Come around, damn it… come… come… pull up… damn it, no… no!" A familiar sound suddenly surrounded her. She felt it more than heard it, and thought it must be a sign from heaven. A rumbling of an engine she had heard many times before was coming from behind her and getting louder and louder as a voice kept repeating in her ears, *I'm here… I'm always here*. "Lilya."

The Yak made one very good pass right in front of her and she watched as the Nazi's 109 ignited into a ball of flames. The German must have keyed his mic as his plane caught fire. She could hear him screaming and whimpering for his mother as his plane broke up and fell down to the sea. As she watched the plane disappear beneath the waves, it was like a new day had risen and a new life had begun. Her old world was gone forever and she could now start anew.

"Are you all right, Kat? Are you wounded?" Matt asked as he banked and pulled up from the fire of the Nazi's plane.

"I'm fine… just fine." Her voice was calm and steady. Lilya's soft words still rang clearly in her head but were ever fading. She grinned, then whispered a heartfelt, "Thanks."

"What's going on up there?" Brevan asked.

"Just threw out some German trash, nothing to worry about." Matt's voice seemed stoic.

"A rookie could have made that shot with me keeping him busy like I did." Kat snickered to herself, knowing what the reply would be.

"Me the rookie? Only a Russian novice would have tried to

crew-cut old Werner's tail." Matt pulled up alongside of her and inspected her plane for damage.

"Looks like you two are the last ones." Brevan had caught up to them and was on the opposite side of her from Matt.

"I wonder if the admiral knew all along it would be you two," Brevan said with a chuckle in his voice.

"Not going to be behind me, haaa!" Matt started to laugh.

"It all depends who hits the water first." Kat's words brought Matt back to actuality.

"That's not a problem!" barked in Brevan.

"What do you mean, Brevan? We still have four hundred miles to reach Sydney and none of us have the fuel to make it. Maybe the admiral knew that also?" Kat was turning angry at what she thought was Brevan's stupidity.

"Do you think they would let the rescue ship run out of fuel? The admiral lied back at the ship. He gave the wrong coordinates for the ship's position. There's really only about two hundred miles left to Sydney."

"Why would he do that?" asked Matt.

"To give the real racers a chance not to fight and just race. If you flyers thought you would use up all your fuel in a dogfight you couldn't be racing, could you? You must be after something else."

"I see his point," Matt replied.

"Throttle up to one hundred sixty knots. That should give us a smooth ride into Sydney." Brevan pulled the Kingfisher into the point position.

"Then he was a nice man?"

"Yeah, he was, Kat. He had his own problems, like most of us, but inside I think he was a pretty nice guy. He did a lot for everyone that would take it. Of course, there are Werners and Rudys everywhere with their own agendas, like ruling the world or killing Germans just because they're Germans."

"But why did he have it out for Sake?" Matt wondered aloud.

"It was personal… I don't know the details, but I do know both men knew the score." Brevan was tired of the fighting, and almost tired of flying. The last couple of months of the war had left him in a shaking mass of turmoil. He flew every one of his missions over Germany, twenty-six in all. But with every new bomber run came the ever-mounting feeling he would not return. Visions of the dead and wounded haunted his dreams night after night. He started drinking, and soon his crew noticed his fear.

It all started when he fell in love with and married an Englishwoman in London. At first, their love was strong, but as the booze became dominant in his life, his love flickered and almost blew out. Soon he was grounded and transferred to Intelligence, where he met the admiral. He had found out later that the admiral had his own bout with the bottle. He never knew the reason, but the admiral seemed to know just what he was feeling, and helped him restart his life. He soon laid his fears aside and Betty gave him another chance, and with the help of this mission and a new son, he was on his way to the good life and happiness once again.

A ray of sunlight interrupted his thoughts and he looked over to Kat. She reminded him of his wife, Betty; small but spunky. "What are you going to do with all that money, Kat?"

"She's going to give it to me... I'm the president of the company."

"You may be the president but I'm the company treasurer... and I'll be handling the profits. Between you and Yokes, we'd be paupers in no time, spending money on this, then that, like it grew out of the ground like a potato. Georgina and I are going to keep you two in line. I'm not becoming an American to starve to death on some white beach in Florida."

"Sounds like a wife already, doesn't she, Brevan?"

"They're all the same... but who in their right mind would change them?"

"Not me."

"Damn right... not you." Kat giggled to herself.

"I'm glad you two are waiting to marry back in the States. It's always better to start your new lives where you're going to live it. Are you looking forward to being an American, Kat?"

"I'm looking forward to being Mrs. Drew... whatever the nationality. I do hope it lives up to its reputation. I think I will enjoy the freedoms you have, but the open wasting of so much bothers me. The Americans don't know what it is to need a simple crust of bread or a warm coat in the winter so you won't freeze." She didn't want to think on those days back home any more. "Enough of such things… Mattie, do all your women marry in white gowns like in the movies?"

"No, Kat. You'll wear whatever you like at our wedding. We're not marrying in the church, so you don't have to wear white."

"Will your mother be unhappy if we don't marry in the church?"

"I'm not marrying my mother… we decide on how we pledge our love."

"Oh… I like that… remember those words for later. I'll use them when I write to Victor."

"Look, you love birds… Sydney Harbor on your right about twenty miles." He made contact with Number Two and got the final heading for their landing.

Matt tipped his wings at Kat. "From here on in it's me and you, forever."

"That's a nice word too… forever."

"Kat, you line up first," Brevan announced.

"Roger… lowering landing gear." She throttled back and waited for the gear to snap in place. "I'm not getting a green light on the landing gear, could you check it for me, Matt?"

Matt lowered the Yak and looked under the Sea-fire. The landing gear was still in the up position. "Kat, the gear is still up… try again."

She tried the lever once more. "Still no light."

"Damn… why is it always you?"

"Been here before. Keep your gear up. There's a grassy length just to the north of the field. Many a pilot has put it down there with no problem." Brevan pointed to the field. "See the grass? It's the whole length of the strip. Just come in slow and cut your engines early."

"No problem. Looks like the field back in Russia. I've belly-landed several times back there."

"Be careful, love." He stuck up his thumb so she could see.

"Piece of crust." She maneuvered into position.

"Piece of cake, you mean." Matt tried to keep his fears to himself. "I'll be right beside you all the way."

"I wonder if I'm getting all my bad luck out of the way," she twittered.

"Boy, I hope so. Check you gauges... is your airspeed ninety knots? That's what I read."

"Yes... right at ninety knots."

"Be smooth, baby... real smooth."

"Like waltzing at our wedding." The propellers went into neutral and stopped spinning. The Sea-fire glided along the grass on its belly as unruffled as you please and came to rest right in front of Number Two and the rescue vehicles. There were no fires or even smoke. The bent propeller was the only apparent damage. The field's rescue team flew into action and had Kat out of the plane and standing with Two, staring at Matt and Brevan as they landed.

Matt hurriedly went over to the swarm of personnel that were busy foaming down Kat's aircraft. He stayed long enough to find out that she was unharmed and with Number Two on the side of the field. He sauntered over to them with a grin on his face. "Not bad... not bad at all. You're going to tell me you can waltz that good?"

"It all depends if you keep your two left feet out of my way." She exposed a mouth-full of whiteness as she tilted her head.

Matt grabbed her and lifted her off the ground, twirling her round and around, kissing her over and over.

Brevan walked up to the celebration. "What next?"

Two turned to the group. "Well, you're free to do whatever you want till 18:30 tomorrow; that's when we're leaving to go back home, on Yokes' C-47." He looked at Matt and Kat kissing, then looked to the heavens. "I miss my wife and kids so bad, I'll never do this again."

Brevan walked up to them. "I know a great place for shrimp."

"I'm starving, let's go." Kat pulled on Matt's arms.

"What are we going to use as money?" Matt asked.

"You are such a *govedo*. We're rich. We won!" Kat's face glowed bright as she suddenly realized their finishing.

Number Two winked at Kat. "Checks will be here tomorrow

morning, bright and early. But in the meantime, here's fifty, go and enjoy."

Kat grabbed the bill, turned from Matt and pulled at Brevan to leave. "Let's go."

Matt stood dumbfounded, then pleaded, "What about me?"

Kat shrugged her shoulders. "I'm with him, he knows where the shrimps are. By the way,… what are shrimps? I hope you can eat them."

The three of them headed for the gate, laughing all the way. Two remained with the field crews to clean up and take care of last-minute details. As he walked over to the hangars, he thought it was a shame to have lost the admiral, but it could not have ended any other way, for either Sake or him. They both needed to get to where their lives were, and that wasn't here on this earth. They were both proud men and a little vain. They lived and died their way and who could question that.

The two were awakened by the sounds of the helicopters landing outside. Matt looked at his watch to find it was 16:00. He nudged Kat and asked, "Were we up all night?"

"Yes, we didn't get to bed till almost ten this morning."

"What the hell was I drinking last night, goat piss?"

"I don't remember, but I think I was drinking the same swill."

"Missy… Missy, my girl, I knew you could do it! First and second, we're millionaires!" Yokes was jumping up and down on the bed, to the great discomfort of Kat's head.

Two came into the room with two checks in his hand. "This one's for you, Miss Katya Yegorova, and this one's for second place, Mr. Matthew Drew."

"You mean she beat me in the race? I want a recount. She didn't land here in Sydney, she crashed. Doesn't landing your aircraft safely mean anything?"

She just shook her head, smiled, then put her hand out for his check. "I'm the treasurer, aren't I, Yokes?… so, hand it over, Mr. President."

He did so, to the laughter of the room. Soon he too was laughing. They boarded the C-47 that afternoon and waved goodbye to Mel and Viktor. While they were in the air, Yokes gave the letter to Number Two. One didn't want to leave anything to chance, so he told his old friend what he had done and that his wife would be waiting in Honolulu instead of California. He told him that there would be many more surprises once he got there.

"I like Boris for a boy's name," Kat said.

"Boris… it sounds like a cartoon character or a spy. Mike, Sam, or maybe Ben. Yeah, one like those or…»

Kat smiled and sat back and made herself comfortable. She happily started daydreaming as Matt rattled on and on with children's names.

Printed in the United States
By Bookmasters